"You know who I am, don't you?" Ryder demanded.

"You're Ryder Tate," Merri said tensely, hating the way he was making her feel.

"That's right, honey. I'm Ryder Tate. Oliver 'Real Estate Tycoon' Tate's son. But then, I don't imagine that comes as any surprise to you, does it?" His gentle eyes had turned icy.

"If you think for one minute my gratitude has anything to do with your money, you're dead wrong, Ryder." Merri's voice was as cold as his, but inside, her heart was breaking.

"If that isn't what all your 'gratitude' is about, I'll eat my fire truck," Ryder said as he pulled her closer. "But, to be honest, I don't care what you're attracted to," he confessed in a husky voice. "I'm willing to be used by you for whatever reasons...."

TUG OF WAR

"Open up," Luke instructed.

Cassle popped her mouth open in a wide and exaggerated pose. He grasped her chin between his fingers to inspect her throat. Their eyes met briefly.

"It's just a himple caze of tonsihites," she garbled as he held her mouth firmly open.

"Could be," he murmured distactedly. "But then tonciletiemosis has the same symptoms."

She frowned. "Whut's 'at?"

"A rare, debilitating disease that...oh surely you've heard of it."

"I'b neber heard ob suzh a diseese!" she scoffed, but her pulse did give a queer little leap at the mere thought of such a malady.

"You're serious? Well," he said in a grim tone, "the voice goes first, then the eyes...then the mouth...well, let's just say it's a heck of a way to go."

Other *Leisure Books* by Lori Copeland:

PLAYING FOR KEEPS/A TEMPTING STRANGER
OUT OF CONTROL/A WINNING COMBINATION
UP FOR GRABS/HOT ON HIS TRAIL
OUT OF THIS WORLD/FOREVER AFTER

SPITFIRE
— & —
TUG OF
WAR

THE BEST OF LORI COPELAND

LEISURE BOOKS   NEW YORK CITY

To Olivia Ferrell and Melodie Adams
special friends who share the agony
and unspeakable joys of being a writer

A LEISURE BOOK®

November 1991

Published by

Dorchester Publishing Co., Inc.
276 Fifth Avenue
New York, NY 10001

SPITFIRE Copyright ©MCMLXXXV by Lori Copeland
TUG OF WAR Copyright ©MCMLXXXVI by Lori Copeland

All rights reserved. No part of this book may be reproduced or transmitted in any form or by any electronic or mechanical means, including photocopying, recording or by any information storage and retrieval system, without the written permission of the Publisher, except where permitted by law.

The name "Leisure Books" and the stylized "L" with design are trademarks of Dorchester Publishing Co., Inc.

Printed in the United States of America.

SPITFIRE

CHAPTER ONE

The slender girl on the narrow bed moved restlessly in her sleep, fighting to draw a deep breath. The air in the small bedroom became increasingly acrid as she tossed about. Damp tendrils of light brown hair clung to the sides of her youthful face as she moaned softly, trying to force her eyes open. Even in her sleep Merri Lambert could sense it: Something was wrong.

A low moan filled the room as her breathing grew more ragged and she fought to reach consciousness. Her eyelids felt heavy, as if someone had placed massive weights on them. It was a few minutes before she was able to force them open, and for a split second she fought to orient herself to her surroundings. She froze as her eyes focused

11

on the thick layer of smoke billowing about her room.

Fire! Her apartment was on fire!

Hurriedly throwing off the blanket, she got out of bed as fear quickly took possession of her muddled senses. Her mind tried desperately to determine what to do. *Don't panic. First and foremost, don't panic!*

Dropping to her hands and knees, she crawled to the bedroom door and groped blindly to determine if it was hot. Instantly her hand jerked back as the heat seared the tips of her fingers. The fire had already reached the hallway! A hysterical sob escaped her as she realized that there was only one way out of the apartment, and it was through that doorway.

The smoke grew thicker in the small room as Merri buried her face in her trembling hands.

She was going to die.

When she and Erica had rented the lovely high-rise apartment a year earlier, they had discussed the frightening thought of a fire breaking out, but the view from the fifteenth floor was so spectacular that they tossed their worries to the wind and rented it.

Now she was fifteen stories up, with no way out but through the front door. She knew enough about fires to know that if the heat had already reached the door, she was trapped.

And what about Erica? Was she already dead? Maybe not: Her bedroom was down the hall from Merri's. Maybe she was sitting alone in her room now, waiting . . . praying . . . crying.

Tears filled Merri's eyes as her body began to shake violently. How long did it take to die of smoke inhalation? Merri bowed her head and began to pray, pleading for a rescue she knew would never occur. Springfield had very few high-rises, and she vaguely remembered the warnings from the fire department that it was difficult to fight a fire effectively in any building over ten stories high. She laughed ironically at the strange thoughts that were running through her brain. She could hear the faint wail of sirens as her mind inanely went over what would happen to the dry cleaning she was supposed to pick up the following day. Had she mentioned to her mother she had opened a savings account a few months earlier for a trip to the Bahamas? What would happen to the $77.29 she had in that account? Had she told her parents how much she loved and appreciated all they had done for her? Had she confessed to Erica that it was she who had put the gravy stain on the new cashmere sweater they shared? Would she *really* have stopped throwing her and Erica's trash in the next-door neighbor's can instead of taking it down to the incinerator herself as she had faithfuly promised to do when Mr. Centers had caught her dumping her garbage in his trashcan again that very morning? *Oh, Lord,* she prayed, *if you'll just get me out of this alive, I'll swear I'll never do that again!*

It was almost impossible to breathe now as Merri lay down on the floor to await the inevitable. Twenty-eight years old and she was going to die. She began to list mentally the things she had never experienced. She had never been married or tasted the joys of motherhood. She had never been so madly in love with a man that he could make her stomach flutter with excitement or her pulse pound in anticipation. The closest thing to love she had ever experienced was the warm feeling she had when she was with Dirk Bennett. Maybe if they had had more time together, something lasting would have developed out of their relationship; but then again, if there was ever a time for honesty, it was now, and she had to admit that she didn't really care all that much for him. How would Dirk feel when he heard she had died? She frowned. That rat fink Yvonne Mathers would be consoling him before they dug Merri out of the rubble!

Her eyes grew heavy as she closed them for what she feared would be the last time. She'd give anything if she had voted yes in the last election instead of her standard no when the city wanted to hire more firemen.

The sound of the door being smashed open barely penetrated her thoughts as she drifted in and out of consciousness. A bright ray of light shot about the room as she heard muffled voices.

"Over there on the floor, Joe. I think I see something." A male voice floated through her dazed senses as she tried to call out but couldn't. Seconds later she was being held by a pair of strong arms, and she peered into the face of what looked to her to be a creature from outer space.

"Are you Darth Vader?" she asked.

The creature shook its head, and it vaguely began to register that what was carrying her was not an alien creature but a fireman with an air mask on.

"Is there anyone else in this apartment?" a second fireman questioned her.

"Erica, my roommate," Merri cried out. "Did you find her?"

"Where is she?" he shot back.

"In the bedroom next to mine. First door on the left," she muttered through a choking gasp. Thick smoke was pouring in the room now as the fireman who was holding her swiftly handed her over to the second man.

"I'll go after her, Ryder. You take this one down and tell them to get more men and equipment up here."

The arms that held her now were also powerful. "Okay. Are you sure you don't need any help? This floor's going to be out of control in another few minutes," the second man warned.

"I can handle it. You get her down safely, then get back up here pronto!" the first fireman instructed before hurrying off into the surging smoke.

The fireman who held Merri ripped off his mask and held it over her face, letting her gulp in several deep breaths of air before he placed it back over his own face.

"I'm going to take you down to the tenth floor," he shouted. "We can't get you out from up here!"

Merri nodded as she wrapped her arms around his neck and held on tightly.

He ran quickly out into the hallway. She gasped

as the searing flames licked at their bodies. Her apartment was directly across the hall from the stairway, and moments later the fireman was clattering down the five flights of stairs, holding her against his chest.

The tenth floor was teeming with activity as they burst out of the stairway exit. Several firemen were hosing down one end of the hallway as the fireman carried Merri to the window overlooking the parking lot.

"How are we going to get out?" she shouted above the roar of the fire.

"Through that window!" he yelled back. "Hey, Jackson! I'm going to take this one down. McFarland's still up on fifteen. Take three or four men and get up there fast!"

The other firemen hurried off as the fireman holding her stepped through the window into a bucketlike apparatus, still clutching her firmly in his arms.

She sucked in large breaths of fresh air and gasped when she realized where she was: *in a small bucket ten stories high!* The bucket swayed as the wind whistled eerily around her scantily clad form. Her arms shot up around the fireman's neck in a death grip, and she heard someone scream at the top of her lungs.

"Don't get hysterical on me, lady." The fireman grimaced painfully as her scream reverberated through his head, and he tried to steady her thrashing form. "It's a long way down there, and I don't think either one of us cares to make the trip."

Instantly she froze and didn't move a muscle. "Will we fall?"

It would be just her luck to be rescued from a burning building, only to fall ten stories to the ground!

"We will if you don't calm down," he warned her grimly. "Now, I know you're upset, but you're safe now, lady. . . . Lady! Get your nails out of the side of my neck!"

By now Merri was clawing and grasping for any kind of hold as the bucket started moving slowly down the side of the building.

Below them the sounds of sirens and police cars filled the air. Shouting could be heard as Merri buried her face against the fireman's neck and prayed that they would make it to the ground. It seemed ludicrous to her that she should pick *this* time to note how sexy his after-shave smelled, but she did. For one brief, fleeting moment she wondered if he was as good-looking as he smelled, smoke and all. But that moment passed swiftly as the bucket jerked to a halt in midair, sending her into another screaming fit.

"What's the matter?" she demanded hysterically.

"Trouble on the ground somewhere," he grunted, shifting her weight in his arms. "Will you hold still?"

"You don't have to be so nasty!" she flared back.

"Lady, I'm standing here, ten stories up, weaving around in a tiny bucket, trying to hold a woman who seems intent on doing the boogaloo, and you wonder why I'm being nasty?" he asked incredulously.

"Then put me down!" she snapped. "I'm perfectly capable of standing on my own two feet!"

"Well, *excuse me.*" He sat her down with a thud. "I hope you enjoy the view!"

She didn't. When she glanced down and saw the tiny specks that were people running around on the ground, she sagged weakly in his arms.

"Don't do that!" she moaned, and threw her arms around his neck. It hadn't taken long for her to decide that now was definitely not the time to assert her independence.

He held her against his broad chest once more as he issued a stern warning: "Don't you even twitch a muscle until we get down on the ground. Understand?"

"Don't forget, I'm a taxpayer and you work for *me,*" she reminded him crossly.

Darn! she wished she could see what he looked like. He might be old enough to be her father, and if so, she was treating him disrespectfully. The way his hat and mask covered his face, she didn't know if he was twenty or ninety!

Turning her face away from him, she noted that he sure didn't feel as though he were ninety years old. His arms held her as easily as if he were holding a baby, and under all that protective gear she could tell there was a solid wall of muscle.

In a few moments the bucket started easing down the side of the building, and she unconsciously tightened her arms around his neck.

"You're choking me again."

18

"I shall be happy to pay for any bodily damages I inflict," she said. "But right now I need something solid to hold on to."

"If I live through this rescue, I may take you up on that." She could have sworn there was a teasing lilt to his voice. It suddenly occurred to her that all she had on was a very sheer nightgown. She blushed. She couldn't help but be aware that one of his gloved hands was holding her just below her breast, and her face grew even redder. Some guys would take advantage of *any* situation!

"Move your hand!"

"What?"

"I said move your hand!" She tried to push his hand from her side. He didn't respond for a minute, but she could sense his irritation.

"Why?"

"Because I don't like strange men pawing me, even if they are trying to save my life!"

"Do you think I'm trying to make a *pass* at you *now, under these conditions?*" he asked in disbelief.

"I don't know what you're trying to do; just move your hand!" she ordered again.

The hand in question fell away instantly. "Darn. You're a real loony bird!"

She stiffened in resentment at his words. "I am not! Just because you're some kind of a pervert who tries to take advantage of a bad situation—"

"Look, lady," he interrupted harshly, "let's just drop this conversation before I throw you out of this bucket. Okay?"

Before she could reply with a scathing answer,

the bucket reached the ground and she was transferred to another pair of waiting arms.

"Where's Joe?" the fireman who now held her yelled.

"Still up on fifteen. Apparently there were two trapped in one of the apartments, so he went to find the second one. Tell the captain we're going to need more men and equipment up there," Ryder called as he motioned for the bucket to be lifted again.

Someone wrapped a blanket around Merri's shoulders as they hurried her over to an area where other residents of the high-rise sat in stunned silence. Children were crying and frightened, and confused people milled through the crowds, searching for loved ones. A nurse and doctor were examining each new person brought down.

The doctor hurriedly examined Merri. "I don't think there are any real injuries," the doctor told her. "You sit here and I'll have someone bring you a cup of hot coffee and another blanket. It's very cold out here tonight, and I see you're not dressed for the occasion." He winked sympathetically and went on to the next patient.

Merri's eyes unwillingly wandered to the bucket creeping back up the side of the tall building, and her heart raced as the figure of the fireman who had carried her down grew smaller and smaller in the roiling smoke. What a horrible job he had. Would he be able to make it out of that burning building alive a second time?

It seemed like hours before the two firemen

appeared at the window on the tenth floor with a bundle wrapped in a blanket. Merri caught her breath as flames shot out on the heels of the two men's hasty exit from the burning room. She anxiously watched the bucket go into motion once more, praying that Erica had been found in time.

Stumbling over thick hoses, she made her way through the crowd and hurried over to the huge tower-ladder truck the bucket was attached to, to await their arrival. Ten minutes later the small bucket finally reached the ground.

"Is Erica all right?" Merri called out fearfully.

Jerking his mask off, the fireman who had brought her down brushed past her as he carried Erica to the first-aid area.

"Is she all right?" Merri asked again, terrified.

The other fireman who had brought Erica down took his mask and hat off, and Merri noted that his face was streaked with dirt, smoke, and perspiration.

"Ma'am, try to calm down. The doctor will take care of your friend. She's safe now."

"But is she all right?" Merri pleaded, gripping his hand.

"I couldn't say, ma'am."

"Did she say anything to you?"

The fireman hung his head. "No, ma'am . . . but that doesn't necessarily mean anything. . . ."

"Oh, no," she moaned, sure that the fireman wasn't telling her all he knew. "She has to be all right!" Whirling around, she started back to the first-aid area in a dead run, wincing as her bare feet met the cold, hard ground. Barreling around the corner, she collided head on with what felt like a brick wall. The unexpected collision knocked both of them to the ground, and Merri lay stunned for a few moments as she tried to gather her wits about her.

The sound of cursing reached her ears as she looked up and encountered a set of steely gray eyes staring into hers.

The other fireman who had been following her he was now trying to help both parties to their feet.

"Hey, Ryder, are you okay?" he asked as his co-worker staggered upright.

"Holy cow! Did the building cave in?" Ryder asked groggily.

"Here, ma'am, let me help you." Joe extended his hand to Merri, who grasped it gratefully and pulled herself up to a sitting position. Tears of frustration formed in her eyes as she gathered the blanket around her trembling shoulders and tried to avoid the glare of the fireman named Ryder. This night would go down in history as being the most miserable one in her life!

"Are you all right, lady?" Ryder's gruff voice penetrated her shattered emotions, and her temper flared.

"Why don't you watch where you're going!" she snapped.

"*Me!*" he returned hotly.

"Hey, you two." The other fireman stepped between them and picked up Ryder's hat, which had fallen on the ground, and handed it to him. "Why don't you take her over to first-aid again while I get back to work?"

"Me? No way." Ryder picked up his hat and jammed it back on his head irritably. "*You* take her to first aid. I prefer the burning building!"

"You big oaf! You act like all this is *my* fault," Merri accused him. From the moment they had laid eyes on each other, he had rubbed her the wrong way!

"Hey, look, lady, I'm just doing my job and you're being a pain in the neck."

"All right, *I'll* take her to first aid; you get back to work before the captain sees us," the other fireman said. Taking Merri's arm, he hoisted her to her feet and pointed her in the direction in which she had been heading earlier. "I'll be back in a few minutes, Ryder."

The doctor and two nurses were bending over Erica as Merri and Joe McFarland walked over. Merri's feet were beginning to feel like two blocks of ice, and she was sure she'd have pneumonia before the night was over.

Merri moaned softly when she saw how pale Erica looked, and ran over to her friend. "How is she, Doctor?"

The doctor frowned. "She's inhaled a lot of smoke. We're going to send her to the hospital for treatment."

"Merri?" Erica called out weakly.

"I'm here," Merri assured her, kneeling down to take her hand.

"Oh, I'm so glad you're all right. I thought . . ."

"I know. I thought you were too. . . . Are you all right?"

"I think so. . . . What happened?"

"I'm not sure. When I woke up, the room was filled with smoke," Merri explained. "I didn't get to bed until after midnight, so the fire must have started sometime after that."

"Excuse me, ma'am, but we need to take her in the ambulance now." A white-coated attendant moved a stretcher next to Erica and, with the doctor's help, placed her on it.

"Do you want me to come with you?" Merri offered.

"I'd feel better if you were checked over again anyway," the doctor said. "Why don't you ride with your friend to the hospital?"

Merri followed the attendants as they loaded Erica into the back of an ambulance. Streaks of red were beginning to tinge the sky as dawn broke over the blazing inferno.

As the ambulance pulled out of the parking area, Merri turned her head toward the place she had called home for the last year. In the distance she could see the firemen working frantically to put out the blaze, and for just a moment a vision of that arrogant clod who had saved her popped into her mind. Was he all right?

She shook her head to rid herself of his image, and her mind drifted back to more pressing issues. What would happen to her and Erica now? All their clothes, personal possessions, photographs— even her birth certificate—were in that building. Feeling dejected and exhausted, she laid her head down and cried.

CHAPTER TWO

The doctors at St. John's Regional Health Center found that Merri had a touch of frostbite on her feet and thought it was advisable for Erica to remain overnight for observation, so the two friends were placed together in a semiprivate room.

Since Merri's parents lived in town, they were notified by the hospital. The doctor had also notified Erica's parents, who lived four hundred miles away, that there seemed to be no serious injuries to their daughter and that Erica herself would call them later in the day and tell them of the accident.

Merri's parents arrived at the hospital thirty minutes after they were called.

"Are you sure you're all right?" Aurora Lambert asked her daughter as she fussed with the pillows and straightened the blanket on Merri's bed.

"I'm fine, Mom," Merri replied for the tenth time since her mother had entered the room.

"And you, Erica? Is there anything we can do for you?" Aurora persisted.

"No, thanks, Mrs. Lambert. I'm feeling much better now," Erica soothed.

"Well, I can't tell you how relieved I am to hear that. I shudder to think of what a close call you girls had."

"Were there any serious injuries, Mom?" Since arriving at the hospital, Merri knew the emergency room was overflowing with residents of the high-rise, but she had no idea if anyone had been hurt badly.

"Oh, dear. Haven't you heard? There have already been three deaths and numerous serious injuries. The fire is still out of control."

Merri's face clouded with apprehension as she thought about the people who had been her friends and neighbors for the last year. "Have they released any names yet?"

"No, not yet. There hasn't been time to notify all the next of kin." Aurora sighed and patted her daughter's hand lovingly. "Thank God they won't be calling us. . . ."

A few hours earlier Merri had been sure they *would* have been calling her parents. An overwhelming sense of gratitude filled her as she thought of the valiant firemen who were still fighting the blaze. They each deserved a medal of honor. All except one. He deserved a rap across the mouth.

Merri yawned and her eyes grew heavier. She

was safe now. But it could have been such a different story. . . .

"Your father's talking to the doctors now. As soon as he's finished, we're going to leave and let you girls get some rest," Aurora promised. "I know you must be exhausted."

"I *am* pretty tired, Mom," Merri agreed drowsily.

Aurora smiled. "Erica is already asleep," she whispered. "I'll just join your father and let you rest now too."

"Okay, Mom," she murmured. "I'll see you later."

A smile gently curved Merri's lips as her mother leaned down and placed a kiss on her cheek.

"You always smell good, Mom." She sighed. Her mother wore a certain kind of perfume that reminded Merri of home whenever she smelled it, no matter where she was.

"Thank you. You smell like smoke," her mother teased gently.

Smoke . . . fire . . . confusion . . .

Merri dropped off to sleep with thoughts running through her head of the strongest pair of arms she had ever been cradled in, the broadest chest she had ever been held against, and the most despicable personality she had ever encountered. The smell of smoke mixed with the most enticing men's after-shave she had ever smelled. She frowned. All those strange and disturbing things kept dancing through her mind as she slept.

After a night in the hospital Merri and Erica felt like two new people. As they ate breakfast in their beds the following morning, their discussion centered on where they would live when they left the hospital later that day.

Merri knew they would be welcome at her parents' house, but both she and Erica had had their independence so long, they decided to find a new apartment immediately.

"They had a vacancy over in Columns Four last week," Erica remembered as she finished her meal and slid the tray out of her way. As she watched her friend rise and walk over to the lavatory, Merri could tell that Erica was still a bit shaky. Standing in front of the mirror for a moment, Erica surveyed her pale features. "Gad! Do you have any makeup with you?" she grumbled.

"No. I left in such a hurry, I forgot to pack everything I needed," Merri said dryly.

"Oh, yeah." Erica looked embarrassed. "Gosh, Merri, what are we going to do? We don't have a stitch of clothing left!"

"Mom said she would bring some of my old clothes by this morning. I left a lot of things over there when I moved."

"It's a good thing we wear the same size," Erica mused, running her fingers through her shoulder-length blond hair. "Well"—she turned from the mirror and sat back down on her bed—"back to the immediate problem. Jane Wilson rented a nice two-bedroom in Columns Four last week, and she mentioned that there was still a vacancy left. What do you think?"

Merri shrugged. "Sounds all right to me. They're nice apartments, and it would be closer to work for both of us."

"Yes, a lot closer, actually. I think we could swing the rent. We would have the use of the tennis court, exercise room, clubhouse, *and* security guards. Let's call right now and see if they still have the opening."

Ten minutes later Erica hung up the phone. "They said we could look at the apartment this afternoon!" she told Merri enthusiastically.

"That's great. As soon as Mom gets here with some clothes, we can check out."

Erica twirled around the room, excited over the prospect of moving into a new apartment. "I'm sorry this fire had to happen—and if I could change the past, I would—but I'm glad we're moving. I think it's time for a change."

Merri smiled. Erica could always make the most of any situation. They had been best friends through high school and roommates in college. When they graduated, Merri had moved back home for a few months, but discovered that no matter how much she loved her parents, she needed her privacy. One afternoon, during a lunch and shopping spree with Erica, Merri confessed her desire to quit her position at a local bank and pursue her dream of opening her own flower shop. She knew it would mean taking night courses to prepare herself for a new career, but she was willing. Erica, with her bubbly personality and endless enthusiasm for new adventures, encouraged her, and within a few months Merri had her own floral-design shop. Two months later she and Erica took an apartment in the high-rise amid loud protests from her parents, who had enjoyed having their daughter home with them again.

"You know"—Erica paused and looked at Merri —"if it wasn't for those two marvelous firemen who saved our lives, we wouldn't be here to have this discussion!"

Merri nodded her head thoughtfully. "I know." Her mind deviously summoned up the image of the fireman named Ryder who had had the audacity to threaten to throw her out of that bucket if she didn't hold still. "But we have to remember, they were only doing their job," she pointed out realistically. "They weren't doing us any particular favor."

"I know, but that still doesn't alter the fact they saved our lives, and I think we should do something to show our appreciation," Erica persisted.

Merri leveled her eyes at her friend. "How are we going to show our gratitude if we don't even know who they are?"

"Well . . . we'll just find out who they are," Erica said simply. "That shouldn't be hard. We'll simply find out which stations were called to fight the fire and go down there and ask for Joe. . . . Did you notice what a doll *he* was?" Erica broke off unexpectedly, forgetting for a moment the purpose of the conversation.

"No. I didn't notice anything about either one of them," Merri answered quickly.

"From what I could tell, he was a *hunk!* I didn't get a good look at the other one, did you?"

"No."

"Let's see, I think his name was—"

"Ryder," Merri supplied.

Erica paused and looked at her friend knowingly. "I thought you didn't notice anything about them."

Merri lifted her shoulders indifferently. "I heard someone call one Joe and the other one Ryder."

"Which one carried you down?"

"Ryder."

"Ah-ha!"

"What do you mean, 'Ah-ha!'?" Merri demanded impatiently. "So I happen to remember his name! That doesn't mean I was sizing him up, Erica, and you should be ashamed to even think such things at a time like this."

"I meant ah-ha! You did notice more about them than you let on. Anyway, as I was saying, I think we should do something to show our appreciation."

"I'll send them a large bouquet of flowers," Merri offered hurriedly, knowing her friend's uncanny knack for getting the two of them into hot water!

"Flowers! Men don't particularly like flowers," Erica protested.

"Well . . . then let's send them a thank-you card. That would be nice," she suggested.

"Not nice enough. Saving our lives should be worth more than a card," Erica continued to insist. "Think of it, Merri. They saved our *lives!*"

"So we'll make it an expensive card," Merri said

stubbornly. "You know, a when-you-care-enough-to-send-the-very-best–type card."

"No, no, no," Erica groaned aggravatedly. "It wouldn't be good enough; besides, I'd kind of like to see what that Joe looks like with all the smoke and dirt off his face," she confessed.

It was Merri's turn to issue the scathing "Ah-ha!" "Good heavens, Erica, they may both be married and have a dozen kids running around at home!"

"Well . . . if they *are* married, we'll politely express our gratitude and be on our way; and if they're not—"

"*N:* fourteenth letter of the alphabet; *O:* fifteenth letter of the alphabet. *No!*"

"You're not being reasonable," Erica said. "What could it possibly hurt?"

"Erica"—Merri pulled herself up in bed and glared at her friend in disbelief—"what about Chuck?"

"Chuck who?" she tossed off lightly. "We broke up the night of the fire. It was a rotten day all around."

A soft knock on their door interrupted their heated debate.

"Come in!" Merri snapped.

Aurora Lambert stuck her head in and frowned. "Are you feeling worse this morning?"

"No. Come on in, Mom," Merri invited in a more conciliatory tone. "Erica and I were just having a discussion, but we're through now!"

Erica's Cheshire-cat smile indicated *she* wasn't through, but for the moment she would let it ride, which she did all the rest of that day and until after dinner the following evening at Merri's parents' home.

When they had checked out of the hospital the day before, they had gone straight over to see about the new apartment. They fell in love with it at first sight and rented it immediately.

Aurora had convinced them to stay at the Lambert home until they could gather up enough household necessities to set up housekeeping again. The new apartment was furnished, so that narrowed down the essentials to sheets, towels, and kitchen accessories. By mid-morning of the second day, they had managed to come up with everything they needed to move into the apartment.

"Let's get out of the house this afternoon and relax," Erica proposed as she and Merri washed and dried the last of the lunch dishes. "It's nice weather for a change."

Merri glanced at the clock on the kitchen wall. It was barely one o'clock. "I don't know, Erica. We still have a lot to do if we're going to try to move tomorrow." In addition to picking up donations from all her friends that morning, she had managed to run by the shop to put in a couple of hours of work.

"Oh, come on. We'll get it all done," Erica protested.

With a resigned sigh, Merri removed her apron and hung it on the peg beside the back door. "All right. Where do you want to go?"

"Just riding."

"Boy, you must not have worked as hard as I did

this morning," Merri heckled her as they put on their jackets. Then they went outside and got into Erica's blue Toyota. Merri knew Erica hadn't gone to work because her office manager had given her a few days off to get settled. She was a top-notch secretary for an industrial plant not far from Merri's flower shop. "Where did you disappear to all morning?"

"Oh . . . just around."

" 'Just riding'; 'just around,' " Merri teased. "Your vocabulary is very limited today."

They drove around for a while, idly exchanging ideas of what they planned to do with the new apartment. Erica suggested that they drive by the high-rise and see the damage in the daylight. The street in front of the building was still blocked off, so they parked the car and walked the remaining distance. The smell of smoke and burnt debris still hung in the air.

As they stood looking up at the charred remains of the once lovely building, Merri shivered. Memories of swaying around in a small bucket ten stories up, a chill wind whipping against her thin nightgown, filtered through her mind, and she could almost hear again the noise, confusion, and cries of distress.

"Don't you think?" Erica prodded again.

Merri glanced at her friend. "What?"

"I said, don't you think it was a miracle we got out alive?"

Turning her eyes back to what once was her home, she murmured softly, "Yes . . . it *was* a miracle."

34

"And who do we have to thank for those lives?" Merri stiffened. "The good Lord, that's who!"

"True," Erica conceded sheepishly, "but besides Him?"

"Are you going to start that again?" Merri asked. She had hoped Erica had given up on the idea of looking up those two firemen.

Erica's nose tilted upward a fraction in that stubborn manner Merri knew so well. "I certainly am, and if you're not polite enough to at least say thank you properly to two men who saved you from the very clutches of death—"

Merri groaned audibly at Erica's theatrics. She knew without a doubt this was going to be trouble, with a capital *T*.

"—then at least don't try to discourage me from dropping by the stationhouse and letting them know how much I appreciate their services!" Erica finished in a stern voice.

"You don't even know what fire station they're from," Merri accused.

"Well . . . it so happens, I do."

"So *that*'s where you were this morning!" Merri accused her.

"Oh, come on, Merri," Erica pleaded. "So I just *happened* to stumble across their fire station! It was a rare stroke of luck, that's all." She discreetly left out the fact that it had taken her the better part of the morning to dig up that information. In view of the fact that almost every fire station in town had been called that night, including off-duty firemen and volunteers, she thought she had done a marvelous job of sleuthing.

"Erica . . ." Merri's voice held just enough hesitation for Erica to take full advantage of her weakening fortitude.

"We'll just run by for a few minutes, express our gratitude, and be back home in thirty minutes. Now, how can you possibly refuse to go along with anything so simple that would make me feel so good?" By now Erica was dragging Merri back down the street toward her parked car. "For the life of me, I can't see why you're making such a big thing out of this."

"Because I know *you*," Merri complained. "And I haven't the slightest doubt I am going to regret this dark hour of my life. You mark my words!"

The Toyota sped down Glenstone, heading for the fire station where Joe and Ryder were stationed. Merri tried every excuse she could think of to talk Erica out of the madcap idea, but she failed. Not that she wasn't grateful to the two firemen; still, she was going to feel awfully foolish when they walked into that fire station. In her opinion a potted mum plant was much more appropriate.

She was still pleading for mercy as they walked through the entrance of the modern red-brick building.

The station was one of the newer ones in Springfield and looked well cared for. The entrance hall had a sofa, and some pictures hung tastefully on the wall behind it. The two women glanced around, and Merri hesitantly pointed at the door on the right marked CAPTAIN.

Erica rapped in a businesslike manner as Merri

tried to make herself invisible behind her. When Erica had knocked a few times, Merri suggested, with a relieved sigh, that no one was in and they should leave.

"That's crazy," Erica whispered. "Someone *has* to be here. What if there's a fire?"

The sound of a TV playing in the background prompted the two to go down the hallway. Merri wiped her sweaty hands on her jeans as they passed a large bathroom with several showers, lavatories, and stools. Gritting her teeth, she silently wished a thousand times she had been firmer with Erica. Thank heaven the bathroom was empty at the moment!

The next doorway they passed was obviously where the firemen slept. A long row of cots stretched across the room. Although the furnishings were very basic, the room was spotlessly clean.

Suddenly they were standing in the doorway of a very large room where several men were undertaking various housecleaning chores. To the left was a living area with several sofas, chairs, and a TV set. There was a small partition separating the living area from another area. A long table was next to the partition.

Erica cleared her throat, then proceeded to speak in a hesitant voice. "Excuse me. . . ."

Ten sets of male eyes turned in their direction, but Merri didn't see Ryder.

"Would any of you happen to know where we could find Joe and Ryder?" Erica inquired.

For a moment there was complete silence in the

room. The ten sets of eyes surveyed the newcomers inquisitively. Mercifully, when the silence seemed to reverberate throughout the entire building, one lone fireman holding a dustcloth in his hand stepped forward, asking, "Who?"

Merri's grasp tightened in apprehension on Erica's arm.

"Uh . . ." Erica gave him one of her most beguiling smiles. "Joe and Ryder. Actually, I don't know their last names. You see, we lived in the high-rise that burned two nights ago, and two firemen, by the names of Joe and Ryder, helped get us out of the building."

"Oh." The fireman nodded. "You mean McFarland and Tate."

Erica's smile was pasted on her face. "Yes . . . if you say so."

"Tate's mopping the kitchen floor, and McFarland's out in the garage, washing the truck." From between his teeth he let out a shrill whistle that cut through the room. "Hey, Ryder! Someone out here to see you!"

Merri huddled closer to Erica. This was every bit the nightmare she thought it would be!

"Yo! Tell them to come in here," a deep voice called out from behind the partitioned area.

"Just step on in the kitchen, ma'am," the fireman offered graciously.

Merri and Erica walked across the room self-consciously as the men turned back to their work.

"Listen, you go on in and thank Ryder, and I'll go find Joe," Erica instructed Merri.

"Don't you dare leave me!" Merri gasped, but it

was already too late. Erica was across the room, asking where the garage was. Merri made a mental note to strangle her with her bare hands when they got out of there.

Taking a deep breath, Merri ducked around the partition, intent on getting her part over with quickly.

A tall man with curly dark-brown hair was mopping the floor when she entered the room. He glanced up and his features grew puzzled, as he failed to recognize her. "Yes?"

"Hi," Merri began rapidly, sloshing across the wet floor. Her mind was on thanking him, not on the fact she was tracking across his clean floor. "I know you probably don't remember me . . . do you?" she added hopefully.

He studied her for a moment. "You look familiar . . . but no, I'm sorry, I don't recall your name."

"You never knew it," Merri assured him quickly. "We were only together one night for a very short time."

One of his eyebrows rose a fraction of an inch and he glanced away from her uncomfortably. "I'm sorry, I think you have me confused with someone else. . . ."

It suddenly occurred to her how she had phrased her explanation, and Merri's cheeks turned red. "Oh, no . . . I didn't mean together *that* way!" she exclaimed, irritated at the way he had looked so instantly guilty.

An immense look of relief swept over his features. "Oh." He let out what sounded to her like a sigh. "Then, what can I do for you?"

"My name is Merri Lambert and you saved my life the other night."

A look of recognition slowly came over his handsome features as Merri surveyed the broad chest she had been pressed up against two nights earlier. He *was* handsome in his uniform, she conceded as she discreetly surveyed his broad shoulders and muscular arms. She noted that his light blue shirt had round patches on the shoulders stating the name of the city, and his navy blue pants hugged his masculine form in a most appealing way. He was so much younger than she had pictured him to be; he was probably in his early thirties.

He turned back to his mopping. "Oh, yeah. I *do* remember you."

"Well, I just wanted to come by and tell you how much I appreciated what you did that night."

"You're more than welcome," he acquiesced politely.

"And if there's ever anything I can do for you, you be sure and let me know," she offered sincerely. "I'd like to be able to repay you in some small way. After all, saving someone's life should be properly rewarded."

Again his left eyebrow rose slightly as he kept on mopping. "There's really no need. I was only doing my job."

"Does your wife like flowers?" she asked impetuously. "I own a flower shop here in town, and if you'll just give me your address, I'll be happy to send her the biggest bouquet in the shop."

"Thanks, but I'm not married."

"Oh?" She paused and leaned closer.

"Pardon me—do you mind?" He gestured with his eyes to her footprints trailing around the room. "I have that fan running so the floor will dry quicker, but you'll have to stop walking where I'm mopping."

"Oh, my goodness." She laughed nervously. "I *am* sorry. Here, let me go back over this for you."

"No, ma'am, really . . . I can do—"

"No, really, I insist," she coaxed, trying to take the mop from his hand.

"Lady . . . I can do it, really!" he snapped, jerking the mop away from her groping fingers. "If you'll kindly step out of my way, I'll finish the floor, then get to the pie I have to bake for supper!"

Merri noted for the first time the canisters, apples, mixing bowls, and spices on a small table. "I'd be only too happy to finish the floor for you so you could get started on your baking," she insisted. Stubbornly they fought over the mop for a minute, both intent on having the last word. "I am *determined* to do something to pay you back in some small way," Merri warned him grimly, realizing she was getting nowhere.

"Well, all right!" he said between clenched teeth. "I can see you're just as stubborn as you were the night of the fire!" He let go of the mop unexpectedly, sending her flying back against the table. A massive cloud of flour fogged the room as a canister sitting on the table tipped over and spilled onto the floor.

Gasping with indignity, Merri went into a spasm of coughing. The fan was blowing the flour around the room like a Minnesota blizzard!

41

She grimaced when she heard him swear as he tried to fight his way through the blinding flour storm to turn off the fan. The flour covered every square inch of his once immaculate uniform.

Deciding this might be the most opportune time to take her leave, Merri coughed once more and yelled meekly above the chaos, "Well, I'm afraid I've taken up way too much of your time already, Mr. Tate. I'll just be running along and let you finish your work." She grinned lamely. "Thanks again. . . . And remember: If there's anything I can ever . . ." Her voice trailed off as she noted the look of wrath on Tate's flour-covered face.

In a flash she ran out of the kitchen and down the hallway, leaving behind a trail of pasty footprints all the way out to the blue Toyota sitting in the parking lot.

CHAPTER THREE

"What in the world happened to you?" Erica asked as she opened the driver's side of the car and peered in at the blob of white hovering in the front seat.

"Don't even ask!" Merri snapped, crunching down lower. "All this is your fault, Erica Marshall!"

"My fault?"

"Yes, your fault! I have never been so embarrassed in my whole life."

"What happened?" Erica demanded again as she got in the car and started the engine. "Didn't you find Ryder?"

"Oh, yes, I found him," Merri said grimly. "And I thanked him properly for saving my life. Then, since I had thoughtlessly tracked all over the floor he was trying to mop, I offered to finish the job for him while he started a pie. . . ."

"And . . . ?"

"And we sort of disagreed over who should do the mopping, and before I knew it, there was flour blowing all over the kitchen and we were both covered from head to toe!"

"Oh, my gosh! Flour! What did he say?"

"Nothing. Absolutely nothing. But if looks could kill, I would be dead right now!" she admitted.

Erica heaved a sigh of resignation. "That's horrible. Then I gather you and Ryder didn't hit it off."

Merri glanced over at her friend crossly. "You might say that."

"I hate to hear it. Joe and I liked each other instantly," she admitted happily. "I found out he's thirty-one and unattached, and he loves Clint Eastwood movies, pepperoni pizza, buttered popcorn, and rainy nights!"

"Well, hooray for you and Joe," Merri said morosely, wondering how in the world anyone could find out so much about a stranger in fifteen minutes.

"Didn't you find out anything about Ryder?"

"Other than the fact he looks horrible in white?" she snapped. "Very little. I didn't go in there to do a case history on him, Erica. If you'll recall, we were only going to thank the firemen for saving our lives."

"Yeah, I know," Erica admitted, "but now that I found out Joe is single, I consider that the biggest stroke of luck I've had in ages!"

"Ryder is single, too, but I don't find that to be as exciting as you—"

"He is? Gee, that's fantastic! Joe said he and Ryder not only work together but are personal friends as well. Wouldn't that be something if we started double-dating—"

"Whoa! Hold on a minute!" Merri cast an instant blight on Erica's fantasizing. "You can just stop that ridiculous train of thought instantly!"

"Why?" Erica turned puzzled eyes in her direction.

"Why? Are you dim-witted?" Merri snapped. "So far I have done nothing but make a complete fool out of myself when I'm around Ryder Tate!"

"If you're talking about that little flour incident—"

"It isn't only the flour incident," Merri interrupted. "We had a small disagreement when he was trying to carry me down in the bucket the night of the fire."

It was Erica's turn to glare at her friend in disbelief. "You had a fight with someone who was trying to rescue you from a burning building?"

"Not a fight exactly." Merri shifted around in her seat and picked at the clumps of flour stuck to her jeans. "He was trying to be bossy, and you know how I hate chauvinistic men!"

"You don't find him attractive?" Erica asked.

"Oh, he's good-looking enough," Merri had to admit. "But this whole conversation is pointless, Erica. I'm absolutely *positive* he would never be interested in me."

"He might be if you let him know you're interested," Erica pointed out.

"Erica! I am *not* interested in him! If you and Joe want to pursue each other's company, then more power to you, but count me out!"

"All right, but I think you're making a terrible mistake," Erica relented grudgingly.

"Then *you* go after him."

"No, I think I'll concentrate my efforts on Joe."

"You'll be lucky if you ever see him again," Merri grumbled under her breath.

"Oh-ho! That's where you're wrong." Erica had heard her and couldn't hold back her gleeful response. "He knows we're moving tomorrow and he's offered to drop by and see if we need any help."

"How nice," Merri noted wryly. "Just as long as he doesn't bring his friend along."

Erica pulled into the driveway of the Lambert home and shut off the engine. Flashing Merri a mischievous grin, she giggled. "How could he? His friend will probably still be pasted to the kitchen floor of the fire station!"

"I certainly hope so!" Merri said sourly. They both burst into giggles as Merri playfully smacked her jacket sleeve in Erica's direction and the small car fogged anew with flour.

After church on Sunday, Merri and Erica ate a hurried lunch, then began to load their possessions into the Toyota and Merri's station wagon.

"It's times like these I'm glad you drive this

tank," Erica commented as she shoved a large box into the back of the station wagon.

"I can't afford two cars, and I have to have something big enough to deliver flowers in," Merri explained, pushing the box back as far as it would go. "Besides, I happen to like old Watson."

"It's a good thing. Old Watson would be doomed to the junk pile if you didn't." Erica surveyed the old car disparagingly. It had definitely seen better days!

"When I get rich, I'm going to buy a new van," Merri proclaimed optimistically as she jumped out of the back. "Until then, speak a little more kindly around Watson. He's sensitive."

"Sorry, Watson." Erica patted one slightly dented fender lovingly. "If you'll just get our meager belongings over to our new apartment, I'll never ask another thing of you."

"She might not, but I will," Merri warned with a gentle pat on Watson's rusted rear fender. Wealth was still a long way off!

It was the middle of the afternoon when the two cars drove between the large pillars leading into the Columns Four apartment complex. For the next two hours Erica and Merri worked steadily, unloading the cars and carrying boxes into their new home.

It was close to five o'clock when a late-model Corvette pulled up to the Columns Four and waited while the security guard cleared the occupants' admittance and told them where to park.

"I still think we should go bowling tonight," Ryder Tate said irritably as Joe McFarland put the

47

engine back into drive and headed for the address the guard had given them.

"Hey, we won't get tied up here very long," Joe promised. "I sort of half promised I'd drop by and see if the ladies needed any help, and I sure would hate to disappoint them."

"How could you disappoint them? You only met them a couple of days ago," Ryder pointed out dryly. If Joe had given any indication earlier that he planned on going there, Ryder wouldn't have come along. He had thought they were going straight to the bowling alley.

"Yeah, but the point is, I might want to build up a friendship with Erica." He gave Ryder a knowing wink.

Ryder shook his head wryly. "Don't you ever get tired of chasing women?"

"Never! Besides, I thought you might want to check out the other one. . . . What's her name . . . Merri?"

"No, thanks."

"Why not? She's a good-looking chick."

"She'd probably knock your head off if she heard you refer to her as a 'chick,'" Ryder warned. "She has a temper."

"Well, what the heck? Let's check them out anyway. You are going to have to learn to stop being so distrustful when it comes to the opposite sex," Joe said philosophically. He parked the car in front of the designated apartment and braked once more. "And you can thank your fairy godmother I'm here to help you, good buddy." He reached for the handle on his door and got out of the car. When he noticed that Ryder was making no move to exit, he went around to his side of the car and knocked on the window. "You coming?"

Rolling down the window hesitantly, Ryder frowned. "No, you go on. I'll wait in the car."

"Oh, come on!" Joe opened the door and adamantly motioned for Ryder to get out. "We'll just stick our heads in and say a quick hello."

Moments later Ryder found himself walking to the door with Joe, his lagging stride testifying to his reluctance.

"She isn't going to be happy to see me," he predicted.

"You don't know that."

"I do know it. She doesn't like me," he insisted, grimacing as Joe punched the doorbell.

"So? You're not here to ask her to marry you," Joe observed. "You need to loosen up, Ryder. There's bound to be a woman somewhere who'll meet your specifications. Maybe this will be your lucky day."

"I'd prefer to pick my own women," Ryder replied defensively. "And stop worrying about my love life, okay?"

"I don't know about you, fella—" He broke off as the door swung open and Erica gasped excitedly.

"Well, for heaven's sakes! Look who's here! I was so surprised when the guard called to announce you!"

Joe grinned. "We just happened to be driving by and thought we'd stop in and say hi."

"I'm so glad you did! Come in!" Erica gestured for the two men to enter the apartment, her face beaming as she smiled at Joe. "You'll have to excuse the mess. We just got here a couple of hours ago."

"Say, this is nice," Joe complimented, glancing around the room approvingly.

"Thanks! I think Merri and I are going to love it. . . . Merri! Come out here. We have company!" Erica called brightly.

Seconds later Merri entered the room, her face falling when she saw who it was. "Oh . . . hi."

Joe greeted her in a friendly manner while Ryder nodded his head politely in her direction.

"Joe and Ryder happened to be in the neighborhood and decided to stop in," Erica explained. "I wonder if we can find the coffeepot. Would you guys like a cup of coffee?"

"No, we can only stay a minute," Ryder explained.

"Oh?" Erica's face fell with disappointment.

"What he means is, we only stopped by to see if you needed any help," Joe clarified, discreetly punching Ryder in the ribs.

"How nice of you to offer! I know you said you might, but I really wasn't expecting you!" Erica's face brightened once more. "I don't know how Merri's coming along in the kitchen, but I'm having a terrible time arranging my bedroom to suit me."

Joe wiggled his eyebrows up and down suggestively. "Joe McFarland, interior decorator extraordinaire, at your service, ma'am."

Erica giggled as he followed her toward her

bedroom, leaving Merri and Ryder standing uncomfortably in the living room, facing each other.

"Well . . ." Merri laughed shakily. "I guess I'll get back to work. Just make yourself at home. I'm sure Erica won't detain Joe very long."

Ryder cleared his throat. "Thanks." He walked over to the sofa and seated himself as Merri disappeared into the kitchen.

The least he could do was ask if *she* needed any help! Snatching up the shelf paper, she measured off the precise size and angrily cut it off the roll. Joe was in there helping Erica; why couldn't Ryder put forth enough courtesy to at least poke his head through the doorway and say, "Oh, by the way, is there anything I can do to help you, Merri?" Not that she would even consider accepting his help, but it would be nice. . . .

"Pardon me."

Merri whirled around and almost fell off the chair she was perched on as Ryder's voice interrupted her silent seething. She hurriedly pasted a pleasant smile on her face and turned to him. "Yes?"

"I was wondering if there was something I could do to help you." He didn't sound very sincere, but Merri guessed it was better than no offer at all. At least now she could have the pleasure of refusing him.

"No, thanks," she replied politely. "I'm just putting in new shelf paper."

He surveyed the disorganized kitchen. "Are you sure?"

51

"Positive," she reaffirmed in a cool tone, turning back to her work.

Walking over to the cabinets she had already placed the new paper in, he peered inside. "I could start unpacking some of your dishes and put them in for you," he offered.

"That's not necessary."

"I figure helping you is better than sitting around, twiddling my thumbs," he confessed bluntly.

Wow! This guy could really make a woman feel wanted!

"Oh . . . well, if you insist . . ." She eyed him warily.

Stepping over to one of the large cardboard boxes, he surveyed the contents, then demanded, "Where do you want the glasses?"

Her lower lip jutted outward at his gruff demeanor. "In the right-hand cabinet on the middle shelf," she said tensely.

He rustled through the boxes and began to bring out assorted glasses. When he had all the glasses taken care of, he used his own discretion in placing the cups and saucers. He noticed that Merri seemed to be a bit testy again this evening, and he didn't want to stir her wrath any more than necessary. From the moment they had met, he seemed to provoke her unintentionally.

Joe had been correct in accusing Ryder of being wary around women. He was—with very good reason. The majority of the women he'd dated had left him with a cold, empty feeling. Coming from a well-known, wealthy family, Ryder had found out early in life that money was the root of all evil and seemed to have undo influence on the women he dated once they found out who he was. Five years earlier, with his parents' understanding, he had decided to leave the golden nest and live an ordinary life, securing a job with the fire department and supporting himself totally. As far as he was concerned, the woman he married would never know of his considerable bank account until the day he married her. That way he could be sure she had married him for love, not money.

Merri watched Ryder out of the corner of her eye, trying to figure him out. Erica had always accused her of being too aloof with men, but she had never found one she wanted to give her independence up for. She didn't have the slightest desire to become encumbered with a "lasting relationship" until the right man came along, and so far she hadn't seen hide nor hair of that particular man. To be quite honest, this fireman had come closest to stirring her senses, but the really crazy thing was, she didn't have the slightest idea *why* Ryder Tate affected her as he did. His mere presence irritated her most of the time. So why was he so fascinating to her?

"Am I doing all right?" he asked, tackling another large box energetically.

"You're doing okay," she admitted reluctantly.

Ripping off another piece of shelf paper, she peeled off the back to expose the self-adhesive surface. The instructions had led her to believe this type of shelf paper would be clean and a snap to apply. Ha! she thought impatiently as she tried to peel off a strip that had stuck to her arm. When she finally removed it, another aggressive piece of paper firmly fastened itself to her hand. Waspishly she tried to shake it off, but only succeeded in turning the paper into a mangled mess. With a snort of disgust she attacked the paper with both hands, intent on being the victor in this unexpected wrestling match. Moment by moment her temper grew, her face becoming angry and flushed as she ripped at the paper, trying to reassert her authority.

Ryder had paused in his work and stood surveying her in bewilderment. It appeared this could very well be a fight to the death.

With an exasperated cry of disgust, Merry flung the wad of crumpled paper on the floor and glared at it.

"May I be of any assistance?" Ryder offered, an amused grin tugging at the corners of his mouth.

"This stupid paper is driving me nuts!" she wailed.

"Would you like to trade jobs?" he suggested in a calm voice.

"Do you think you can do any better?" she chided in an indignant tone.

"I don't think I can do any worse," he reasoned, eyeing the crumpled shelf paper on the floor.

"I only have two more shelves. . . . I think I'd rather do this than unpack."

Ryder shrugged his shoulders. "Whatever you think." He walked back to the table and dug into the box once more.

Five minutes later, war was again raging hot and heavy between Merri and the shelf paper.

"Why don't you let me finish that and you do something else?" Ryder suggested as Merri, infuriated, threw down another piece of mutilated paper.

"Be my guest!" she relented curtly. Climbing down off the chair she had been standing on, she offered him the roll of paper. "It is totally impossible to line that top shelf!"

"Have you thought about using another kind of paper?" he asked with maddening composure. Picking up a previously discarded roll of the nonadhesive type of shelf lining, he casually unwrapped it. "This shelf is irregular. We'll just cut a piece to fit as close as possible and use these short nails to hold it in place."

Meticulously he measured the size they would need and cut it off the roll. "Now, I'll hold it in place while you hammer in the nails."

Moments later the paper was lying neatly on the shelf. Ryder held the nail firmly in place. "It's your turn," he teased with an easy grin.

Merri found her stomach suddenly filled with butterflies. They were in very close proximity at the moment, and it was impossible for her to ignore the smell of that wonderful, sexy after-shave he wore.

She swallowed uneasily and gripped the hammer nervously. Her body was pressed against his muscular form as they stood on the kitchen chair together.

"Is there something wrong?" he asked uneasily,

realizing for the first time their nearness to each other. Her light floral perfume drifted up to tantalize his senses as he inched away from her slightly.

"No . . . nothing," she murmured, noting for the first time what a clear, beautiful shade of gray his eyes were.

"Just give it a light tap on the head," Ryder encouraged, referring to the short nail he was holding.

"Yes . . . I know how . . ." she assured him, mesmerized by his handsome features looming so close to hers.

Their gazes met and held for a moment, and neither one could think of anything to say. Almost every man Merri knew would have taken full advantage of this moment and kissed her, but Ryder seemed to have no inclination in that direction. In fact, their closeness seemed to be makng him very uncomfortable.

Reaching out in a daze, she rapped the nail much harder than she had intended to.

An agonized cry of pain erupted throughout the room as she groped to prevent Ryder from falling off the chair. "Oh, my gosh! Was that your finger?" she cried, aghast that she should do such a thoughtless thing.

Ryder was in so much pain, he couldn't speak. She watched helplessly as he wrung his hand, sucking in deep, anguished breaths. His finger was throbbing like an abscessed tooth as she helped him off the chair.

"I am *so* sorry," she apologized. "I should have been more careful!"

The yelps of pain coming from the direction of the kitchen brought Joe and Erica in to investigate the commotion.

"What happened?" Erica demanded, anxiously surveying Ryder's pale face.

"Ohhh, I missed the nail and hit Ryder's finger with the hammer," Merri said.

"You *what?*" Erica glared disapprovingly in her friend's direction. How were they ever going to get anywhere with these two guys if Merri didn't cooperate?

"We were trying to put shelf paper on the top shelf! I certainly didn't mean to."

"Let's take a look at it." Joe walked over and gripped Ryder's hand. A low whistle followed as Joe winced. "I'll bet that hurts like the blue blazes."

Ryder's finger was already beginning to swell and showing signs of turning blue around the nail as he fought to overcome the excruciating pain and stand upright. "Don't worry about it; it was just an accident," he mumbled in a strained voice.

"Here, we'd better run some cold water over it," Merri urged as she pulled him over to the kitchen faucet. "I don't know anything else to do for it except maybe wrap it in ice," she apologized.

"I think you'd better," Erica cautioned. "It's swelling awfully fast."

They all dutifully oohed and aahed in sympathy as Merri made a makeshift ice bag out of a kitchen towel and wrapped it around his hand gently.

"There. Does that feel better?" she asked hopefully.

"Really, it will be all right," Ryder reassured her once more, but she knew he was only trying very hard to be polite.

He swore and jerked his hand out of the way as she accidentally dropped the empty ice tray she had picked up to refill. She couldn't believe she was such a klutz in his presence!

"Oh, good grief! Did it hit your finger again?" she gasped.

Erica quickly stepped in and took the tray away from Merri. "I think you'd better let me do this.

"Joe and I were just about to come in and see if you two would like to go out for a sandwich," Erica announced as she filled the tray with water and replaced it in the refrigerator.

Ryder glanced at Joe with panic-stricken eyes. "I don't think so. . . . We have to be running along now," he hedged.

Erica frowned in disappointment. "Are you sure? I know your finger hurts, but maybe something to eat will take your mind off it. Ebenezer's has marvelous food."

Joe placed a friendly, reassuring arm around Erica's waist as the four walked into the living room. "I'm afraid we'll have to take a rain check tonight. How about tomorrow night?"

Merri couldn't help but notice the look of disbelief Ryder shot in his friend's direction.

"What about it, Ryder? You don't have anything going for tomorrow night, do you?" Joe asked innocently.

"Nothing definite, but—" Ryder began.

"Great! How about seven o'clock?" Joe turned to Erica and grinned boyishly.

"Seven would be fine with me! What about you, Merri?"

Merri glanced at Ryder uneasily. This was horrible! She knew he wanted to take her out about as much as he wanted a case of malaria.

"I really don't think—"

"Good! Then it's all settled. Ryder and I will be by around seven tomorrow evening," Joe interrupted.

They all said polite good-byes and Erica let Joe and Ryder out the front door. The minute the door closed, Merri rushed over to Erica and exploded. *"Why did you do that?"*

"What?"

"Force Ryder into taking me out on a date!"

"I didn't *force* Ryder to ask you for a date," Erica scoffed. "Whatever are you talking about?"

"It was as plain as the nose on your face the man does not want to go out with me." Merri groaned. "Couldn't you see how green his face turned when Joe mentioned it?"

"His face turned green because his finger was about to fall off, you goofball! How could you have missed the nail?"

"I don't want to go out with him," Merri told her stubbornly, ignoring her question. "I won't be here tomorrow night when they come. You can tell them I got tied up at work."

"And spoil my evening with Joe?" Erica gasped. "If you didn't want to go with Ryder, you didn't have to agree. All you had to do was say no!"

"Erica, you are making me ill." Merri slumped down on the sofa and stared at the ceiling. "I am a total basket case around that man and I don't know why!"

"Maybe because you find him attractive," Erica suggested, flopping down beside her. "He is, you know."

"I realize that, but he isn't the least bit interested in me."

"Well, maybe that's because you have shown so little gratitude to him!"

"I told the man I was grateful to him for saving my life," she said in an exasperated tone. "What do you want me to do, throw *him* in a burning building and come to *his* rescue?"

"No, but I told Joe over and over how grateful I am to him, and even though he says he was only doing his job, you should see the way he beams when I bring it up. Men eat up compliments and praise, you know."

Merri closed her eyes and pondered Erica's words. Maybe she was right. She had only apologized one time, and that apology seemed to have gotten lost in the flour storm. Maybe Ryder Tate didn't think she was grateful enough. That would explain his cool indifference to her and his reluctance to go out on a spur-of-the-moment date.

She gave a long sigh. She hated to admit it, but Ryder did appeal to her. Perhaps it would be to her advantage to put forth a little more effort to show her appreciation of his heroic act the night of the fire. "Maybe you're right," she relented. "I'm going to try my best to show him how much I appreciate what he did, but I still absolutely refuse to go out with him. I have my pride."

"If you don't want to go out with him, that's your mistake and I can't force you to," Erica said.

Merri let out another long sigh. "When I feel like I've sufficiently paid him back, I want your word you'll butt out. I am not now—nor do I ever plan to be—personally interested in Ryder Tate."

Erica looked momentarily surprised at her friend's lack of tact, but accepted it in a congenial way. "You've got it. But don't be surprised if something totally unexpected develops out of all of this."

"And don't *you* be if it doesn't!" Merry warned her friend.

CHAPTER FOUR

True to her word, Merri deliberately kept herself busy at the flower shop long after her normal quitting time. Since Easter was only a few weeks away, plus the fact she had two weddings to prepare for, she barely noticed the couple of extra hours work. When she arrived home, she ate the hamburger she had bought at a fast-food restaurant and took a hot shower, feeling very proud of herself for getting out of the impromptu date so easily. She would have loved to see the look on Ryder Tate's face when he showed up that evening and Erica told him Merri had been unavoidably detained. A devilish grin tugged at the corners of her mouth, then sagged momentarily. Maybe she wouldn't want to see his face. He might have been as relieved to get out of the date as she had been!

No, she countered. He might not have been overjoyed at the prospect of spending an evening with her, but still, he was a single man, and although she wasn't a raving beauty, she was reasonably sure she didn't make men run for the nearest latrine to retch.

Yes, she decided with a confident toss of her brown curls, Ryder Tate had probably been *very* disappointed. Too bad. Maybe the next time they met he would show a little more respect.

It was after one o'clock in the morning when Merri heard Erica's key in the front door. Her date must have been a roaring success for Erica to stay out so late on a work night. Slipping out of bed quietly, Merri padded into the kitchen, where Erica was fixing herself a cup of hot tea.

Erica turned from the stove and smiled brightly. "Hi! Did I wake you? I'm sorry."

"I wasn't sleeping," Merri dropped into a chair at the table and yawned. "I thought I would fall asleep the minute my head touched the pillow, but I didn't. How was your date?"

"Fabulous. Want some tea?"

"No, thanks." Hiding another wide yawn, she eyed Erica accusingly. "It must have been. Do you realize what time it is?"

"Not really. What time is it?"

"One fifteen."

"No kidding?" Erica brought her cup of tea over to the table and sat down. Reaching for the sugar bowl, she stirred three heaping teaspoonfuls into the hot liquid. "Joe and I didn't realize how late it was getting."

Merri groaned inwardly. This wasn't encouraging at all. Erica was already showing unmistakable signs of being bitten again by that little love bug, which seemed to be drawn to her like a magnet!

"I don't see how you had such a fabulous time with an extra person dragging along," Merri pointed out.

Erica glanced up from the rim of her cup. "An extra person?"

"Ryder Tate." Merri refreshed her memory.

"Oh." Erica blew on her hot tea, then took a sip. "He didn't come."

"He didn't *what?*"

Erica shrugged. "Ryder couldn't make it tonight. He sent his apologies. It really worked out just great," Erica said in a relieved voice. "That way I didn't have to tell him *you* were detained and couldn't keep the date either."

"He stood me up! That low-down chiseler stood me up!" Merri sprang to her feet and began to pace the small kitchen angrily. "Can you beat that?"

"For the life of me, I can't see why you're getting all bent out of shape," Erica remarked calmly. *"You* were the one who was going to stand *him* up. What's the difference?"

"I'm not sure, but there is!" Her pacing increased in intensity. "The very nerve of that guy!"

"Well, if you ask me, you deserved it."

"Me? What did I do? I agreed to go on the date!"

"But then you backed out!"

Merri slapped her hand down on the table irritably. "That doesn't make any difference," she argued. "He agreed to go, too, and he didn't know I had decided not to go, therefore *he* stood *me* up!"

"What brilliant reasoning." Erica groaned. "If you don't want to go out with him, why should you care what he does?"

"It's the principle of the thing," Merri fumed.

Erica rose from the table and took her cup over to the sink. "I'm afraid that's something you'll have to work out yourself, because I'm going to bed."

Merri followed Erica through the apartment, still grumbling crossly under her breath.

"If I were you, I would stop grumbling under my breath and do something about it if it really upset me that much," Erica ventured.

"It doesn't upset me!"

"No, I can see that it doesn't. Sorry." Erica paused at the doorway to her bedroom and looked at her friend sympathetically. "I really am sorry, but you did ask for it." Without another word Erica entered her bedroom and closed the door, leaving Merri silently seething by herself.

The following morning Merri was at the flower shop by seven A.M. Because sleep had eluded her most of the night, she had decided to come in early and begin work on plan A, being intellectually and cleverly designed to pay back one Ryder "Hotshot" Tate for saving her life. On the remote and highly unlikely prospect that plan A should fail, she had proficiently drawn up plans B and C and was prepared to put them into action within a blink of an eye. Somehow, some way, she had to get this monkey off her back.

By the time her two employees, Cleo and Megan, arrived for work at nine, Merri had constructed what she thought to be her most impressive piece of work to date. A gargantuan floral offering in the shape of a large horseshoe filled the entire working area of the small shop: profusions of red, white, and blue blossoms massed together to form a most impressive piece of art. A large streamer proclaimed in bold black lettering: THANK YOU, RYDER TATE! YOU'RE THE BEST! If that didn't let him know she was grateful, then she didn't know what would!

"What in the world is that?" Cleo Jarmen eyed the stupendous wreath with awe as she removed her jacket and hung it on the Victorian clothes tree.

"Isn't it something?" Merri beamed proudly at her newly created offering.

"Yeah . . . well . . . it really *is* something," Cleo agreed. She slowly circled the mind-boggling assemblage of gladioli, mums, carnations, and daisies. "Who ordered such an elaborate . . . something?"

"No one. I'm sending this to the fireman who saved my life," Merri told her. "Think he'll like it?" She stood back once more to survey the array looming before her.

"I don't know about that, but I think you can safely assume he's never received anything even remotely like it before." She paused and perused it thoughtfully once more. "Don't you think perhaps it's a bit . . . large?" The massive wreath was totally out of character with the usual delicate creations Merri was known for.

Merri eyed the wreath critically. "No. . . . I wanted something rather ostentatious."

"Then you've hit it perfectly," Cleo said with a tinkling laugh.

"Good, I thought so too." Merri stuck the last piece of greenery into the wreath and brushed her hands off in satisfaction. "How about delivering this for me."

Cleo's face paled. "Me?"

"Yeah. Since I'm the one sending it, I don't think I should be the one to deliver it," Merri reasoned, washing her hands and applying a dab of hand lotion. "While you're at it, you might as well make the hospital deliveries too."

An hour later the three had completed the hospital orders for the morning and had the station wagon loaded. The large wreath barely fit in the back of the wagon, so the women had to place some of the smaller bouquets in the front seat.

"You'd better go to the hospital first," Merri cautioned, rearranging a bouquet designed for a new mother and her baby. "Oh, wait a second. I guess I should put some sort of note on the wreath you're taking by the fire station." She ran back into the shop and returned a few minutes later with a small note card and attached it to the wreath. She had signed it with a simple *Thanks again, Merri Lambert*.

"I envy you, Cleo," Merri sighed, breathing in

the mild spring air. "I think spring is finally going to get here and I'm stuck in the shop all day."

"I'll be glad to stay and let you do the deliveries," Cleo offered hurriedly. She didn't want to hurt Merri's feelings, but she dreaded the thought of taking that monstrous wreath to the fire station. Maybe with a little luck . . . "What if Ryder Tate isn't on duty today. Don't firemen work twenty-four-hour shifts, then have a string of days off?"

"Yeah, I think so, but he works the same shift as Joe McFarland, and Erica mentioned that Joe would be working today."

"Oh." Cleo started the station wagon. "Well, ol' Watson and I will be back as soon as we get our work done."

"Take your time," Merri called as she watched Cleo back out of the drive. A great sense of relief assailed her as she walked slowly into the shop, savoring the mild temperature. At least she had made an effort to repay Ryder Tate for her life. Granted, it was a very small gesture, but a sincere one nevertheless. She paused for a moment and tilted her face upward, drinking in the feel of the warm sunshine. Missouri had had a long, hard winter that year, and spring was slow in coming. But, she reasoned contentedly, it couldn't be too far off. The next day would be the first day of April, and although there would be lots of April showers to bring May flowers, the temperature would be warmer and the trees would be shooting forth their new leaves. For a moment she stood with her eyes closed, silently thanking the Lord and Ryder

Tate that she could be there that very day, enjoying the smells and sights of this new spring.

Immediately after lunch Megan and Merri went to work on the bouquets for the Williams wedding that would take place that evening. Weddings were some of Merri's favorite events. She loved the glow and excitement, and in some small way she always felt a part of the happiness that surrounded such affairs. When the phone rang around two and Megan announced it was for Merri, Merri carefully laid down the yellow rose she was arranging in the bridal bouquet and went to answer it.

"This is Merri. May I help you?"

A male voice cleared his throat nervously. "Merri Lambert?"

"Yes?"

"This is Ryder Tate."

"Oh, yes, Mr. Tate. How are you?" She leaned back on the stool at the counter and prepared herself for his lavish thank yous, which she considered totally unnecessary. The floral wreath had been her pleasure.

"What in the hell is this thing you sent me?"

Merri blinked in surprise. "You mean that beautiful floral wreath?"

"Is that what it is? I thought it was a portable greenhouse," he replied crossly.

"No, it isn't a portable greenhouse!" Good grief, was she dealing with a moron?

"Are you under the mistaken impression someone passed away in my immediate family?"

"Of course not. The flowers are just my small way of reiterating my profound gratitude for your extreme bravery," she returned with saccharine sweetness, trying not to let her temper seep through the conversation. She was still upset over his failure to show up the night before. "I had planned on telling you in person last night," she stressed in an overly friendly tone, "but you were unable to keep your commitment."

"Yes, I'm terribly sorry," he mocked. "And I understand you were unavoidably detained also."

Merri made a sassy face into the receiver. "Yes, I was. I am so sorry too. I really hated to miss the opportunity of seeing you again."

"I'm sure."

"Didn't you care for the flowers?"

"They have certainly amused the other men," Ryder told her. "Especially the big banner that says 'Thank you, Ryder Tate. You're the best!' They're all still trying to figure that one out."

Merri cringed as it suddenly dawned on her how that must sound to the other men. "I . . . I didn't mean to embarrass you. . . . I only meant—"

"Oh, I know what you meant, Miss Lambert," he interrupted curtly. "Perhaps I haven't made myself clear on this matter of my saving your life. I would have rescued anything that happened to be breathing that night, Miss Lambert. You see, that's my job," he explained in a voice dripping with patience. "In addition to putting out the flames, I am supposed to carry to safety anyone I happen to stumble over. Isn't that neat? I can assure you, there is absolutely nothing personal about who I

70

rescue and who I don't. Now, does that make you feel a little better?"

"Are you trying to be facetious?"

"No. Are you trying to get on my nerves? If you are, you're on the right track," he stated without the least bit of tact.

"I certainly am *not* trying to get on your nerves," she snapped. "It may have been a very impersonal act on your part, but it was *I* who thought I was going to die! I have every right to show my appreciation."

"Miss Lambert, I assisted in saving your friend, Erica, that night, too, and *she* isn't bugging the hell out of me. Why do you feel like you have to?"

"Oh, for heaven's sake! Erica's more interested in Joe than she is in you," Merri shot back without thinking.

There was dead silence on the other end of the line as Merri's words sank in. "Is that what this is all about?" Ryder asked in a steely tone. Here was another pushy woman, only this one beat all he had ever seen!

"If you're trying to imply that I desire your company, then listen closely, Mr. Tate: My only desire is to pay you back in some small way for saving my life. When I'm convinced I have accomplished that, you can go to the Devil for all I care."

"Look, this conversation is getting to be a drag. I accept your gratitude and I ask only a small favor out of you."

Merri let out a sigh of relief. "You do? That really makes me feel better. What's the favor?"

In a voice that sounded as if he were gritting

every tooth in his mouth, he whispered in a loud hiss, "Please don't *ever* send me flowers at the fire station again, and *get off my back!*"

She jumped nervously as she heard the loud click on the other end of the line. He had hung up on her! Furiously she slammed the receiver back into place, her face turning beet red.

Drumming her fingers irritably on the counter top, Merri sizzled. Well, it was plain he was going to make this hard on her. She hadn't thought she would have to resort to plan B so soon. Obviously he hadn't appreciated the flowers or her gratitude. Now that he had tactlessly pointed out her glaring blunder, she could see where he would be a *little* embarrassed by the banner—a poor choice of words on her part. Maybe the flowers had been a mistake, but plan B would not fail to catch his attention. Whether he liked it or not, Merri was forced to repay him not only for saving her life but for embarrassing the pants off him in front of his co-workers. And come hell or high water, she *was* going to repay him. No one could ever accuse Merri Lambert of not paying her debts!

The following Saturday morning dawned bright and clear. The alarm had gone off a little before six, and a groggy Merri had fallen out of bed in a daze. A hot shower and three cups of coffee later, she still was finding it difficult to keep her eyes open. She would have welcomed sleeping late that morning, but she knew that today would be her only opportunity to implement plan B. The weatherman was promising mild temperatures after a rather frosty start to the day. Shivering, she climbed into the front seat of her station wagon a little before seven and drove to the address Erica had secured from Joe the night before.

Ryder Tate lived in an apartment complex just off Sunshine Street on Ingram Mill Road. After a hurried stop to get another cup of coffee and two glazed doughnuts at a local convenience market, Merri pulled up in front of his apartment building and parked. There was very little astir at that ungodly hour of the morning. She sat sipping her coffee and munching on her doughnuts for a few minutes before she went to work. Her eyes fastened on the old wreck parked in Ryder's driveway. The car was a four-door sedan at least fifteen years old. It not only needed to be washed, it was screaming for a new paint job as well. Deciding that the car fit his personality to a tee, she licked the sticky glaze off her fingers and opened the car door. Removing a large shopping bag from the backseat, which was filled with cleaning supplies, she zipped her jacket up against the brisk early-morning wind and started up the drive.

She stood grimly surveying the old car. It was a piece of junk in her opinion, and certainly not worth the effort she was about to undertake, but that would be all the more reason why he'd appreciate her efforts.

Reasoning that a single man's pride and joy was usually his car, she had decided plan B would include a complete washing, waxing, and interior cleaning of Ryder's car. A small gesture, to be sure, but it was the only thing she could think of that

73

would be sure to please him. She had purposely picked this early hour to do the chore, as Joe had said Ryder liked to sleep late on his days off. Joe had told Erica that both he and Ryder would have this Saturday off, so Merri had decided it was the day to put plan B into operation. By the time Ryder got up, she would be gone and his car would look like new. She had already written a nice, polite note to leave on the windshield, apologizing for sending him the flowers and embarrassing him in front of his friends. In the note she thanked him yet again for saving her life, and signed it. After another quick glance at the car, she grimaced and quickly amended her earlier glowing prediction of "looking like new" to "looking a little better."

A small gray-haired poodle with pink ribbons shot out of the bushes in her direction as she placed her sack of cleaning supplies on the ground and blew on her cold fingertips. The dog continued to close in on her, his yapping becoming more fierce as she backed away uneasily and eyed him with authority. She wasn't about to let a dog that size bluff her out! Moments later Merri found herself pinned up against the car as the dog stood at her feet and growled menacingly.

"Get out of here, doggie," she hissed, glancing around frantically to see if anyone had heard the commotion. "Go home!"

The little dog bounced up and down on his hind legs, barking obnoxiously, daring her to make a move. She didn't have the slightest idea whether the dog would bite or not, but he was doing a marvelous job of keeping her in suspense.

Deciding that the pet's owner had probably let him out for his early-morning ritual and would doubtlessly be calling him in before long, Merri decided to wait him out. When the dog got bored with terrorizing the intruder, his barking ceased and he calmly raised his little furry leg and relieved himself on her white tennis shoe.

She was still angrily telling him *exactly* what she thought of his crude conduct when a sleepy-looking man flung open one of the apartment doors and gave a sharp whistle.

The dog bounded off happily for home, leaving his very uncivilized calling card on Merri's left foot.

Squishing back out to the station wagon to retrieve the hose she had brought along, she railed at Ryder Tate under her breath for having put her in this miserable position. Why couldn't someone else have saved her life? she thought angrily as she hosed down her foot with the cold water.

Four hours later Merri stood back and surveyed the car. She was exhausted, but she had to admit she had done an excellent job. The old car glistened in the spring sunshine, its newly washed and double–Turtle Waxed surface gleaming proudly.

She devoted the next thirty minutes to crawling around the inside of the car and hand-vacuuming the upholstery and floorboards to a spotless perfection. This was absolutely the best job she had ever done on anything in her entire life! she marveled contentedly as she rubbed the last tiny streak out of the windshield. Too bad she wouldn't be there to see Mr. Tate's face when he walked out of his apartment and saw his car. Naturally he would find the note right away and immediately know who had done it all. He would probably rush back in and call her to thank her properly this time for the effort she had put forth. Without being rude, she would accept his thanks and tell him she now considered her debt to him repaid. She would inform him that it had been nice meeting him, then with cool aplomb would say *"Adiós, amigo"* and hang up on *him*. . . .

Her happy musings were rudely interrupted when she heard someone pecking on the car window. Glancing up from her unladylike position on the floor, where she was vacuuming under the seat, she frowned. Good grief! It was *Tate!*

An impatient rap sounded on the window again as she switched off the hand vacuum and straightened up to face her adversary.

Slowly rolling down the window, Merri met his stern gray gaze sheepishly. "Yes?" she asked in a perturbed voice.

"What do you think you're doing?"

"What does it look like?" Her eyes unwillingly wandered over his strikingly virile frame. He was wearing a bright red shirt tucked neatly into the waistband of a pair of tan-colored dress slacks, and he looked and smelled devastatingly male. He was wearing that same after-shave he had been wearing the night he rescued her. It annoyed her to no end that he somehow managed to get better-looking every time she saw him!

"It looks like you've been very busy this morning," he acknowledged, his puzzled eyes giving the car a quick once-over. "What's going on?"

Merri climbed out of the car, trying her best to straighten her tumbled hair into some semblance of order before she had to face him. Every time he saw her, she looked as if she had been run over by a train!

Without a word she reached into her purse and handed him the note she had written. It was not the way she had planned it, but she guessed she could accept his thanks in person.

Ryder unfolded the note and began to read the short message explaining why she had spent the morning cleaning his car. Merri cautiously watched him for a reaction.

Moments later he glanced over at her, a slow grin creeping across his face. "You've been out here all morning cleaning this car?"

"That's right." Merri began to gather up her cleaning supplies, anxious to return home and crawl into bed for the rest of the afternoon. "You don't have to thank me," she pointed out politely. "As the note said, I wanted to do this for you."

"Oh, I wasn't going to thank you," he assured her. "But the man down at the garage who loaned me this car probably will." His grin broadened devilishly.

Merri froze and whirled around to face him. "What do you mean, the man at the ga— Isn't this your car?"

"This piece of junk? You actually thought this was *my* car?" he asked incredulously. "I can't believe you! The garage loaned this junker to me while they were working on my van."

"Of course I thought it was your car! It was sitting in your driveway!"

"And you've worked your tail off cleaning it all morning?" He let out another whoop of delight. "Boy, that's rich!"

"I fail to see one thing amusing about this, Mr. Tate! Why in the world didn't you say something before I got this mess cleaned up?" she demanded as he began to laugh at her stupidity.

"Me?" he cackled. "I didn't have the slightest idea you were out here!"

Her face grew darker as his laughter increased. "Look at that," he crowed. "You've even *waxed* this old jalopy!"

"Oh, yes. I did." She smiled sweetly. "And vacuumed it, and did all the windows, and hand-washed every inch of the whitewalls. Isn't that hilarious?"

He roared with delight. "It certainly is!"

Merri calmly walked over to the hose and picked it up. Ryder was obviously going into hysterics and needed help. Turning the nozzle on full blast, it was her laughter that filled the air now as he screamed and started running across the yard, trying to escape her vindictive pursuit.

She managed to drench him, and she was reasonably sure she had washed off every trace of that darn sexy after-shave he wore when he finally made it to the safety of his apartment and slammed the door shut.

A few seconds later she turned the hose in the

direction of his bedroom window, which was opening, and shot the water full blast in Ryder's face once more.

"Hey, you crazy lady!" he yelled through the tiny crack. "Why don't you just give up trying to pay me back? You'll never be able to do it!" he taunted. He was getting tired of trying to convince her he didn't need any payment for saving her life, so now he was going to have to try and make her mad enough to leave him alone!

The rush of water drowned his words again as he finally slammed the window down in annoyance and went to change his clothes.

When Merri was convinced he wasn't coming back out, she gathered the cleaning items into her sack and got into the station wagon, still seething at his asinine ingratitude. She would pay Ryder Tate back for saving her life if it *killed* her— which, she was beginning to suspect, it very well might!

CHAPTER FIVE

So plan B was down the tubes. It was a disturbing fact, but nevertheless true.

The following Monday morning Merri sat at her desk and turned the sticky problem over in her mind. Paying back a person for saving her life was certainly not the easiest thing she had ever done, especially when fate had dealt her the extreme misfortune of trying to deal with a man as ungrateful as Ryder Tate. She still seethed when she thought of how that thankless ninny had stood and laughed in her face! What she should do is give up on trying to show her gratitude and forget he even existed!

Her eyes narrowed thoughtfully. Then why didn't she? Well, if she was truthful, she had to admit there was something about that rascal that

intrigued her. His ability to reject her simple gratitude was annoying enough, but the way he was
completely overlooking her as a woman was becoming downright irritating!

And she still had plan C.

Plan C was a little more complicated than A and
B, but very workable all the same. Deciding that
she was definitely going to have to pique the man's
interest in her as a woman before he would consider letting her repay him for saving her life, she
was going to be forced to resort to crafty feminine
wiles. She much preferred to think of it as the act
of a brilliant, intellectual woman who could outwit
the pants off a certain conceited jackass, but she
doubted Ryder Tate would view it in the same
light. Regardless, it was worth a try. It would mean
she would have to be out of the shop most of the
morning, but a short phone call to Cleo took care
of that problem.

Picking up the phone again, she dialed the oper-
ator and got the number of the fire station where
Ryder worked. Since he had been off over the
weekend, she knew he would be back on duty
today, and Erica had mentioned that Joe was
working the day shift. So that meant Ryder was.
. . . Seconds later the phone was answered and
plan C was thrown into full operation.

Merri took a deep breath and pinched her nos-
trils closed. "Does the fire department still get cats
out of trees?" she whined in an exaggerated nasal
twang.

"Now, that depends, ma'am," the fireman began politely.

"Well, I'm a resident of the Columns Four apartment complex, and a neighbor's cat seems to be stuck in a tree," she interrupted. "It's just a-sittin' up there a-screamin' at the top of its lungs, and I'd sure go up there and get it if I could, but I have this here lumbago in my back. . . . You ever been plagued with lumbago?" she asked with a whine.

"No, I don't believe so. . . ."

"Well, it ain't no picnic, sonny," she assured him. "I certainly hope you send someone over here to get the poor cat down afore he has a nervous breakdown."

"Did you say Columns Four, ma'am?"

Merri, exuberantly proud of her dazzling plan, rushed on, "Is Ryder Tate working today?"

"Yes, ma'am. But if you're a resident of Columns Four, we—"

"Would it be possible to send him over to get the cat?" she twanged.

"Are you a friend of Ryder's?" the fireman asked suspiciously.

"Well, sort of," she hedged.

"If we were to come out, he probably could," the fireman conceded. "But if you live in Columns Four—"

"Oh, I'm sorry, sonny, but I have to go now. I hear that poor old cat a-screamin' his silly head off again," Merri interrupted before he could grow more suspicious. She didn't care to push her luck any further, and the man had said Ryder could come. She slammed the phone down and breathed a sigh of relief.

The trap had been baited.

Now to find that old cat that had hung around her back door since the day she had moved into the apartment.

Seconds later the unsuspecting cat let out an indignant screech and dug his claws into the tree limb. Since she had been a child, Merri had always been the biggest tomboy in her neighborhood, so she had no difficulty shimmying up the tree in the backyard and placing the cat on a low branch. The cat hung on and watched her with fascination as she hurried back into the house to put on her shorts and halter top to sun in. Granted, it was a bit early in the season for sunbathing, but it was a surefire way to catch Ryder Tate's eye when he arrived to get the cat out of the tree. And when she caught his eye—*really* caught it—it would all be downhill from then on. What man could refuse a pretty girl trying to repay him a debt of gratitude?

By the time she got back outside again, the cat was lying on the back porch once more.

"Oh, good grief, you dumb cat! Get back up in that tree!" Ryder would be there any minute, and that darn cat had decided to pick this time to try her patience! Scooping the furry ball up in her arms, she made the long climb back up the tree again, scraping the skin off her leg in several different places before she got the cat positioned properly.

Seconds later the cat jumped lithely out of the tree and stood looking up at her as if she were just a little bit off.

Abrading what little undamaged skin was left on

her knee, Merri slid back down the tree in exasperation. She returned to the apartment, and a few minutes later she was grimly spreading tuna on the branch to hold the cat's attention. How she was going to explain the tuna to Ryder, she wasn't sure, but she would think of something.

The cat dug into the unexpected treat and docilely sat on the branch.

Striking her most sexy pose, she stretched out on the chaise longue and waited for the rat to take the bait.

She heard a truck pull up in front, and a few minutes later the sound of footsteps approached.

"We had a call there was a cat in a tree," a deep voice announced.

Merri kept her eyes closed, wetting her lips sensuously before she spoke. It wasn't Ryder's voice, but he was undoubtedly standing there silently, ogling her luscious body.

"Oh, really! I haven't noticed one," she fibbed. "Perhaps one of my neighbors phoned in," she said in a sultry voice. She sure hoped Mr. Tate was getting an eyeful, because she was freezing to death!

The cat was meowing at the top of his lungs, and was very unhappy now that his stomach was full and he had been left all alone.

"I think I've found the trouble," the second voice noted with a trace of laughter.

That wasn't Ryder's voice either! She cocked one eye open cautiously.

The two firemen standing over her were both old enough to be her father!

"Oh . . . uhhh . . ." She sat up quickly and pulled her top up in embarrassment. "I do believe it's in that tree right there," she said in mock surprise. She laughed nervously. "Can you beat that? I didn't even notice it!"

One of the fireman propped a ladder against the tree and climbed up to retrieve the screaming cat. "Good lord! There's tuna up here!" he yelled in disbelief.

"Tuna!" the other fireman shouted incredulously, then turned to look at Merri in bewilderment.

Merri turned five shades of red and shrugged her shoulders innocently. "Darn neighborhood kids. They'll do anything for a joke!"

When the cat reached the ground again, he sped away like a bolt of lightning, heading for the neighbor's yard as fast as his four legs could carry him.

Scrambling off the lounge chair, Merri trailed behind the firemen as they walked back to their truck, still shaking their heads.

"I bet you guys get a lot of useless calls like this one," Merri prodded, wondering where in the devil Ryder was!

"Oh, we don't usually get cats out of trees any longer, but we weren't exactly sure what the situation was over here," the one fireman noted. "The call we received was rather vague."

Merri's face fell in disappointment. "Well, when you get back to the station, be sure and say hi to Joe McFarland and his friend. . . . Let me see, I

85

believe his name's Ryder Tate," she said, hoping she didn't sound so guilty.

"Tate and McFarland?" Both fireman looked at each other quizzically. "They're not at our station."

"I thought . . . Well, darn it!" she caught herself. "I thought they were!"

"No, their station wouldn't be the one to respond to your neighborhood," one of them explained, stowing the ladder on the truck. "Come to think of it, it *was* one of the men from their station who called," he said thoughtfully.

Son of a gun! Plan C had just taken a nose dive.

"Oh, ma'am"—the fireman looked at her sympathetically—"are you aware your legs are bleeding?" They both glanced down at her scratched and mutilated legs.

"Oh . . . yeah. I shaved my legs this morning and got a little careless," she lied weakly.

The answer seemed to satisfy him, and he climbed in the truck and waved a friendly goodbye.

Merri stood watching the truck drive off, her lower lip sagging. Well, Merri Lambert was no quitter! Before the sun set tomorrow night, plan D would be rolling. She shivered miserably and ran into the house to put some clothes on before she caught pneumonia.

Removing a sheet of clean paper from her desk drawer at work that afternoon, she rolled it into the typewriter and pursed her lips thoughtfully. Plan D was, without a doubt, destined for success.

It took her the better part of an hour to compose the legal-looking document she would mail to Ryder. It contained a simple stubborn statement informing him that she would not rest until she felt she had in some small way paid him back for saving her life in a way that *he* would accept. That seemed to be the bugaboo: getting him to accept anything!

The paper listed three foolproof ways to pay him back. All he had to do was take a pencil in his grubby little hand and mark one of the square boxes she had painstakingly drawn next to the three choices. Nothing could be simpler.

Even for a man of his caliber.

The choices were: (a) housecleaning services for one entire month; (b) laundry services for one month; or (c) secretarial services for one month.

Ryder Tate may be an ungrateful nerd, but he certainly wasn't addle-brained. He would jump at this once-in-a-lifetime offer or she'd eat every Boston fern hanging in the shop!

During her lunch hour she dropped the letter in the mailbox, feeling quite confident she would hear from him soon.

When an entire week had passed and she still hadn't heard one word from him, her temper surfaced again and she decided to take matters in hand once more. If Ryder wanted war, then she was more than happy to haul out the big guns!

"What happens now?" Erica asked as she spooned sugar in her coffee at breakfast one morning after watching Merri stew in her own juices for the last week. "Are you ready to activate plan E?"

"Certainly not. Plan D still has every opportunity to work," Merri pointed out in a carefully controlled voice.

Erica laughed and shook her head hopelessly. "You and Ryder beat anything I've ever seen. Why don't you just give up? The guy obviously isn't interested."

"Interested! Do you think I'm going through this degrading situation because *I'm* interested in *him?*" Merri asked incredulously.

"Well, aren't you?" Erica reached for a slice of toast and buttered it thoughtfully. "He's eligible . . . you're eligible . . ."

"He's a complete boor and I would die before I would let him know I was interested in him!" Merri bit her lip too late to hold back her confession.

"Ah-ha! You *are* interested!" Erica seized the opportunity to corner her friend. "I knew it all along!"

Merri frowned, then dropped into the chair opposite Erica. "All right, I admit he has piqued my interest . . . but only because he's so . . . so uninterested! What's wrong with me? Have I got warts on my nose!"

Erica playfully surveyed Merri's features. "Other than that one large one between your eyes, I haven't noticed any," she teased.

"That isn't funny, Erica. What am I going to do?" Merri pleaded. "Joe accepted your thanks and you've had several dates with him since. Ryder won't give me the time of day—not that I really care," she added defensively. "But it still makes a girl wonder what she's doing wrong!"

Heaving a resigned sigh, Erica leaned back in her chair to face Merri's worried countenance. "Joe is going to wring my neck if he finds out I've broken my word and told you what I'm about to, but I can't let you go on tearing yourself apart like this. You haven't done anything," she assured Merri. "Ryder has been the one holding back."

"What do you mean?" Merri's spirits picked up at Erica's words. She knew the lagging relationship had all been Ryder's fault, but it was nice to hear someone else confirm that fact.

"Now, you have to promise you won't *ever* let Ryder know about this conversation," Erica pleaded nervously.

"Why would I tell him anything?" Merri snorted. "Our conversations are not exactly cordial, you know."

"Well . . ." Erica bit her lip and paused. Joe was going to murder her if he ever found out she had told!

"Oh, come off it, Erica! Either tell me or go to work!" Merri demanded impatiently. The suspense of not knowing what dark secret about Ryder Tate loomed on the horizon was killing her.

"Well . . ."

"Erica!"

"Ryder doesn't like women," Erica said quickly, unable to hold back any longer.

Merri's face paled. "Doesn't like wom— You mean he's—"

"Oh, ye gads, no! I didn't mean that!" Erica exclaimed hurriedly. "What I mean is, Ryder doesn't like pushy women—you know, women who try to force their attentions on him."

"Well, la-di-da," Merri mocked. "Does he really think he's so irresistible that women fall at his feet and try to *force* themselves on him!"

"Laugh if you want to, but it's the truth," Erica said. "Have you by any chance ever heard of Oliver Tate?"

"The real estate magnate? Who hasn't?"

"Did you know he has a son?"

Merri pondered the question for a moment. "I think I heard that mentioned somewhere, but I heard the son doesn't want any part of the Tate wealth, that he disassociates himself from the pomp and grandeur—"

"That's right," Erica interrupted. "So much so, several years ago he stepped out of the gilded cage and now lives a very simple life working at a job of his own choosing."

"A fireman! Ryder Tate is Oliver Tate's son!" Comprehension was slow in coming, but when it did, it nearly floored Merri. "Why in the world would *anyone* with that kind of money be risking his life as a fireman?"

"Because he wants to," Erica explained simply. "Joe said that he and Ryder have been friends since childhood, and Ryder always resented the fact that people were impressed by his money rather than him. After college Ryder tried working in his father's business, but found that only made him more unhappy. So, when Joe went to work for the fire department, Ryder put in his application, and a year later he was hired."

"But what has all this to do with Ryder not liking women?" Merri persisted.

"It all goes back to the Tate fortune. Joe said that Ryder was sick and tired of the meaningless relationships he had had during the last few years. I know this is going to sound crazy, but Joe says Ryder's very shy and maybe just a little insecure when it comes to women. He always felt women were more interested in his money than they were in him, so when a woman comes on strong with him—like you've been doing lately—it scares the puddin' out of him," Erica explained.

"Shy, my foot!" Merri scoffed. "He didn't appear shy to me."

"No, but I really think he is, Merri. And if Joe ever finds out I've told you all of this, we are *both* going to be in hot water!"

While Erica was talking, Merri was assessing the situation. She could see where a man would resent a woman chasing him for his money, and maybe she had come on a bit overpoweringly; but if he thought that was why *she* was trying to show her gratitude, then he was all wet and she wouldn't hesitate to tell him so.

"Do you promise?" Erica demanded.

"Promise what?"

"That you'll never breathe a word of this to Ryder or Joe. I told you only so you would stop beating your head against a brick wall. Ryder obviously thinks you know who he is and what you're after."

"Oh, he does, does he?" The flags of battle shot

up her private mast as Merri stood up and began angrily to pace the small kitchen. "Well, that conceited jackass has another thing coming," she fumed. "The very nerve of him thinking I'm after him or his stinking money!"

"Now, Merri," Erica reasoned, "if you'll stop to think about it, he has a point."

"Yes, I noticed. It's right on the top of his egotistical head."

Erica groaned and took her cup over to the sink. "I wish I had never started this fiasco of trying to pay them back for saving our lives. If it weren't for the fact that Joe and I are getting along so marvelously—"

"Oh, you don't have to worry," Merri broke in. "Mr. Tate will never know I know his true identity unless he brings it up, but he will be made aware of the fact that there are some women in this world who aren't gold diggers!"

Erica eyed her warily. "*Now* what are you going to do?"

Merri glanced up and smiled slyly. "Why, continue to try and pay him back for gallantly saving my life," she purred sweetly. "Then, when he sees what a nice, wholesome girl I am—one who will be totally shocked to find out that a poor little serf girl like herself is associating with a millionaire—I'm going to lower the boom on that moron and tell him exactly what I really think of him and his money!"

"You're heading straight for trouble," Erica warned her. "Besides, he isn't about to let you pay him back. It looks to me like even you've noticed that!"

"You just watch me," Merri replied smugly. "Ryder Tate isn't going to know what hit him. And by the time he does, he won't be so quick to lump all women in one category!"

Marching over to the telephone, she snatched up the receiver and heatedly dialed the number to the fire station, which Erica had scribbled on the chalkboard they used for messages.

"Ryder Tate, please," she asked in a voice dripping with sugar. Covering the receiver with the palm of her hand, she whispered to Erica, "If he's not at work today, can you call Joe and get his home phone? Hello, Ryder?"

"Yes?" The voice that was beginning to haunt her drifted casually over the line.

"Hi, this is Merri."

"Merri Lambert?"

She wasn't going to let his cool indifference upset her this time. "Hey," she proceeded in an overly friendly voice, "what's happening?"

There was a disbelieving pause on the other end of the line before he finally answered in a frosty voice. "Not much. What's going on with you?"

"Not much." She turned her back away from Erica's inquisitive stare and lowered her voice. "I was wondering if you got my letter. . . ."

"The nutsy one?"

Merri stiffened at his snappish manner. He was going to be difficult again!

"I sent only one," she clarified tersely.

"Then I got it," he conceded. "I don't have any idea what it means, but I did get it."

Merri cleared her throat, then plunged in. "It means exactly what it says. I would like to pay you—"

"Ms. Lambert," he interrupted curtly, "I really wish you would consider me 'paid back.' Now, if you'll excuse me, I'm at work, and I really should get back to the roast I'm fixing for dinner. The other men want gravy with it, and I haven't the slightest idea how to go about making gravy."

"Do you always cook their dinner?"

"We take turns. But after they eat my gravy tonight, I feel reasonably sure they're going to ask me to work out in the garage," he said confidently.

"Oh, well, back to the reason why I called." Merri gripped the receiver, forcing her pride back down her throat. "I was wondering if you would be free to stop by the apartment tomorrow evening." Realizing that he would think she was being pushy again, she hastened to add, "I would like to discuss the letter I sent you and clarify certain points."

There was a disgusted grunt from his end. "Merri, I don't think this is necessary. . . ."

"You might as well accept the fact that it is, Mr. Tate. Now if you'll only let me get on with this, we'll have it over and done with before you know it."

"Look, I hate to be so blunt with you, but I'm not looking for any action at the moment."

"Nor am I!" she fired back. "If it will make you feel any better, I can personally assure you my

94

offer is sincere and entirely without any strings attached!"

The glacial tone of her voice cooled his rapidly rising temper and made him pause. Was it possible she *was* just nutsy enough to want to show her gratitude and nothing else?

"I still think this is a waste of my and your time, but yes, I'm free tomorrow evening," he admitted reluctantly. Maybe it was better to get this thing out of the way once and for all and get her off his back.

"Thank you. What time may I expect you?"

"Would seven o'clock be convenient?" he inquired in a tense but polite voice.

"That would be most convenient," she accepted haughtily. "If you have no objections, I'd like to make this a business-dinner meeting. I planned on working late at the shop tomorrow, so I won't get a chance to eat before you arrive. We'll go dutch, naturally," she stipulated coolly. The last thing she wanted him to think was that she was hinting for him to buy her dinner, and she certainly wasn't going to buy his!

"Might as well," he agreed. "That way the whole evening won't be shot to hell."

"My sentiments exactly." He had such a way with words.

"I have to go, I smell the roast burning. Say, you couldn't tell me how to make gravy, could you?"

"I could, but I have to take the garbage out," she said sweetly. "See you tomorrow night." She quickly hung up and stuck her tongue out at the phone.

"He's really going to come by?" Erica asked in amazement.

"Sure he's coming by," Merri told her. "And when I get through with Ryder Tate, he isn't going to know what hit him!"

Merri was afraid she wouldn't have time to shower and change clothes before Ryder picked her up the following evening, but she did. She had dropped off some last-minute deliveries, and it was nearly six thirty when she arrived home.

Erica had left a note explaining that she and Joe had gone out for the evening, so when the doorbell rang a little before seven, Merri was still struggling to hook the back of her dress together as she ran to open the door.

"Hi." Merri motioned for Ryder to step into the apartment, her hands still working at the obstinate clasp.

"Hi. Hope I'm not too early."

"No, I'm almost ready," she promised. "Just as soon as I get this darn hook fastened."

Her hands worked uselessly for a few more minutes until he finally took heart and stepped forward. "You want me to get that for you?"

"Would you mind?" Merri glanced at him shyly, trying very hard to dismiss how nice he looked this evening. Charcoal-gray dress slacks attractively hugged his athletic build. A light-gray sweater with a cranberry stripe fit very nicely over his trim waist and emphasized his masculine frame. The darker gray sport jacket was casual, yet reflected good taste and excellent breeding. And as usual he smelled so tempting, it was very hard to keep her mind impartial and remember that she was out to prove a point to him . . . nothing more.

The touch of his hands as he effortlessly fastened the clasp sent unbidden shivers racing along her bare skin. She drew in her breath and waited for him to finish, silently chastising herself for being so aware of him as a man.

"Nice dress," he observed casually. "I always like that particular shade of blue."

"Thanks. It's old," she confessed nervously. Moving away from him, she went to the hall closet and withdrew a light sweater. "I thought it might be nice to eat at Ebenezer's tonight, if you don't mind," she suggested.

"If that's what you'd prefer," he agreed, helping her slip the sweater on. Merri couldn't understand why she felt so ill at ease with him, but she tried to brush away the anxiety as they moved toward the front door.

The early spring air had a bit of a nip to it tonight as they walked out to the customized luxury van parked in front of the apartment. Ryder held the door open for her as she climbed into the passenger seat, and she murmured polite thanks.

"This is very nice," she complimented as he got in on the driver's side and started the engine. The plush interior was decorated in shades of brown and gold, and she noted that the van could easily seat eight people comfortably. There was a plush sofa and table in the rear, and a small refrigerator and television built into the interior. Obviously not in the price range of every city fireman!

"I like it," he agreed as he pulled out on Sunshine and turned left.

She just bet he did. It looked like a very convenient den of iniquity to her! "I've been hearing a funny noise in the rear end lately that has me a little worried," he said, trying to make conversation. "I put it in the garage for a couple of days, and I thought the mechanic had it figured out, but I guess he didn't. I'm still hearing it. Oh, by the way"—he glanced over at her and tried to smother a grin—"they said to tell you their old loaner car looked better than it had in years."

Merri blushed at the thought of her foolish blunder. "I should send them a bill!"

Ebenezer's was only a few minutes' drive from Merri's apartment. Merri felt her pulse leap when Ryder's hand touched the small of her back when he opened the restaurant door and ushered her in ahead of him. Because it was a weekday evening, the restaurant wasn't as crowded as usual; however, there would still be a short wait before a table was available.

"Let's step in the bar and have a drink while we're waiting," Ryder suggested, his hand finding her waist and guiding her into the lounge.

Merri found a table while Ryder went to the bar to get their drinks. She heard him speak cordially to a couple of men and pause to chat for a moment. She stiffened as two very attractive women sitting at another table called out to Ryder. He returned their greeting politely, then made his way back to where she sat.

"I hope I made the right choice for you." He set

a drink down in front of her and offered her a napkin.

"Oh, this will do fine," she assured him. "I really don't like the taste of any of it."

By the time their table was ready, she was feeling much more at ease. To her surprise he was quite fascinating and knowledgeable and conversed about a variety of subjects during the meal.

Lingering over coffee, she found herself telling him all about her life while he revealed practically nothing about his.

When she finally glanced at her watch, she realized they had been sitting at the table for two hours. "My goodness," she murmured. "Is it that late?"

"A little before ten isn't late," he chided good-naturedly. The evening had been much more pleasant than he had anticipated also.

"It is when you have to get up at six in the morning," she protested, feeling a small seed of disappointment when she realized that the evening was nearly at an end.

"By the way, how's your finger?" she asked, picking up his hand to examine the finger she had whacked with the hammer.

"I think I'll probably lose the nail," he conceded, staring at the still black-and-blue swollen fingertip.

"I really am sorry," she said sheepishly.

The lazy smile he gave her assured her he was no longer upset. "I believe you wanted to talk to me about the letter," Ryder prompted as he signaled the waitress for the check.

"Yes . . . I . . . I was absolutely sincere in my offer. I honestly would feel better if you would let me repay you . . . even in this small way, for saving my life."

Ryder studied her earnest face, trying to discern if she was being truthful. "As I've said many times before, Merri, it's not necessary. I was only doing my jo—"

"I know, I know, you were only doing your job, but it was much more than that to me. Please, just mark off one of those boxes and hand the letter back to me," she coaxed. "You won't even have to know I'm around. You'll have free maid, laundry, or secretarial services for a month and I'll salve my conscience." Her smile was totally beguiling. "What could be simpler?"

"I don't like it," Ryder grumbled, but she could see he was beginning to weaken.

"But you'll do it?"

"Just how do you propose to offer your, uh, services to me and still carry on with your job?" he procrastinated.

"Oh, I've already thought all that out. That's alternate plan D," she told him smugly.

He looked at her blankly. "Plan D?"

"Uh . . . yeah . . . I sort of work with a certain plan in mind. But you don't have to worry!" she promised. "I'll be in your service only a month. I figure I'll have to be gone from the flower shop only two mornings a week for that month, and the other two ladies who work in my shop can handle things while I'm gone."

"If I do sign this ridiculous paper, you will have

to make me a solemn promise that you won't be under my feet for the next month," he warned sternly.

Merri glared at him impatiently. "Are you afraid I'll interfere in your personal life, Mr. Tate?" she asked, her eyes drifting over to the two women who had spoken to him in the bar earlier, and were now dining just across the aisle from them.

"That's exactly what I'm hoping to prevent," he replied curtly. "I rather like the way I live right now, and I don't want anyone interfering in it."

"I thought you didn't like women . . ." Merri accused, then caught herself abruptly. He hadn't said a word about women!

His eyes narrowed. "Who told you that?"

"Told me what?" she asked innocently.

"That I didn't like women?"

"No one," she hedged. "You just don't seem the type to chase a lot of women." She continued to cover her tracks and lay it on thick. "And you plainly stated on the phone yesterday you were not looking for any 'action.' Those were your words, not mine," she reminded him. Merri knew that excuse sounded as flimsy as it actually was, but it was the best she could come up with on the spur of the moment.

Ryder studied her for a few moments before he finally reached into his coat pocket and withdrew the letter addressed to him. Removing a pen from his inside pocket, he hurriedly checked one of the boxes and handed the letter back to her. "I want you to know this is the most stupid thing I've ever done in my life"—he frowned—"and if I thought for one moment I could get you off my back any other way—"

"I shall be more than happy to get off your back as soon as I feel I have done the right thing," she said crossly. She picked up the paper and glanced at the box he had checked. Rats! Maid service!

"Just be sure that you do," he advised, leaving money on the table for the waitress and sliding out of the booth. "I hope I made myself clear yesterday when I said I wasn't interested in any action."

"So? Who's offering you any?" she snapped back, sliding out of the booth and trailing him through the restaurant. "*I*'m certainly not," she declared.

"You don't know what a comfort those words are to me, Ms. Lambert."

"No more so than they are to me, *Mister* Tate!"

Neither one said a word on the ride back to Merri's apartment. Merri sat on her side and seethed silently at the way he suddenly seemed paranoid that she was going to jump over the console between them and attack him! If she had the nerve, that was exactly what she would do just to see his reaction.

"Will you leave me an extra key under your doormat so I can begin my job one day this week?" she asked coolly as he deposited her unceremoniously at her doorstep.

"Yes, but you let me know what day you'll be there so I can make other plans," he ordered gruffly.

"By all means."

"And at the end of this month we're even, and I

don't want to hear another word about this grate-fulness business. Agreed?"

"Agreed."

Ryder turned and started back down the walk.

"Oh, Mr. Tate?" she called to him.

He turned and looked back at her. "Yeah?"

"For someone who isn't looking for action, that sin bin you're driving is very incriminating!" Merri opened her door and slammed it shut so fast, he didn't have time for rebuttal.

A sofa, a television, and a refrigerator! Who did that clown think he was kidding!

CHAPTER SIX

How could she have been so stupid to include the choice of housekeeping on that list? Merri asked herself for the umpteenth time in the last two weeks. What with the Easter rush at the flower shop and the extra job of cleaning Ryder's apartment, she had barely had time to breathe. Her personal life had gone down to minus zero too. Dirk Bennett had called numerous times to ask her out, but she had had to refuse his offers. Not that it broke her heart: Dirk was okay, but her real interest seemed to be homing in on one Ryder Tate. He was an enigma to her—one that was becoming more complex every day.

True to his word, she had not seen hide nor hair of the recalcitrant millionaire fireman on the four occasions she had been to his apartment to clean. A millionaire fireman! That in itself was ludicrous.

Her new cleaning job wasn't a strenuous one, because he was as neat as a pin—infuriatingly so! She barely had to do anything to his bachelor domain other than the normal dusting and vacuuming. Most of her time was spent in the bathroom, uncapping the bottle of that enticing after-shave he wore and smelling it. It reeked of being a "playboy" fragrance, and that made her even madder, considering the fact she had had no success whatsoever in turning his roving eye. She had hoped she would at least run into him a few times on Monday and Friday mornings, but he had made sure to stay away on her days to clean.

Business was slow in the shop this morning as she got up and poured herself a fresh cup of coffee. The thought kept nagging at her that there must be something wrong with her looks. She understood Ryder's indifference toward women, but after all, he was human . . . wasn't he? A pretty woman should always be able to turn a male's head and tempt him just a little. . . . She knew for a fact that he wasn't leading a monk's life, because she had found wedged between the sofa cushions when she cleaned Monday a tube of shocking-pink lipstick that hadn't been there on the previous Friday. A strange tingle of jealousy hit her as she thought of Ryder Tate with a woman wearing shocking-pink lipstick. All she could find out about their time together was that they left a big greasy mess in the kitchen. She had found all the dirty spaghetti dishes in the sink on Monday morning.

Sipping her coffee thoughtfully, plan E began to take shape in her head. It was up to her to make Ryder notice her. She had been approaching this problem all wrong. True, in the beginning she had only wanted to repay him for saving her life, but he was becoming more of a challenge to her as each day passed. Suddenly it seemed crucial to her that she teach Mr. Tate a valuable lesson: All women were not necessarily interested in a man for his wallet alone. It would sure do her heart good to see him come to heel for once in his egotistical, self-centered life. She would treat him so sweetly and nicely that he would fall for her like a ton of bricks; and then, when he confessed his secret identity and told her about his family's money and how he loved her and wanted to marry her and have her live in the lap of luxury the rest of her life, she would politely turn up her nose and tell him she didn't *want* to marry a rich man. She'd walk away from him, and from then on he might view women just a little differently!

She reasoned he *had* to be all those nasty things she called him behind his back; why else would he act as if she didn't exist? After all, she wasn't that bad! He probably considered her beneath him: She wasn't good enough to associate with a Tate!

Well, she was going to change all that. She had written down the schedule he kept in his apartment for the days he worked at the fire station, and today was not one of them. If she was real lucky, she could take him by surprise.

Slamming her cup back down on her desk, her eyes blazed in defiance. "Cleo, I've decided to go

106

over to Ryder's apartment and clean this morning. Can you and Megan take care of things here?"

Cleo came into the room, a long-stem rose stuck between her teeth, and looked at Merri in surprise. "Sure, but this is only Thursday," she reminded her boss.

"I know, but I'm going to clean his apartment a day early."

"Will you be back this afternoon?"

"It depends," Merri hedged, gathering up her purse and sunglasses.

Cleo frowned. "On what?"

"On whether I'll be able to trap the lion in his own cage," she answered. Scooping up the keys to Watson, she waved and left the shop whistling the tune "On the Road Again."

On the drive over to Ryder's place Merri tried to decide what the best way would be to let herself in the apartment. She could enter the apartment as she usually did, with his spare key, and run the chance of walking in on his privacy—which could prove to be very embarrassing; but if she rang the doorbell, he would probably refuse to let her in, since he had warned her repeatedly that he didn't want her underfoot. The thought that he might not be home at all, even if it was his day off, never entered her mind until she was halfway there.

Merri heaved a relieved sigh as she pulled up in front of the apartment and saw the van sitting in the driveway. He was home.

Retrieving the cleaning supplies from the back of her station wagon, she scurried up the walk and removed the spare key Ryder kept under the front doormat.

Unlocking the door, she let it swing open as she picked up the cleaning supplies and started to tiptoe in. Her left foot was still up in the air when she glanced up and saw Ryder standing not three feet away from her, his gray eyes staring at her.

"What do you think you're doing?" he asked her calmly.

"Well, for heaven's sake! What are *you* doing here?" She grinned guiltily as her sack dropped out of her arms onto the floor.

"I live here," he replied. "I believe the question should be, What are *you* doing here?"

"I work here," she answered brightly. *Shoot!* She had hoped to sort of ease up on him, not greet the king of the jungle the moment the cage door was opened.

"Not on Thursdays you don't," he reminded her.

Merri glanced at him and noticed that the right side of his jaw was puffed up as though he had nuts stuffed in it, and he seemed to be having trouble pronouncing his words. "Are you drunk?" she asked sharply.

"No! What a thing to barge in here and ask," he said indignantly.

"Well, what's wrong with you? You look like a chipmunk and you're not talking very clearly," she demanded.

"I just had a tooth pulled at the dentist," he grumbled. "The feeling is just beginning to come back to the right side of my mouth."

"Really?" She moved closer and peered at him sympathetically. "Can I do anything to help?"

"Nothing," he refused her offer hurriedly, taking a cautious step backward. "What are you doing here today?"

"Oh . . . I thought I'd clean today instead of tomorrow. I'm expecting to be very busy at the shop tomorrow," she lied. "I never dreamed you might be here today, but now that I'm here"—she took his hand and dragged him toward the sofa before he could voice an objection—"you just lie down here and I'll get you an ice bag to put on that jaw. It looks terrible."

"No, thanks—"

"I wouldn't think of letting you suffer here all by yourself," she interrupted, nearly shoving him down on the sofa. This was even better than she had hoped for! What a perfect opportunity to show him what a nice, helpful person she really was. . . .

She tucked an afghan around him and patted his shoulder comfortingly. She heard him grunt and grab his jaw as she accidentally knocked against the sore part amid her motherly cluckings. "Did I hit your jaw?" she asked.

He sat up and spit weakly into a wad of tissues he had been clutching in his hand. "Oh, Lord, I think you've started it bleeding again."

"I'll run into the kitchen and get the ice bag and some aspirins." She grimaced, realizing she wasn't going to make a very good impression on him at this rate.

Her hand accidentally grazed his jaw again as

she jumped up to get the promised items. "Oh! I'm so sorry!" she gasped. "I don't know how I can be so clumsy!"

"Just get me the damn ice bag before I hemorrhage to death," he ground out crossly as he sank weakly down on the sofa, both hands protectively holding his swollen jaw.

Within minutes she had secured the ice bag from the hall closet and filled it with ice cubes and water from the refrigerator. Her fingers worked to get the stubborn cap back on the bag as she anxiously glanced into the front room to see how he was doing. His face was much paler than it had been when she first arrived, and she prayed he wasn't losing a lot of blood due to her klutziness.

Rushing back in, she placed the ice bag gently on his swollen jaw. "There, does that feel better now—"

Her words died in her throat as he lunged off the sofa, distraughtly trying to pull his drenched, clinging shirt away from his body. Ice cubes were dropping onto the floor as he pranced around like a deranged wildcat!

"What's the matter now?" Merri demanded crossly. Men could be such babies! All this commotion over having a simple tooth pulled?

"The lid came off the bag, you idiot!" he shouted in a garbled voice.

"It did? I thought I had it screwed on tight," she said in a mystified voice. "Well," she sighed, "I don't think you're helping your jaw one bit with all that bouncing around. Why don't you sit down and let me fix you some hot soup for lunch? I bet you haven't had a thing to eat since you got home from the dentist, have you?"

"Only one small bag of peanut brittle I ate on the way home," he said sarcastically.

She ignored his answer.

Ryder unbuttoned his shirt and flung it off his back in one irritable motion and slumped back down on the sofa. Merri tried hard not to gawk at his broad, incredibly sexy chest. She nervously wet her lips and glanced away, trying not to let her mind dwell on the delectable light brown hair spread across the width of it, and how silky and soft it looked; but it was darn hard to ignore, so after a few moments she quit trying and let her eyes drink their fill.

"I'll get you some soup," she told him cheerfully when he mercifully pulled the afghan back over his chest and closed his eyes.

"I don't want any soup," he grumbled. "Just go do your housework and let me lie here in peace."

"It's bean soup," she coaxed.

"That's all I need to make my day: a bean lodged in the cavity of the extraction," he muttered crossly.

"Then I think you should at least take some of these pain pills the dentist gave you." Merri had found them on the kitchen counter. She went to get them and a glass of water and was back quickly. Ryder dutifully sat up and took his medicine as she left to get a pillow for his head.

"Are you sure you wouldn't like some—"

"I don't want any soup!"

Sheez! Merri decided he had his mind set on

being a pain today. "Well, if you get hungry, let me know. I'm going to start cleaning."

He didn't answer as she reached over his head for a clean wad of tissues to hand to him and knocked a dish of peanuts over, sending the nuts ricocheting off his sore jaw once more.

"Oh, horse hockey! . . . Here!" She stuffed the tissues in one of his hands as he moaned and rolled over on his stomach.

"What have I done to deserve this?" he pleaded to a higher authority as she scurried out of the room quickly. He was still muttering under his breath about how, if he had to do it over again, he would leave her in the burning building! Now, that was gratitude for you!

When Merri reached the sanctuary of the kitchen, she sagged against the counter in relief. Boy, everything had certainly gone wrong in plan E! Maybe she should scrap it and start plan F. No, it was too soon to do that. Maybe after he took a little nap he would feel better. *Then* she'd try to impress him. Granted, it was a long shot, but she had to try.

For the remainder of the afternoon she worked quietly around the apartment, trying her best to keep from disturbing Tate. Around five she heated up some tomato soup and placed it on a tray along with a gelatin dessert and a pitcher of lemonade.

As she tiptoed into the living room she noted with uneasiness that the sofa was empty. She glanced around the deserted room. Surely the rat wouldn't have gotten up and snuck out on her . . . would he?

The faint sound of a television reached her ears, drifting in from his bedroom. Apparently he had decided to go to his own bed sometime during the afternoon and she hadn't noticed.

A few minutes later she was placing the tray on his night table and scolding him mildly. "So this is where you disappeared to. When did you leave the couch?"

"About an hour ago," he murmured sleepily, the effects of the pain medicine still lingering in his system.

"I heated up some tomato soup and made a fresh pitcher of lemonade. Would you care for a glass?" she inquired pleasantly.

Ryder turned over on his back and groggily opened his eyes. "I've got a terrible taste in my mouth. I think I'll go into the bathroom and rinse my mouth with mouthwash before I try to eat."

Merri helped him rise from the bed and he disappeared into the small adjoining bathroom. She heard the water running and a few minutes later he came back out to lie on the bed again.

"Whatever's in that medicine has made me crazy," he confessed, his voice still sounding very drowsy.

"How's the pain?"

"There isn't any."

His voice sounded so little-boyish that Merri found herself reaching over and soothing his back, her fingers magically massaging all his aches. "Do you feel like eating your dinner before it gets cold?" she asked gently.

His sighs of contentment as her hands slipped

upward to massage his shoulder muscles assured her that he wasn't interested in eating. "All I want to do is lie here and let you do this to me all night," he murmured.

Merri's pulse jumped at the husky, almost intimate sound of his deep voice, and she wondered why he was suddenly so capable of turning her insides to mush. This man was beginning to represent a real danger, and she would have to be very careful not to let her feelings override her common sense. She would simply get into, then get out of, this relationship as quickly as possible. As soon as she proved the point that not all women were after Ryder Tate's money and that he would be a very desirable man if he didn't have a penny to his name, she would hurriedly exit, unscathed, from this troublesome encounter.

Her hands explored the taut ridge of muscles on his broad shoulders as she bit her lower lip in contemplation of this touchy situation. Maybe, just maybe, if she was very discreet, this might be the appropriate time to make a subtle but very effective move.

Her hands trailed slowly down the bare skin of his back, pausing to knead the skin at the waistband of his slacks.

The slight tensing of his body indicated her move had not gone unnoticed.

"Does that feel good?" she asked pleasantly, growing increasingly anxious as she tried to decide how far to go without seeming obvious. Holy moly! She didn't know about him, but it sure felt nice to *her!*

"Yeah . . . it feels okay," he confessed cautiously, a note of suspicion creeping into his voice.

So far, so good. She smiled complacently. "Ryder," she began hesitantly, "I hope you do realize how very much I appreciate your saving my life."

"I believe you have mentioned it a couple of times," he drawled lazily, letting his body relax under her hypnotic ministrations.

"Well, I believe in letting people know when they're appreciated," she reasoned. "Too many times we fail to tell people what we really think of them."

"That's true," he agreed.

The tip of her nail trailed playfully around his waist, causing a rash of goosebumps to break out on his skin. He shifted around uncomfortably on the bed.

"Am I hurting you?"

"No, I'm just a little ticklish," he confessed, trying to control the surge of desire that had suddenly shot through him.

"Oh. Well, as I was saying, I think people should be more caring about each other and when someone does something nice, I think they should let the other person know they appreciated their efforts . . . especially in our case. Why, you endangered your own life to save mine!" she marveled.

"I don't mean to disillusion you, but you have to realize that I was only doing my job," he pointed out for what seemed to him the hundredth time since they met.

"Oh, I know that, but I'm still very happy to have the opportunity to do something nice for you. After all, we might never have met if it hadn't been for the fire," she admitted, letting her finger continue its onslaught. "I might never have found out what a truly nice person you are." That was stretching it a bit, because he certainly hadn't been very nice to her, but somehow she sensed he could, if he really wanted to. . . .

"Yeah, perish the thought," he said dryly. Her hands were becoming more aggressive with each passing word, and he couldn't quite figure out what she was up to.

Merri's hands paused. "You really don't like me, do you?"

A firm hand shot out and Merri's eyes widened as he hauled her down on the bed beside him. "What is this all about?" he asked her as their gazes met for the first time.

Merri caught her breath as she felt the broad, bare chest she had been admiring all afternoon press against the fullness of her breasts. Their faces were only inches apart now as his eyes surveyed her flushed, rosy features carefully.

"I . . . I don't know what you mean," she said in a weak voice, trying to defend herself as her hand crept disgracefully up to touch the soft mass of hair that lay like a thick carpet across his chest.

"Come, now, Merri. I think you're more than aware of what you've been doing the last few minutes." He pulled her closer. "What's your game, lady?"

"I told you, I'm only trying to repay you for saving my life." She tried to squirm away as his arms wrapped around her and held her like two bands of steel.

"Oh?" One of his dark brows lifted in blatant skepticism. "I see. Well, why don't we stop all this pretense of sending flowers, making phone calls, washing cars, and playing housekeeper and get right down to what you're really after, sweetheart." His hand reached out to touch one of her breasts through the thin fabric of her blouse.

Merri's breath quickened as he gently massaged it and spoke to her softly. "You could have saved yourself a lot of time and trouble if you had let me know a little earlier that this was what you were after," he chided. His actions were calm and deliberate, and showed not the least bit of affection for her.

"You . . . you actually think that's what I'm trying to do? Get you into . . . bed?" she whispered in disbelief. An unwilling moan escaped her as his hand slipped under her blouse and ran up her rib cage.

"It is, isn't it?" His fingers slipped under her bra to investigate her delicate softness once more. "I must admit, I haven't been getting the message. In fact, to be honest, I really didn't know what your game was, Ms. Lambert, but I should have guessed."

"Ryder . . ." Her voice trailed off as he buried his face in the perfumed fragrance of her neck and began to kiss her. She had to put a stop to this nonsense! He had most certainly gotten the wrong impression of what she was trying to do!

"Ryder," she began again, "you have com-

pletely misunderstood what I'm trying to do. . . .
I'm not that type of woman. . . ." She groaned as
his mouth found the pulse at her neck and sucked
on it gently. "What about your tooth?" she reminded him inanely.

"I told you, it doesn't hurt. It's only a little sore.
. . . Just be careful where you touch," he said, his
hands sending goosebumps over her skin now.
"And don't tell me you're not 'that kind of a
woman.' I should have seen it from the beginning,
but I didn't. You know who I am, don't you?"

"You're Ryder Tate," she said tensely, hating the
way he was making her feel so cheap.

"That's right, honey, Ryder Tate, Oliver 'Real
Estate Tycoon' Tate's son. But then, I don't imagine that comes as any surprise to you, now, does it?
I knew it would only be a matter of time before Joe
told Erica, then Erica told you. . . ."

"No, it isn't a surprise," she admitted, "but if you
think for one moment my gratitude has anything
to do with your money, you're dead wrong, Ryder." Her voice was as cold as his now.

"Yeah. Well, you'll have to admit, it looks mighty
suspicious. If that isn't what all this 'gratitude' is
about, I'll eat the fire truck." His teeth nipped
almost angrily at the lobe of her ear as he pulled
her back against him roughly. "But, to be honest, I
don't care what the hell you're attracted to right
now," he confided in a husky voice. "I'm willing to
be used, whatever your reasons. . . ."

It took a moment for his crass words to sink in,
but when they did, Merri reached up and
slammed him across the face sharply.

"Darn it!" He sucked in his breath and pulled away from her abruptly, rubbing his sore jaw angrily. "What did you do *that* for?"

"I don't like your attitude, Mr. Tate!" Merri slid off the bed and angrily straightened her blouse. "If you think for one, conceited, egotistical moment I am interested in climbing into your bed for the sole purpose of snagging a rich husband, then you are all wet!"

He lay back on the bed and grinned at her insolently, still cupping his abused jaw. "Tell me another one, sweetheart."

"You don't think you're all wet?" she asked innocently.

"Nope."

Her hand reached for the pitcher of lemonade on the tray she had brought in earlier. "Really?"

"Really." He yawned and stretched. "Don't feel bad, tootsie. You're no different from any other woman I've met in the last few years."

Tootsie!

"I suppose a woman has a right to seek out a man who can give her the finer things in life, but I'm afraid you're going to have to look for some other sucker to make your dreams come true. *This* rich man is looking for a little different breed in a—" His sentence ended in a high shriek as she snatched the pitcher off the tray and dumped the contents over his head.

"You can just take your wallet and your snobbish disposition and stick them up your nose, Ryder Tate!" she bellowed.

"Now look what you've done!" he shouted, picking a slice of lemon out of his hair and throwing it on the floor in a fit of temper. "You not only got it all over the carpet, you've got it all over my bed!"

"Oh! Stick a sock in your mouth, you chauvinist pig! I'll clean it up!" she shouted right back. She moved closer and shook her finger under his nose threateningly. "Just don't ever let me hear you even so much as insinuate I'm after you for your stinking money! I am only trying to be nice to you and repay a debt of gratitude, and you'd better not forget it! Besides. I thought it was your father who was so filthy rich! You're only a fireman, and you couldn't bring home a king's ransom from that job, so why are you so worried about some evil woman coming on to you to get to your precious money?"

Ryder jerked off his belt and defiantly stripped off his trousers as Merri gasped and turned away.

"That was crude! Couldn't you go into the bathroom to do that?" she demanded.

"Couldn't you have found somewhere else to pour your damn lemonade?" he countered sarcastically. "And don't worry, I have money, sweetheart! Lots of stocks and bonds and business investments and trust accounts and doting grandparents. . . . You name it and I've got it! And no woman is going to get her hands on it unless she loves *me*, not the money." He stomped into the bathroom to wash the lemonade off and change into clean clothes, still railing away at her through the closed door.

"The woman I fall in love with is not going to know a thing about the money until our wedding day. That way I'll be sure she's marrying me for who I am, not what I possess!"

"You're being unfair," Merri stormed as she stripped the wet linens off the bed. "Sure, maybe women who wear shocking-pink lipstick and leave the kitchen sink stacked full of dirty spaghetti dishes are only interested in money, but all women aren't like that!"

"Are you complaining about your job?" he argued above the sound of running water. "I was under the distinct impression my 'maid' would be happy to clean up any mess I happen to leave!"

"She does not clean up after your girl friends!" Regardless of how angry she was with him, Merri was having a hard time keeping her jealousy under wraps. She took out a clean sheet and put it on the bed.

"Well, I hate to disappoint you, but 'Shocking Pink' doesn't even know about my money, and she isn't my girl friend."

"I'll just bet she isn't," Merri grumbled. She finished making the bed and sat down on it.

"What?"

"I *said* maybe *some* women are interested in nothing but money, but there are a heck of a lot of us that aren't!"

Ryder stepped out of the bathroom, buttoning his clean shirt. "You show me one who isn't and I'll show you fifty who are."

Merri wanted to point at herself and say, "Here, blind man, here's one who could fall in love with you at the drop of a hat and eat dirt for the rest of her life if you returned that love," but she couldn't. He would never believe her now. Oh, why had she ever let Erica talk her into trying to show him her gratitude? He would never believe she wasn't after his money.

"I think my mouth's started to bleed again," he announced, reaching for the box of tissues again. Merri noticed that he was beginning to tremble as he sat on the bed and dabbed halfheartedly at his mouth.

"Are you cold?"

"Wouldn't you be if you had just gone swimming in a bucket of lemonade?" he told her caustically.

"Oh . . . here! Get into bed." Merri turned back the blankets and eased him down onto the pillow. "Do you need another pain pill?"

"I can get it myself!"

"I am the maid, remember?"

Reaching for the glass of water on the bedside table, Merri dumped two pills into his hand and helped him take a sip of water in order to swallow them. She noticed he was still shaking like a leaf, even though she had put an extra blanket on the bed.

"Are you still cold?"

"Yes, I'm still cold; no, I don't want any soup; yes, I want a pain pill; no, I don't want anything to drink; yes, I'm still hurting . . ." he rattled off impatiently.

"Oh, shut up and scoot over," she demanded. He was still being obnoxious, but she was concerned about him.

"What do you think you're doing now?" Ryder

eyed her warily as she slipped off her shoes and crawled under the covers with him.

"Getting you warm."

For the first time that day a tiny grin crept across his features. "I'm not up to par at the moment, Ms. Lambert. Have a heart."

"You can wipe that smug look off your face, macho nerd. I am only doing this to prove I am a nice person, contrary to those who might believe otherwise."

Ryder gave a disbelieving grunt as she punched him in the ribs.

A tired sigh escaped her as she laid her head down on the pillow. Within a few minutes Ryder relented and reached out, wrapping his arm around her waist and pulling her warmth closer to his shaking body.

"You will soon see I have no interest in you whatsoever, other than to get this month over with and repay my debt to you," she assured him sleepily. It had been a long day and she was exhausted. She would just lie there awhile until his pain medicine took effect and he got warm and drifted off to sleep; then she would get up and go home.

"You don't like me?" he complained against the softness of her hair.

"I didn't say I didn't like you." She couldn't say that. In fact, she was beginning to like him entirely too much. "I merely said I wasn't after you for your money."

"Are you going to stay all night with me?" he inquired politely.

"No, I'm going home as soon as you go to sleep. You obviously don't like me and haven't appreciated a thing I've done for you today," she scolded, just a little hurt that he was so totally indifferent to her.

"Who said I didn't like or appreciate you?" His mouth brushed her cheek softly. Had he kissed her and she missed it?

Merri's voice turned gentle. "You certainly haven't acted as if you like me." It felt so good to lie there in his arms. She moved over a little and found her arms drifting up around his neck.

This time when Ryder Tate kissed Merri Lambert, she knew it.

"What was that for?" she asked breathlessly as they broke apart and he buried his face in her hair once more.

"I don't know . . . probably because I'm indebted to you for being so nice to me today," he whispered.

Merri snuggled contentedly against his chest as they both started to feel warm and cozy and drift off to sleep. "Ryder . . . thank you."

"For what?"

"Oh, for saving my life," she said, wanting to add, "and for making me realize how nice love can be." Love? Was she actually in love with Ryder Tate?

"My pleasure. . . ." His voice floated away as he drifted off to sleep.

Merri sighed happily and closed her eyes. He said it was his pleasure, not just his duty. That sounded so much nicer.

CHAPTER SEVEN

When Merri opened her eyes the following morning, she was shocked to find she was still cuddled against Ryder's warm body. She blinked, amazed to think she had spent the whole night with him, no matter how innocent it had been!

Easing away from him carefully, she slid out of bed and started for the bathroom, still finding it hard to believe she had slept so soundly all night.

"Where are you going?" Ryder asked in a sleepy voice.

"I . . . I'm going to the bathroom, then I have to get to work. I can't believe I've spent the night with you!"

"Yeah, it was a real wicked orgy," he agreed drowsily.

When she returned a few minutes later, he had

rolled over onto his back but his eyes were still closed.

"Don't you have to work today?" she asked quietly.

"No, I'm taking a couple of days off."

"How's the jaw?"

"As long as you stay on that side of the room, I think it will be fine," he murmured.

Merri hurriedly ran her brush through her hair and threw it back into her purse. "Well, I have to be going. By the time I run by the apartment to shower and change, I'm going to be late for work."

"I think I'll go back to sleep," he said as he yawned.

She had hoped he would say something a little more encouraging than "I think I'll go back to sleep," since they had just spent the night together; but then, all they had done was sleep. . . .

"Well, see you around," she called brightly, and left the bedroom as he rolled back over and covered his head.

All day at work her mind kept going back over the night before and the devastating kiss they had shared just before they had gone to sleep. The very thought of the way his mouth had felt on hers made her insides turn to jelly. Ryder Tate could claim he wasn't interested in any "action," but she was sure that if that darn medicine had not done its job so effectively, their night together would have turned out very differently. And what would she have done if he had made a pass at her? Because she was afraid to answer that question, it made her all the more uneasy. Somewhere be-

126

tween plans A and E she had fallen in love with Ryder. It was as simple—or as highly complicated —as that. Now, how easy was it going to be to walk away from him when the time came?

When she left the shop at five, she couldn't help but wonder if he had eaten anything all day. Not that he wasn't perfectly capable of fixing himself something; nonetheless she was beginning to feel rather protective toward him, although heaven only knew why she should after the way he had treated her.

After a quick stop at the grocery store to pick up some more soup and a package of instant pudding, she decided to drop them off at his apartment. She had noticed that his cupboard as well as his refrigerator was nearly always bare. If he wasn't there, she would put the soup and pudding in the cabinet and then would feel more confident that he would have something to eat when he wanted it.

Tate's van was still in the drive when she pulled up and parked in front of his apartment. Trying to gather up enough courage to face him again, she sat for a moment and enjoyed the spring afternoon, mulling over in her mind the two bouquets of flowers she still had to drop by the church later on. There was to be a small, informal sunrise wedding in the church garden in the morning, and the bride wanted the bouquets delivered tonight.

When she glanced up a few minutes later, she was surprised to see Ryder jogging toward her station wagon. Her heart did flip-flops as she took in the white tennis shorts and red polo shirt he was wearing. Along with his sexy chest, he had the cutest pair of legs that she had ever seen. And to think she had slept next to *that* last night!

"Hi! I didn't expect to see you again so soon." Ryder walked up to her car and leaned in the open window. The smell of his familiar after-shave filled the car as she drew in a tantalizing whiff and smiled at him.

"I thought maybe you hadn't eaten today, so I stopped by and picked up some soup at the store. Here, you can take it in and I won't even have to get out of the car." She reached around to the backseat and handed the grocery sack to him.

"Thanks, but I had a late lunch."

"Your jaw must be doing better," she observed lightly.

"Yeah." He reached up and rubbed it carefully. "It's still a little sore, but it's improving. Joe and I even managed to get in a game of tennis this afternoon."

"That's great!" Merri leaned back and smiled, trying to delay her leaving. "So, what have you done all day except sleep and play tennis?"

"That's about it," he confessed, "but I'm afraid I'm going to make up for it this afternoon."

"Oh?"

"Yeah. My kid brother has a paper route and he's got a touch of the flu. Mom called and wanted to know if I could deliver his papers for him this evening."

"I thought the Tate family was filthy rich," Merri teased. "Surely the boys wouldn't have to hold down a job if they didn't want to."

"They wouldn't, if they didn't want to," he agreed. "It just so happens, they want to."

"Do you and your parents get along? I mean, they don't resent the fact you're not . . ."

"That I live my own life?" he supplied. "Not in the least."

"I . . . I didn't mean to pry," she said quickly, noting his defensive tone. "Well, look, I haven't anything to do for the next couple of hours. Why don't you let me help you deliver the—"

"I wouldn't think of it," he interrupted. "You've . . . you've already done too much as it is," he added.

Well, how nice: He had *finally* noticed her efforts! she thought elatedly.

"But I wouldn't think of letting you do this by yourself," she insisted, hopping out of the car enthusiastically. "I know how much work those paper routes can be, but with two of us working, it won't take any time at all to get those papers delivered."

Ryder shuffled along behind her bouncing steps, grumbling under his breath. Merri paused and put her hands on her hips and smiled at him pertly. "Now, quit your grumbling. Can you honestly see me *not* offering to help you, Ryder Tate?"

He grinned back in defeat. "No, but I can always hope, can't I?"

"Well, if it will make you feel any better, you can help me take some flowers by the church tonight. Deal?" She held her breath, praying he would accept her casual invitation.

"I suppose that's the least I could do for the girl I

slept with last night." He gave her a wink that sent her pulses racing.

Merri glanced around self-consciously to see if anyone had heard his playful remark. She laughed nervously. "Yeah, I suppose it is."

Draping his arm around her neck, he took uncommon delight in her obvious embarrassment as they ambled up the sidewalk together. "Uh . . . by the way, why don't you be my bunkie tonight? I'm feeling much better today, and—"

"I can't," she refused, before he could elaborate on his suggestion.

"But I thought you wanted to repay me for saving your life!" he exclaimed in mock disappointment.

"Oh, I will," she assured him sweetly. "If I have to spend the rest of our lives trying, I'll do it!" she promised with a wicked grin.

Ryder groaned and held his front door open for her. "Just shoot me and put me out of my misery right now," he pleaded, but she noticed he still had a grin on that disgustingly handsome face of his.

Dark thunderheads had been gathering on the horizon all afternoon, so Ryder decided the papers should be wrapped in an orange protective covering, assuring that subscribers of the Springfield *Leader and Press* would have a dry paper to read should the spring thunderstorms materialize. It took longer than Ryder expected to get the papers rolled and wrapped, so they were running at least half an hour behind schedule as they loaded the bundles of papers into the back of Watson and

130

carefully surveyed the list of addresses Ryder's mother had brought by earlier.

"Are you sure this piece of junk will make it?" Ryder asked for the third time. "I still think we should take my van."

"The van will be harder to throw the papers out of," Merri reasoned, "and Watson is perfectly capable of delivering papers. He delivers flowers every day."

"If you say so." Ryder scratched his head. "I haven't done anything like this in a long time."

"It'll be a snap," Merri promised. "You want me to drive?"

"No, I'll drive. How good is your aim?"

"Perfect. The boys always chose me first on their baseball teams when I was a kid because I could throw a perfect spitball," she bragged.

"How nice. Of course, I don't suppose there's a lot of demand for women who throw spitballs nowadays."

"No," she agreed with a grin. "But I was a legend in my time."

"Well, legend, you just be sure you hit your target," Ryder warned as they both got into the station wagon. "Pete has to pay for any damages he's responsible for, so be careful."

"Trust the bomber," she drawled, blinking her eyelashes at him in a flirtatious manner.

The very first paper she threw, she "bombed" a windowpane, shattering the glass all over the lawn.

"What the dickens . . . ! I thought you said you were a good shot!" Ryder sputtered as he hur-

131

riedly gunned the car away from the scene of the crime. "I'll have to pay for that window!"

"I'll pay for the stupid window," Merri dismissed curtly, reaching for another paper. Darn! She was rustier than she thought. "Just give me a minute to get my arm warmed up, then I'll be okay," she promised.

Ryder grunted and turned the station wagon toward the next house on his list.

Merri threw the next several papers without incident as they drove up and down the streets, delivering the evening news.

After seventy papers Merri's arm was beginning to feel as if it were going to fall off. That, coupled with Ryder's constant nagging to "Be careful! Be careful!" every five minutes, was beginning to take a toll on her disposition.

"Be careful!" he snapped again as a paper whizzed through the air and struck a porch light.

"Don't get so shaken up! I didn't break the light. I only tilted it a little!"

"If I couldn't throw any better than that, I'd quit!"

"You think you can do any better?" She angrily lobbed a paper and cringed as she heard something shatter. "What'd I hit this time?"

"Well, ace, you just beheaded a ceramic reindeer," Ryder replied calmly.

"No kidding?" Merri turned and looked at the deer head rolling across the lawn. "Hm. I guess I'm going to have to practice up on my spitball sometime."

"I wish you would have just let me deliver the

papers by myself." Ryder cringed as one of the subscribers stumbled off a porch, trying to dodge an orange bullet that had been fired out of the station wagon. "This little excursion is going to cost me a hundred dollars, not to mention Pete's job!"

"Do you want to throw these stupid papers yourself?" she challenged. "If you think it's easy, you're out of your mind. Pull this car over and I'll drive, and you can see just how easy it is!"

She irritably zoomed another paper out the window, and they both watched as a dog scooped it up in his mouth and started to run with it.

"Now, look at that!" Ryder accused. "You've done it again!"

"Stop this car!" she demanded. Enough was enough!

Ryder slammed on the brakes as Merri tumbled out of the car and took off in hot pursuit of the four-legged thief. She might not be able to do anything about the porch light or the poor reindeer's fatal accident, but she could get *this* paper back!

She ran across the yard, her mouth pursed in grim determination as she chased the dog. She was reasonably sure she was gaining on him when her feet became entangled in a bush and she went sprawling across the freshly cut lawn. For a moment she just lay there, staring at the darkening sky, counting to ten.

A large hand reached out and placed the confiscated paper in her hand. "Are you by any chance looking for this?"

"How did you get that?" she groaned.

"The dog dropped it the minute you started chasing him." Ryder reached down, grasped her hand, and pulled her to her feet. "Just look at you," he said, trying to brush the grass stains off her ruined clothing. "You look like something that dog dragged in!" He withdrew a snowy-white handkerchief from his pocket and diligently wiped her dirt-smeared face.

"Thanks. You always say the nicest things," she muttered crossly.

"I think you'd better drive and let *me* throw the rest of the papers," he ordered, letting her lean on him as she limped back to the car.

"With pleasure!" she acceded gratefully.

"I hate to be the one to tell you this, honey," he chided as he carefully helped her in the car, "but I think the ol' spitball legend has bit the dust!"

By the time the papers were finally delivered and Ryder had showered and changed clothes so he could help Merri deliver the flowers to the church, it was growing very late.

"We're taking my van this time," Ryder announced as they walked down the drive.

"Why don't you follow me over to the apartment and I'll clean up and leave Watson there?" she suggested.

It was nearly nine o'clock by the time Merri had showered and she and Ryder had gone to the shop for the wedding bouquets. After taking a short tour of the shop, he helped her carry·the white wicker baskets of blue and yellow daisies out to the van to load.

"You need a van in your business instead of that

134

station wagon," Ryder noted as he slammed the door and helped her into the passenger seat.

"I know, but I don't have the money right now," she replied. "Why don't you give me yours?" she teased.

"As far as I'm concerned, you can have it," he teased back. "That noise I keep hearing is beginning to really worry me."

"You think it's serious?"

"Sure sounds to me like it is, but the mechanics can't find anything."

Merri told him what church they were going to as he started the van and pulled out of the drive.

All of a sudden it seemed very natural to Merri to be riding along with Ryder and exchanging small talk. They talked about the rainy spring they had been having, and the fact that they both loved McSalty's Bear Pie pizzas and childhood friends. They were both surprised to find out they had gone to the same high school.

"How old are you," Merri laughed, "or would you rather not say?"

"I'm still young enough to say." He grinned. "Thirty-one. How old are you?"

"Twenty-eight. Let's see, I was probably a freshman when you were a senior. I'll have to get my old yearbook out and see if I can find your picture."

"Don't you dare. I was a skinny kid with long hair and zits," he protested with another grin.

They pulled up in front of the church as a low clap of thunder rumbled ominously in the distance.

"Looks like we'd better get these unloaded in a hurry. I don't like the looks of that cloud bank moving in," Ryder cautioned.

"I'll have to go next door to the parsonage for the key to the church. I'll just be a moment." Merri left and was back in less than five minutes with the key in her hand. "The minister said to leave the flowers on the altar and someone will bring them out to the garden in the morning."

While Merri unlocked the church door, Ryder gathered up the baskets of flowers and followed her in. A dim light was burning at the altar as the couple walked down the carpeted aisle and paused for a moment to admire the beauty of the sanctuary.

"I've always wondered what this church looked like on the inside," Ryder confessed. "It's really very beautiful, isn't it?"

"I think all of God's houses are beautiful," Merri admitted softly. "Especially this one. Do you know that couples who don't even belong to this church want to get married here because it's so lovely?"

"I can see why."

"Come on, I'll show you the garden where tomorrow's wedding is going to take place."

Merri took his hand and led him over to double French doors opening out onto the garden. Even though it was too early for summer flowers to be blooming, it was still an exquisite setting for a wedding.

"Isn't this nice? I think this is where I would like to have my wedding when the time comes." She sighed and leaned her head against the doorframe.

"Can't you just envision the bride in her gown of pristine white, and the groom, proud and tall, standing next to her?"

Ryder chuckled. "No, not really." His voice took on a teasing lilt. "You expect to be standing there anytime soon?"

Merri laughed. "Heavens, no!"

"I guess you're waiting for some rich guy to come along and sweep you off your feet," he probed lightly.

"Not that either. Just some ordinary guy who loves me, wants a little cottage with a white picket fence and two children," she told him softly. "Those are the important things to me, and I couldn't buy them no matter how much money I had," she added, hoping he would get the point.

"You're not dating anyone?"

"No, not seriously. I was seeing a man named Dirk Bennett before the fire, but I've been so busy lately I haven't even seen him." Merri paused, then asked shyly, "What about you? Are you seeing anyone?"

A jagged streak of lightning lit up the small garden, and the thunder rolled once more as she held her breath and waited for his answer.

"No, not anyone special," he said. "I try to avoid headaches as often as possible."

The first few drops of rain plopped at their feet as they stepped back and closed the French doors. "We'd better get going before it starts raining hard," Ryder said in a tone that sounded sad, as if he didn't want to leave the peaceful setting.

When they left the church, they had to make a

mad dash for the van as the skies opened up and poured buckets.

They were both laughing as Ryder opened the side door of the van and they fell in breathlessly, trying to wipe the rain from their faces.

"Go sit on the sofa and I'll see if I can find something for us to use to wipe ourselves off," Ryder offered as he switched on the interior lights.

Seconds later he handed her a towel he had taken out of an overhead storage shelf, and she stood up and began to rub herself dry, shivering from her rain-soaked clothes.

Ryder took an extra coat he kept in the van and wrapped it around her snugly.

"Now you'll be cold," she protested, noting he was as wet as she was.

She reached out and started to hand him the towel and suddenly found herself staring into his beautiful smoky gray eyes, alive with the beginnings of desire. As far as she was concerned, she would be content to spend the rest of her life looking into those eyes, and it was never more clear to her than it was at that moment. It was true: She couldn't deny it any longer. She was falling hopelessly in love with Ryder Tate.

Ryder took the towel she offered him, his eyes still locked hypnotically with hers, and gently looped it around her neck.

With agonizing slowness he pulled her face toward his. "Come here, my little damsel in distress . . ." he whispered in a husky voice.

She was amazed that she could make her trembling limbs move at all, but somehow she did, moving closer to him. That incredibly wonderful smell of his after-shave played havoc with her tingling senses as her arms melted around his neck and she drank in the masculine touch and feel of him.

"I don't suppose you'd have any objections if I kissed you?" he asked in a voice that had dropped to a low, sensual timbre.

"No . . . I can't say that I would," she had to admit.

She couldn't help but notice he was trembling as hard as she was as he reached behind her to switch off the interior light.

"You know, I've been fighting against doing this very thing since the night I carried you out of that burning building," he said softly.

"I can't imagine why you would fight it," she teased lightly. Her fingers found their way into the dark curly locks of his hair.

"Because I still don't know how to figure you out," he confided. "You are a constant headache to me . . . yet—"

"What's to figure out? I'm a normal woman trying to pay a guy back for saving her life. I am not after your money, your body, or a lifetime commitment."

"That's what you say. . . ."

"But you still think I'm up to something," she sighed.

"I don't know, Merri. I really don't know. I wish I could believe differently," he murmured. His eyes gazed into hers deeply, seeking an answer only he could find.

"I'm sorry some other woman hurt you, Ryder. And there was one who did, wasn't there?" she guessed in a tender voice. There *had* to have been. No man would carry such deep scars if he hadn't been in the heat of a battle at one time in his life.

"That was a long time ago," he dismissed softly. "I haven't thought about her in years."

"Yes you have," she disputed gently. "Every woman you've come in contact with in the past few years has, in some way, reminded you of her. Well, I'm *not* her, Ryder. I'm me, Merri Lambert, and I'm standing in the arms of a man whom I want nothing more from than the kiss he just offered."

A bright flash of lightning lit up the dark interior of the van, and Merri caught a brief glimpse of a tender smile on Ryder's face as he said affectionately, "That man will be more than happy to make good his offer."

Then she felt his mouth touch hers—lightly at first, as if he weren't sure what his reaction would be, then more firmly as he realized he had lost his long-fought battle.

Merri's eyes closed, deliciously savoring the feel of his lips on hers. They felt cold from the rain, and he tasted faintly of his after-shave. This wasn't their first kiss; yet both could sense a turning point about to take place in their rocky relationship.

"I think we should go somewhere a little more private," he suggested a few minutes later as their lips parted unwillingly. "You didn't want to get home early, did you?"

"No, I'm in no hurry," she assured him quickly, her mouth still savoring his tantalizing kiss.

Merri had no idea where they were going as they sped down the highway. Nor did she care. This feeling of contentment she was experiencing with Ryder Tate was new and completely satisfying.

After a twenty-minute drive Ryder finally pulled the van off a country road and stopped.

"Is this what you call the boonies?" Merri asked, her eyes taking in the deserted wilderness he had brought her to.

"You might say that. Any objections?" He glanced at her.

"No, I feel safe with you," she answered demurely.

"You shouldn't. We could get in a lot of trouble out here," he pointed out solemnly.

"I know." Her gaze met his in the dark interior of the van. "I live for danger," she bluffed.

"Come on, let's get comfortable," he invited lightly.

Minutes later they were each enjoying a glass of white wine Ryder had taken out of the refrigerator and poured into two paper cups.

"You have all the comforts of home," Merri complimented as she took a sip of the chilled Chablis.

"You want some cheese and crackers?"

"No, thanks. The wine is perfect."

The sound of rain pelting down on the van lulled them into a peaceful silence as they relaxed and enjoyed their drinks.

Before long, Ryder finished his wine and set the

cup down on the table in front of the sofa. As he slowly rose to his feet he pulled her up with him.

"Now, let's see. Where were we before we were so rudely interrupted?"

"Mmmm . . . I think that must have been when you were kissing me," she said pensively. "Yes . . . yes, I'm sure that's where we were."

"Really? Well, if you say so." He leaned closer to her and sipped tantalizingly at her lips before he greedily took full possession of her mouth.

A surge of raw desire shot through Merri as she leaned against his masculine frame and parted her lips to allow his tongue to merge with hers. The kiss left them both weak and shaken and longing for more when they finally broke apart.

"You mind if we try that again?" Ryder asked as his hands traced lazy circles across her back.

"Not at all; take as much time as you need," she offered graciously. *Take the rest of my life if you want it!* she invited him silently.

Together they sank down on the sofa as his mouth closed more fully over hers, his tongue seeking hers again.

Amid the sound of thunder and rain beating a staccato tempo on the roof of the van, they lay on the small sofa and exchanged long, smoldering kisses, both caught up in a sensual web in which nothing or no one existed but each other and the dark, rainy night.

So many questions kept floating in Merri's mind as their fervent kisses grew longer and more passionate. What would happen when he found out she was merely setting out to prove a point to him

142

and had foolishly fallen in love with him before she got the job done? In a way she was as bad as all the women he had tried to avoid in the past few years. However, stating that she wanted nothing more from him than these kisses was very untruthful. She didn't care about his money, but she was beginning to want much more from him than an evening of unbridled kisses. Would he ever believe she wasn't a devious female out to get what she could from him?

Ryder's mouth trailed down to her ear, and she shivered as he hesitantly spoke the words she had known would be coming: "I want to make love to you."

How was she to answer such a request? Never one for casual affairs, the old Merri started to whisper her heartfelt refusal; but the new Merri, who had fallen so deeply in love with this man, would not let the words escape. Instead she found her hands reaching down to unbutton his shirt in silent acceptance of his proposal, realizing for the first time how very weak she was in his presence.

"I . . . I'm not prepared . . ." she murmured as he eased up and slipped out of his shirt. He tossed it on the floor and his hands moved to rid her of her clothes.

"I'll take care of it," he promised as his mouth gently moved her hair to one side and stayed to explore the silkiness of her throat.

"Ryder . . . I hadn't planned for this to happen," she pleaded, knowing without a doubt he would think this was all in the realm of her calculated plans to ensnare him.

"Shhh," he cautioned, kissing her unfounded worries into silence. "Just let me love you."

Their kisses turned to sighs of pleasure as her bare skin met the rough texture of his hair-matted chest and their bodies blended. Words were no longer needed between them as their passion flared and they slowly began to acquaint themselves with each other, their kisses saying what words could not.

Ryder began to explore the sensitive area below her ear, wanting her desire to be as great as his. When his mouth found the gentle swell of her breast and sucked gently, she cried out softly and nestled against him in an age-old feminine instinct that sent his passion soaring.

"Have I ever told you how beautiful you are?" he asked in a ragged voice. "How I love the color of your eyes, the fragrance of that sexy perfume you wear—everything that makes Merri Lambert a very special person?"

"No, but I'm willing to stay here the rest of my life and let you convince me," she whispered. Their mouths blended once more, his tongue exploring the dark moistness of her honeyed mouth, sending a sudden gush of warmth surging through her.

Here was the man she had been waiting for all her life. So, why was this moment so frightening to her?

He moaned and drew her closer to him. "I'd like that too."

Too soon they became unable to bank the fires,

and their bodies cried out for complete fulfillment.

As Ryder prepared to claim her as his he paused and gazed lovingly into her eyes. "Are you sure?"

"I'm sure," she whispered. Tomorrow would surely find her confidence gone and her common sense returned, but tonight was his to claim.

He gently lowered his large frame over her slender body and the night became a magical one in which a lovely princess was caught and suspended in time with her handsome prince. Moments or hours could have passed, but neither of them noticed as their union turned ragged and wanting, joyful and wondrous, then powerful and explosive as they cried out each other's name and succumbed to the showering of sensations that had overtaken their bodies.

When they were finally ready to speak once more, Ryder rolled over onto his back and contentedly cradled her in his arms. "I think you and I are going to get along well together, my fair damsel."

"I think you may be right, my handsome prince," she conceded, snuggling closer to his broad chest. "You are getting much nicer than you used to be."

"Oh, you haven't seen anything yet," he bragged in all his chauvinistic modesty.

"Ryder . . ." The nagging thought that he might misunderstand why she had let him make love to her threatened to shatter her tranquillity. "You don't think I—"

"You're right: I'm trying not to think," he replied in a drowsy voice.

He still had that touch of defensiveness in his voice, even though it was tempered with the brushing of his lips in feather kisses across her temple.

It was apparently too soon for Ryder to know his feelings, and she wasn't going to press the issue, especially when she was on such rocky ground.

The drive home was made in silent companionship. There seemed to be no need for words, but a certain closeness prevailed as he reached over a couple of times and stole a languorous kiss from her at stop signs. When he walked her up to her door with his arm around her, the good-night kiss they shared told her he was becoming more involved than he cared to admit.

"I'll give you a call tomorrow," he whispered, his mouth still touching hers lightly.

"All right," she whispered back. "I'll be looking forward to it."

When she let herself in the dark apartment, she could barely wait for the next day to see him again. She was finally in love, and it felt both wonderful and terrifying at the same time. It was all she could do to keep from awakening Erica and telling her the good news, but she decided to keep her joy to herself until she saw how things developed. After all, tonight was the first indication that anything serious could develop out of their tenuous relationship. She also knew she had to take one day at a time and try to win his love instead of rushing headlong into an affair that would only leave her hurting. No, she wanted that stubborn fireman for a lifetime, and she was willing to put all her efforts and planning into reaching that goal.

She closed her eyes; then they flew back open. She had been right! That van *was* a sin bin, and she had fallen in headfirst!

CHAPTER EIGHT

During the night the storm passed. The town awoke Friday morning to a glorious sunshiny day, one perfect in every way—just right for the wedding Merri knew would be taking place at the church as she lingered over her coffee. Her mind kept going over the night she had just spent in Ryder's arms, and she wondered if it had been a big mistake on her part. Obviously he wasn't in the market for a permanent relationship—at least not with her. She had to force herself to stop her foolish daydreaming and dress for work. By reminding herself repeatedly that he said he would call today, she was able to make it to the shop on time.

The day seemed an entire week long. Each time the phone rang, Merri scooped up the receiver eagerly, hoping to hear Ryder's voice. When it inevitably turned out to be a customer wanting to place a flower order, it was all she could do to keep her disappointment from seeping through her voice. What if he didn't call? What if last night had only been a pleasant distraction for him and he had gone back to his former suspicions of her and decided not to call? And worst of all, what if she was back to square one and plan F?

It was late in the afternoon before Ryder finally relieved her misery.

"Hi. Sorry I'm so late in calling, but I've been tied up all afternoon," he apologized in a breezy voice. That idiot didn't have the slightest idea of the sheer agony he had put her through all day!

"Ryder? My goodness! I'd almost forgotten you said you would call," she said in the most convincing voice she could muster up.

"You did?" It did her heart good to hear a touch of disappointment in *his* voice now.

"Well, not really," she relented. "But it was getting so late, I thought maybe you had forgotten."

"No, I didn't forget. In fact, Joe wants us to double with him and Erica tonight."

"That's sounds like fun. Where are we going?"

"Joe suggested we make it a casual evening and play it by ear. We'll grab a bite to eat and then take it from there. How does that sound?"

"Fine. What time will you be by?"

"Around six thirty. Think you can wait that long to see me?" he teased in an intimate voice.

"I'll force myself. It will be hard, but I think I can handle it."

Ryder gave a soft chuckle. "You know something? I've thought about you all day long."

Merri's heart fairly sang at his innocent confession. "I hope they were all nice things," she said happily.

"They were. Maybe, if you're real good tonight, I'll tell you a few of them," he offered in a sexy voice that made her stomach a shambles.

"I'll try to be on my best behavior," she promised.

"Well, that certainly won't be any fun," he chided.

"You might be surprised," she challenged.

"In that case I'll see you around six thirty."

When she hung up the phone, Merri felt like jumping in the air and clicking her heels together. Ryder Tate had thought about her *all day!* Things were going much better than even she had planned.

When the two handsome men came to pick them up that evening, Merri and Erica were ready and waiting.

"I don't know about you, Ryder," Joe commented in a lazy voice as he surveyed the two women standing before them, "but I think we've hit the jackpot tonight."

"I think you could be right," Ryder agreed, stepping forward to help Merri on with her sweater. "I think I'll take this one if you don't mind," he teased Joe, glancing down at Merri.

"Don't mind at all," Joe drawled in a fair imitation of W. C. Fields, "I'll take this little chickadee and try to content myself with her." The kiss he and Erica exchanged laid to rest any speculation that the fireman was unhappy about his fate.

"I think you two had better break it up," Ryder warned, pushing Joe's reluctant frame toward the doorway. "You're steaming up the windows."

"Come on, baby! We're in Ryder's van tonight, so you and I can continue our greeting in the privacy of the backseat," Joe promised, winking at Erica affectionately. It was becoming increasingly clear that Joe and Erica's relationship was deepening with each passing day.

When they were settled in the van, the men gave the girls the option of where they would like to eat.

"I would even be good enough to take you to the Vintage House," Ryder offered big-heartedly, "but none of us is exactly dressed for it."

"No, I didn't wear my tux tonight," Joe groaned. "What a shame."

"You tightwad." Erica punched him in the ribs. "You wouldn't have taken me there if you *had* worn your tux."

"I didn't say I would take you there," Joe defended, "Ryder said *he* would take us there."

After ruling out several of the town's better-known establishments, Merri finally broke the impasse. "Would anyone think I'm absolutely crazy if I suggested Calvert's? They have the most delicious raisin-bread pudding I've eaten."

"A cafeteria?" Ryder glanced at her in surprise.

"Sure . . . but if anyone objects . . ."

"We don't object," Erica and Joe chorused.

Merri noted that they were too busy kissing to object if she had suggested they take a picnic lunch to the sewer disposal plant and eat it!

"You sure are easy to please," Ryder noted with an amused smile. "Most women would have picked a more expensive restaurant."

"I think you'll find that the more you get to know me, the more you'll see I'm not like *most* women." She winked suggestively at him, hoping he would get the not-so-subtle point.

"I think I might like that," he said, his voice suddenly taking on a serious note.

"What? Eating at Calvert's?"

"No, getting to know you better," he stated simply.

"You certainly have my permission," she assured him softly. Their eyes met and sent a tingling message to each other as Merri recalled his kisses of the night before. From the moment he had picked her up that evening, Merri had felt a certain intangible intimacy between them, one she wished she had the privacy to explore more fully.

"Hey, Ryder, turn on the radio and let's hear some romantic music," Joe enticed, reaching over to pull Erica into his lap.

"Radio doesn't work," Ryder apologized. "I've been thinking about putting a stereo system in for a long time, but I haven't had the time to take the van into Wally's Stereo Shop to have it installed."

Joe let out an appreciative whistle. "That eight-hundred-dollar system you were looking at the other day?"

"Yeah. Nice, huh? But I don't have time to fool with it right now. I'm still worried about that whine in the rear end."

"You had the differential checked?"

"Three times, and the wheel bearings, too, but no one has been able to come up with the problem. I have a fellow coming by tomorrow to take a look at it again. If he can't come up with the source of trouble, I may just get rid of this thing," he joked. Ryder turned to Merri. "He's been after me for the last month to sell him the van."

Merri was digesting the conversation silently, her mind latching on to the fact Ryder didn't have the time to have his desired stereo installed. She could always get a few hours away from the shop. . . .

When the van pulled into the lot of the South Oaks Center shopping mall, plan F was fully formed in her mind.

As the two couples started toward the entrance of the cafeteria, Ryder pulled her back and put his arm around her waist as Erica and Joe ambled on ahead of them.

"I don't know if this double-dating was a wise idea or not," he said in a doubtful voice.

"Why not? Joe and Erica are fun," Merri noted.

"Sure, but it isn't that," he conceded. "The thought just occurred to me I'd rather be alone with you tonight."

Merri glanced up and smiled at him invitingly. "What would you do differently from what you're doing now?" she prompted in her sultriest voice.

"You keep looking at me like that, and it won't

153

take me long to show you," he told her, pulling her closer and giving her a very promising kiss.

"You sure have changed your tune," she accused in a teasing lilt. "Not very long ago you were telling me to get off your back, out of your life, and off your case."

"*I* said those nasty things?" he asked incredulously.

"Every word, and then some."

He grinned engagingly. "Remind me to eat those words first chance you get."

By now they were standing in line in the cafeteria, waiting their turn.

Ryder leaned his arm on the wall behind her and pulled her closer to him as they talked quietly. The outside world didn't exist, and they simply enjoyed each other's company.

"How was your day?" he asked softly, as if he were honestly interested in what she had done that day.

"Very hectic. I've had such a rash of weddings lately, and I still have another large one tomorrow afternoon. If April is this busy, I hate to think of June."

"I would think you're the type who would love doing all those mushy weddings," he observed good-naturedly.

"I do." She smiled. "Every last mushy minute of them."

"Well," he said in mock resignation, "I'll have to admit, there are a lot of suckers in this world. It's a crying shame the way you pushy women are leading us poor unsuspecting men to the altar like a

154

bunch of cattle to the slaughterhouse. . . ." He laughed as she gently punched him in the stomach.

"I don't see anyone leading *you*," she pointed out.

"And I hope you never do." He chuckled. "But if that time ever comes, I might consider letting you do the flowers, since you're so crazy about weddings."

"You are all heart," she said sourly, but accepted his fleeting kiss gratefully.

They got their food and found a table for four. The couples lingered over their evening meal while Ryder and Joe entertained the ladies with outrageous stories about events they were supposed to have encountered in the line of duty as firemen. By the time Joe finished telling the story of how Ryder had tried to carry a three-hundred-pound man down seven flights of stairs, they were all laughing hysterically.

"I can just see you macho men wandering around the fire station, washing windows and mopping floors," Erica teased when the conversation got around to how the two men spent their time when they were on duty.

"We do things other than housework," Joe pointed out hastily. "We go to school two hours a day and study Monday through Friday."

Merri patted Ryder's hand sympathetically. "And I know you get stuck with some of the cooking. How was your brown gravy?"

"Enough to gag a maggot," Joe said with a grimace.

"I seem to remember your 'hamburger surprise' wasn't anything to write home about, either, Joe," Ryder said. "Each one of us has to wash our own dishes, and whoever cooks has to do the pots and pans. I hate those greasy pots and pans," he confessed.

"I'll take the pots and pans any day," Joe offered. "It's wiping those trucks down every time they're taken out that drives me up a wall!"

"You sound real efficient," Merri concluded. "You guys are going to make someone real nice wives someday!"

When they finally finished their meal and left the cafeteria, Joe suggested they go to Lucy's, a local disco.

Glancing at Merri, Ryder hedged. "I have a better idea. Why don't I drop you off at your car and you and Erica go. I thought I might take Merri over to meet my folks, then we can come out later on if we want."

Merri could hardly believe her ears when Ryder said he wanted her to meet his parents, but she decided to defer to his wishes, even though the thought sent cold chills running down her cowardly spine.

The transfer of the other couple to Joe's Corvette was easy, with Ryder and Merri faithfully promising to join them when they left Ryder's parents, if it wasn't too late.

"What is all this about meeting your parents?" Merri asked as they drove away from Joe's apartment.

"I thought you might be interested in seeing how the rich folks live," he told her.

"No, I'm really not," she said politely. "But if you're asking if I'd like to meet your parents, then yes, I'd like that, even though I can't imagine why you would want me to."

"I can't either," he admitted, "but for some crazy reason it seems important to me."

By now they were driving in one of Springfield's oldest and most expensive neighborhoods. The sheer magnitude of the houses was enough to make one hang out the car window with his mouth gaping open in astonishment. Merri had passed these homes many times in her life, but never dreamed she would one day be dating a man who had lived in one of them.

When Ryder turned into the driveway of one of the most elaborate homes on the block, Merri groaned, her eyes drinking in the loveliness of the old mansion. She knew from her childhood memory how elegant and lush the surrounding grounds were with their kidney-shaped pool, white stone cabana, tennis courts, and masses of flower beds blooming all summer long. "I just knew this had to be the one."

Reaching down to switch off the ignition, Ryder glanced at her and asked, "Why this one?"

"Because when I was a little girl, I used to think a handsome prince lived here," she confessed.

"And now that you know who lived here . . . ?" he prompted.

"I realize the prince is only a common frog who

157

is paranoid that someone is going to steal his pad." She grimaced. "What a waste of manhood."

"The frog might be waiting for that legendary kiss that's supposed to turn him into a real nice prince," Ryder pointed out. He leaned over and captured her mouth as her arms wrapped around his neck. They kissed hungrily for a few minutes, oblivious to their surroundings.

"I think we had better stop this before your parents look out the window," she murmured as they broke apart and he buried his face in the fragrant mass of her lustrous hair.

"I think I'd rather stay out here all night and forget about going in," he said, nibbling at her earlobe.

His warm breath sent prickles of delight racing across her skin, and when his hand slipped under her blouse and found the soft mound of her breast, her breath caught momentarily as he chuckled wickedly against her ear. "Then again, it might be better to go in and get this over with so we can still have some time to ourselves this evening."

Their kiss was longer and more demanding this time as his hands ran smoothly over the velvet texture of her skin.

"Ryder . . . I don't want to be a wet blanket . . . but I do think we'd better stop," she protested as his hands grew increasingly bolder. She broke off the kiss with reluctance. "Anyway, this seat is for the birds when it comes to trying to neck."

"I was just thinking the same thing," he muttered, but he still pulled her mouth back down to his and continued his onslaught of kisses.

When the kisses and his fevered caresses reached the boiling point, Merri pushed his hands away gently and sat up. "This has got to stop," she whispered in a ragged voice. "Your parents . . . what in the world will they think of a girl who will sit in a van in front of their home and blatantly neck with their son?"

"The living quarters are in back of the house, worrywart. I'm not quite that deranged," he scoffed. "But if you insist, we'll go in and ease your conscience."

By the time Merri had straightened her hair and reapplied her lip gloss, Ryder was back to trying to distract her in a most disgraceful way.

"Ryder Tate! I am going to tell your mother," she warned as she gently slapped his hand away from her leg for the third time in five minutes.

"Go ahead, and I'll tell your mother what her daughter tried to do to me the day I had my tooth pulled, and what you did to me last night," he mocked. He straightened up and ran his hands through his unruly hair. "Does that put the fear in you?"

"Not in the least. Both times I was only trying to show you I thought you were a nice guy, money or no money," she replied, opening the car door and climbing out.

"Not to mention the small fact I'm head over heels in love with you," she whispered under her breath so quietly, he couldn't hear her.

"What happens when you decide you've paid

me back for saving your life?" Ryder asked as he joined her and they strolled up the sidewalk to his parents' house.

"Then I suppose I'll tell you good-bye and we'll go back to our old lives," she said with a touch of sadness to her words.

"Just like that, huh?"

"You don't believe I can do that?"

"I don't believe you would be foolish to throw away what you have going for you," he said calmly.

"Which is . . . ?"

"Let's not play cutesy, Ms. Lambert. You have me eating out of your hand and you know it." His voice had lost its earlier playfulness and only sounded bitter now.

Merri paused and turned to face him, guilt hanging heavy in her mind now. "Ryder, I confess that at first, other than paying you back for saving my life, I deliberately set out to . . ."

"Teach me a lesson," he finished stonily.

". . . teach you a well-deserved lesson," she continued sheepishly. "And you have to admit . . ." She stopped and glared at him soundly. "You knew?"

"I suspected. After all, you haven't been very discreet in your efforts to prove you're just a poor little girl who would never *dream* of marrying a rich man."

"I wouldn't marry you if you were the king of Siam," she said heatedly. "I wouldn't marry *anyone* with your attitude, and you can just bet your bottom dollar that as soon as this month's over, I'll be out of your life for good, and you and your rotten money can live happily ever after!"

Ryder inserted his key in the door, completely ignoring her fit of temper. "I'll bet," he taunted, then opened the door, bowed gallantly, and ushered her in politely. "Welcome to the prince's palace."

The 'prince's palace' almost took her breath away as they stepped in the elegant foyer and paused.

"Wow!"

Ryder glanced at her sharply. "It's only a house."

"You didn't let me finish," she accused him. "I was going to say 'Wow, it's only a house.'" Her grin was so contagious that Ryder's defensive stance slackened immediately.

"Yeah, wow, isn't it? Come on, I'll show you the rest of it and you can 'wow' all the way through," he chided.

An elderly man appeared in the doorway as they crossed the massive foyer and started up the winding stairway.

"Oh, Ryder, I didn't know it was you!"

Ryder turned and smiled affectionately at the family butler. "Hi, Graves. Where're Mom and Dad?"

"Your father flew to Kansas City this morning on business, and your mother decided to join him," Graves announced. "They won't be back until sometime late tomorrow evening."

"Pete go with them?"

"No, Master Peter just left for the evening. I'm

afraid if you wanted to speak with him, you're a bit too late. His touch of flu passed quite rapidly, and he is ready to kick his heels up again. This being the weekend, and with your parents gone . . . well, he tends to take advantage of the freedom."

"Most teenage boys would," Ryder agreed with a guilty grin.

"I remember, sir," the butler said dryly.

Ryder's grin widened as Graves's eyes rolled in remembrance. "Well, I'm going to show Merri— Oh, I'm sorry. Merri Lambert, this is Graves Larsons. He's been in the family . . . how long now, Graves?"

"Forty-two years, sir."

"Forty-two years." Ryder whistled appreciatively. "I hadn't realized. Well, as I was saying, I'm going to show Merri through the house."

"Very good, sir. I was just about to retire to my quarters for the evening. Will you and Ms. Lambert be needing anything?"

"No, you go on. I'll lock up when we leave."

Graves bowed respectfully and backed out of the room.

"Wow. Nice little butler you have there," Merri complimented. "But don't worry, I'm not impressed."

"Now you're getting the hang of it." He grinned. "Money can't buy everything."

"No, but it's way ahead of whatever can." She instantly wiped the smile off her face. "However, I don't want any."

Ryder put his arm around her waist and they

climbed the staircase together, chuckling over their playful teasing.

The house was all Merri had ever thought it would be, and more. What seemed glamorous and overwhelming to Merri seemed commonplace and ordinary to Ryder.

"You should be ashamed of yourself," Merri chided as they walked back downstairs, their arms still entwined. "God has given you all these marvelous things to enjoy and you turn your nose up at them."

"See? I knew you would be overly impressed. What's wrong with a simple life, with a common, ordinary man to come home to every night?" he complained.

"Not one blessed thing. But what's wrong with having money?" she asked. "As long as it's made honestly and spent wisely, I really can't see what you object to."

"I don't object to the money in itself," Ryder explained. "What I object to is the way people worship it and let it change them."

Merri reached over and pinched his nose. "Not all people, Fireman Tate. This woman, the one you haven't thought about in years, is she the one who worshiped your money?"

Ryder laughed bitterly. "She sure didn't worship me. Only what I could give her."

"Then she was a real jackass," Merri declared firmly. "And only another jackass would care what a jackass does."

Ryder glanced down at her in surprise. "I really hadn't thought of it that way."

"Obviously not. Let's see the rest of the house," she dismissed curtly, turning away to walk ahead of him. If he wanted to pine over a lost love who had soured him on all women for the rest of his life, he would have to do it without her sympathy.

Ryder reached out and caught her arm. "Merri."

"Yes?" She refused to look at him for fear he would see the tears gathering in her eyes.

"Thanks. I think I needed that."

Relenting, Merri turned and tenderly placed her hand on his cheek. "My pleasure," she said sweetly. "Believe me, you lovable little jackass, it was my pleasure."

CHAPTER NINE

"And I think you will agree with me when I say I've saved the best for last." The tour of the house was nearing completion as Ryder paused in front of a set of double doors and smiled.

"If you have a topper to what I've just seen, I don't know if I can take it or not," Merri cautioned. For the last thirty minutes they had wandered in and out of rooms filled with antiques and priceless works of art. If the house contained any more surprises, it would be hard to believe.

"It may not top anything you've already seen tonight, but it's a very special room to me and I hope you'll like it." With those words he opened the door and stood back for Merri to enter.

The scene before her nearly took her breath away as she stood staring at hundreds of lush green plants surrounded by massive windows and sky-lights. Glancing upward at the domed ceiling, she could see thousands of tiny stars twinkling in the heavens.

"Oh, Ryder . . . a solarium," she said in awe as her footsteps carried her among the rich foliage.

"Yeah." He turned around, closed the door, and slid the lock in place. "When I was a kid, this was my favorite room to play in. I used to stay in here for hours and make up all kinds of games. I could be anything from Tarzan to a great safari hunter."

"It is beautiful," she said with a sigh.

"Almost as beautiful as you are," he agreed softly.

The change in his voice made her glance up unexpectedly to catch the wistful look in his eye. "Would you like to see my hideout?" he asked.

"Would it still be here?" she marveled.

"Sure. Knowing mother, she has forbidden Graves to touch it. She always said she wanted it for her grandchildren to play in." Ryder took her hand and they wound through the greenery until they came to a small gurgling fountain built into the center of the room.

"Tarzan needed a river to live by," he explained as Merri *ooh*ed over the unexpected treat. "We have to crawl from here," he warned.

They both dropped to their knees and crawled a few feet under the hanging vines into a small room closeted from the outside world.

"This is marvelous," Merri exclaimed with de-light, glancing around at the assorted rugs and pillows that were thrown on the floor. "Why, any child would be thrilled to spend his days playing here! When I was a child I had to play in a deserted lot across the street from my house!"

"It was okay," he reasoned, lying down and propping his hands behind his head. "But there were lots of times I wished I'd had a deserted lot to play in instead."

That intangible note of longing filled his voice again as he lay staring up at the ceiling, recalling his childhood days.

She reached over and tousled his hair affectionately, "Poor little rich boy, huh?"

His grin was chagrined. "Something like that."

Merri toyed with the tassel on one of the pillows. "Have you brought many girls here to see your private domain?"

"Nope. In fact, this is the first time I've ever brought a girl home—period." He reached over and tweaked her nose. "How does that suit you?"

Merri's puzzled gaze met his. "I have to wonder why?"

"I have to too," he confessed. "And I don't have an answer yet."

His steady gaze met hers as they sat silently for a moment. "Last night was something very special to me, Merri," he revealed quietly.

"It was for me too." Her hands closed around the pillow more tightly.

"Come here," he ordered in a most persuasive voice as he held his hand out to her. "Let's play jungle."

"Uh-oh. That sounds like trouble!"

"Trouble!" His gray eyes widened in such innocence, she thought she was going to laugh out loud. "Me, Tarzan; you, Jane. How could any trouble come out of that combination?"

"Why, I can't imagine how," she agreed, just as innocently. "I suppose you want me to sit here and eat bananas with you and discuss the astronomical price of owning a decent grapevine nowadays."

"Exactly! Come here."

She went into his arms, knowing it would probably be one more mistake in her ever growing list of blunders concerning Ryder Tate, but nevertheless she was willing to take whatever he was offering, no matter how small.

They kissed in unhurried, sweet reunion as she lay down next to him, wrapping her arms around his waist, his hand coming up to cup her breast.

His mouth slid down to nip sensually at her shoulder as she pushed herself closer to his now familiar body. No longer was she shy and hesitant about what she wanted. It was lying right there in the circle of her arms.

"My, my. Jane is getting naughty right out of the chute," he chided as her hand slid under the back of his shirt and worked its way up the ridge of rippling muscles that played across his back.

"Are we playing cowboys and Indians or Tarzan and Jane?" she mocked.

"We'll play anything you want, sweetheart," he murmured huskily as his mouth captured hers once more.

They rolled over and he slid on top of her, his tongue driving deep into her mouth as his hands cradled her hips.

"Tarzan needs his woman," he coaxed. "Does his woman know what she wants?"

"She knows what she wants," Merri whispered. "She wants you, Ryder Tate."

A low moan escaped him as he deepened the kiss they were sharing in demanding mastery. It was hard to believe that this man could touch every fiber of her being and leave her wanting more; and yet he did—with such ease, it frightened her. Yes, she wanted him, but not for this brief moment in their life; for eternity. It nearly broke her heart to think what a slim thread of life this relationship was holding on by. She really had no hopes of having a permanent life with Ryder; she knew she'd have one that was doomed for a painful separation in another short week when her "contract" with Ryder was up.

They dropped their clothes one item at a time as they teased each other with agonizing playfulness.

"I suppose Tarzan is prepared for a romp in the jungle with Jane," Merri said pointedly.

"Ummm. Tarzan is boy scout in spare time. Always prepared for Jane."

Ryder's lips began a slow assault to find the erogenous zones that made her sigh in pleasure and beg for more. Whispers of pleas and murmured words of love filled their small hideaway as each strove to bring the other to the pinnacle of pleasure without sliding over the top.

Merri felt she was being consumed by a fire as she buried her face in his neck and moaned his name.

"What is it, sweetheart?" he pleaded. "Tell me what pleases you."

"You . . . you . . ." she answered hoarsely. "I want you." An unbearable hunger was tearing at her body, and she begged for it to be assuaged.

They came together explosively as Ryder's hands lifted her. The world seemed to burst around Merri, and she drowned in the powerful, fiery sensations. He slowly began to alter his rhythm to hers, taking them to a higher plane, their passion threatening to consume them as they neared the peak of desire.

The end was sudden and powerful. Waves of fulfillment washed over them, and they softly cried out the other's name. Ryder still held her tightly in his embrace as he kissed her face and eyes and uttered words of pleasure while they slowly floated back to reality.

"You know, you're getting pretty good at that," he complimented her, tenderly stroking the damp tendrils of hair away from her face.

"You'd be surprised to know how very little experience I've had on the job," she laughed softly.

"No I wouldn't. Some things are rather hard to hide," he chuckled.

Merri sighed and buried her face in the warmth of his neck. "When you walked into my life, I seemed to lose all sense of right and wrong, black and white."

She couldn't help but wonder how he could have shared such a perfect moment with her and yet refuse to admit that what they had was something very special. Would he ever realize that, or in the end, would he simply dismiss her along with all the other women who had drifted in and out of his troubled life.

They lay in each other's arms, content with the world for a very long time before Ryder finally stirred and strained to read the hands of his watch. "It's getting late," he noted regretfully.

"Yes, I know. We should be going. I have a big day tomorrow," she said in a drowsy voice.

"You said something about another wedding?"

"Yeah. Another one of those mushy things," she teased, and kissed him again.

"I don't know how you work with that old station wagon," he fretted.

"Watson? He's great, even though I have to admit, he's almost seen his day."

"Are there a lot of flowers to be delivered tomorrow?"

"Ummm . . . it's going to be an elaborate affair."

Ryder turned over and propped himself up on his elbow. "I'll tell you what: Why don't you take me to work in the morning, then keep my van. It's a lot roomier than Watson, and it'll make your day ten times easier."

Merri traced the contours of his face lovingly. "Why, that's very generous of you, Tarzan."

Ryder shrugged resignedly. "That's true, Jane, but I suppose I'm just a born sucker for sexy jungle women."

It puzzled her how he could say those intimate things to her, yet never once voice his true feelings.

"Well, if you're sure . . ." she accepted, before he could reconsider his rash offer. It was the perfect time to implement the clincher to their tottering relationship: the unfailable plan F. It would be tricky business to get down to the stereo shop first thing in the morning and have the music system that Ryder wanted installed in his van in view of all the work she still had to put in on the wedding, but with a careful balancing of her time, and with Cleo's assistance, she could swing it. Inasmuch as money was the least of Ryder's worries, she would simply charge the system to his account and he could pay for it later on. If this plan failed to make him realize she loved him and wanted nothing more than to please him, then she was going to throw in the towel. If he could still be skeptical of her intentions after all she had gone through for him, failing to realize that she loved him for himself—for no other reason—then what else could she do?

Ryder yawned and sat up, rubbing his neck. "Yeah, I'm sure. Just have it back around five. There's a guy coming over to the station to take a look at it."

"Okay, I will," she promised obediently, her mind rejoicing in the look of sheer joy she would be seeing on his face when he saw his new stereo system! She had to hand it to herself: She was a mental giant!

After dropping Ryder by the fire station early the next morning, she kissed him good-bye and promised to have the van back by five. Other than the annoying noise he kept complaining about, Ryder seemed to be very proud of his van, and no doubt wanted to show it off to one of his friends. Well, he was going to be even prouder when she returned it that evening!

She was the first customer at the stereo shop, the name of which she had heard Ryder mention to Joe the night before. Because the salesman knew Ryder and knew the system Ryder wanted to purchase, she had no difficulty charging the entire $842.37 to Ryder's account. And, owing to a cancelation in their work schedule and her incredible luck, the salesman offered to have the stereo installed while she walked over to a nearby restaurant and ate breakfast.

By eleven o'clock Merri was clicking her fingers and swaying to the fantastic sound blaring out of the four-speaker system as she drove to the flower shop. Wow! AM, FM, and cassette, with eight-inch sub-woofers, coaxial speakers, all being pushed by 140 watts of amplification! Ryder would go out of his gourd when he heard this! She knew he would be nearly delirious with excitement when he found out what she had done.

The day went along smoothly as she and Cleo efficiently moved the masses of floral bouquets to the church and arranged them along with the baby-blue– and yellow-colored satin ribbons on the altar and the pews. Megan was left to watch the shop and carry on business as Cleo and Merri moved back and forth between the church and the shop all afternoon. By four o'clock the church was a mass of gardenias, lilies of the valley, and gold candelabra waiting expectantly for the bride and groom to exchange their holy vows.

"Oh, hey," Merri exclaimed, glancing down at her watch, "I'm going to have to leave in a few minutes. I promised to get the van back to Ryder by five."

"Give that thoughtful man a kiss for me," Cleo ordered. "That van has made the day much less hectic."

"I will. He's a real sweetie to loan it to me," Merri said affectionately as she arranged the last gardenia around the towering wedding cake.

Cleo paused and glanced at her knowingly. "I think he's become much more to you than 'a real sweetie,' hasn't he?"

Merri's finger traced the blossoms of the fragrant gardenia as she felt a tug of pain on her heartstrings. "Yes, he's very special to me," she admitted softly.

"And are you special to him?"

"I don't know. I hope so," she said, sighing.

Cleo glanced at the clock on the wall and turned back to her chores. "I'll finish up here if you want to go on. I'll take a cab back to the shop when I'm through."

Merri gathered up her supplies and her purse and hurried out to the parking lot. It was nearly four thirty, and the traffic would be getting heavier. She'd have to hurry.

It was nearly five when she pulled up at the fire station, the stereo going full blast. She waved at Ryder, who was standing beside the brick building, talking with another man.

Wheeling up to within three feet of them, she braked and grinned mischievously. Crooking her index finger mysteriously, she motioned for him to step over to the window of the van.

Casting an apologetic look to the man he was visiting with, Ryder walked over to the van and paused as he heard the loud strains of music coming from the interior.

"Hi, Tarzan!"

"What's up, Jane?" He kissed her lightly, his face suddenly turning puzzled. "Did the radio start working again?"

"Nope! Guess again!" she replied happily.

Ryder leaned into the window and surveyed the dash. His face suddenly turned positively green as his eyes fastened on the new blaring in-dash stereo.

He swore in the most ungentlemanly manner she had ever heard him use, then shouted at her, *"What in the hell is that?"*

Merri drew back from the window, her eyes widening in disbelief. "The new stereo you wanted."

"The *what?*" His eyes distraughtly took in the expensive system, and he looked as if he were ready to strangle her.

"The new stereo . . ." She paused, then gathered her courage and straightened her shoulders defiantly. Good grief! What was his problem? "I said, this is the new stereo system you wanted for the van. . . . You know, the one you couldn't find time to have installed," she prompted. "Since I

175

had extra time, I took it by the stereo shop first thing this morning and had it installed."

"*You* paid for it?"

"Of course not! I don't have eight hundred and forty-two dollars and thirty-seven cents to throw away on stereos!" she snapped. "I charged it to *you.*"

"*Eight* hundred forty-two dollars and thirty-seven cents. . . ."

"Well, for heaven's sake! You wanted it. I thought you would be happy! The salesman said you wanted this very system . . . and now you're standing here acting as if it's the end of the world?"

"Merri, dammit, I just sold the van!"

"*Sold it!*" She screamed in stunned amazement.

"That's right. That guy over there is a mechanic. Because of that funny noise I haven't been able to pinpoint, I decided to sell the damn thing to him!"

"Well, how was I supposed to know that?" she demanded irritably. She was going to give up on all those foolish plans she had concocted. Not one of them had worked out.

"You're just like all women! You think I'm made of money," Ryder stormed. "Now I'm going to lose all my profit on the van and it's all your fault!"

"Well, that does it!" She snatched up her purse and the empty box the stereo had come in and jumped out of the van angrily. "I have had it with you, Ryder Tate! I don't want ever to see your face darken my door again!"

"*You're* mad at *me?*" he asked incredulously as she shoved him out of the way and started walking. "That *has* to take the cake! *I*'m the sucker who's out a bundle of money! You come back here while I'm talking to you!" he demanded, trailing along behind her. "*I*'m the one who's out eight hundred dollars, so where do you get off being mad at *me?*"

"Just shut up, Ryder Tate! We're back to *your* money again, aren't we?" It had stung her pride when he had accused her of thinking he was made of money! Any other man could have made the same remark and it wouldn't have bothered her, but she knew what he was thinking. "Well, you can take your money and stick it, mister, because I couldn't care less about it—or you!"

His expression turned instantly hurt. "That doesn't surprise me . . . that you don't care for me personally," he clarified in a strained voice. "I knew you were just like—"

"All the other women? Well, you're right as usual! I am greedy and conniving and have only wanted your money all along, but I see now you were too smart for a girl like me," she lied, her eyes filling with tears. "Here!" She rummaged around in her purse and withdrew the crumpled letter she had carried with her ever since the night Ryder had signed it in the restaurant nearly a month earlier. Finding a ball-point pen, she scribbled PAID IN FULL across the paper and thrust it angrily into his hand.

"We're even now. You find someone else to be your whipping post." She angrily wiped at the tears streaming down her face. "I sincerely hope you find what you're looking for in life, Ryder. Obviously it isn't me."

"Merri . . ." Ryder reached out and tried to touch her, but she jerked away from him. She couldn't help but notice that his eyes were growing suspiciously wet now. "Look, I'm sorry. . . . I lost my temper for a minute, that's all. I know you were only trying to help."

Merri faced him hopefully, still ineffectually wiping her tears. "Do you really believe I care whether you have money or not, Ryder?" She *had* to know his true feelings.

"It doesn't matter anymore. . . . You're welcome to anything I have," he said in a dead voice. "If the money is important to you, then I'm more than willing to let you share whatever I have. Maybe in time I can make you love me, because I love you, Merri. If you are interested in only the money, then I don't care . . . it doesn't change the way I feel about you—" His words were severed as she let out an exasperated cry and mashed the empty cardboard stereo box with all his warranties and instructions over his head.

"As I said, I don't ever want to see you again, Ryder Tate!" She whirled and stormed off down the street in the direction of the nearest bus stop. She'd had it with that conceited imbecile!

Ryder stood in the driveway, the papers fluttering dejectedly around his feet as the man who had been witnessing the entire fracas hurried over to him.

"Wow! What happened?" he asked as he helped Ryder take the box off his head.

"I think I must have said the wrong thing," Ryder confessed as he watched Merri's flouncing figure disappear down the street.

"Well, if you don't mind, I'd like to take another look at my van," the man said, glad that the wild woman wasn't his problem.

"No, I don't mind," Ryder grumbled as he turned and, disheartened, shuffled along behind him. "But I can tell you this: It's got one hell of a stereo in it." Suddenly his face brightened somewhat. "Listen, about that dangerous noise I've been hearing in the rear end: If you want to reconsider your offer to buy . . ."

CHAPTER TEN

It had been one unbearable week since that fateful day plan F had bombed so miserably; seven wretched, lonely days since she had seen Ryder and heard the sound of his voice, felt her heart tumble over at the sight of his crooked smile, felt the touch of his lips on hers. . . .

Merri sat at her desk at work the following Saturday morning and stared out at the cloudy day, recalling the happy news Erica had shared with her at breakfast that morning. Joe had given her an engagement ring, and their wedding would take place in late summer.

"I am so happy for you," Merri had told her with complete sincerity. "Of course, I insist on doing your flowers."

"Do you honestly think I would have it any

other way? Besides, Joe and I figured you would give us a good discount."

Merri laughed. "You always were so sentimental!"

"Oh, Merri! Joe and I are both so happy. We realize this has all been so sudden, but I always knew that when the right man came along it wouldn't take me a minute to recognize him."

Merri smiled. "What can I say? I'm thrilled for both of you. Maybe someday the right man will come along for me."

The happiness faded from Erica's eyes as she caught Merri's hand and apologized softly. "I wish things could have been different between you and Ryder."

The tears that had never been far from Merri's eyes all week swam to the surface at Erica's kind words. "Thank you. I do too." She smiled dismally despite the thickening lump in her throat.

"What happened to the girl with all the plans?" Erica chided gently. "It isn't like you to give up on something you want."

"Ryder doesn't want me, Erica. I can't go on trying to prove to him I love him when he continues to think I have ulterior motives."

"Does he know you fell in love with him long before you knew who he was?"

"Did I?"

"I'd stake my life on it. I think you fell in love with him the moment you met him," Erica stated.

Had Merri loved Ryder all along? At the moment she could not remember when she hadn't loved him. Would she be able to fall out of love with him as easily as she had fallen in love with him? She seriously doubted it.

The tinkle of the bell over the front door sounded as she sighed and got up to wait on the customer who had just entered the shop.

Ten minutes later she was halfheartedly trying to help a lady decide what to buy, when the bell over the door sounded once more. She did a double take when she saw Ryder walk in and glance around the showroom. He spotted her instantly, although she had immediately squatted down behind a potted palm tree to avoid him. The very nerve of him ignoring her all week, then showing up there unexpectedly and upsetting her! Her eyes narrowed angrily and she stood up and addressed the customer again.

"Have you thought about a nice cut-flower arrangement?" Merri asked politely, completely ignoring Ryder as he walked toward her.

"Cut flowers? That might be nice . . . but I really can't decide. What's this plant called?" The lady wandered over to examine a flowering azalea plant as Ryder made his way over to Merri and stopped.

"I want to talk to you," he stated impatiently.

"I'm terribly sorry, but I'm waiting on another customer. Cleo will be happy to wait on you." She turned her head coolly and called for Cleo. "Cleo! We have another—" She broke off, gasping as he picked her up in his arms.

"*What do you think you're doing?*" she protested in disbelief.

The customer turned around, her mouth dropping open as Ryder flushed and nodded to her politely. "Me, Tarzan . . . she, Jane." He grinned weakly.

"Well . . . I've never . . . !" The woman eyed him in extreme disgust.

"I can believe that," Ryder muttered under his breath, and started out the front door with Merri still clasped firmly in his arms.

"I don't know what you think you're doing, but I warn you, I am going to scream my head off if you don't take me back this instant," Merri yelled, struggling with all her might to free herself from his tight embrace.

"I take that to mean you're still mad at me," he grumbled, hefting her up more securely in his arms as he strode briskly down the street.

"You bet I am, you ungrateful chicken-plucker! I don't know where you get off coming into my shop and hauling me off down the street after I haven't heard one word from you in a week!" she ranted.

"You don't have to tell me how long it's been," he snapped. "It's been the most miserable seven days of my life. I hope you're happy!"

"If you were so miserable, then why didn't you call?" she asked him stonily.

"I needed a little time to sort through my feelings and give this fight we've been having some serious thought," he replied, completely ignoring her ravings, "and I'm ready to admit that part of it was my fault. I'm sure in the heat of anger I phrased my feelings in all the wrong words. Will you hold still? I'm not very good at eating crow, and you sure aren't making it any easier for me."

183

He threw her up over his shoulder and smacked her bottom soundly as they continued down the street.

"You were only telling the truth," she accused petulantly. "You have always thought that I was up to something devious when I was totally innocent in every instance . . . except the time I put the tuna in the tree," she granted crossly.

" 'Put the tuna in the tree'?" He stopped and turned his head to face her at close range.

"Never mind. That isn't important any longer," she dismissed quickly. "The important thing now is for us to admit we will never reach a workable solution to this sticky problem and get on with our lives. I'm sure if you look hard enough, you'll find some Ms. Goody Two-Shoes clone who will be happy to live with you in a thatched hut and eat grass for the rest of her life just to prove money doesn't mean anything to her. Is that the kind of wife you want?"

When Ryder had to think about that question for a moment, her temper boiled over again. "Well, is it?" she demanded as she pounded on his back.

He hurriedly surrendered. "No! No, that's not the kind of wife I want," he hastened to assure her before she broke every bone in his body.

"I should say not!" she agreed hotly as she felt herself slipping. "And you'd better not drop me, you fool!"

"I'm not going to drop you. How much do you weigh, anyway?" he grunted, clasping her tightly

184

once more as she kicked him angrily. "You feel a lot heavier than you look!"

"Put me down if you're going to insult me!"

Cars were beginning to honk and people stared at the warring couple as Ryder continued down the street, unperturbed by her shouts and demands.

"No, because if I put you down, you will turn your haughty little back on me and stomp off."

"Faster than you can blink an eye," she spit back.

"Now, see? That's your problem: You fly off the handle and don't stop to think things through," he accused. "Take that stereo incident. I'll grant you that it was a nice thought on your part, but don't you think I had the right to get a little upset?"

She stubbornly refused to answer him.

"All right. I can see you're not exactly receptive to discussing your shortcomings at the moment, so let's move right along to some of mine. That should be a subject more to your liking."

She remained silent, waiting to hear what he had to say.

"I'm willing to admit I've been too hard on you, Merri, but you have to admit you have given me good cause to be."

"I haven't done anything but try to pay you back for saving my life," she denied coolly.

"I know that . . . now," he added softly. "And I'm sorry I haven't trusted you and accepted what you've been trying to do in a more appreciative way. But you have to confess, you came on pretty strong at first. What else could I have thought?"

"You could have viewed my actions for what they were. I was only trying to be nice," she hissed, but her heart had begun to soften. "And that still doesn't alter the fact that you think I'm after your money," Merri added as the fight slowly drained out of her.

When Ryder realized she was now willing to listen to what he had to say, he gently set her down on the sidewalk and took her hand as they began to stroll slowly down the street.

"Maybe at first I did, but not anymore, Merri. I love you. I thought I made that clear the other day."

"Oh, Ryder!" she cried in exasperation. "The only thing you made clear was the fact it didn't matter if I cared about your money or not—which, by the way, I don't, whether or not you want to believe me! But if I'm going to be honest with you, I have to confess I *do* like money. Not that the lack of it has ever occupied much of my time, but I do enjoy the nice things money can buy. I like expensive clothes, nice cars, and not having to worry about where the next meal is coming from. But even to suggest that I would choose the man I marry on that basis alone is ludicrous."

"What basis would you choose your husband on?" he asked quietly.

"On the basis that he loved me, first of all. Then I would pick a man whom I could laugh with, who would listen to my problems even if they were silly ones. I'd pick a man who would make my stomach flutter every time he walked into the room. I want a man who is kind and gentle yet

186

knows when to be firm with me. I need that at times," she acknowledged, "but most of all, I want a man who trusts me no matter how suspicious my actions may be."

"Money wouldn't figure in the picture?"

"Well, I would want him to have a job," she conceded. "I can't see how that would be too pushy on my part. I'd want us to be able to work together for the things in life that seem important to both of us: a home, our children's future education, a retirement fund . . . things like that."

"Then I don't see where we have any problem at all," Ryder said thoughtfully. "I can successfully fill every one of your qualifications, except maybe the one about making your stomach flutter every time I walk into a room. . . . But I'm more than willing to work hard on that one."

Merri's footsteps faltered as she paused and looked at him in amazement. "Are you asking me to marry you?"

"Yes, I am. Will you?"

She whirled back around and started walking ahead of him angrily. "No!"

"Well, why in the hell not?" he demanded, running to catch up with her flying footsteps. She was beginning to give him an ulcer!

"Because you're rich!"

Ryder groaned painfully. "I've spent half of my life running from greedy women who wanted nothing but my money, and now I fall hopelessly in love with a girl who doesn't give a tinker's damn about the size of my bank account; in fact, she tells me she won't marry me because I'm rich! That stinks!"

"Well, it may stink, but it's the truth. If I married you, every time I'd want a new dress or some extravagance I couldn't really afford, I would feel guilty as sin."

"Why?"

"Because I would constantly be thinking you thought I loved you for your money!"

"Do you love me?" he asked hopefully.

Stepping blindly out into an intersection, Merri gritted her teeth and confessed her love loudly and openly. "Yes! I love you. Since the day I first met you I've been in love with you, although I can't imagine why, after the insults I've had to put up with—" Her words were cut short as she heard Ryder yell her name and jerk her back to safety as a car came careening around the corner, narrowly missing them both.

"Watch where you're going, you idiot!" Ryder shook his fist and shouted angrily at the speeding car.

"My gosh! I could have been killed," Merri gasped, reaching out to steady her trembling body against his broad, reassuring frame.

"Crazy lunatic!" Ryder mumbled, and pulled her closer to him. "Are you all right, honey? Lord, if anything happened to you . . ." He buried his face in her neck and hugged her.

Merri stiffened, her face breaking out in a radiant smile. "Ryder! Do you realize, you just saved my life *again?*" she cried, hugging him back gratefully.

His face sagged. *Here we go again!*

"You did! Twice you have saved my life!" she pointed out lovingly.

A slow grin began to creep across his face now as the meaning of her words sank in. "I did, didn't I?"

"You certainly did! And I don't know how I'll ever be able to thank—" She stopped, her expression turning sullen once more. "Don't worry. I'm not even going to try to thank you this time." She wasn't about to go through all of that again!

"Oh, now, hold on a minute!" Ryder planted his feet firmly on the ground and stared at her stubbornly. " 'When a person saves another person's life, she should have the decency to try to pay him back,' " he recited, imitating her voice as best he could. "Your words, honey, not mine."

"But you won't let me pay you back. . . ."

"Oh, yes I will," he corrected. "But I name the terms this time."

"Such as . . . ?"

"Marry me. And nothing less," he stated flatly.

"You're just doing this to make me feel better," she accused, wanting so very much to believe he loved her enough to trust her with his future happiness.

He gazed down at her tenderly. "No, I'm doing it to make *me* feel better. You've just put me through the most miserable week of my life," he confessed, "and if you don't believe I'm sincere, you just try me, lady."

She went into his arms with a strangled sob and buried her face against his shoulder as she started to bawl. "I love you . . . you wonderful idiot."

"Then what's all the fuss about?" He picked her up and swung her around. "I love you, too, you more wonderful idiot."

"Oh, Ryder, what am I going to do with you?" She lifted her head up and his hungry mouth found hers. They stood on the sidewalk, kissing passionately as the passing traffic honked and beeped its loud approval.

"You're going to marry me and live happily ever after with your arrogant chicken-plucking rich prince. What else?" he asked when they finally ended the kiss.

"And you'll never doubt that I love *you* no matter what?"

"I may need a little reminding at times," he conceded solemnly. "Old habits die hard sometimes, but I'm not averse to learning new ones. Especially with you teaching me." He cupped her face in his two large hands and gazed at her tenderly. "If there's one thing I've learned from all this, it's the fact that no matter how much money a person may have, there are still some things in the world he can't buy."

"You mean the love of a good woman?"

He grinned. "Well, certainly the love of this one particular good woman."

They wrapped their arms around each other's waist and slowly walked back the way they had come. Life now held all the promises both of them had ever dreamed of, and it would have been very difficult to find another handsome prince or lovely princess as happy as they were in the whole wide world . . . except perhaps in England.

TUG OF WAR

CHAPTER ONE

To just say that it was a beautiful day would be doing an injustice to Mother Nature.

The sky was that brilliant, breathtaking blue that makes a person want to lie out under a big old shade tree and stare at its magnificence for hours on end. A soft breeze teased the air with the tantalizing smell of the flowers blooming colorfully along the highway, and Cass rolled down the car windows to allow the achingly familiar smells of her childhood to recapture her senses.

The verdant, gentle swells of the hillsides spread out before her with open arms, as if to say they welcomed one of their children home once again.

She took a deep, intoxicating breath of the sweet air and let it out slowly. New York City was wonderful, full of excitement and a million new things to see and do every day, but Rueter Flats, Texas, was home and always would be.

Actually, she was just a little surprised to find that she was looking forward to coming home for her vacation this year.

Always before there had been a tiny seed of resentment nagging at her when she would have to spend her precious few weeks of freedom in Rueter Flats, but somehow this year seemed different.

With a touch of renewed guilt, she was reminded of the fact that she hadn't seen her parents in well over two years and it was no wonder that they were beginning to get annoyed with her continuing excuses.

And to be honest she had seriously toyed with the idea of giving them yet another reason as to why she wouldn't be home again this summer, but then she reminded herself that they were getting along in years and she wouldn't always have them around to make excuses to.

Oh, they had all been perfectly valid excuses. There had been that bad snowstorm last Christmas and she had decided to stay in the city for the holidays instead of making the long trip home. And the year before that she had decided to take advantage of an unexpected Aspen ski trip instead of taking a summer vacation.

But this year it was time to stop making excuses and pay an obligatory visit home.

Maybe it wouldn't be so bad this time. The weather certainly looked as if it would cooperate and she had to admit the slow, lackadaisical way of life of the citizens of Rueter Flats would be a far cry from the hustle and bustle of New York.

So absorbed in her thoughts, she nearly whizzed by her intended cutoff. She slammed on her brakes, came to a dead halt for a moment, then hurriedly backed up to make the turn, chuckling softly under her breath at the thought of what a pileup that would have brought on in the city.

Concentrate on your driving, Cass, she reminded

herself as she shifted her sleek silver Jaguar into second gear and gunned it on down the road.

Once again her thoughts drifted back to years past as she sped along the back roads leading to her childhood home.

She was quite sure that leaving Rueter Flats wasn't on the high-priority list of most women of that town, but it had always been high on hers.

Oh, it was a nice town. She couldn't argue that. It was just small and exceedingly dull with a population of around fifteen hundred. But by now Ellie Sweetwood would surely have done her best to increase that statistic. She shook her head with amusement at the thought of her former childhood friend and schoolmate. When Ellie Poston married Teft Sweetwood she became a baby machine, but then there were a lot of women in Rueter Flats who were like that.

Now, take her sisters for instance. They were having kids with alarming regularity and they couldn't be happier. They would smile and simply shrug their shoulders when an impending birth was announced and state without apology that they were married to their "good ole boys," whom they laughingly said kept them "barefoot and pregnant" most of the time.

Their husbands were barely eking out a decent living on their small scraps of land, but not one of them ever raised a voice in complaint.

But they couldn't help but be thrilled with Cass's new life. She had such an exciting, glamorous life, while they on the other hand had the same boring, monotonous existence day after day.

Clearly they thought the sun rose and set in their

"successful" sister, yet, strangely enough, never once had any one of them expressed a desire to trade places with her.

Their eyes may have shone with pride when Cass came home and regaled them with stories of the advertising world, but that light was decidedly pale compared to the one that glowed so radiantly when they looked at their husbands or cradled one of their sleepy children's heads against their bosoms after a long day of picnicking and swimming with all the McCason family gathered about them.

Cass had never been able to understand their complete contentment. Their way of life was a far cry from what she wanted. Being a dirt farmer and raising a passel of towheaded kids wasn't for her, and once more a tremendous feeling of gratitude washed over her when she thought about what her parents had sacrificed in order to scrape up enough money to put her through college.

But it had paid off, and the right person had an opportunity to view her work, and before she knew it she had landed a job with one of the most prestigious advertising agencies on Madison Avenue.

Now their daughter was settled in a career that afforded her luxuries that her parents had only heard about. Cass had been bright, talented, and eager to achieve, and each year brought her one more step up the ladder of success. Yes, for a girl who came from practically nothing but a hole in the road in Texas, who was now driving a Jaguar, living in a luxury apartment in the heart of Manhattan plus enjoying a career that was going nowhere but up—well, she wasn't doing bad at all.

She heaved a sigh of pure contentment. Yes, sir. The rest of the McCasons could have her share of the farm life. She'd take the big city any day.

A swell of pride engulfed her as she thought about the newest piece of information she had to pass on. What would her family think when they heard of this latest advancement at work? In September, when Rolland Hendricks retired, Cassandra Beth McCason was going to be made vice president of Creble and Associates. Sure, there was more than one vice president at Creble's, but still the title was impressive.

Mom and Pop would be proud when they heard that bit of news. They would probably throw one of those big parties they were forever having and invite the entire town to come and celebrate their daughter's newest success. Her relatives would gather from miles around to see the little McCason gal who had gone to the big city and struck it rich. She had to snicker at that thought. She was a far cry from rich, but she had to admit she was doing extremely well. And it felt good.

No longer did she have to shop at the local discount stores for her clothes and save up for weeks just to purchase some small luxury item she wanted. She was wearing cashmere and pearls now. And having her hair styled in the finest salons instead of having to wash it herself, and eating croissants for breakfast every morning instead of corn flakes.

Now if she wanted anything, she just whipped out her American Express Card and bought it.

A small smile of satisfaction tugged at the corners of her mouth as she sped along. In fact, she was at the point now where she was buying things she really didn't need simply because it felt good.

Yes, sir. No more grubbing in the dirt for Cass Mc-Cason.

She had it made.

About eight dogs of assorted breeds ran out to meet her as her car turned across the old cattle guard, their yelps setting up enough racket to wake the dead. Nipping at the shiny chrome rims of the fancy sports car, they chased it down the rutted lane until she brought the car to a halt in front of a weather-beaten, two-story farmhouse that seemed forever in need of a new coat of paint.

At the sound of all the clamor the front door flew open and two happy children clamored off the porch and headed for Cass as fast as their little legs could carry them. She cringed as she saw the condition of their hands as they whooped around the car like a bunch of wild Indians and somehow managed to touch every square inch of the shiny new vehicle before she could bring it to a complete halt.

"Oh, boy! Auntie Cass. This here's a neat car," the older of the two proclaimed in awe. "I bet it costed lots of money, huh?" His chubby hands ran reverently down the length of the car as he circled it excitedly.

Cass hurriedly got out of the car and slammed the door shut. She raced around the side of the car and put out a beseeching hand. "Yes, lots of money. Please, Billy Ray, don't touch the hood that way!"

"Gosh, is it neato," the smaller one chimed in as three of the bigger dogs, still yapping at the tops of their lungs, jumped up on Cass and started to lap at her face.

Staggering under the weight of the smelly animals, she felt her Gucci heel sink down in the soft ground at the precise moment her eyes took note of one of the speckled bird dogs doing his "thing" on the rim of her tire.

"Billy Ray! Get that dog!" she demanded.

Billy Ray was too busy inspecting the fascinating new object that had just pulled into his drive to heed Cass's frantic pleas.

"I'll get him, Auntie Cath," the smaller boy offered, and before she could stop him he had picked up a large rock and hurled it in the direction of the dog, who was still standing next to the car.

"No! Bobby Ray!" But her words came too late.

The sickening thud of the rock striking the car caused Cass to shut her eyes in despair and sag against the car weakly as the remainder of the dogs gathered around her feet, still barking rambunctiously.

"There, Auntie Cath. He'th going now." The child grinned proudly as the bird dog quickly lost interest in the new company and sauntered away from the car in search of a shade tree.

"What in the world is going on out here?" The screen door swung open and a plump, silver-haired woman stepped out on the porch and shaded her eyes to see what all the commotion was about.

Her eyes lit with joy when Neoma McCason saw her youngest daughter slumped against the car, smiling weakly back at her.

"Hi, Mom."

"Cassie!" With amazing agility for a woman her

age, Neoma was off the porch and hurrying toward the car as Cass jerked her shoe out of the dirt and inspected the grubby heel that was caked with mud.

By now her mother had reached the car and engulfed her in a big bear hug as she laughed and returned the embrace eagerly.

"Hi, Mom."

"Hi, darlin'. I wasn't expectin' you until late this evening." For a moment Cass closed her eyes and drank in the familiar smell that held her tightly pressed against an ample bosom. Neoma always smelled like freshly laundered clothes and homemade bread, with just the tiniest scent of roses mixed in.

"I made better time than I thought I would," Cass told her as she wrapped her arm around her mom's waist and they began walking toward the house. "Where's Pop?"

"Down in the barn. He's got a sick calf he's been working with all day." Neoma looked her daughter over hungrily, her generous mouth breaking into another huge smile. "My, you look good, honey. Real good. And that fancy new car! Is that yours?"

"Yeah." Cass grinned back. "Pretty nice, huh?"

"Never seen anything like it," Neoma marveled, her gaze running pridefully over the shiny sports car.

"It's a Jaguar," Cass announced proudly, just as if that would ring any bell with her mother. To Neoma a Jaguar was an animal. Always had been and always would be.

"Oh? Well, it's right nice," she praised, then diverted her attention to the two rowdy boys still racing around the fancy automobile. "Billy Ray and Bobby Ray, you git on down to the barn with your grandpa.

200

We don't want you puttin' any scratches up your Aunt Cass's new car."

Too late for that, Cass thought as her eyes grimly searched for further signs of missing paint on the fender where Bobby Ray had thrown the rock.

"Aw, Grandma!" They both raised their voices in protest as Neoma shot them a warning look. "No back talkin', now. You go on and do what I say before I take a switch to your behinds!"

The boys grumbled a few more chosen words between them before they raced off to seek other pursuits.

"They're really growing," Cass marveled as they walked toward the house.

"Like ragweed," Neoma sighed. "The baby's in the house. You've never seen Joey Ray, have you?"

"No, just pictures of him." It never ceased to amaze her the way her sister had named all her children after their father. You would think one Ray in the family would have been enough, but no, in addition to the father being named Ray, there was Billy Ray, Bobby Ray, and now Joey Ray.

"How is Rosalee?" Cass inquired of her middle sister.

"Why, she's as healthy as a horse. She left the kids with me today. Had a doctor's appointment." Neoma grinned knowingly. "She thinks she might be in the family way again."

Cass shook her head in amazement. "Lord, I hope not."

"Why, Cass McCason. What a thing to say," her mother admonished, clearly shocked that her daughter would say such a thing. "Her and Ray want another baby."

"Why in the world would she want another child? They have three already, and the baby's not even a year old yet. How many more Rays can the family stand?"

"Ray says he wants a whole house full before he stops," Neoma laughed.

"Well, he's certainly on his way," Cass acknowledged as they stepped up on the porch.

"I'll have to call Rowena and Rachel and Pauly and Newt to let them know you're in early. They're all a-comin' over for supper, but they'll want to come sooner when they find out you're home," Neoma was saying.

A tiny shudder ran through Cass as she thought about her brother and sisters and all their families under one roof, but she tried to force as much enthusiasm into her voice as she could. It wasn't that she didn't love every one of them, it was just when they all got together everything was so . . . disorganized and boisterous. "Yes . . . I'll be glad to see all of them again. . . ."

Both women glanced up as a late-model pickup came rolling into the yard and the driver gave a couple of toots on the horn in a friendly fashion and stuck his arm out the window to wave at Neoma.

Neoma smiled and waved at the driver as he proceeded on down to the barn lot.

"Who was that?"

"That's the Travers boy—Luke, you remember him, don't you?"

"Oh, brother. That wild hair." Cass remembered

him all right. He had been a thorn in her side the entire time they had been growing up.

He had pestered her unmercifully in grade school, terrorized her in junior high, and by the time they had reached high school she had stopped speaking to him altogether.

That had never seemed to bother him, though. In fact, it had become a little game between them to turn their noses up at each other every chance they got, and living in such a small town, that was quite often.

But along about the time they both graduated she had dismissed Luke Travers from her mind, and last she had heard he had left town to join the Navy, which was probably the best thing that could ever have happened to Rueter Flats.

Her gaze absently followed the pickup until it stopped in front of the barn.

But apparently the bad seed had returned.

As wild as Luke Travers had been, Cass wouldn't have been a bit surprised to hear he was off making license plates in the big house somewhere.

Neoma chuckled at Cass's disgruntled observation of Luke. "Yes, he used to be quite a rounder in his younger days, but the boy's really settled down since he came home. Dad and I were talking about just how much he's changed the other night."

"Boy? Really, Mom. He's hardly a boy any longer. He's my age or older," Cass reminded.

"Well, thirty years old isn't exactly ancient," Neoma agreed good-naturedly as she opened the screen door to the kitchen. "Luke's turned out to be a real fine man, Cass. He's the local vet around here and your little brother Wylie's taken a real likin' to him."

"A veterinarian! Luke Travers is a veterinarian!" Now that was hard to swallow. He had barely made passing grades in high school because he was too busy getting into trouble all the time.

At the mention of her youngest brother Cass's face clouded with concern. "You mean you actually let Wylie associate with him? Now what in the world would a nine-year-old have in common with a thirty-year-old, Mom? Especially that thirty-year-old!"

"Now why should that upset you?" A slow grin spread across her features again. "Oh, my. I had forgotten. You and Luke never did get along, did you?"

"No, we didn't. I didn't like him and he didn't like me."

Neoma clucked in a motherly fashion. "Never could understand why. I have to admit he was a might ornery at times, but I don't think he was all that bad."

"Oh no? Then how come every time anything bad happened in this town they went looking for Luke Travers?"

" 'Cause he usually was the one who did it," Neoma had to agree. "Either him or that Falk boy, but that was a long time ago, honey, and they were usually just harmless little pranks. When Luke came home from the service he had turned into a real fine man. Then he up and went off to college and before we knew it he was back with a handful of them real fancy-soundin' degrees," she boasted. "It turned out he had become a veterinarian and the people of the town welcomed him with open arms. You know the closest vet around Rueter Flats is old Milt Turner over in Macon and he's gettin' blind as a bat."

Cass could hardly believe Luke could be that

changed. Not the Luke who used to push over outhouses with people still sitting in them or throw sacks of burning cow manure on her front porch.

"I still find it hard to believe you would let Wylie associate with him," Cass complained.

"I don't see why not. They fish and hunt together all the time. Uriah's health isn't what it used to be, so Luke's been filling in for him. I appreciate the time he finds to spend with the boy."

"What's the matter with Pauly? Why can't he take Wylie hunting and fishing?" The thought of her little brother being in the company of someone as unsavory as Luke Travers annoyed her, especially when there were certainly enough men in the McCason family to provide that service quite sufficiently.

"He does when they have the chance, but Newt and Pauly have been real busy lately," Neoma excused. "And they have their own family to look after."

"Well, I don't like it," Cass complained once more as they walked into the large, airy kitchen.

The tantalizing smell of pot roast simmering in the oven filled the air as Cass paused and drank in the familiar surroundings.

This room—this house—had always been the same for as long as Cass could remember. It was as if she had walked out the door only twenty minutes ago instead of two years.

A massive round oak table sat in the middle of the room laden with jars of homemade jellies, pickles, and preserves her mother had set out for the evening meal.

She could see several delectably browned pies cooling on the counter and the smell of apples and cinnamon still mingled enticingly in the air with that of the pot roast.

The pictures Cass and her brothers and sisters had made in grade school hung on the brightly papered wall above the old refrigerator. Colorful rainbows and comical-looking stick characters that had the names Mom and Dad and Pauly and Cassie and Rachel and so on scrawled boldly beside them.

Newt had even attempted at the age of three to draw a picture of their old dog, Whiskers, and the family still went into hysterics at the finished product. The dog resembled a deranged chicken more than the valued family pet, but Newt still insisted there was a definite resemblance, so the picture had remained on display.

On the long oak buffet that sat along the wall were pictures of Grandma and Grandpa McCason and Grandpa and Grandma Kinley, plus a photograph of every child and grandchild of Neoma and Uriah.

There was one of Cassie in her prom dress and Newt in his high school cap and gown. There was Rachel and Jesse's wedding picture and Rosalee and Ray holding their first child and happily smiling into the camera. A beaming Cassie proudly displaying her college diploma and grinning, and Wylie wrestling on the front lawn with one of the dogs.

Crisply starched calico curtains hung at the glistening windows and the old linoleum was scrubbed to shiny perfection. Neoma McCason was well known for keeping a clean house, even though for years she had seven young children running in and out all day long.

Now there was only nine-year-old Wylie left at

home, but the house hadn't looked any different when Cass and all her brothers and sisters had lived there.

A feeling of contentment washed over her, the sort of feeling that can be brought on only by poignant memories and the smell of the old honeysuckle bush blooming outside the kitchen door. So many years of happiness had been spent in this house, and Cass suddenly realized how much she had missed being with her family.

Wylie came into the kitchen carrying Rosalee's youngest child and a round of excitement broke out as Cass viewed her newest nephew for the first time, then hugged her younger brother affectionately.

"I can't get over how much you've grown!" she exclaimed, holding him back away from her to get a closer look. He was at least five inches taller than when she had last seen him.

With a shy grin, Wylie mumbled some excuse about eating a lot, then quickly handed the baby to his grandmother. "I saw Luke drive in a while ago. I want to go see him."

"He's down at the barn with your dad," Neoma cautioned. "Don't get in their way."

"I won't!" Grabbing an apple from the bowl of fruit sitting on the buffet, he was out the door like a flash of lightning and on his way out the door.

"Well, I'm going to change the baby's diaper and get him settled down for a nap before I peel the potatoes for supper. Fix yourself a glass of tea, honey. I won't be long."

Neoma hustled out of the room while Cass went over to the cabinet to retrieve a glass. After she poured the drink she sat down at the table and waited for her mother to return.

She absently took a sip of the tea, trying to fight the small seed of curiosity that was beginning to grow inside her concerning Luke Travers. Funny, but she couldn't remember exactly what he looked like except he had blond hair and was sort of gangly.

When he had driven into the barnyard earlier she hadn't paid that much attention to who was behind the wheel of the truck so she didn't know if he had changed in looks. Probably not, unless he had just gotten homelier.

He had lived with his grandmother while he grew up because his parents had run off and left him. She remembered that much about him. The Travers's place was about three miles down the road from the McCason homestead, but she remembered her mom saying Minnie Travers had died a few years ago.

She looked out the window. I wonder if he still lives there? Her mom hadn't said anything about him being married, but that didn't mean he wasn't. As wild as he was, he had probably been herded to the altar by way of a double-barrel shotgun. Yes, he was probably married to one of the local girls and had several homely-looking kids running around the house. Pushing her glass back, she rose and glanced toward the door her mother had disappeared behind earlier. It would take a few minutes for her to get the baby settled. In the meantime maybe she should just run down and say hello to her dad.

Yes, it was all coming back to her now, she thought as she quickly slipped out the door and hurried down the path that led to the barn. She was only going to say hello to her father, not to see what that annoying Luke Travers looked like now.

She could almost guess.

He was probably still blond, gangly, and ugly as a mud fence. Undoubtedly age had improved neither his looks nor his disposition in the slightest.

CHAPTER TWO

Funny how time had such a way of being so fickle.

The familiar smells of hay and cattle surrounded her as she stood in the doorway for a moment trying to adjust her eyes to the dim interior of the building.

Uriah McCason was bent over a small heifer talking to her in soft, soothing tones while a younger man held the animal down and administered medicine with a syringe.

The calf's bellow was a weak, pitiful one as the elderly man continued to stroke the animal with a large, comforting hand. Uriah had been up since three that morning trying to save the calf, but there seemed to be little hope for its survival.

"Pop?"

With a weather-beaten face lined with fatigue and a lot more winkles than she had remembered, he turned his head to seek the sound of the voice that had called out to him. Standing in the shaft of sunlight, Uriah's eyesight, which was not as good as it once had been, could barely make out the slender form of his middle child, but when she called his name again he broke into a radiant smile.

"Cassie?"

"Yes, Pop. It's me."

"Well, come on over here, girl. Let me get a closer look at you."

Cassie stepped into the barn and walked over to her father, still amazed to see how he had aged in the time since she had last seen him. Why he must be nearing seventy, she thought with a jolt as he stood up and extended his arms out for her to come into.

Two bands of steel pulled her gruffly up against a broad chest that always smelled like sunshine and Red Man chewing tobacco, and his powerful grip belied the fact that Uriah McCason was no longer a young man.

She closed her eyes and returned the embrace with loving affection. "How are you, Pop?"

"I guess I'm doing okay for an old man. How's my Cassie girl?"

Uriah had always called her his "Cassie girl" and she smiled up at his tall six-foot-two stature and winked playfully. "Cassie girl's doin' great, Pop. Just great."

"So I've heard, so I've heard." Uriah held her back and inspected her with a critical parental eye. "Too skinny. Ain't got any meat on your bones at all. Don't they feed you up there in that big city?"

"Sure they do. And if you knew how hard I had to fight to stay 'skinny' you'd be ashamed for even mentioning it."

"Hogwash. You're goin' to make yourself sick if you don't start eatin'. Mom will have to fatten you up a little like she has your sisters. You'll never get a man lookin' like that."

"So who's having trouble getting a man?" she bantered with mock indignity.

211

"Luke, you remember our little Cassie, don't you?" Uriah put his arm around his daughter and turned her around to face the man who was still working quietly with the calf.

Six feet of solid muscle, thick dark blond hair with sunlightened streaks and a pair of the most arresting, cobalt-blue eyes Cass had ever encountered, glanced up and smiled politely at her.

Cassie had noticed that Luke, if indeed this was Luke Travers, had looked at her when she first came in, but then quickly turned his attention back to his work.

This man kneeling beside the calf was so ruggedly handsome it was almost impossible to associate him with the gangly, blond-headed boy of her youth. She just couldn't believe he had changed so much.

The man rose slowly to his feet, giving her another polite but distant smile.

His brilliant blue eyes met her gaze solidly. "Yes, I remember Cassie." He extended his hand. "It's been a while since you've been back."

No, it just couldn't be Luke Travers, she fretted as she tried to maintain her wavering facade. This man was too suave . . . too smooth . . . too . . . male. . . .

Whether it was from force of habit or just because he was Luke Travers, she suddenly felt her nose tilting upward with just the slightest hint of distaste as her hand was swallowed in his large one. "Yes. I live in New York and I don't get to make the trip back home as often as I would like," she acknowledged.

The way he had said "It's been a while since you've

been back" irritated her. It was almost like an accusation instead of a mere observance.

His eyes ran carelessly over her, taking in the designer silk dress and the string of cultured pearls she was wearing with cool detachment. The look wasn't insulting or even provocative, just inquisitive.

She felt resentment stir anew as she recognized the reserved, almost snooty look he had always managed to give her while they were busy ignoring each other in high school slowly come over his face as he withdrew a small cheroot out of his shirt pocket and stuck it between his even white teeth.

"That's what I hear." He cupped his hand to his lighter as he lit the small cigar. For a moment she thought he had completely dismissed her, but then he commented, "You work in some little office up there, don't you?"

He knew it was a poor choice of words, but he had intended it that way. She looked every bit as sassy as she had back in high school.

Her spine stiffened even more at the offhanded way he referred to her work. "I'm creative director of Creble and Associates," she corrected curtly. "It isn't a 'little office.' It happens to be a very big, highly successful advertising agency—on Madison Avenue." She doubted that would mean anything, but just in case it didn't, she wanted to enlighten. "You *have* heard of Madison Avenue?"

The blue of his eyes narrowed resentfully, then he smiled and conceded courteously, "Yes, I believe I have heard of Madison Avenue."

"Then you know that I don't work in a 'little office,' " she snapped.

He bowed his head in mock contrition. "Sorry. I stand corrected. *Big*"—he stressed the word obediently—*"highly* successful office in New York City."

She had to fight hard to keep the growing anger from showing on her face. "That's right."

Somehow they had both forgotten that Uriah was there watching this almost childish display of rudeness take place between them.

"Little office" indeed! Who did he think he was? Everyone in Rueter Flats knew how well Cass was doing and she would bet her bottom dollar Luke Travers knew it too. Well, she wasn't going to let him get under her skin. She was a little more mature than when they had been in high school together and she wouldn't allow him to irritate her this time.

She smiled at him, making it plain he was only something to be tolerated while they were in Uriah's presence. She literally forced civility back into her voice. "My goodness, it is so good to see you again. It's been a long time." Not long enough, but that was beside the point. "I understand you joined the service when I left for college."

"That's right." He reached over and picked up several instruments lying beside the calf and began to replace them in a brown leather bag.

"I hope they saved your job at the filling station," she remarked pleasantly. If he could be insulting, she could too. "A good grease monkey's hard to find."

"No, I gave it up when I decided to go to college," he remarked in an easy tone, then glanced up at her expectantly. "But I bought the service station a few years ago. You need gas?"

"No . . . I . . . I don't need gas. . . ."

"Oh. Well, when you run out, I'd be happy to tell Red to give you a discount while you're here." He went back to packing instruments while her pilot light went up another notch.

Damn! He'd *bought* the only gas station in Rueter Flats! If that wasn't enough to unnerve her, she still had to face the fact that he had gone to college too. She had always taken great pride in her degree, thinking that she was the only one in Rueter Flats who had one.

"You say you went to college?" she found herself probing in a decidedly petulant voice a few moments later.

"That's right."

"When?"

"A few months after I got out of the service." His first thought was to ignore the highfalutin little snit. She was baiting him and he knew it. He had seen her standing on the porch with her mother when he had driven up, decked out in her fancy designer clothes, lookin' as pretty as a Rocky Mountain sunrise. Neoma must have mentioned that he was the veterinarian coming to check on Uriah's sick calf.

His gaze skipped back over her broodingly. He had forgotten how damn good-looking she was and it rankled him to admit she looked every bit the part of the highly successful woman she was touted to be.

She had always been cute when they had been growing up, but she had become a real beauty. . . . He quickly shifted his attention back to his work. She might look good, but he'd bet his last dollar she was still the same old Cass McCason, by far the most ill-tempered little heifer he had ever met.

"Why, Luke's got him all kinds of degrees since you last seen him, honey." Uriah decided this had gone on long enough. He had to chuckle to himself. Two ornery kids! He would have thought that in the twelve years since they had seen each other they would have managed to outgrow all that childish animosity. "Like he mentioned, Uncle Sam put him through college right after he got out of the service and he's a veterinarian now." Uriah beamed at Luke proudly. "Not only that, but he runs his own ranch too. Got two thousand prime acres he has to look after on top of everything else."

Luke could tell that impressed her about as much as it would if she had stuck her high-priced fancy shoe in a pile of cow dung.

"Really." She tried to disguise her growing confusion. Luke's grandmother, Minnie Travers, had nothing but a run-down old farm when she had left years ago and Luke had been a juvenile delinquent still working at the local gas station.

Now all of a sudden he had a college degree, a reputable job, and a huge chunk of land Uriah was referring to as a "ranch," and . . . blond curly eyelashes that a woman would kill for. Not to mention other stunning assets. . . .

Well, it was too much. "What ranch?" she asked skeptically.

"Why, Luke took the acreage Minnie left him when she died and turned it into one of the finest cattle ranches around here. Didn't you see the big sign announcing THE SUNDOWNER when you drove into town?" Uriah exclaimed.

Yes, she had seen the sign. It had been quite impressive but she had never dreamed it belonged to anyone she knew, let alone Luke Travers. "Yes, I saw it. . . ." Her gaze reluctantly crept back up to meet Luke's amused one. "Is that yours?"

A slow, extremely aggravating grin spread lazily across his face now as his blue gaze met hers almost triumphantly. "My, how times are a changin', huh?"

She slumped against a bale of hay and sat there for a moment just looking at him.

Luke Travers could probably buy and sell her three times over.

It was hard to swallow.

"That's very nice," she finally managed. "I never realized your grandmother had so much land."

"She always had the land. She was just never inclined to run cattle on it."

"And you are?"

His smile still held that edge of cockiness. "Yes, I've acquired a few head."

Uriah nearly choked on that one. A "few" head consisted of at least fifteen hundred of the best beef cattle around. "Well, I'll bet Mom's got supper almost on the table," Uriah intervened brightly. "I'll have her set another place if you can stay, Luke."

Luke gathered up the remaining instruments and prepared to depart. "Thanks, Uriah, I hate to miss one of Neoma's meals, but I'll have to pass. I have another stop to make on the way home."

"You sure, boy? I think I smelled pot roast when I went in earlier," he tempted.

There was no doubt that Neoma's tender pot roast, swimming in rich brown gravy, was Luke's favorite, but the temptation was quickly overcome when he

217

glanced at Cassie and saw the look of sheer relief cross her face when he declined the offer.

For a brief, devilish moment, Luke considered retracting his refusal and accepting her father's offer just to see her squirm, but then thought better of it.

He didn't care for her company any more than she cared for his.

"Sounds good, Uriah, but I'm afraid I'll have to make it another time," he apologized again.

"Well, sure, but now you are going to be at the party for Cassie Saturday night, aren't you?" Cassie tried to motion to Uriah that it didn't matter, but he seemed persistent in getting an answer out of Luke.

"Can't really say," Luke hedged. "I'll keep it in mind, though."

That still wasn't good enough for Uriah. When Cassie came home he wanted all his friends there to welcome her. "At least promise you'll drop by, even if you can't stay long."

Luke chuckled as he realized he wasn't going to be let off the hook. "Okay. I'll stop by sometime during the evening," he relented.

He meticulously avoided looking at her.

And she went out of her way to avoid looking at him.

"Where's Wylie?" It suddenly dawned on her that her little brother wasn't in the barn.

"He was here a while earlier but he decided to go down to the pond and fish before supper," Uriah answered. "Guess one of us ought to go down and get him."

"Don't hold out too much hope on the calf," Luke

cautioned again as the three of them walked out of the barn. "The odds are against her making it."

"Yes," Uriah sighed. "I was afraid she wouldn't. I hate to lose her, sort of got attached to the little booger, but I'll see that she's comfortable." Uriah had lost many a calf over the years and it still never failed to bother him. He glanced toward the pond thoughtfully. "Cassie, you take Luke up to the house and get him something cold to drink before he leaves. I'll go get the boy."

She would much rather go after Wylie, but she didn't want it to seem obvious so she managed to sound almost cordial when she agreed. "Okay, Pop."

Uriah broke off and walked in the direction of the pond as Luke and Cassie proceeded to the house.

At first neither one made an attempt at conversation. Cassie was intent on trying to keep up with Luke's long-legged strides and Luke was intent on ignoring her.

But the house was a small distance from the barn so Cassie decided to at least be sociable. "Mom says you and Wylie have become good friends."

"Yeah, he's a good kid," Luke complimented.

They walked on in silence and a few moments later she tried again. "It's good of you to take your free time and spend it with Wylie. Do you have children of your own now?"

Now why did she ask that! He would think she was trying to pry into his personal affairs!

But if he thought her remark was out of context, he didn't show it. Instead, he kept on walking, his eyes straight ahead. "No, I don't have any children of my own."

She spoke before she thought. "You mean that you know about," she teased, then was horrified she had been so crass.

For a moment his pace slackened and he turned to focus a very frosty, highly indignant blue gaze squarely on her. "No," he stated again, pronouncing the word so emphatically that even a one-year-old could have understood him. "I'm quite sure I do not have any children—anywhere."

She felt her face redden like a prairie fire. "Pardon me," she apologized in the same tone he was using with her. "I was only teasing."

His gaze flicked over her coolly one more time, then he turned and started walking again.

She decided to forget the sociable bit. It wasn't working. As they approached the backyard of the farmhouse their eyes fell on the shiny new Jaguar sitting next to the well house.

"That's mine," Cassie announced as she watched his eyes run over the car appreciatively.

"That would have been my first guess."

"It's a Jaguar," she taunted, ashamed she was being so repulsive, yet unable to stop herself.

"I know what it is. We have picture books here in Rueter Flats."

She looked at him sourly. "Pretty nice, huh?" She had no idea why she was baiting him like she was. He could probably buy a Jaguar just as easy as she could, yet she'd bet anything that he would try and pretend indifference to the car.

People around Rueter Flats might have books with pictures in them, but they sure didn't see a Jaguar every day of their lives.

But to her surprise he was relatively nice about his answer. "Yes, it is nice. Is it new?"

"Almost. I bought it six months ago."

He walked around the car, inspecting it closer. "It has a scratch on the right front fender," he informed calmly as he circled back to stand beside her.

Cassie frowned when she remembered the rock her nephew had thrown earlier. "Oh, I know. Bobby Ray threw a rock at the dog and it was standing in front of the car," she complained.

"Well"—Luke started for the house again, leaving her standing beside the car rubbing at the scratch irritably—"if you're going to spend your money on a Jaguar, you'd better learn to take care of it."

"I do!" She objected to that! "It didn't have a scratch on it before I came here."

He looked as if he doubted that, but he wisely decided to let the issue drop. "While you're here you might take it over to Dave Levell's garage. You remember him, don't you? He went to school with us during our senior year."

She remembered. Dave had never had the sense to get in out of the rain, let alone work on an expensive car.

"Yes, I remember Dave. Don't tell me you actually let him work on your cars."

"Yes, he's done some work for me in the past," Luke relayed offhandedly. "And he's darn good."

"Well, thanks, but I'll wait until I get back to New York," she said with a final swipe at the angry scratch.

Dave Levell might be good enough to work on Luke's old heaps, but she sure didn't want some local yokel working on her Jag.

"It was only a suggestion," Luke dismissed mildly.

He stepped up on the porch while she still trailed a few feet behind him. Seconds later the screen door banged loudly shut in her face.

Well! she seethed, then angrily jerked the door back open.

This was the same old Luke Travers she remembered!

CHAPTER THREE

When Uriah and Neoma gave a party folks would come from miles around. The McCasons would shove the furniture out of the way and the entire house would be opened up to their friends and relatives. There would be enough food and drink to feed a small army, and the dancing would go on long past midnight. Such was the occasion of Cassie's homecoming and celebration party the following Saturday night.

Cassie grumbled under her breath as she stood before the mirror in her bedroom and frowned at her reflection. It was going to be impossible to make her hair look decent in this wilting humidity. Uriah had never invested in air-conditioning, so consequently the house was still like a steam oven from the day's heat. She could have literally wrung the water out of the air, and every time she created a bouncy, long, dark brunet curl with her iron, it fell right back out again.

"Lordy, lordy, the place is really beginning to fill up and I'm about to melt." Rachel burst through the doorway and hurried over to the bed and flopped down comfortably, cradling her infant child in her arms. "The baby's hungry. You don't mind if I feed him up here while we talk, do you?"

"Of course not. Go right ahead. I'm just trying to do something with my hair." Her sister Rachel was as pretty as she had been in high school, even though that was four babies and eleven years ago. She had the same dark hair and brown eyes as her other sisters, and she had always been the bubbly, vivacious one of the family.

"Your hair always looks so pretty," she praised as she began mechanically to unbutton her blouse. "But then you're pretty all over."

Cassie grinned at the lovely compliment while her eyes were unwillingly drawn to the ritual of Rachel breast-feeding her child. Her sister's eyes radiated with love as she fed the child. Cassie knew it was the way God intended for an infant to be fed, yet the whole process left her feeling a little uneasy. It looked—quite painful, actually.

"Doesn't that hurt?" she asked as the baby sucked noisily for a few moments.

"No, not at all. Who does your hair?" Rachel changed the subject momentarily.

"Oh, a man by the name of Stephan." Cassie picked up the curling iron again and wrapped it tightly around another strand of hair.

Rachel closed her eyes dreamily, trying to envision what it would be like to have a man named Stephan cut her hair. "Stephan. That sounds real nice. What's that style called?" she asked.

"I'm not sure. It's something Stephan does exclusively." Cass surveyed the tapered sides, not at all sure she liked them. Somehow it lacked the sophistication she was striving for.

"It's real nice," Rachel praised once more. "Your hair's gettin' real long. I like it that way."

"Thanks, it's easy to care for—usually. Where do you go when you get your hair cut?" Cassie asked conversationally.

Rachel sighed. "I usually cut it myself. Nellie Sooter's the only one around here who has a beauty shop."

Cassie lifted one brow disdainfully. "Nellie Sooter? Why she must be eighty years old by now."

"Yeah, eighty-two," Rachel said wistfully. "She gave me a permanent last summer that Jesse said looked like I had run into a high-voltage wire." She giggled. "Took me three months to grow it all out. Since then I do my own."

Cassie shook her head in disgust at the lack of services offered in Rueter Flats as she released the curling iron and the curl fell flat on her head once more.

Her brown eyes flashed angrily. "Cripes!" She threw the iron back on the dresser and unplugged it. "I can't do anything with this mop!"

"Don't need nothing done to it," Rachel assured. "It looks good, Cass. Real good." Rachel picked up the baby and put him over her shoulder to pat his back gently as Cass strolled over to the closet to select what she would wear for the evening. The customary denims and Western shirt usually worn at these informal gatherings would be far too hot in this heat. She thumbed through her clothing and finally withdrew a lightweight skirt and matching blouse in a pretty shade of red.

"What do you think about this?" Cass held the ensemble against her and studied herself critically in the mirror. The simple cotton creation was her newest purchase and this would be the first time she had worn it.

"It's truly lovely," Rachel sighed as she settled the baby to her other breast. "It's such a pretty color."

"It's called summer red," Cass murmured absently as she carefully studied her selection, then decided it wouldn't be too dressy.

She began to dress and their conversation drifted off to earlier days when they had shared this room together. The same wallpaper—bright splotches of red and yellow flowers—still adorned the wall, and the double bed with the yellow chenille bedspread still had its place in the middle of the room.

They laughed over the stories of lost loves and of the dreams they used to share together while they were trying to get to sleep at night, and both agreed those times were some of the happiest ones in their lives.

"Oh, I know it's wishful thinking, but I sure wish you lived back home again," Rachel sighed. "We used to have such good times. We miss you, Cass. The whole family does."

"And I miss all of you, but New York is my home now," Cass reasoned as she sat down on the side of the bed to tie the matching, mid-heel ankle pump she had just slipped on.

"I know it is," Rachel conceded with that same touch of wistfulness in her voice. "But I was hoping you had sorta got your fill of the big city and was ready to come home now. You know, Pop's health isn't what it used to be."

At the mention of her father's health Cass frowned. "What's wrong with Pop? He looks fine to me."

226

"Oh, nothing in particular," Rachel comforted. "It's just, I don't know. He just doesn't seem to have the bounce he used to have."

"Well, he's almost seventy," Cass pointed out gently as she slid off the bed and walked back to stand before the mirror. "I imagine we'll lose some of our bounce by the time we reach that age."

"I suppose so, still . . ." Rachel's voice trailed off undecidedly. "I guess I just can't stand the thought of Mom and Pop getting old."

Cass laughed softly. "I know. But I think that's only natural."

"Yes, I guess so. You really don't think you'll ever come back here?" Rachel's eyes held a faint glimmer of hope, even though she knew Rueter Flats would never hold a candle to New York City in Cassie's eyes.

"No." Cassie smiled, hoping to cushion her disappointment. "I don't think so. I have my work there and it's important to me."

"Can't really blame you," Rachel conceded as the baby finished his dinner and she rebuttoned her blouse. "Not much to attract you around here. Not even many eligible men unless it would be Luke Travers or Seth Holoson or Bray Williams."

Her grin turned defiantly wicked as she watched her sister for the reaction she knew would soon be coming at the mention of Luke. Cassie had never particularly cared for Luke, strange as that might be. Rachel had always thought he was exciting, a real free spirit.

Cassie picked up her blusher and dabbed it irritably on her cheeks. "Luke Travers would be the last reason I would come back," she said curtly.

"Yeah, I know, but I bet you were a little surprised

to see how good-lookin' he is now." Rachel's grin widened. "Not that he wasn't always nice-looking, but since he's gotten older . . ."

"I've seen him only once since I got home, but he looks like the same old Luke to me," Cassie snapped, but she felt her hand involuntarily hesitating as her memory conjured up Luke's virile good looks.

Well, perhaps not exactly the same, and yes, she had been surprised at his vast improvement, but then men's looks always seem to enhance with age.

"Luke's about the best catch around here," Rachel insisted. "Seth's all right, but Bray's gettin' a little old and crotchety. I think he'll probably be a bachelor all his life. But now that ole Luke, he has all the available girls absolutely swooning over him, not to mention all the unavailable ones," she giggled.

"Good for ole Luke, but this is one who'll never swoon over him." Cassie pitched the blusher down on the dresser and reached for a small bottle of perfume.

"He still rankles you a little, doesn't he?"

"Me? Heaven's no. Until I came home day before yesterday I hadn't given Luke Travers a thought since we were in high school together."

"I think you're still mad at him because he took Sybil Wilson to that dance instead of you," Rachel heckled playfully.

Now that was really the last straw. Cassie whirled around to face Rachel defensively. "What a thing to say, Rachel Murdock! I didn't actually want Luke to take me to that dance!"

"You did too." Rachel said matter-of-factly. She was absolutely sure her memory served her correctly. "I remember it like it was yesterday. We were all standing around after school one day and the subject of the Friday-night dance was brought up. Luke asked you if you had a date and you mistakenly thought he was asking you for a date."

Cassie felt her face flood with color. "I wouldn't have gone to a dog fight with Luke Travers," she denied sheepishly, but she did remember the incident and it had been highly embarrassing.

Luke had asked her if she had a date in front of all their friends. She didn't have a date and at the time she theorized it would be better to go to the dance with Luke than not go at all.

After all, not every one in town despised him quite the way she did. Some of the girls she ran around with foolishly thought he was "cute." But not her. She would only be going with him so she wouldn't have to show up without a date. But he had promptly made it known he was only asking if she had a date out of curiosity, that he was planning on asking that wild Sybil Wilson to go with him.

Well, that was only fitting. They were both as fast as New York cab drivers.

"That's not the way I remember it," Rachel persisted until Cassie was forced to shoot her a highly annoyed reminder that she was getting tired of the subject.

"Oh, my." Rachel quickly heeded the familiar warning signal and quickly jumped up to investigate the tantalizing fragrance Cassie was irritably dabbing behind her ears. "What's that wonderful smell?"

Cassie was relieved to hear that Rachel was going to finally drop the subject of Luke Travers. Strange how mention of that long-ago incident with Luke still had the power to annoy her. "It's called Giorgio." She held the bottle out for Rachel to get a better whiff.

Rachel inhaled the rich scent appreciatively. "Smells real expensive. Jesse got me a bottle of Windsong for my birthday and I thought it was just about the nicest thing I'd ever smelled, but this would just fairly take your breath away."

Cassie smiled and brushed a small amount behind Rachel's ear. "Go find Jesse and see what he thinks of it."

"He'll die, he'll just die," Rachel exclaimed, inhaling deeply of the intoxicating scent floating around the room.

Cass didn't know if she had done her sister a favor or not. More than likely another resident of Rueter Flats would be on its way by tomorrow morning, she thought ruefully as Rachel happily scurried out of the room to find her husband.

Casting one last critical eye in the mirror, she decided she would have to do.

Besides, she wasn't out to impress anyone. It would just be the same old friends and neighbors she had known since she was a baby at the party tonight.

Luke Travers suddenly appeared back in her thoughts and she shrugged him away immediately.

And she had not wanted to go to that dance with him, she denied emphatically to the mirror once more. Swiping up a tube of lip gloss, she applied it to her lips with swift, efficient movements. And if he was the best catch in four counties, then the poor women of Rueter Flats were fishing in the wrong hole.

The party was in full swing when she came down the stairway five minutes later. Several of the men had brought their guitars, banjos, and fiddles and they were standing in the corner of the living room tuning up their instruments.

A murmur went up as she stepped into the parlor.

She was immediately greeted by a sea of friendly faces crowding around, all wanting to talk to her at the same time. As she passed through the crowd exchanging hugs and handshakes, she soon became caught up in the festivities of the occasion. Everyone wanted to tell her how good it was to have her home and congratulate her on her upcoming promotion with Creble and Associates.

"Tom and Karen! It's wonderful to see you again," she exclaimed as she shook hands with a couple of her former classmates. "And this can't be little Jacob?"

A beaming child of around six years old stared up at her angelically as she paused and patted the top of his curly brown head.

"Yeah, can you believe how he's growin'?" Karen said proudly.

"It's hard to comprehend. He's going to be as tall as his dad if he keeps on at this rate," Cass praised.

At six foot five, two hundred and fifty pounds, Tom Metsker had always been an imposing sight in the community and it looked as if his son was following in his footsteps. Cass eyed Karen teasingly. "I thought by now Jacob would have another brother or sister to play with."

The look Tom and Karen exchanged was a tender

one and Cass immediately realized she had hit upon a touchy subject.

"Oh, we've been tryin' real hard," Karen murmured.

"Just don't seem to have much luck," Tom confessed with a soft chuckle as he took his wife's hand and squeezed it lovingly.

It always came as a surprise for Cass to hear such a nice soft voice come out of such a large man.

Cass reached out to pat her hand reassuringly. "Well, I'm sure one of these days you'll hear the patter of little feet racing through the house."

"I sure hope so," Karen sighed. "Isn't it just wonderful about Rosalee?"

"Yes, Ray seems to be real excited about becoming a father again," Cass agreed, then excused herself a few moments later and moved on through the crowd.

An hour later she was out of breath and her face flushed happily with exertion as she danced first one and then another dance with the men of Rueter Flats. Some were eligible, some were married, and some were nearing eighty years old, but she found herself enjoying the old-fashioned clogging with each and every one of them.

She had been raised on Saturday-night dances just like this one, but she hadn't realized how much she had missed them.

There was just something about briskly two steppin' around the crowded floor to a fast-paced tune that the chic discos in New York couldn't quite compare with.

Around ten another murmur went up in the crowd as Cass was standing at the punch bowl with a former classmate, Seth Holoson. They had just danced the last two dances and decided to sit the next one out. Seth handed her a cup of punch as she glanced over to the doorway to see what all the excitement was about.

With a frown, she saw Luke enter the room.

Moments later he was surrounded by every eligible woman in the room from sixteen to sixty. She watched with utter amazement as they fluttered around him and, in her eyes, made absolute fools of themselves.

"There's Luke Travers," Seth remarked needlessly as he tilted his cup up and took a drink of the cold liquid. "You remember ole Luke, don't you?"

"Yes." Cass turned her eyes back to Seth and smiled. "I remember ole Luke." Even on the remote possibility she had forgotten him, everyone she had come in contact with since she returned home seemed bent on jogging her memory when it came to Luke Travers.

She turned her attention back to Seth and they made idle conversation for a few moments as they stood and drank their punch. Cass was determined to ignore the latecomer. By arriving as late as he had, she was well aware this was Luke's devious little way of stating he was there only in deference to Uriah, not to celebrate Cass's homecoming.

Well so what, she thought. He doesn't bother me one little bit. But when her mind repeatedly refused to focus on what Seth was saying, she realized with growing frustration that as bad as she hated to admit it, it did bother her.

He was a stunning man, much as it irked her to acknowledge that, and men didn't usually give her such a cold shoulder. Especially not at her own party!

233

It was downright degrading for him to deliberately ignore her this way.

Her gaze involuntarily found its way back across the room and paused once more. What did he have that had all those silly women in such a dither? Was it the way his pants fit snugly to his muscled thighs, or that his chest was uncommonly broad, or that his waist was sleekly trim? She quickly snapped her head back around. Get a hold of yourself, Cassie! He's just a man, for heaven's sake!

It irritated her to think that it was quite possible Luke was one of those men who took the ladies' breath away and wasn't even aware of what he was doing. Of all the things she could accuse him of, and they were many and varied, being stuck on himself had never been one of his faults—but of course up until now he had no reason to be.

He was dressed casually tonight, in denims and a red plaid shirt. He was wearing an attractive honey-colored leather vest that made his hair look even blonder. As he had entered the room he had taken off a large Stetson and handed it to one of the young teenage girls to take care of.

The girl had giggled with delight and Cass could almost see the excited way her heart had fluttered when he winked at her playfully.

He should be ashamed of himself for tantalizing a girl that age, she thought reproachfully, then carefully forced her attention back to Seth.

But try as she would, Luke's appearance put a damper on her evening. Oh, he didn't bother her personally. On the contrary, he ignored her as steadfastly as she ignored him. Even when they danced past each

234

other they carefully turned their heads in opposite directions.

She had to allow him one concession, though. He had good taste in his women. The girl he had been dancing with for the last hour was a real looker and they made a striking couple.

She was petite, with platinum-blond hair and an ivory complexion like one of those Kewpie dolls Cassie had won at the fair one year. He was tall and tanned, with golden hair and twinkling blue eyes.

The girl wasn't familiar to Cass, but then there were a lot of unfamiliar faces in the crowd tonight. Whoever she was, it was clear she didn't view Luke with the same distaste that Cass did.

Once more she deliberately forced her attention elsewhere. Still, to her utter dismay, the next half hour found her eyes constantly searching the room to see where he was and what he was doing.

Finally, a little before midnight, she gave up trying to ignore his presence and slipped quietly out the back door for a much-needed breath of fresh air.

A huge, round moon hung suspended over her head as she began to stroll toward the corral. Its silvery beams lit her path. The air was richly perfumed with the scent of honeysuckle as she wandered over to the fence and paused. One of the horses neighed softly and ambled over to where she stood.

"Hi there, girl." Cassie rubbed the mare's nose affectionately.

The horse whinnied low and nuzzled deeper into the palm of her hand looking for a treat.

"No sugar cubes tonight, but I'll bring you one tomorrow," she promised.

A low, grunting sound caught her ear and her gaze was drawn to where her car sat down by the barn.

Because of the party, Uriah had suggested she park the Jaguar out of the way so the party guests would have plenty of room for their cars and trucks.

The bright moonbeams made the little sports car glisten like a rare jewel in a nest of black velvet, and once again a feeling of pride overcame her.

The car was the nicest thing she had ever had, and it made her feel good to know that she had worked hard to earn it. Not that it was all hers—yet. But it would be in thirty-six more payments.

Once more the strange, grunting sound reached her ears and she could have sworn she saw the car rock back and forth.

Giving the horse one final pat, she began to edge toward the barn, a puzzled frown on her face now.

A loud snort rent the air and her eyes widened as she stepped backward a fraction. She paused and listened for a moment, then began to move forward again. She couldn't imagine what was going on because the noise sounded exactly like one of Uriah's old sows grunting—but that would be impossible. It was nearly midnight and the pigs were all asleep.

But to her growing puzzlement the noise sounded again and the car definitely moved this time.

Stepping around the vehicle, her mouth dropped open in outrage as she saw a huge pig rubbing up and down on the front bumper, grunting with contentment as it calmly scratched itself back and forth, back and forth. . . .

It must have weighed close to five hundred pounds,

and each movement caused the small car to vibrate up and down in a most unnerving manner.

"Good grief!" Cassie squealed about the same time the old sow did, and the still night air exploded. "What do you think you're doing!" she demanded. "Shoo! Shoo! Get out of here!" She bolted toward the sow as it shrieked frantically and went down on the ground for a minute before it could gain enough traction to jump back up and run.

She was flinging her arms at the animal, yelling, enraged to think that the Jaguar would have yet more damage done to it. At the rate things were going, she would have to take her car back to New York in a brown paper sack!

An enraged Cassie, hot on the heels of a terrified pig, came racing around the car just in time to run head-on into the solid wall of a man's chest.

The pig squealed again and ducked between his legs while Cassie slammed into his chest like a bullet. For a moment it looked as if they were both going down, but the man finally managed to steady both of them.

"What in the . . . !"

Cassie caught her breath and looked up into familiar blue eyes and her heart sank. Oh, brother. It would have to be him! He had undoubtedly seen the whole fiasco with the pig and her car and no doubt he would have a field day laughing behind her back and telling the humiliating story.

Still so mad she could barely speak, she drew herself up indignantly and stepped back from him, her brown eyes sizzling like a hot bed of coals.

"You—he—that darn pig—rubbed on my bumper and left pig hairs and now I have a scratch and no telling what else. . . . Oh, you! . . . I thought pigs were supposed to sleep at night!" She broke off when she realized she was literally yelling at Luke as if it was all his fault and jabbing at the pig, who was now heading full speed toward the barn lot.

Luke was looking at her as if she had lost her mind. He had been on his way to the barn to check the sick calf again before he left for home when he had heard all the commotion.

To her mortification she burst into tears and began sobbing. She knew she should have stayed home this year! "Oh—you—don't you dare repeat this to anyone!" she warned as she shook her finger threateningly under his nose, then marched angrily off in the direction of the house.

To her further humiliation she felt one of the heels on her new shoes snap like a broken bone. Gritting her teeth with pure rage, she reached down and picked up the broken heel and, further enraged, hurled it at Luke's head.

With a look of sheer disbelief, he hurried ducked as it went sailing past his ear. He cautiously straightened back up in time to watch her storm off to the house in a real snit, still trying to figure out what she had been so hysterical and mad at him about.

Whatever it was, it apparently concerned her fancy car, and whatever had happened, she deserved it for being so uppity!

He had been right all along. She was still the meanest little heifer he knew.

CHAPTER FOUR

A vacation was supposed to be a restful time, a time when one had nothing to do but loll around and dread the thought of going back to work, but Cassie's vacation had been the exact opposite.

She had been so busy running around seeing old friends and visiting in the homes of each brother and sister during her brief stay that she had barely had time to catch her breath.

Returning home late Tuesday afternoon after an extended shopping session with Rosalee and her children, Cassie rushed up to her room and kicked off her shoes, stripped down to her slip and panties, then flopped down on the bed with a sigh of relief. The bed felt like sheer heaven.

She hadn't known a day could be so long!

Shopping in Macon seemed like such a good idea at first. Cassie was thrilled that she was able to take her nephews out and buy them each a shiny new pair of leather cowboy boots. Of course the baby wasn't quite ready for boots yet, so a tiny pair of Nikes was purchased for him.

Cassie loved to see the way their eyes lit up as they preened proudly in the shoe-store mirror, announcing for all those who cared to listen that their Aunt Cassie had bought the shoes for them!

But the newness of the shopping expedition wore off quickly and the children had become fussy and hard to get along with.

Hoping that a good lunch would improve their dispositions, Cassie treated them all. The meal did nothing to restore the children's good nature, but Rosalee enjoyed the unaccustomed luxury so much that at least Cassie felt better.

By the time they had finished wiping hands, scraping macaroni and cheese off tiny faces, and digging smashed green beans from beneath clenched fingers, Cassie was beginning to see the folly of her earlier suggestion.

"I want a thucker now!" Bobby Ray demanded.

Cassie glanced at Rosalee. "Can he have a 'thucker,' Mom?"

"Oh, sure," Rosalee consented blithely, and Cassie had to wonder if she had considered what they were going to do with all the sticky faces and hands.

But it was when the baby decided to do his "thing" as they were pushing his stroller through the crowded maze that Cassie knew the shopping spree had been a horrendous mistake. Of course about this time the two older boys quickly decided they needed to use the public facilities, too, so Cassie was forced to halfheartedly offer to change Joey Ray's diaper while Rosalee assisted the two older ones.

Several times she was sure she would gag herself to death before she finished the awesome task of getting a clean diaper on Joey Ray, but fifteen minutes later she was tucking him neatly back into his stroller with a sigh of relief.

By now Billy Ray and Bobby Ray had every hand dryer in the room blowing full blast and Cassie's head was pounding like an African war drum.

The rest of the afternoon had been a blur of sticky hands and more dirty diapers, and Cassie had never been so glad to finally call it a day.

If a vacation was what she had wanted, she would have to hurry and get back to work, she thought dryly as she closed her eyes and luxuriated in the glorious silence.

And to top it all off, her throat was beginning to bother her again. This past winter had found her with a sore throat more often than not, but she had hoped that with summer's arrival she would finally have a reprieve.

Oh well, day after tomorrow she would get in her Jag and head back to New York. When she got back home she would see her doctor and the sore throat would disappear for another few weeks.

Thank goodness vacation would be over for another year.

But she honestly didn't know how Rosalee kept her sanity.

She must have been more exhausted than she realized because the next thing she knew Neoma was gently shaking her shoulder to awaken her for dinner.

"Supper's on the table, hon."

Raising sleep-filled eyes, Cassie murmured something about not being hungry and tugged the pillow over her head.

Neoma chuckled softly and pulled the corner of the

spread up over her gently. It wouldn't hurt to let her sleep a little longer. Uriah had eaten early and driven into Macon for a meeting, and Wylie had gone to a baseball game with Luke, so it would just be her and Cassie eating together tonight anyway.

Her hand reached out and tenderly touched the wisps of dark hair that fell around her daughter's face, a loving smile touching the corners of her mouth now. Cassie looked like she did when she was a child. Her face was warm and flushed with sleep and she looked so very young and innocent to Neoma.

When Cassie had first moved to New York, Neoma had spent many a restless night lying beside Uriah, both of them tossing with worry about their daughter's welfare. But Cassie had made it fine. She had made them all proud, and Neoma had to admit that she was no longer a child. She was a lovely woman now, and Neoma was so glad to have her back home for a while. She sighed softly, then turned and slipped quietly out of the room. She would keep a plate warm and she could eat when she got up.

But when she returned a couple of hours later, Cassie was still sleeping as soundly as before. A small seed of concern began to take root as she bent over her daughter and once more nudged her shoulder.

"Cassie, you'd better wake up, dear. You won't sleep a wink tonight if you don't."

Cassie could hear her mom's voice calling from somewhere far away, but the warm cocoon of sleep that had enveloped her was reluctant to release her from its pleasant hold.

"Cassie?" Neoma was becoming more than a little concerned now. It wasn't at all like Cassie to sleep this long in the afternoon. "Cassie. Can you hear me? Wake up!"

Her mom's voice was sharply insistent this time and Cass tried to force her eyes to unlock. "What?" she murmured drowsily. Her mouth felt dry and hot and she was vaguely aware of a deepening ache in her throat.

"Goodness." Neoma heaved a sigh of relief and sat down on the edge of the bed. "I was beginning to get worried about you."

"Worried? Why?" Cassie rolled over and tried to focus her gaze on her mother but seemed to have a hard time doing so.

"You didn't want to wake up, and that's not like you at all."

"Yes . . . I know. . . . I'm just so tired. . . ." She swallowed and the action proved to be extremely painful. Her right hand shot up to touch her throat. "My throat hurts," she complained.

"It does?" Neoma's hand immediately went to her daughter's forehead and she frowned. "Land's sake, Cassie. You're burnin' up with fever."

"I am?" The news was more than a little disturbing. If her throat was this sore and she was running a fever again, it could only mean that she was in for another bout of tonsillitis. Twice in the past few months she had missed several days of work due to the annoying recurrence. "Surely not. I was feeling fine earlier."

"It sure feels like it to me, but there's a sure way to find out." Neoma slid off the bed and went in search of a thermometer. Moments later she was back, shaking the mercury down as she walked. "Have your tonsils been bothering you again lately?"

"Every once in a while," Cassie admitted as she obediently opened her mouth and Neoma peered into her throat.

"Oh, my."

Cassie's heart sank. Neoma had said that in the glum, tsking way mothers have that assure you you're in for big trouble. Shaking her head worriedly, she placed the thermometer under her daughter's tongue.

"We should have had those things out long ago," Neoma fused as she plumped the pillow and clucked like the typical mother. "Doc warned us that you were going to have nothing but trouble if you didn't."

"I know." Cassie had heard that a hundred times, but she cringed when she thought about having the operation at her age. A sudden chill assaulted her and she began to shiver uncontrollably as Neoma hurried over to the closet and withdrew a couple of lightweight blankets to drape over her. The room was at least eighty degrees but Cassie felt it had suddenly dropped to below zero.

"Tha-n-kk-s, M-om." She was barely able to talk now as intermittent chills shook her slender frame.

"Dear, dear," Neoma twittered worriedly. "I think I'd better go call Doc Lydell and see if he can run over here."

Any other time Cassie would have voiced a stern protest, but she had been through tonsillitis enough to know that she would have to have an antibiotic to get over it. Simple aspirin wouldn't do this time. "I think you'd better," she agreed, then huddled down deeper into the blanket.

But a few minutes later Neoma was back with bad news. "He's not home. Mildred said he had surgery over in Macon today and she doesn't know what time he'll get back. He may even spend the night over there if the patient doesn't do well."

"Well, it's not exactly an emergency," Cassie pointed out around the thermometer, which was still stuck in her mouth like an ice pick. "Just give me a couple of aspirins and we'll call him in the morning."

Withdrawing the thermometer, Neoma's brow furrowed deeper. "I don't think we should wait till mornin'. You have a hundred and four temperature."

"It's been that high before."

"I don't care. That's dangerous for an adult to have that high a temperature. Uriah will have to drive you over to the emergency room in Macon. Doc Lydell will surely still be there. I don't want to take the chance that the fever will go any higher."

"Mom, really—"

"Oh, dear!"

Cassie's head shot up from beneath her pile of blankets. "What?"

"Your father's not back yet—he went to a Grange meetin' tonight. . . . Well, I'll just call Ray to come and take you," she decided.

"Rosalee said Ray had to go to a deacons' meeting at the church tonight," Cassie murmured.

"Oh, my stars, that's right. Then I'll call Pauly—"

"Pauly and Newt have gone fishing."

"Oh, dear me." Neoma sank down on the bed in dismay, realizing that Cassie was right. Pauly and Newt had stopped by earlier and borrowed some of Uriah's tackle before they went on down to the river. She reached over to feel her daughter's forehead again. "You're hotter."

"No, I'm not."

"Yes, you are."

"No, I'm not."

"Don't argue with me. You're hotter than a two-dollar pistol."

The sound of a truck pulling into the graveled drive finally broke the impasse as Neoma sprang to her feet and rushed to the window. "Thank goodness. It's Luke bringing Wylie home," she announced with a rush of relief. "He can take you to Macon."

"Mom!" But before Cassie could stop her, Neoma had spun on her heel and left the room in a flurry of excitement. With a disgusted moan, Cassie jerked the blankets up over her head and scrunched lower in the bed. All she needed to top a perfectly miserable day was Luke Travers's company!

But with much to-do about nothing, Neoma returned a few minutes later dragging a puzzled Luke along behind her. "She's right in here, Luke. She's being ornery, but I want you to take a look at her and see what you think."

He paused in the doorway, his gaze quickly locating Cassie, who was lying in the middle of the bed vibrating like half-set Jell-O.

She felt her face growing even hotter with embarrassment as he eased cautiously over to her bedside.

"What's going on?" he asked quietly.

Neoma had run out of the house yelling at him just as he had dropped Wylie off and started to pull out of the drive. She had babbled something about Cassie needing a doctor and he'd better get upstairs quick!

Cassie made an apologetic face. "Mom is overreacting a little."

246

He stepped closer to the side of her bed to examine her flushed features more accurately. "How high's your fever?"

"I'll bet it's shot even higher than it was when I took it a while ago," Neoma fretted. "You're a doctor, Luke. Tell her she's taking a chance if she waits until morning to get some medicine."

"Mother." Cassie shot her an annoyed look. "Luke is a veterinarian, not a people doctor."

"Well, I'll bet there ain't a whole lot of difference, is there?" Neoma prompted hopefully to Luke.

"Nope, dealing with one jackass is just about like dealing with another," Luke agreed, with just the suggestion of a grin on his face for her mother's sake. He leaned over the bed. "Open your mouth, Cass, and let me have a look."

"I will not!" This was beginning to get ridiculous. She wasn't about to let him peer into her throat!

"Don't give me a hard time," he warned with the familiar edge of impatience he always used when addressing her.

"Don't give me one. I said no."

"Fine with me," he said indifferently, and promptly stepped back from the bed. "She won't let me look in her throat, Neoma."

He sounded exactly like he was tattling on her!

"Now, children," Neoma pacified. "This is not the time to be ugly to one another. Now, Cassie. You sit up there and let Luke look at your throat," she ordered in a tone that Cassie knew meant business.

It was quite unnerving to be ordered around like a child again, but Cassie began to slide back up from the depths of the blankets and glare at Luke hostilely.

"This is a waste of time. I don't need you to look in my throat and tell me I'm sick! I know I am, but Doc Lydell is out of town and I don't want to have to go clear over to Macon tonight to see him."

Luke took the flashlight Neoma extended to him. He was clearly turning a deaf ear to her pleadings. "Open up," he instructed.

She popped her mouth open in a wide and exaggerated pose. He grasped her chin between his fingers to inspect her throat. Their eyes met briefly.

"It's just a himple caze of tonsihites," she garbled as he held her mouth firmly open.

"Could be," he murmured distractedly as he pointed the rays of light down her throat. "But then tonciletiemosis has the same symptoms."

She frowned. "Whut's tonciletiemosis?"

If he thought trying to carry on a conversation with your mouth propped open like a jack-in-the-box was easy, he was nuts!

Luke lifted a disbelieving brow. "You've never heard of tonciletiemosis?"

"Nooob . . . whut ees hit?" Her eyes broaded farther.

"A rare, debilitating disease that . . . oh surely you've heard of it." He was acting as if she was kidding him.

"I'b neber heard ob suzh a diseese!" she scoffed, but her pulse did give a queer little leap at the mere thought of such a malady.

"You're serious? Well," he said in a grim tone, "the voice goes first, then the eyes . . . then the mouth. . . . Well, let's just say it's a heck of a way to go."

Her eyes widened more fearfully as he finished his examination and tapped her now gaping mouth shut.

"Well?" she prompted.

"Well, what?"

"Do I have tonsillitis?" She knew he was only trying to scare her with all that foolish talk about toncile-tiemosis, but yet with Luke you never knew. . . .

"It's entirely possible."

"Possible! Of course I have tonsillitis! Any fool can see that!"

Luke was unperturbed by her self-diagnosis as he turned his attention back to Neoma. "Or she could have strep throat. There's no way of knowing until they get some cultures on that throat."

"That's what I thought!" Neoma exclaimed triumphantly.

Cassie groaned with exasperation as a new round of chills assaulted her.

"Well, that settles it. Uriah will just have to take her back to Macon when he gets home this evenin'," her mother announced.

"Probably be a good idea." Luke nodded. "Well, guess I'll be running along. Oh, by the way, Cass, I don't think it is tonciletiemosis, but you can never be too careful. If your temperature goes up another notch, and you feel the skin around your neck and facial muscles begin to sag. . . ." He shook his head pensively. "Of course, I'm not a 'people doctor,' but I'd still strongly advise you consult another doctor real quick."

When Neoma left to see him out Cassie was still peeping up over the blankets looking considerably more concerned than she had been a few moments earlier.

"She'll be all right," Luke comforted a few moments later when they were out of Cassie's hearing range. "It's her tonsils all right, but it would be wise to get a culture taken."

"Yes, that's what we'll do, but I have no idea what time Uriah will be back. Sometimes those Grange meetings last till midnight."

"Well"—they paused as they reached the kitchen and his fingers toyed with his large Stetson—"you know I'd be more than happy to take her, but she wouldn't hear of it."

"You would?" Neoma's face brightened at his suggestion. "Now let's not be too hasty. She just might change her mind and decide it's best for her to go."

Luke shook his head negatively. "Not a chance. Not with me, at least."

Neoma smiled deviously. "If you're serious about taking her, you wait right here."

Luke shrugged and pulled out a chair from the kitchen table. "Don't get your hopes up," he warned as he pitched the hat on the table and made himself comfortable. "I guarantee you, she won't go."

"Wylie, you fix Luke something cold to drink," Neoma ordered as her youngest son walked into the kitchen looking for a snack. "I'll be right back."

Ten minutes later Luke was finishing his glass of tea when to his surprise Neoma and Cassie walked into the room.

He shot to his feet, hardly able to believe his eyes. Cassie was wearing a heavy sweater and carrying her purse, but the scowl on her face assured him she wasn't any too happy. She planted herself in the middle of the kitchen floor staring at him sullenly, but it was obvious she had consented to make the trip.

"Uh . . . you ready to go?" he asked cautiously.

"If I must."

Reaching for his hat, he motioned for her to precede him. "We'll take my car," she stated curtly. She didn't want to be indebted any more to him than was necessary.

"No, we won't," he said pleasantly. "We'll take my truck."

"Don't be an ass about this, Luke. I'm already imposing on your time. I don't intend to argue about this. We'll use my car and my gas."

"We'll take my truck and use my gas or we don't go," he stated flatly.

He wasn't about to drive her hot-shot car.

"For heaven's sake, Cassie. You can settle this later," Neoma intervened. "Now go get in the truck."

She looked at Luke sourly. If it wasn't for the fact that there was just the tiniest chance that she might have this . . . horrid tonciletiemosis thing, she would tell him what he could do with his truck and his farfetched diagnosis!

"Are you coming or not?" he challenged.

"I'm coming, I'm coming," she muttered, but the look she gave him made it plain she was doing so under duress. She swept around him haughtily and headed for his truck.

"I really appreciate what you're doing," Neoma told Luke as he prepared to follow.

"It's all right, Neoma. I'm glad to do it for you."

"Cassie—well, she don't mean to be so spiteful,"

251

Neoma apologized. "She's just a little stubborn at times."

Luke's gaze followed the young woman, who was carefully making her way out to his vehicle. "Yes, I've noticed that." He'd like to turn that fancy little tail end of hers over his knee and give her a sound paddling, and he just might if she kept defying him. "How did you ever talk her into letting me take her to the hospital?"

"Oh," Neoma sighed, "I just told her I knew someone who had died of that tonciletiemosis thing, and she shouldn't be taking any chances."

Luke's grin was definitely guilty now as he dropped his eyes in repentance. "Aw, Neoma. I was only teasing her about tonciletiemosis. There isn't any such disease. I only made that up to get under her skin."

"Oh, I know that!" Neoma grinned. "But it worked like a charm, didn't it?"

"Yes, I guess it did." He sighed and stuck his hat back on his head. "Well, this ought to be interesting."

"She'll be fine once you're on the road," Neoma predicted.

Cassie was still slowly gaining on the truck when Luke stepped out the door and hurriedly caught up with her. The fever was making her light-headed and she suddenly found herself very unsteady on her feet. Before she knew what was happening he had picked her up in his arms and was carrying her the rest of the way.

"Will you put me down!" she protested indignantly.

"You're staggering around like a Saturday-night drunk," he observed calmly.

"I am perfectly capable of taking care of myself!"

"Maybe so, but right now I'm taking care of you, so you might as well pipe down." He reached the truck and shifted her to his knee unceremoniously as he opened the door.

Moments later she was meticulously being tucked in the front seat and the door was being slammed with the authority of someone who was confident he had the final word.

Or so he thought.

CHAPTER FIVE

"I still say we should have taken my car," Cassie continued to grumble thirty minutes later as they bumped along the highway to Macon in Luke's truck. The Jag rode like a dream while this truck rode like a lumber wagon, and she didn't hesitate to tell him so.

"Well, Her Majesty will just have to put up with the inconvenience," Luke retorted. "If I'm taking you, you're riding in my vehicle."

"Look at your gas gauge," she complained. "You're running on fumes, you know."

"I have plenty of gas," he argued.

"Does your E on your gauge stand for something different than the E on my gauge?" she persisted.

"I don't know. What does your E stand for?" For someone who supposedly felt bad, she sure could be a pain in the butt.

"Empty."

"Well mine means almost empty. That's what you get for buying those high-priced pieces of junk. My truck will run another twenty miles once it reaches the E," he said smugly.

She ignored his tacky reference to her Jaguar. He was only jealous and she knew it. "Why, oh why, did this have to happen now?" she lamented woefully. It suddenly seemed as if the whole world was against her. "I'm leaving for New York day after tomorrow and I'm going to feel awful for the drive home!"

"Stop feeling so sorry for yourself," he complained. "Maybe you'll leave, and maybe you won't."

"Now what's that supposed to mean?"

"It means you may go back to New York and then again you may not," he repeated. "That throat looks pretty bad to me and, personally, I don't think you'll be going anywhere in the next couple of days."

"Don't bet on it. I'll get back to New York if I have to crawl."

Luke glanced over at her impatiently. "You really hate it here, don't you?"

"Yes." The rapid, sharp affirmation hurt her throat. "I mean no, I don't hate it here," she added softly, trying to temper her harsh words. "I always enjoy being with my family and I love seeing old friends, but I can't deny I'll be happy to get back home."

"This is your home," he returned quietly.

"Not anymore." Even as she said the words she felt a terrible feeling of disloyalty to all those who loved her and were so terribly proud of her.

"That's too bad. I found that all the years I was gone I missed the town very badly," he confessed.

It would have been much easier on her guilt if he had picked this time to be his usual, arrogant self.

A humble Luke Travers was frustrating.

"Are you warm enough?" He reached over and tucked the sweater around her closer, changing the subject for the moment.

A nice Luke Travers was even harder to take.

"Yes, thank you."

"It's not much farther now," he noted as he eyed her feverish glow in the lights of the dashboard. "Can I do anything for you?" He had to admit she looked pretty miserable.

"No, I'm fine . . . really." She hugged the warmth of the wool around her tighter, trying to still another round of chills. "Just ge-t me to th-e hospital s-o I can get some re-l-ie-f."

"Neoma said Uriah had to go to Macon tonight," Luke said conversationally as he tried to adjust his side vent for a better flow of air. The temperature was extremely uncomfortable, but since Cassie was having chills he had left the air conditioner off and rolled down his window.

"Ye-s, he-'s at some mee-t-ing."

"He going to have to learn to take it a little easier," Luke pondered. "His blood pressure has been acting up lately."

"He's always had high blood pressure," Cassie pointed out. "Are you hot?" She noticed he was perspiring heavily and periodically mopping at his brow.

"A little." He smiled at her and shook his head. "Looks to me like you'd be burning up in that sweater."

"I wish I had two more," she confessed, and huddled deeper into the warmth. "Why should Dad take it easier? He's always enjoyed wor-k-ing hard." She returned to their earlier conversation, puzzled as to why her father's health kept popping up. First Rosalee, then her mother's vague reference, and now Luke had mentioned he was worried about him.

"I know he has, but he's not a young man anymore,

and I think he's been pushing himself too hard lately. Were you aware he stayed up with that calf again all last night?"

She hadn't known that. For a week and a half the calf had clung precariously to life, and for most of that time Uriah had been at its side. "Well, he shouldn't be doing that," she agreed. "But he's used to working hard."

"Maybe so, but he doesn't seem himself lately."

"Is the calf going to make it or not?" It seemed to Cassie that was what was putting all of the pressure on her father at the moment. He had babied the calf like he would one of his own children had they been ill.

"She's a little scrapper, but I don't see how she's held on this long. The calf has a rare disease that's almost always fatal, and I think it's only a matter of time before it dies."

"Then Dad will lose it?" For some reason the calf had taken on a special meaning for Uriah and she knew its death would hurt her father deeply, especially after he and Luke had fought so long and so hard for its life.

"I could be wrong, but yes, I think we'll lose it," he confirmed softly.

Her gaze fell back uneasily on his gas gauge. The needle wasn't even rocking now. "Luke . . . don't you think you should try to find a gas station?" He was making her extremely nervous. She never let her tank get that close to being empty.

"No, I have plenty of gas."

The lights of the hospital loomed in the far distance as Luke flipped on his turn signal, then shot off the exit ramp. "Besides, we're almost there now. I'm going to take the access road and we'll make better time . . ." As he spoke the truck sputtered a couple of times, then began to jerk along erratically.

Cassie glanced over at him worriedly. "What's that?"

"What's what?" he asked innocently as he began to pump the gas pedal rapidly.

"That noise."

"I don't hear anything."

By now she didn't either. The engine had belched one final time and then stopped altogether. They rolled along another quarter of a mile before the truck glided to a complete halt.

She slowly turned her head to face him. "Well"— she drummed her fingers impatiently on the seat— "what now?"

He grinned sheepishly. "I'll check under the hood. It acted like the fuel pump."

"No, it's not the fuel pump," she stated calmly. "You're out of gas."

"No, I'm not out of gas," he denied again. He jerked the door open and got out.

"You are too!" she exploded. "I had a perfectly good car sitting there with a full tank of gas, but we had to take your truck. Didn't I tell you ten minutes ago you were running low on—" Her words were severed as he slammed the door shut and stalked around to the front of the truck.

Stubborn! Stubborn man! He was out of gas! She seethed.

After tinkering unsuccessfully under the hood for a few minutes, he returned to poke his head in the window once more. "It . . . uh . . . doesn't seem to be the fuel pump."

She patiently folded her hands in her lap in complete martyrdom. "Somehow, that doesn't surprise me at all."

He glanced around, trying to decide what to do. "I guess I'm going to have to call a wrecker."

"Where?" As far as she could tell, there wasn't a place between here and the hospital where he could use a telephone.

Luke's gaze fell in the direction of the hospital, then back at her sheepishly. "Looks like the hospital's about the closest. Think you can make it?"

Her head shot up. "You mean . . . walk?"

"Well, yeah . . . or I could go make the call, then send a cab back for you," he offered.

Cassie tried to judge just how far the hospital was from where they sat. It couldn't have been more than a mile or so, yet the thought of walking there when she felt so bad was not the least bit appealing.

"Maybe another car will come along and give us a ride," she pleaded.

"That's possible, but it's getting pretty late and this road isn't traveled all that much."

With a low groan, she grabbed the handle and pushed the truck door open. She supposed she had no other choice but to walk, but the thought irked her. Especially when she knew she would have been there by now if they had only taken her car.

"Oh, this is appalling. I have to walk to the hospital when I'm sick and it's freezing cold—"

"Just stop your squawking. You'll live, but I may not." He was there to lift her down onto the ground, then carefully button up the heavy sweater so she wouldn't get chilled again. She grumbled and muttered and blustered irritably under her breath, but she complied patiently as his large fingers ran into trouble securing the tiny pearl fasteners.

"Why don't they just put zippers on these things?" he complained.

"They wouldn't be as pretty."

"But they'd work better."

"Hurry, I'm freezing again." She shivered radically.

"Lord, Cass. It has to be a hundred out here!" he groaned. His face was beet red and as flushed with heat as hers was.

It was several moments before he finally completed the task of buttoning her sweater, and by now perspiration was rolling in streams down the sides of his face. "There. You shouldn't get cold now," he said with the complete confidence of a man who was standing at the gateway of hell.

He reached up to remove his hat and run his shirt sleeve over his brow. It was obvious he was sweltering.

"I'm still a little chilly," she confessed meekly.

He sighed and shifted his weight to one foot, a habit she was beginning to recognize when he was trying to be agreeable. "You want my hat?" He didn't have anything else to offer her in the line of warmth.

She nodded gratefully. It was crazy, but even her ears felt cold.

The hat was ridiculously large on her, but by now she was past caring about fashion. "How do you think you're going to see?" he chided as he tried to adjust the hat so that she would still have partial vision.

"It's fine. You wouldn't happen to have any gloves . . . would you?"

"Gloves?" He looked at her blankly. "We're just going about a mile down the road."

"But my hands are like icicles," she objected.

Gloves . . . gloves . . . ? He thought for a moment, and then began to rummage around under the seat of his truck and jubilantly came up with a ragged, crumpled-up pair a few moments later.

"They're not much to look at, but they'll keep you warm," he told her as he helped her slip them on. He stepped back to survey her and the sweat beaded anew on his forehead. "Surely you're warm enough now?"

She peeked back at him from beneath the wide brim of his hat and grinned. "I think so."

"Good, I'm about to have a heat stroke," he confessed with an audible sigh of relief. He absently tucked an errant strand of her dark hair beneath the hat.

"Hey, look. Why don't you cheer up? You don't have that many problems. God's still in his heaven, we've finally got you warm enough, the hospital is just a ten-minute walk from here, Doc Lydell will give you an antibiotic, and in no time at all you'll be on your way back to New York."

She gave him a wavering smile. Maybe he was right. Maybe it wasn't so bad after all.

"As far as I can see, you've got only one problem."

"What?"

"You forgot to put your dress on."

Her gaze flew down to her sweater and it belatedly occurred to her that during all the rush she had completely forgotten to get dressed!

"Oh, for heaven's sake! Why didn't you say something sooner!"

He shrugged and reached into his pocket for a smoke. "I was thinkin' about it, but I didn't know how to bring up the subject without embarrassing you."

Gathering the sweater around her throat tightly, she scowled at him menacingly. "Well, you could have at least given me a clue!"

They started off down the road and Cassie prayed no one she knew would see her. Even in New York anyone walking down the highway at night, with the temperature hovering around eighty-five, wearing a slip, a sweater, gloves, and a gigantic cowboy hat, would look a little odd.

"I'm sorry about this," Luke apologized as they walked along.

"You should be. If we had taken my car—"

"I said I was sorry," he stated again sharply.

"You just didn't want to ride in my car," she accused, feeling decidedly out of sorts with the whole world. He wouldn't let her take the Jag and now she was wandering around half dressed, like some pervert! For some strange reason she and Luke had always been competitive with each other. It was silly, but nevertheless it was true, and now that she had become highly successful in her field and could afford a nice luxury car, he was going to try and ignore it.

Taking her car to the hospital would have meant an admission on his part that she was doing just as well as he was. But it was clear he wasn't about to do that. He just couldn't stand it that Cass McCason was driving a Jaguar and he was still driving a pickup!

"That's ridiculous. Why should I mind riding in your car?" he asked indifferently.

"Because it is my car."

"And you think that worries me?" he asked incredulously.

"Doesn't it?"

"If all I had to worry about was what kind of car you drove, I'd give up!" he informed her irritably.

Cassie didn't have the strength to continue the argument. Luke noticed her weakness, and he put his arm around her and half carried her into the hospital. They didn't speak because it was clear that Cassie was too sick to talk.

As far as Cassie was concerned, she just wanted to get this miserable night over and start back to New York the day after tomorrow.

As far as Luke was concerned, day after tomorrow couldn't come fast enough.

When they reached the hospital there were a few inquisitive stares as Luke held the emergency-room door open and let her enter. The nurse who was sitting at the desk glanced up as Cassie marched up and asked for Dr. Lydell to be paged.

While they took her to an examining room Luke went in search of a telephone. She immediately stripped out of her bizarre wardrobe and asked the nurse for a blanket to wrap around her. It was twenty minutes before the doctor arrived to examine her, only to confirm what she already knew.

She had another raging case of tonsillitis.

"Those things are going to have to come out one of these days," he warned as he tossed the tongue depressor into the wastebasket.

"I know. I just dread the thought."

"Nonetheless, they're not doing you any good. I want you to see your doctor and discuss the possibility of having them removed the minute you return to New York. In the meantime, I'll try to patch you up until you get back home."

"Thank you. I will," she promised, immensely relieved to know it wasn't that horrible tonciletiemosis thing.

He peered through his wire-rimmed glasses at her and winked playfully as his gruff tone softened. "See that you do, young lady, and no more excuses." He turned and gave the nurse some brief instructions, then turned back to her. "Was that Luke I saw out in the hall a few minutes ago?"

"Yes, Dad was at a meeting so he offered to bring me over here." She left out the part about having to walk the last mile because he had run out of gas.

"Hmm. Good boy. Good boy."

"Hmm," Cassie said, unimpressed.

"Guess he and Marilyn Hodges haven't gotten serious yet or I'd have surely heard," he speculated, more to himself than to anyone else.

"Marilyn who?" Cassie's ears unwillingly perked up at the mention of Luke's private life.

"Marilyn Hodges. Oh, yes, I suppose you wouldn't know her. She opened up an interior decorating shop here in Macon about a couple of years ago. Lovely girl, just lovely," he praised.

"And Luke's going with her?" Strange that made her stomach feel a little fluttery all of a sudden.

"Oh, they're seen together occasionally," Doc chuckled. "The whole town's sort of been hopin' something will come out of it. It's high time he took a wife and settled down." He sighed—almost romantically. "They make such a nice-lookin' couple."

The image of the small blonde dancing in Luke's arms the night of the party stampeded her mind like a herd of buffalo. They were a nice-looking couple. And Marilyn had gazed into Luke's eyes like a lovesick calf. . . . Cassie shook the disturbing image away. "Luke hasn't mentioned her to me."

"No, I suppose not," he mused, then chuckled knowingly. "Well, it's good to see you again," he said pleasantly as he sat down at a small desk and reached for a prescription pad. "It's been a while since you've been home."

"Yes, I'm afraid it has been."

"Staying very long?" he inquired as he began to write on the pad.

"No, my two weeks are nearly over. I go back home day after tomorrow."

"Oh? Well"—he ripped the piece of paper off and handed it to her—"that's too bad. I know Uriah and Neoma love havin' you." His face suddenly turned a bit more somber. "By the way, how is your dad?"

"He's fine."

"Good. Good. I'm glad to hear he's been takin' care of himself. I warned him a couple of months ago he needed to slow down." He pointed to the prescription he had just given her. "You can have that filled at the pharmacy here in the hospital before you go."

"Thanks. I will." She safely tucked the piece of paper into her purse. "It was good to see you again."

"Good to see you again, Cass. Take care of yourself." He left the room as Cassie was hurriedly crawling back into her sweater.

The nurse had informed her that Luke was taking care of the truck while the doctor completed his examination. He had left word he would be at the front of the emergency exit when she was ready to leave.

By the time she had the prescription filled he was waiting for her.

"What did the doctor say?" he asked as she got into the truck and shut the door.

"Tonciletiemosis my foot! He said I had plain old tonsillitis." She plopped his hat back onto his head forcefully. "Just like I thought."

"Lucked out, huh?" He readjusted the hat, then glanced in the rearview mirror before he put the truck into gear, then pulled out onto the road. Cassie noticed the truck was running like a top and the gas gauge was registering full now, but she wasn't about to ask him how he accomplished that. It couldn't have been easy since there were only two gas stations in Macon and they both closed by 10 P.M. "Did he give you a prescription?"

She winced as she thought about the shot the doctor had given her, and where he had unceremoniously placed it. "Yes. He not only gave me a prescription, he gave me a shot too."

Luke chuckled. "And I don't suppose it was where you wanted it?"

"No, a little lower than I would have preferred," she verified.

And for the first time since she had known Luke Travers, he actually looked at her as if she were a woman and not some common housefly that continued to annoy him.

Strangely enough, his eyes had that unmistakable light of male appreciation as his gaze slid casually over her slender body in a most complimentary yet disturbing way. Moments later she could hardly believe it when he grinned at her and teased, "I always thought being a medical doctor would have more advantages than being a veterinarian."

She scowled disapprovingly at him, but she had to admit that for some crazy reason her pulse was suddenly beating faster. "Dr. Lydell asked about you," she said sweetly.

"Oh?"

"Yes. He wanted to know if you and Marilyn were serious yet," she said innocently.

"Oh?" He reached into his pocket and withdrew a cheroot and stuck it in his mouth as he punched in the lighter on the dash.

"Yes, that's what he asked." She watched him light the cigar in silence; all of a sudden he had chosen to remain infuriatingly evasive. "I told him I didn't know," she added, hoping to keep the subject alive a little longer, although she had no idea why.

He looked over at her through a cloud of smoke he had just exhaled. "That would be a tough one."

"Well, you're not . . . are you?"

"What?"

"Serious about Marilyn," she snapped. Good grief! You would think he had gone stone deaf!

His lids lowered in the sexiest manner and, again, her pulse did this funny little beat. "Now I can't believe that would be a question that would cause *you* to lose any sleep."

She cleared her throat nervously and felt herself blushing. She was thankful they were back out on the highway now and he couldn't see her as well in the dim lighting. "Well, of course I wasn't asking for my own information," she excused. "I just thought I should know if the subject ever came up again."

"Why in the world would the subject ever come up again?"

She shrugged lamely.

He turned his attention back to the road.

"Well?"

"Marilyn and I date each other occasionally."

"And?"

"We have a nice time together."

"That's it? You have a nice time together?"

"For the present, that's it," he verified calmly.

She was dying to ask him more about this mysterious woman, but she didn't dare. He would think she was asking because she was personally interested, which couldn't be farther from the truth.

"Do you feel better now?" he inquired a few minutes later.

"I wasn't upset because I thought you were serious about Marilyn!" she shot back defensively.

He shook his head in complete disgust. "I didn't mean that. I meant, are you still chilled."

This time she did blush. All the way to the roots of her hair. How could she have made a blunder like that? "Oh," she said meekly. "No . . . I'm fine . . . thank you."

"Let me know if you start again. I stopped and

picked up a heavier coat from a friend of mine in Macon in case you need it."

The completely unexpected gesture touched her heart and she had to admit that was very nice of him. "Thank you. I will."

They rode for another few moments in silence, then like a fool she blurted out, "I suppose Marilyn was the blonde on your arm at the party the other night?"

Once more he turned to level a stern, blue-eyed gaze in her direction, totally confused by now why she was suddenly so interested in Marilyn. "As I recall, I danced with several women that night, but Marilyn is blond and I did dance with her several times."

"So it must have been Marilyn," she concluded, trying to keep her voice light now.

"Why don't you try and get some sleep?" he suggested a little while later. "The shot is making you drowsy."

"I'm not the least bit sleepy," she argued, but on second thought she decided to take his suggestion.

She had made a big enough fool of herself in front of him for one day.

She snuggled down on her side and pretended to doze the rest of the way home.

But she was keenly aware that he sat next to her. In the dim interior of the cab, she wondered for the hundredth time how he could be the Luke Travers she used to know.

He was still as arrogant as ever, but somehow she sensed he could be tender with a woman if he wanted to be. A small smile curved her mouth as she thought about how he tried to button her sweater with his large fingers. He had been kind, almost tender, in his clumsy ministrations. And stopping by to borrow a heavy coat from a friend in this heat must have taken some nerve. She hoped it had been a male acquaintance. Her sleepy gaze found the coat lying between them on the seat and she breathed a sigh of relief. It was a man's garment.

Yes, she bet he could be extremely gentle with a woman when he made love to her. . . .

He was concentrating on the road, deep in thought now. He was probably thinking about Marilyn. Marilyn with her blond hair and blue eyes and knockout figure.

She drowsily tried to focus on his profile as she grew warm and sleepy. Ruggedly handsome, virile, masculine, strong chin, just the right size nose, long, beautiful lashes, blue—incredibly blue—eyes . . . and he had a dimple in his left cheek when he smiled. . . .

Things became increasingly hazy after that. She was vaguely aware of the truck ceasing its rocking motion. Then she was lifted into a set of incredibly strong arms and carried into the house.

She remembered murmuring a soft protest that she was able to walk, yet her arms clung tightly around a warm neck that smelled faintly of soap and a musky after-shave.

The chest she was pressed tightly against was broad and comforting, and whoever was carrying her did so with the greatest of ease and gentleness.

Somewhere, far, far away, she could hear her mother thanking Luke for taking her to the hospital, then her shoes were being slipped off and she was being slid between cool sheets that smelled like they had been dried outdoors in the fresh sunshine.

Then Neoma was saying good night to Luke and he was saying good night to Neoma. . . .

She was aware her throat didn't hurt nearly as much as it had and she sighed softly as she snuggled down deep within the cocoon of the blankets that had carefully been tucked around her.

The faint click of the lamp beside her bed being turned off registered only briefly as the room was plunged into complete darkness.

Then something strange happened that caused her pulse to jump erratically in that funny way it had done twice already this evening.

Something warm and soft touched her forehead so very lightly she barely felt it. Then that delicious, gentle warmness touched her eyes, then her nose, then traveled down slowly until it touched her mouth.

It lingered only briefly, as if it somehow knew it was partaking of forbidden yet completely irresistible fruit.

She thought the warmness tasted musky . . . and sweet, and it made her think of Luke.

She tried to will her eyes back open so that she might draw that wonderful feeling back down to her, to sample and explore that sweetness, but the darkness that held her so tightly increased its hold until it completely overpowered her.

Tomorrow she would think about how nice it was, she promised herself as she dropped deeper and deeper into the strange black void that totally encompassed her now, or even more important, what it was. . . .

CHAPTER SIX

The heat of his kisses seared a molten path down the long, silken column of her neck.

"No, darling. It's wrong. We cannot allow ourselves to give in to this madness," she cried out.

"Wrong? Wrong? How can you say it's wrong when you know it's what we both want," he argued with a tortured groan.

He kissed her again passionately, his tongue swirling hotly in her mouth, and she hated herself, but she felt her defenses weakening.

"But Carolyn . . . we must think of Carolyn," she pleaded, knowing that within moments she would cast all sanity aside and let him make love to her . . . even as his wife, and her best friend, lay dying in the hospital after a crazed psychopath had tampered with the anesthetic in a simple operation to remove a plantar's wart from her left foot.

How could she do this to Carolyn, who had been like a sister to her?

She could only plead love. From the moment she had met Dr. Josh Mitchell she knew this hour was inevitable. He was like a jungle animal and she his powerless prey. . . .

The screen door banged shut as Wylie entered the living room, abruptly interrupting the soap opera Cassie was deeply submerged in lying on the sofa.

By the condition of his dusty face and even dirtier baseball suit, she could only guess that if his team hadn't won, then he had at least played hard that afternoon.

"Hi, how did it go?"

"Okay."

"Did you win?"

"No, but it was close." He disappeared into the kitchen and came back a few minutes later with a handful of cookies and a tall glass of milk.

Cassie glanced up from the screen and smiled as he plopped down in a chair across from her and began hungrily to gobble down the snack. "What was the score?"

"Twenty-six to five."

Her mouth dropped open. "And you consider that close?"

"Yeah," he returned between gulps of milk. "We got beat thirty-five to nothin' last week."

She laughed at his enviable optimism and turned her attention back to the television. Since watching soap operas was a rarity to her, she found herself fascinated with the complexity of the story line. If anyone ever thought they had a problem, this program would cure them of complaining forever. After watching what these poor people went through day after day, one would have surmised their everyday problems were minor in comparison.

"You feelin' better?"

"Yes, I think I am." Between the medicine and the

shot the doctor had given her last night, she thought she could feel a small improvement in her throat today.

"You still going home tomorrow?"

"Yes, I still plan to." She grinned at him impishly. "Are you going to miss me?"

"Yeah." He quickly polished off the last oatmeal-raisin cookie in his hand and wiped his mouth clean with the sleeve of his shirt. He was a little embarrassed at her probing questions and he wished she'd stop putting him on the spot like that. But he guessed he shouldn't mind. She was pretty nice . . . for a sister.

"I'll miss you too. Maybe we can arrange for you to come and visit me in New York next summer," she tempted. "I could take you to see the Statue of Liberty and the United Nations building. We can go for a ride through Central Park or take a sight-seeing boat around Manhattan Island. I know this neat little place that makes terrific hot-fudge sundaes we could go to afterward. Would you like that?"

"Yeah, that would be okay," he admitted. "But it would have to be after baseball season."

"Oh, sure. After baseball season," she agreed.

He looked around uncomfortably. "Where's Mom?"

"Down at the barn with Dad."

"Wonder what we're having for supper?"

"I think I might have heard fried chicken mentioned. You think that would do?"

Every member of the McCason family knew fried chicken was Wylie's favorite.

"Yeah. That would do." He grinned.

"And it seems to me I might have smelled a chocolate cake baking earlier."

Wylie's eyes grew rounder. "I hope she made it with fudge icing." He shot to his feet. "I think I'll go check."

While he was checking on the evening meal Cassie watched the remainder of the soap opera, experiencing a sharp pang of disappointment when she realized she wouldn't be able to see tomorrow's episode. She sincerely hoped that Eve and Josh were able to control themselves. Carolyn had enough trouble as it was.

The sound of the screen door slamming again captured her attention once more. She glanced up and saw her mother standing in the doorway, white-faced and shaken.

Cassie's blood immediately ran cold. She had seen that look on her mother's face only one other time in her life. The night Pauly had been involved in a bad tractor accident and it had been hours before they knew if he would live or die.

"Mom?" Cassie cautiously lifted her head from the pillow. "What's wrong?"

"Get Doc Lydell on the phone."

"What's wrong?" Cassie asked again blankly.

"Just get the doctor, Cassie. Quickly!"

"Dad . . . is it Dad?" She knew she should be making some sort of move to do as her mother had instructed, but some strange paralysis was keeping her imprisoned on the sofa.

A strangled sob escaped her mother as she moved across the floor and grabbed for the telephone. "Go down to the barn with your daddy, Cassie. Stay with him until I can get help."

Springing off the sofa, Cassie barely heard her mother dialing the phone as she slipped her shoes on with trembling fingers, then raced out the front door. Wylie had heard the commotion and followed on her heels out the doorway. They ran toward the barn as Cass's heart pounded in her throat. She didn't have the least idea what she would find when she got there.

What she found when she opened the door was her big, strong father, a man who had never stayed in bed a day of his life, lying on the floor beside the small calf. His eyes were closed and his face was pasty white, and Cassie's heart nearly stopped as her steps faltered in uncertainty.

Was he still breathing?

She had no way of telling, but he was lying so still and lifeless it made her grow weak with fear.

The calf lifted a wobbly head to stare at the new intruder, and then with a pitiful sound it fell weakly back down on the soft pile of hay someone had lovingly placed it on.

Hesitantly, she reached out to touch her father's shoulder. "Pop?"

Instead of the familiar, booming voice she would have once heard in response to her call, there was only the eerie sound of the wind whispering through the walls that echoed back to her.

The heat in the old barn was blistering, and combined with her nerves and recent state of health, she felt her body begin to weave with dizziness.

"Pop," she pleaded, willing him to open his eyes and look at her. But his eyes remained closed as her trembling fingers began to search for a pulse. It was several moments before she was able to locate one, but with a cry of relief she finally felt the sign of life she had been searching for at the base of his throat. It seemed very weak, but it was definitely there.

Tears were running down her cheeks now as she buried her face in her hands and wept with gratitude. He was still alive!

"Is he dead?" The sound of Wylie's shaken voice brought her momentarily back to her senses. He was staring at his father, his face an ashen gray.

"No . . . no. He's still breathing." She drew his small frame into her arms and she felt his body trembling nearly as hard as hers was.

A shaft of sunlight spread across the floor of the barn as she heard the door open once more. She raised tear-laden eyes to see Luke step into the barn, his eyes quickly assessing the scene before him.

With cool efficiency, he strode over to Uriah and knelt down. Within moments he had made a hurried examination of the older man and glanced back over at Cassie. "It's okay. He's still alive."

She nodded mutely, for once immensely thankful for his presence. "Were you here . . . ?"

"No, Neoma just called."

She glanced back to Uriah. "Is it his heart?"

Luke shook his head negatively. "I think he's had a stroke. Get me that old blanket over in the corner."

"But it's so hot. . . ."

"Do as I say, Cass," he instructed softly.

In a daze, Cassie did as she was told and seconds later Luke was making her father as comfortable as possible. "Neoma called an ambulance. It should be here in a few minutes." Luke began to speak to Uriah in loud tones, trying to elicit some sort of response.

"Mom . . . she should be here with him. . . ."

"She's still trying to locate Doc Lydell." As he spoke Neoma rushed into the barn and rushed back to her husband's side.

"Is he . . . ?"

Luke shook his head. "I haven't been able to get a response out of him, but he's hanging on, Neoma."

"Uriah . . . Uriah, please, dear God . . . answer me. . . ." Her voice broke off in a sob as she laid her head on the width of his broad chest and held him tightly. "Doc is going to meet us at the hospital, darling. . . . Hang on," she pleaded.

Luke stepped over and, in a gesture that made Cassie's heart wrench, took Wylie aside and talked to him for a few moments until she could see his trembling begin to subside. He spoke in soft, soothing tones, yet she knew he was helping the child to accept a situation that called for maturity far beyond his years.

When at last they heard the faint wail of a siren in the distance, Luke put a protective arm around the young boy's shoulders and they walked out of the barn together.

Only when her father had been placed in the ambulance and was on his way to the hospital did Cassie break down again. Neoma was riding with him, and as soon as Cassie informed the rest of the family what had happened, she would follow.

She was still in the barn, carefully folding the old, musty-smelling blanket, when Luke came looking for her.

It was a useless gesture.

The old blanket was worn out and dirty, but some-

278

how by performing the simple everyday task it made the events of the last half hour more bearable.

"Are you ready to go?" Luke's deep voice barely intruded on her state of numbness.

"Yes . . . I need to call Pauly or Newt first. They can call Rosalee and Rowena and Rachel."

"I called Newt just a few minutes ago. He said they would meet us at the hospital."

Cassie felt a tremendous sense of relief that she wouldn't have to be the one to tell them. "Thank you, Luke."

She glanced up for the first time and saw him standing there in a shaft of sunlight. The rays made his hair look like spun gold, and the blue eyes that were usually alive with combativeness had lost a great deal of their sparkle now. It wasn't hard to see that his concern for her father was as great as hers.

"Thank you," she whispered again.

"Will you let me take you to the hospital, Cass?"

"Yes. I'd appreciate that."

She walked toward the doorway, and when she was even with him she looked up and started to thank him for helping Wylie earlier, but her eyes suddenly welled over with newfound tears.

He started to speak, but then changed his mind as his arms automatically opened to her and, without the slightest hesitation, she went into them.

Never had a man's chest felt so comforting or so welcome as the dam of emotion inside her completely spilled over.

He held her close as her racking sobs dampened the front of his shirt, and she wept out her fear to him.

"What . . . if . . . he . . . dies . . . ?"   Death

was something she had never associated with her parents and she wasn't at all sure she could deal with such an unexpected turn of events.

"He'll have the best of care," Luke comforted. "We have a good hospital in Macon and Uriah's a strong man." He pried her gently away from his chest so he could see her as he spoke. "Try to look on the bright side. He's still alive, and that's something we can be thankful for."

"I know, but he looked so . . . so helpless." Her arms went around his middle and she buried her face back into his chest.

Her nearness, her vulnerability, her dependence on him at the moment made him almost heady. This was not the Cass he knew, not this warm, sweet-smelling, totally intoxicating woman. All of a sudden he found himself wondering what it would be like to fully taste the soft mouth that was always looking for a fight with him, or to look into her eyes and see desire and need instead of the usual defiance and rebellion that seemed to be there.

What would it be like to hold her body next to his, unfettered by clothing, unhampered by the sense of unspoken competition that always engulfed them? What would she do if he tried to kiss away her fears the way he longed to right now . . . ?

He pulled himself back to reality and silently chided himself for such inappropriate thoughts at a time like this.

With a reassuring pat, he gently lifted her away from him once more and smiled down at her encouragingly. "You better go do what all you women do to your faces before we go to the hospital," he prompted.

"Yes, I must look a mess," she hiccuped. "I'll only be a minute."

True to her word, five minutes later she was seated between him and Wylie and they were on their way to the hospital. For Wylie's sake they kept the conversation light and as normal as possible under the circumstances.

The entire family had gathered by the time they arrived. They were huddled in the small waiting room, apprehension and disbelief written on each face.

"I can't believe it," Rosalee cried. "He was fine this morning. Ray talked to him around nine and he didn't say a thing about feeling bad."

"Has anyone talked to Doc Lydell yet?" Cassie inquired expectantly.

"No, Mom came out a few minutes ago and said they were still running preliminary tests," Pauly said. "But it looks like a stroke."

It seemed longer than it actually was before they received any hopeful news. Late in the afternoon Dr. Lydell finally emerged to speak with the family.

"He's a lucky man," he began. "It was a stroke, but a relatively mild one."

There was an audible sigh of relief from the family.

"How is he now?" Cassie prompted.

"He's resting comfortably."

"Is Mom still with him?"

"Yes, I've allowed her to remain with him for the time being, but I want him kept extremely quiet for the next few days. Visitors will be limited," he warned. "Now why don't all of you go on home and get some rest yourselves? He'll be well taken care of and you'll be notified of any change if it becomes necessary."

"Don't you think someone should stay here with Mom," Rowena protested as the doctor disappeared back into the intensive care unit.

"I'll stay," Newt volunteered.

"And I'll relieve you," Pauly offered.

After considerable discussion concerning who would relieve whom, the family finally disbanded and went their separate ways.

Luke and Cassie decided to take Wylie to the coffee shop and feed him since it was now well past his dinnertime.

The hamburger tasted like cotton in Cassie's mouth, but she forced herself to keep up a cheerful demeanor for her brother's sake. He was taking Uriah's illness extremely hard. He barely touched his plate, choosing to spend most of the time questioning Luke about whether or not he thought his father would really be all right.

Before they left the hospital they stopped by the intensive care unit and spoke with Neoma for a few moments.

She looked drained and ten years older than she had when Cassie got up this morning, but there was a hopeful light shining in her eyes now.

"He spoke to me a while ago." She smiled. "He told me not to worry, he wasn't about to go anywhere without me." Her tears misted anew, then her brave facade crumbled as fast as it had manifested itself. "Ain't that just like him to joke about a thing like that? We've been together forty-seven years." She shook her head in wonderment. "Forty-seven years. Whatever in the world would I do without him?"

Cassie reached over to console her mother. "He'll be

fine, Mom. And he means what he says. He wouldn't think of going anywhere without you. You know that."

"Cassie, honey." Neoma took her hand. "What about you? Are you still planning on going back to New York in the morning?"

She hadn't thought about that. In the midst of all the confusion, leaving for New York had been the last thing on her mind. "No, I wouldn't dream of going back with Dad still in the hospital," she assured her.

"Well, I suppose it would be all right." Neoma tried to sound encouraging, but Cassie could still hear indecision in her voice. "Doc says Dad should be just fine. . . ."

"I know, and I'm sure he will be, but I'd just feel better if I stayed here until he gets out of the hospital."

"But what about your job?"

"I have a very understanding boss," she promised. "I'll stay and take care of Wylie while you nurse Pop back to health."

"Your sisters could do that, honey. We don't want to put any hardships on you."

"Mom, I wouldn't dream of doing anything else," she scolded gently. "Now stop worrying, okay?"

"You're a good girl, Cassie, and I appreciate your thoughtfulness. Doc Lydell said he could arrange a room for me here at the hospital so I can stay close to your dad. I don't expect I'll be home much in the next couple of weeks." She turned to bestow a big bear hug on her youngest son. "Now you behave yourself and mind what Cassie says, you hear?"

Wylie hung his head sadly. "I will."

"And see that you don't get behind with your chores."

"I won't."

"Luke." Neoma took his hand, her eyes shining with love for him too. "Take care of my children while I'm gone."

"I will, Neoma. You take care of Uriah."

"Oh, I will. I can promise you that."

The mood was lighter on the ride home, although Wylie seemed to be lost in a world of his own. In an effort to cheer him up, Luke stopped by the local Dairy Queen and bought them all chocolate cones, but Wylie ate only half of his. When they arrived back at the farm he went directly into the house without a word.

"You think he's all right?" Cassie asked Luke as she fell in step with him. He had told her earlier he needed to check the calf again before he went home.

"He'll be fine. It just sort of threw him for a loop. When you're nine years old you never think about losing one of your parents," Luke pointed out as he lit one of the cheroots he was fond of smoking.

"You don't think much about that when you're thirty," Cassie confessed.

"No, I suppose you wouldn't." The almost wistful way he said it reminded her that Luke had never experienced even having his own set of parents to be concerned about. Rumor had it that they had left him with his grandmother when he was barely old enough to crawl and just never returned to claim him.

"I guess you were too young to remember your parents?" As a rule, Cassie would never have pried into his personal life, but somehow the last few hours had drawn them closer to each other.

"The only thing I remember about them is the fact that they ran off and left me." The tone of his voice stated emphatically he was still very bitter about that. "That was a hell of a thing to do to a kid."

"But your grandmother loved you very much," Cassie said tenderly, trying to ease the pain she had unintentionally brought on.

"Yes, she did. She was a good woman, but it still wasn't like having a dad to play ball with or a mother who fixed pot roast every Sunday."

Once more she fought the urge to take him by the arm and make him stop walking long enough to tell him that it didn't matter.

They had reached the barn by now and suddenly Cassie felt apprehensive. The day had been hard enough on her emotions, and if the little calf that Uriah had fought so hard for had died while they had been at the hospital, she honestly didn't know if she could stand it.

"Luke." Her footsteps faltered and she paused.

"What?" He paused, too, and turned to look at her.

"I'm . . . I'm afraid."

"Afraid? Of what?"

"I'm afraid . . . the calf might have . . . you know."

In the soft rays of the moonlight she saw his tired features soften with realization of her newest fear and it suddenly occurred to her he must be near exhaustion. He had been out late the night before taking her to Macon, then back up bright and early this morning to check on the calf before he went on with his other work.

"Yes, that's possible," he said carefully. He flipped the cigar out into the darkness and there was a shower of red sparks as it hit the ground.

"Do you think it . . . has?"

"I don't know, but if it has it's just one of those things that happens in life, Cass. We've worked very hard to save it, but if it wasn't meant to be, then it just wasn't meant to be."

"I know. It just doesn't seem right . . . not with Dad getting sick too."

"You're right. Life stinks at times." He smiled at her encouragingly. "So, you learn to hold your nose and go on."

She smiled at him timidly. "Maybe you'll have to teach me how."

"Simple." He reached out and pinched her nose together. "Just like that. Then tell the world to get off your back."

They both laughed delightedly.

"So, scaredy-cat, what do you think? Think we're brave enough to go take a look?"

She wasn't brave. Not in the least, but for some reason she didn't want him to have to go in there alone and face whatever lay beyond the door.

"Yes."

He started to push the door open and her hand reached up and stopped him. "Wait."

She was so near him now she could smell his after-shave, and her pulse gave a tiny flutter. She could never remember a time she was so acutely aware of a man. Her hand dropped away hesitantly, confused by these new feelings she was having toward him. "Okay, I think I'm ready now."

For a moment so brief that later Cassie would have to remind herself it did occur, their eyes met and held in the moonlight. They were so close it would have required little or no movement on his part to lean over and kiss her.

And, strangely enough, that was exactly what she wanted him to do.

His gaze ran over her moon-drenched features and he felt his breathing quicken, along with an unexpected ache growing inside of him. Lord, she was beautiful. Even after the day she had spent, she looked fresh and bright-eyed. Bright-eyed and bushy-tailed. That's how his grandmother would have stated it. How many men had there been in her life who had looked at her in the moonlight like this, then gone on to claim her lips the way he wanted to right now?

A soft breeze had kicked up and tossed her hair about her head appealingly. He didn't necessarily like the way she was wearing her hair nowadays. It was too chic for his taste, but he couldn't deny that it was still beautiful. He preferred the way she wore it in high school. She used to pull it back in a ponytail or just let if fall loose around her shoulders in a soft halo. He caught the faint scent of the floral shampoo she used and it brought to mind once more how she had allowed him to hold her in his arms earlier today. He would never have thought, not in a million years, he would ever have the privilege of holding her in his arms, however innocent it might have been.

"Luke?" Her voice snapped him out of his daydreaming and he quickly let his eyes drop away from hers.

"You ready?" he asked.

"Yes."

He pushed the door open and stepped inside. It was so quiet and so dark. She eased over closer to him.

"I don't hear any breathing," she whispered.

He took her hand supportively. "There's a light around here somewhere."

"Over by the grain bin," she instructed.

He started to edge in that direction and she moved with him. "I can get it," he offered.

"I think I'll come with you . . . if you don't mind." Her hand clasped his tighter.

They carefully made their way across the room in the darkness. "I hope no one's left a pitchfork lying around," Luke noted. The pain in his lower half was excruciating enough.

When they reached the wall where the light switch was located, he fumbled around and quickly found it. "You ready?"

She squeezed his hand harder and clamped her eyes tightly shut. "Go ahead."

Light flooded the old barn now as she heard Luke's surprised, "Well, I'll be . . . will you look at that!"

Her eyes popped open and she could hardly believe what she saw. Standing in the middle of the room on decidedly wobbly legs was the small calf, just looking at them.

"Wha . . . look at her! What's she doing?"

"Looking at us." Luke grinned.

The calf bellowed, not a good strong one, but a definite improvement over what she had been doing.

288

Luke walked over and knelt down beside it, his grin growing paternal. "Hey, little one. You had us worried there for a while."

The calf bellowed again, a little stronger this time as she nuzzled a shaky head in Luke's large hand. Luke glanced up at Cassie and his grin widened. "I think she might be hungry."

There was a great deal of scurrying around as they located a bottle and Cassie ran to the house to warm milk. With great joy they watched as the calf took the first substantial nourishment it had had in weeks.

Later, as they walked back to the house, Cassie was still on cloud nine. "She beat the odds, didn't she? She didn't have a chance and she came through with flying colors. Can you believe that! I can't wait to tell Dad."

Luke had to grin at her enthusiasm. There was once a time when Cassie wouldn't have taken any special interest in the outcome of a small, sick calf.

"Yes, she's a fighter, all right."

"You must love your work," she praised. "And you're so good at it!"

Praises for Luke Travers from Cassie McCason. What other wondrous miracles could this magical night possibly hold?

"Thanks, but the credit belongs to a higher source," he acknowledged. They had reached the back door now and she paused to say good night. "I don't think I'll be able to sleep at all," she sighed. "Too many things have happened today."

"Are you feeling better?" he asked.

"Gosh, I've been so busy I've forgotten all about me." She swallowed, then smiled at him. "I think I'll be fine."

"Well, take a hot bath and don't forget to take your medicine," he cautioned. "You're far from well, yet."

"Oh, Luke," she sighed again and gazed up at him, and once more he felt the wall of defense he had tried to build around himself crumbling. "That little calf has restored my faith in miracles."

He smiled down at her. "I'm glad."

"Against all odds. She did it against all odds. Doesn't that make you just want to shout?"

Actually, it made him want to kiss her, but he had to admit that would be against all odds, and it would probably take more than a mere miracle to tip the scales in his favor.

"Yeah, it's real nice," he said softly. "Real nice."

CHAPTER SEVEN

By the grace of God, Uriah's health began slowly to improve. Cassie's assumption that she had an understanding boss proved to be accurate. Rand Creble had told her to take as much time as she needed and return to work only after she was satisfied she was no longer needed in Rueter Flats.

Dr. Lydell was pleased with Uriah's recovery and predicted that he would be back home in no time at all.

Wylie seemed to be the only one who wasn't taking the illness in stride. The change of schedule had thrown him for a loop. He was used to large meals on the table three times a day, Neoma humming around the house while Uriah was tending the stock. Although Cassie tried to maintain the same homey atmosphere, it just wasn't the same.

She could see Wylie's confusion growing with each new day.

As bad as she hated to admit it, Luke had been the only stabilizing force during this crisis. Not only for Wylie, but in a strange sort of way he had made the days easier for her.

Her brothers came by to help feed the stock and to

assist in the general everyday running of the farm. Rosalee and Rowena and Rachel did what they could to help, but their own families demanded the majority of their time, so the burden of keeping affairs running smoothly still fell squarely on her shoulders. Running a farming household in Rueter Flats was a far cry from working in a large advertising firm in New York, but it seemed like any time a major crisis popped up Luke was somewhere nearby to prevent it from turning into a complete calamity.

But to be honest, things could have been worse.

There had even been days when she had found herself enjoying the simple pleasures of country life. She loved to wake up to the sounds of the birds chirping early in the morning and the way the old rooster crowed her awake long before she would normally be rising in New York. She developed a habit of taking her coffee and sitting out on the porch to watch the sunrise each new day. It was a beautiful, almost awesome sight the way that big old fiery orange ball came sliding slowly out of the eastern sky. Although the day would usually be blistering hot, the early hours of the morning were delightful.

She was in the kitchen washing the breakfast dishes about a week after Uriah's stroke. Neoma had kept a constant vigil at his bedside, coming home only long enough to gather up clean clothing and see how things were going. Between daily telephone calls from Rosalee, Rowena, and Rachel, Cassie found it hard to keep up with all her chores. This morning she had been determined to get an earlier start than usual, before the telephone started ringing.

While she worked she had the radio playing and

several times she paused, aghast at times, to listen more closely to the commercials she was hearing.

True, she shouldn't be surprised at the amateurish, hickish way they went about advertising their local products, but still the creative side of her cringed when she heard such slogans as "Buy Grabe's Soap and Stop Your Mopes!" or the one advertising a new figure salon over in Macon that really sent her into fits: "Fatty Patty, Plump and Round, Join Slenderella for Just Pennies a Pound! Take That Fat Off Day by Day, Then the Men Will Start to Say, Hey!" Then they would go into a peppy little singing jingle giving the telephone and address of the new salon.

It would be amusing if it wasn't so pitiful.

If she had been a "Fatty Patty," she would die before she joined an establishment that called the whole town's attention to her problem.

What this area needed was a good advertising agency, she decided absently as she went about her dusting.

She glanced up a few minutes later as she heard a truck pull into the yard. Thinking that it was Pauly coming to feed the cattle, she went to the back door to meet him.

But it was Luke who got out and waved at her. She found herself smiling ear to ear and waving back at him. Darn, now she wished she had taken more time with her appearance this morning. She had showered and put on her regular attire of shorts and a T-shirt, but completely skipped the makeup routine.

"Hi! What's up?" she called.

"Pauly called and said one of the mares isn't acting right this morning. I'm going to check her," he called.

"Want some coffee first?"

"No, thanks. I'd love a cup but I can't spare the time."

"Oh, okay." She watched him walk to the barn, feeling a little let down that he couldn't visit for a while. Neoma had been right when she said he had changed. He had. A full 180-degree angle.

Actually, he was quite tolerable now.

She went back to her work but changed her mind a few moments later and went in and put on makeup, then dabbed a couple of drops of perfume behind her ear. A few minutes later she started out the back door with two cups of coffee in her hand.

Luke was in the barnyard with the mare, just completing his examination when she walked up.

"Hello there," she greeted again.

He glanced up, then quickly lowered his eyes back to the animal. Damn! Those shorts and that tight T-shirt shot his blood pressure up at least twenty degrees. "Hi."

"I thought since you didn't have time to come to the house, I'd bring your coffee out here." She smiled prettily and extended one of the cups to him. "Two teaspoons of sugar and a smidgen of cream. Right?"

"Right. Thanks." He stood up carefully, trying to ignore the way the T-shirt hugged her small breasts. But they weren't too small . . . actually just the right size . . . for him.

"What's the matter with it?"

"Nothing," he said absently, his gaze involuntarily going back to the tantalizing sight straining beneath the soft fabric. "They look great to me."

"Great? I thought it was acting strange."

He suddenly realized he was thinking about an entirely different subject. "Oh . . . the mare. Uh . . . I'm not sure yet."

She cocked her head and smiled at him puzzlingly. "What did you think I was talking about?"

"I'm sorry. I'm afraid my mind was wandering," he apologized, and she could have sworn he blushed, although it was hard to tell beneath his dark tan. He took a sip of his coffee, then grinned at her lamely.

"I have some coffee cake in the house if you're hungry," she tempted.

"Sorry, but I really can't today," he apologized again, then handed her back the cup. "I've got a couple of more calls to make, then I have to run out to the Pixley farm and pick up a piano for Reverend Copley."

"Oh, yes. Mom said Louella died and left her piano to the church."

"Yes. I told the Reverend I'd go pick it up for him today."

"Gosh, I wonder how Morgan's getting along by himself," Cassie mused. The Pixleys were an elderly couple who had no children and Louella had been the center of Morgan's life for nearly seventy years.

"I think he's pretty lonely." Luke had turned his attention back to the horse while they talked. "I try to stop by and visit with him a couple of times a week."

"That's awfully nice of you. I'll bet he appreciates the company."

"He seems to."

"I should make time to go by and visit with Morgan before I leave. Louella used to be my Sunday-school teacher," Cassie recalled fondly. "We used to have

295

wiener roasts and hayrides out at the Pixley farm when I was growing up."

Luke glanced up from his work. "I know. I was there at most of them."

"Oh, well sure you were," she said apologetically. How could she have forgotten? He used to torment her to death during those hayrides, stuffing hay down the back of her blouse and telling the most off-colored jokes he and his buddies could come up with behind the preacher's back.

She studied him more closely as he reached into his bag and prepared to give the horse an injection. That Luke Travers certainly grew up. Now he was a very thoughtful . . . incredibly fascinating man.

Why hadn't he married? If rumors were true, he could have had his pick of the available women he knew. An uncomfortable feeling stirred in her stomach at the thought of Marilyn. How serious was he about her? He had never mentioned her name except for the night she had brought up the subject on the way home from Macon.

Suddenly the memory of something warm and sweet touching her mouth that night after he brought her home from the hospital and carried her to her bed rushed back to her. Goose bumps welled up unexpectedly as she recalled the musky, exciting taste. The after-shave Luke wore smelled exactly like that memory had tasted. But it was ludicrous to think he would have kissed her.

For as long as they had known each other, up until the day Uriah had gotten sick, he had acted as if he couldn't tolerate her, let alone want to kiss her. Perhaps it was only the high fever she had that night that had made her imagination run away with her.

Her eyes played across the broad expanse of his back as he knelt down beside the animal and spoke to it in soothing tones. His shirt could not conceal the ripple of heavily corded muscles as he ran his hands consolingly over the mare, all the while talking to it as if it understood what he was trying to do. He was such a strong yet gentle man, and he spoke with such tenderness to the edgy mare that it quieted down immediately at his command.

What would Luke Travers be like when he made love to a woman? Would he still exhibit that same tenderness and sensitivity he was showing now or would his passion be as intense and as powerful as his magnificent body seemed to suggest?

The mere thought turned her knees to water.

"You doing anything special this afternoon?" she heard him ask while she was still thinking things she shouldn't be. It wouldn't do at all for her to suddenly find Luke attractive . . . in that sort of way. If they had been worlds apart as children, they were light-years apart now. She knew without even asking that he was content with his life here in Rueter Flats, while she on the other hand would never dream of leaving New York and moving back home. Yes, a romantic relationship between them would be highly improbable.

"Beg your pardon?" She hurriedly brought herself back to reality, even though her breathing had suddenly picked up its tempo.

Luke straightened up from his kneeling position and began to remove the rubber gloves he had put on earlier. "I asked if you were doing anything in particular this afternoon."

"No, nothing in particular. Why?"

He had been debating for the last five minutes whether or not to ask her if she would like to go with him to the Pixley farm, but he had finally come to the conclusion that all she could say was no, and he was fully prepared for that event. "I thought you might like to ride over to Morgan's with me when I go to pick up the piano." He turned back to the horse and shut his eyes, waiting for the refusal—or explosion, whichever came first.

She didn't have to be asked twice. "Yes, I'd like that."

"You would? Well, that's great." His shoulders went limp with relief. "I'll pick you up a little after noon," he offered, trying to keep the elation from spilling over in his voice.

"I'll be ready."

Around eleven Cassie found herself heading for the shower again. It was the second time this morning she had bathed, but she wanted to look nice for Morgan.

When Luke came to pick her up at noon, she looked prettier than a field of daisies. "You didn't need to dress up," he told her as he held the screen door open. The scent of her perfume drifted tantalizingly up to him as she ducked under his arm and walked out. But she had noticed he had showered and changed too.

"I didn't. I just thought a skirt and blouse would be cooler," she explained. The blue cotton peasant skirt and matching blouse were casual enough for any occasion. The blouse was worn off the shoulders and displayed enough creamy skin to quickly assure Luke that he was going to be perfectly miserable for the rest of the afternoon.

He helped her into his truck and then took his place behind the wheel. The cool air enveloped the cab as they drove out of the barnyard and headed north on the highway.

"What's Wylie up to today?"

"He's playing with the Edwards boy. They've been building some sort of a tree house all morning."

"Is he doing any better?"

Cassie sighed. "I don't know what's bothering him. He knows Dad is improving every day, yet he's been acting so strange."

"I've been meaning to take him fishing, but I've been tied up lately. I'll try to do it in the next few days."

"That would be nice."

Luke glanced over at her and grinned, the same devilish little grin he used to distress her with years before. "If you're a good girl, we might ask you to come along with us."

"I'm always good," she teased.

And he wouldn't have touched that line with a ten-foot pole.

The afternoon turned out to be one of the most pleasant Cass had spent in ages. Morgan was beside himself with joy when he learned he would have company for the afternoon. He made a huge pitcher of fresh lemonade and they sat their lawn chairs out under a large oak tree and patiently listened to him reminisce about his life with Louella.

At times his eyes would mist with unshed tears, then before they knew it he would be back to relaying some happy occurrence that would return a smile to his wrinkled old face.

The late afternoon shadows were growing lengthy across the lawn when Luke finally got up and folded his chair. "We hate to leave, Morgan, but Cass needs to be getting back home. Wylie will be wondering where she is."

The old man immediately got up also and folded his chair too. "I understand. I'll just call my neighbor to come help you load the piano."

Sawyer Middleton came driving up in his long black Cadillac twenty minutes after Morgan made the call.

Sawyer was in his fifties, pudgy, and always looked like someone had thrown him in a sack, shaken him up, then dumped him back out again.

"Luke, how are you, boy?" he greeted as he wallowed the big nasty-looking stogie he always smoked around in his mouth. Sawyer's family owned the majority of Rueter Flats, and their flamboyant life-style sometimes rubbed the citizens of the town the wrong way, but the Middletons were good about looking out for the best interests of their town.

Luke stepped over to shake Sawyer's beefy hand. "How's it going, Sawyer?"

"Fine as frog hairs." He beamed. His attention was instantly diverted to Cassie. "Lord almighty. Ain't you turned into a looker. The big city sure does look good on you, honey."

Cassie blushed at the blunt way Sawyer had of stating what he was thinking. "Why, thank you, Sawyer."

"Heard you're working in some big advertising agency up there in New York. Ya like it?"

"I love it," Cassie confessed.

"Hear you're doing right well too. Got yourself another big promotion, did you?"

"She sure did," Morgan chimed in. "We got us a right smart little gal here, Sawyer."

"Well, it's a pity she likes it so well up there," he sighed as he took his lighter out of his pocket and tried to reignite his cigar. Cassie studied the large diamond ring that was wedged tightly on his pinky. It must have cost him a mint. A huge puff of blue smoke boiled around his head as he continued, "When I heard you was back I kinda hoped you might be talked into opening up your own agency."

Cassie looked at him blankly. "In New York?"

"No, not in New York," he scoffed. "Right here in Rueter Flats."

"An advertising agency here in Rueter Flats!" Cassie burst into laughter. "Why, I wouldn't make enough money to buy corn flakes."

From the corner of her eye she saw a sudden, annoyed scowl cross Luke's face.

"Well, maybe not here in Rueter Flats," Sawyer retracted thoughtfully, "but Macon sure is big enough to accommodate such an agency. Why, folks around here have to go clear into Houston to get a good agency to represent them. Anything closer stinks."

Cassie would have to agree with him on that point. The local advertising she had heard on radio and television did indeed reek of inexperience.

"I think you're wasting your time, Sawyer," Luke stated quietly. "I don't think you could get her back to Rueter Flats with a whip and a chair."

Cassie shot him an offended look.

"Likes it that well up there, huh? Well"—he

shrugged his shoulders good-naturedly—"if you ever change your mind, Cass, let me know. I'll sure give you all of the Middletons' business."

Cassie's ears picked up. All of the Middletons' business. Mercy, that would practically support a small agency. And in a grand style too.

"Well, let's get this piano loaded." Sawyer grinned. "I got me a date with Estelle Mooney tonight." He wiggled his brows playfully at Luke and Morgan. "Oo-la-la. I'm tryin' to get her to marry me."

Cassie shook her head, laughing again. Sawyer had been married at least five times but he was apparently not at all discouraged by his deplorable record.

As Luke and the neighbor carried the old, upright piano out of the house and loaded it on the truck, Cassie saw Morgan quickly turn away and walk out behind the house to be alone.

She wanted to go to him and put her arms around him, to comfort him, but how would you comfort someone who had lost a part of themselves? The piano apparently represented just another part of Louella he was losing.

By the time they had it loaded, Morgan came back around the house to see them off. But Cassie noticed he never once looked in the back of the truck.

"Stop by and see me anytime you're in the neighborhood," he invited. "I've always got some fresh lemons on hand." His eyes unexpectedly misted again. "Louella always made sure we had lemons for folks that come by to see us."

Cassie reached over and hugged his neck lovingly. "I'll come and visit again before I leave."

302

"I'd like that," he said. "Tell Uriah I'm thinkin' about him."

"I will."

"It was real good seein' you again, Cass." Sawyer pulled out a large snowy handkerchief from his pocket and wiped at his heavily perspiring brow.

"It was nice to see you, Sawyer."

"Listen." He replaced the handkerchief in his pocket and leaned a little closer. "Don't dismiss that idea we were talkin' about earlier too quickly. You give it some thought. You hear?"

"I hear." She smiled.

Morgan turned and slowly made his way back into the house as Sawyer went to his car and Luke and Cassie got back into the truck.

"I'm not sure it's a good idea to let that piano ride like that. It might be wise to tie a rope around it."

Cassie leaned up in the seat and peered out the back window. "It looks like it's jammed in there pretty tight to me."

"It barely fit," Luke acknowledged.

"Then it should stay there without any trouble."

"I don't know. . . ." Luke eyed the situation carefully, then reached down and started the engine. "The thing probably weighs a ton. It should be all right. I'll take it easy."

They bumped along the gravel roads carefully and the old piano didn't budge an inch. When they reached the highway Luke felt confident enough to begin to pick up speed.

If the piano hadn't moved on the gravel roads, it sure wasn't going to move on the paved ones.

They were riding along, talking and thoroughly enjoying each other's company, and Luke was thinking more about the low cut of Cassie's blouse than he was the church's new piano.

By the time he went to make the sharp turn onto the highway leading home, they were fairly well flying low.

Luke was trying to light a cigar to take his mind off the scenery when the truck whizzed around the corner and all of a sudden there was the most horrifying clamor coming from the back of the truck. Sort of a Ping! Ping! Bong! Bong! Bong!

It sounded as if someone was trying to play the piano with a sledgehammer.

Frozen in their seats, Cassie cautiously turned her head to meet Luke's worried frown. Neither one of them had the nerve to look in the back of the truck.

"What was that?" she whispered.

"I don't know."

"It sounded like the piano fell out of the back of the truck," she said needlessly.

"It couldn't have!"

The truck slowed to a crawl and they both hazarded a glance at the bed of the pickup at the same time.

"It's gone," she announced grimly.

"Oh, hell."

"Luke." She was peering out the side of her window now, her hand clamped over her mouth in revulsion. "I think I see it. . . ."

He leaned over and his distraught eyes followed in the direction she was pointing. The piano was lying in pieces at the bottom of a culvert.

"Son of a . . . gun! What do we do now?"

"We'll have to pick up what's left of it and try to

explain what happened to Reverend Copley," she reasoned.

"How?"

"I don't know, but we can't leave it lying out there."

It took them well over an hour to gather up the remains of the piano. As Luke slid the last of the pieces into the truck he peered at her worriedly. "How are we ever going to tell him what happened?"

He could kick himself for not having his mind on his business. If he had watched the piano half as much as he had watched her gaping blouse, this would have never happened!

"The church will never get over this," he moaned. "Now I'll have to go out and buy them a new piano and I don't know a thing about buying pianos and—"

"Ooohhh. We'll just explain that it was an accident," she consoled as she stepped over to give him a reassuring hug. She could see he really felt bad about the loss and she didn't know anything else to do.

"I don't know, Cass. Everyone in the congregation was looking forward to having that piano," Luke fretted as his arms tightened around her possessively to return the embrace. "And what's Morgan going to say when he finds out what I did to Louella's piano?"

"He'll understand," she assured again, but she had been wondering the same thing.

She patted him on his back consolingly.

He patted her on her rear reassuringly.

"We'll tell him together," she promised. "It'll be just like getting up the nerve to go into the barn the night the little calf was so sick. You remember? Neither one of us had the nerve to go alone, but together we made it and everything turned out all right. And that's exactly how this will be."

But she felt considerably less brave as they pulled into the churchyard a half an hour later and Reverend Copley ran out to meet them with a grin the size of Texas on his face.

He peered anxiously into the back of the truck and the grin slowly began to fade as he viewed the mangled keyboard hanging out of the tailgate. "My word . . . what happened?"

Luke took a deep breath and pushed the truck door open reluctantly. "We better start looking for a new piano tomorrow," he whispered under his breath to Cassie. "But we'll make sure they deliver it."

As if the piano incident wasn't upsetting enough, when they arrived back at the McCason farm Wylie was nowhere to be found.

"I can't understand it," Cassie complained. "He hasn't touched the lunch I left, either."

"Maybe he's still over at the Edwards'," Luke suggested.

"He shouldn't be. I told him to be home by supper and it's way past that time." She picked up the phone and dialed the neighbor's number. Moments later she replaced the receiver, a frown forming on her face. "They said they can't find Davy, either."

Luke took off his hat and ran his fingers through his hair wearily. "They've probably lost all track of time. They'll be getting hungry before long."

"Do you think so?"

He replaced his hat and smiled at her. "I know so.

306

I'll go down and check the mare and I'll lay you odds he'll show up by the time I get back."

But Wylie had still not returned when Luke came back from the barn. By now it was growing dark and a dark cloud bank was moving in from the north.

"Luke, I'm worried. He's never stayed out this late before and it looks like a storm's coming up."

"Did you call the Edwards again?"

"Yes, and they're worried too. What shall we do?"

Luke sighed. "Let's go look for him."

"Do you have time?"

He glanced at his watch. "Can I use your phone?"

"Sure, go ahead." She walked over to the sink and made a pretense of getting a glass of water, wondering who he was going to call.

He didn't use the directory, but quickly dialed the set of digits by heart. "Hi," he said when the phone was answered on the other end. He leaned casually against the wall as he talked. "I'm afraid I'm not going to be able to make it tonight.

"No, I'm over at the McCason place. Wylie seems to have disappeared and I'm going to help Cass look for him."

Cassie would have given fifty dollars to know who he was talking to!

"Sounds good. Maybe tomorrow night.

"Yeah, I'll get in touch with you later." He placed the receiver back on the hook and glanced over at her. "You might as well ride over to my house with me. I have to pick up a few things, then we can leave from there."

"What if Wylie should show up here?"

"Leave him a note and tell him we're looking for him. Tell him to call my house as soon as he gets in."

Cassie hurriedly wrote the note and called the Edwards to inform them of her plans and asked if they had any suggestions where they should begin their search.

"Surely he's just lost all track of time." She tried to bolster her sagging spirits.

"I'm sure it's that or something equally simple," Luke agreed. He reached in his pocket for a cheroot.

"You smoke too much. It's bad for your health," she reminded.

"Don't start nagging me. I'm trying to be nice to you."

"I'm not nagging you. I'm only pointing out a well-known fact that smoking is harmful to your health."

"I know."

As they walked out the back door Cassie glanced over at him, her stomach doing that funny little flip-flop at his nearness.

"I hope this doesn't spoil your evening."

"It won't."

"The person on the phone didn't mind?"

"Didn't seem to." He struck a match and lit the cigar.

Oooooo! He could be so irritatingly tight-lipped at times.

"She wasn't upset?" Cassie tried a sneakier approach.

Luke paused, his blue eyes narrowing. "Did I say it was a she?"

"No . . . no. I just assumed . . ."

They started walking again.

"Then she didn't mind?"

"No, he didn't."

She was ashamed of herself, but she couldn't keep her face from brightening. "He . . . didn't?"

"That's right. He. I was supposed to have a beer with a couple of buddies tonight." He finally glanced down at her and she could see a faint smile tugging at the corners of his mouth now. "Okay?"

"Oh, okay." She shrugged indifferently. "I mean it doesn't really matter who it was, I just wanted to make sure I wasn't imposing upon your evening."

"Rest assured, you aren't."

She didn't know how "assured" she was by the whole matter, but she had to admit it did make her feel a lot better just knowing that he hadn't had a date with Marilyn.

CHAPTER EIGHT

The storm moved in while they were en route to Luke's house. He lived only a few miles down the road from the McCason farm, but by the time they had pulled into his drive the rain was pelting down on the windshield in big fat droplets.

"We'd better make a run for it," he warned.

They had barely reached the porch when the heavens opened up in a deluge and the wind and lightning began in earnest.

"I hope Wylie has taken cover," Cassie shouted above the wind.

"Give the kid a break, Cass. Of course he's taken cover. He's got a brain."

Luke opened the door and let her into the living room just as his phone started ringing. In three long strides he jerked up the receiver and barked, "Dr. Travers."

That was the first time Cassie had ever heard him refer to himself as a doctor and a thrill of pride shot through her.

"Yeah, Neoma." He shot Cassie a worried grimace.

"Is that Mom?" Cassie rushed over beside him.

"Don't tell her about Wylie yet. She'll only worry," she cautioned in a hushed whisper.

"Yeah, we've been looking for him."

Neoma said something and Luke's brow raised. "With you? How did he get over there?"

"Is he with her?" Cassie gasped.

"Wait a minute, Cassie's about to blow a fuse." Luke handed the phone to her and stepped back.

"Mom? Is Wylie there in Macon with you?"

"Yes, he and the Edwards boy decided to come and visit Uriah today. They hitched a ride in the back of a milk truck."

"Oh, good grief!" Cassie sank down on a chair and breathed a sigh of relief. "I bet you think I'm some baby-sitter to let that happen."

"I've already told him it was a foolish thing to do, but he seems to be taking his father's illness so hard, maybe it's best he spend a little time over here with him."

"I'll drive over and get him right now," Cassie promised.

"No, don't do that. It's getting late and I think it will do him good to spend some time with his daddy. I think he'll see that Uriah's really going to be fine and then he'll feel a whole lot better about the situation."

"But where will the boys sleep?"

"I'll make special arrangements with the hospital to let them sleep in my room tonight, then you can come over tomorrow and get them. Uriah wants to see you, anyway."

"Is he feeling better?"

"Much. The doctor thinks he'll be able to come home in another few days."

"Oh, that's wonderful . . . but, Mom, how did you know I was over here?"

"I called home first and when I didn't get an answer, I called the Edwards. They told me you and Luke were going to go out hunting for the boys so I thought to try his place."

"Well, I'm sorry I didn't watch Wylie closer." She went on to explain how she had spent her day and the disastrous incident with Louella Pixley's piano.

"Oh, how terrible," Neoma sympathized. "We needed that piano for our Sunday-school class."

"Luke's going to buy the church a brand-new one," she consoled. "Reverend Copley is elated."

When she hung up the phone it had been decided that she would drive to Macon early the next morning and retrieve the adventurous boys.

"Well at least he made it all right," Cassie said thankfully. She raised her eyes to meet Luke's and she suddenly felt uneasy. She had felt his gaze studying her as she had spoken with her mother and he was still staring at her with a strange light in his eyes, even now. She remembered the embrace they had shared earlier and she wondered if he was thinking about the same thing.

Granted, it had been at the intersection of a busy highway, with semitrucks and cars whizzing around them, but the impact was no less devastating than if they had been in a candlelit room with soft music.

Her gaze shyly dropped away from his and she gave a small nervous laugh as she smoothed her hand across her hair. "Well. All this trouble for nothing. As you said, he was perfectly all right." She hazarded a quick glance at him again. "If you hurry, you can take

312

me back home and still keep your date to have that beer with your friends this evening," she offered.

"No," he said easily. "I'm bushed. I'll catch them another time. If you're not in any hurry, I'll just go and clean up."

"No, I'm not in any hurry," she agreed quickly. "With Wylie gone, I don't have a thing to do until tomorrow morning."

She had no idea why she was so relieved he hadn't taken her up on her suggestion to keep his date, but strangely she was.

"Make yourself at home. I won't be long."

While he was gone Cassie entertained herself by exploring the house. It was an old two-story farmhouse, but it had been well taken care of.

The downstairs had a large living area, a small den, a massive kitchen that was furnished with all modern appliances, and a large utility room with a commode and lavatory.

The living-room furniture was masculine, yet in extremely good taste. The room was decorated in shades of oatmeal and browns with splashes of navy blue throughout for accent. Two plaid love seats sat facing each other in front of a stone fireplace, with a massive round table made of glass sitting between them.

She surmised the bedrooms would be up the steep, carpeted staircase because she could hear the shower running somewhere overhead.

The den was all his. Comfortable mahogany and leather furniture, a beautiful oak desk, and rows upon rows of books in the shelves lining both walls told her this was the room Luke spent most of his time in. There was a small lamp burning on the desk, illuminating the pile of assorted papers he had strewn about. But otherwise the entire house was immaculate and orderly.

He came down the stairs while she was sitting on one of the love seats thumbing through a magazine.

He was still combing his hair as he entered the living room.

"My, that didn't take long," she complimented as she glanced up at him. The fresh smell of soap and after-shave drifted about enticingly and it made her slightly heady as she tried to focus her attention back on the article she had been reading.

Why was he affecting her this way? He was just a man, she reminded herself. A very forbidden man, because if she continued to let herself keep dwelling on his good looks or the size of his biceps in that short-sleeve shirt he was wearing . . . or the attractive way his hair was styled . . . or that devastating masculine after-shave he wore . . . well, it wouldn't be long before she would be entertaining some sort of idiotic, harebrained idea that they might . . . well, that would be totally ridiculous!

She was going back to New York in a few days, and by the time she got around to visiting Rueter Flats again, Luke would probably be married to Marilyn.

She threw her magazine down angrily.

Luke's gaze shot over to her expectantly as he slid the comb into the back pocket of his clean denims. "What's the matter?"

"Nothing." She stood up and smoothed her skirt nervously. "Are you ready to take me home?"

"No. Actually, I was thinking about making us an omelet," he said, grinning. He had no idea what had gotten her dander up, but suddenly she seemed to be on the defensive with him again. "How about it?"

"That isn't necessary," she refused crisply. "I can eat something when I get home."

"I can't see why you would want to do that when I've just offered to make your dinner," he chided.

Their eyes met stubbornly for a few moments and she felt herself weakening. She wanted to stay. She wanted to be with him—but she didn't want to be with him. Not when he was making her feel so confused, so uncertain. But time was growing short. Soon she would be gone.

"Oh, all right," she finally relented, mentally shaking herself for being so asinine about this. Luke had been the perfect gentleman all day and never once had he made any sort of pass at her. Her imagination or guilt for thinking such preposterous thoughts was her problem, not his.

She trailed along behind him, complaining to herself about the way his denims clinched his bottom so suggestively. No wonder the women in Rueter Flats drooled over him! His pants not only squeezed his bottom, but they were indecently tight in the front too. She had noticed that the minute he walked into the room.

Sure, he was a prize specimen of manhood. But did he have to advertise it so blatantly?

All of a sudden he stopped and she ran into the back of him. "Oh . . . I'm sorry," she mumbled.

"Did you say something?"

Oh, no, she hoped she hadn't been thinking out loud. "No." She grinned at him guiltily. "I didn't say anything."

315

They walked into the kitchen and he flipped on the lights. There was an island bar in the center of the room with various copper cookware hanging above it. Reaching for a large skillet, he placed it on the stove and busied himself dragging the ingredients for the omelets out of the refrigerator.

At his suggestion, she made the toast and brewed a pot of fresh coffee. The earlier tension began to dissolve as they sat down at the bar and ate their dinner, relaxing for the first time that day.

"I wonder if it's still raining?" she asked later as they leisurely sipped coffee in the den.

Luke was sitting at his desk, preparing to light an after-dinner cigar. "It was the last time I looked out."

She could see brief flashes of lightning illuminate the window behind his back as he began absently to sort through the day's mail. The fragrant smell of his cigar filled the room pleasantly and a feeling of lethargy stole over her. It felt uncommonly good to sit here with him and listen to the soft patter of rain outside the window.

"Do you live here alone?" she asked.

"No, I have a housekeeper and three other employees who help me run the ranch."

"The housekeeper lives here in the house with you?"

"No, I built a small guesthouse out back a few years ago. She lives there." He opened a long white envelope, briefly scanned the contents, then pitched it back on the desk.

She was curled up in the big old chair that sat before his desk and she began to grow warm and drowsy as he continued to read his mail. Before she knew what

316

had happened, her eyes grew heavy and she began to nod.

Luke glanced up and a tender smile curved his lips as he observed her sleepy condition. The light from the lamp made her hair look shiny and lustrous and his fingers longed to touch the thick mass and see if it was as soft as he had imagined it to be.

She was slumped over like a child now, breathing softly as he pushed his chair back and stood up. She was exhausted and needed to be put to bed.

Walking around to the front of the desk, he knelt down beside her and reached out to gently awaken her when his hand paused.

Her skin had the flawless beauty that other women envy, and the subtle aroma of her perfume rose up to taunt him anew. Her face was warm and rosy and he felt his passion stirring, not for the first time that day. Of all the women he had known, she was the loveliest —and the most unobtainable.

He had no idea why he was torturing himself with thoughts of her, thoughts that were totally ridiculous. She had been on his mind both day and night since she had walked in Uriah's barn that day a little over three weeks ago. He could tell himself all he wanted that she was not the woman for him and that he'd better let well enough alone, but why was he constantly having to remind himself of that?

They were exact opposites. She loved her career and the big city, while he gloried in his work and small-town life. For one brief moment he let himself wonder what it would be like if they were actually to fall in love with one another.

His gaze lovingly ran over her again. It would never

work, Travers. Let it be. She seemed to be willing to coexist with him now without that constant sparring they had once indulged in. He would be a fool to try and change their relationship. If it wasn't for the fact that her father had taken ill, she would be back in New York, still detesting the ground Luke Travers walked upon. She was city and he was country and the two would mix like oil and water. He knew that.

He knew he would be walking down a blind alley if he ever once let himself touch her . . . hold her . . . kiss her. . . .

As if she could sense his presence, her eyes slowly opened and her brown eyes met his blue ones. "Umm . . . hi."

"Hello."

"Did I fall asleep?" He was kneeling beside her, so near she could smell his familiar scent, and it made her grow weak with desire.

"Yes. I guess you were tired." He knew this was the time to move away, to break this slender thread of intimacy that was threatening to draw them closer, but some invisible force rendered him powerless.

"You must be tired too." Her fingers reached out and lightly caressed his cheek and lingered there.

Fire raced unchecked through the nerve ends where her fingers touched. "Yes . . . a little," he confessed in a voice that had suddenly grown a little husky.

She gazed back at him sleepily, with eyes as warm and soft as a doe's. "Still raining?"

"Umm . . . still raining."

"Luke?"

"Umm?"

It would be dangerous and completely insane, but

she suddenly wanted this man to make love to her. She continued to gaze at him solemnly, searching for the right words to relay these lunatic, almost absurd feelings, but coming up depressingly empty-handed each time.

How do you tell a man you want him to make love to you?

After several long moments without speaking, his hand involuntarily reached out to stroke away a stray lock of her hair from the corner of her eye.

"Cass? Was there something you wanted to ask?"

The shyness had returned full-force, yet she reasoned if he wasn't going to make some sort of move, she would have to. It amazed her that he couldn't sense what she was asking.

"Cat got your tongue?" he prompted again teasingly.

She shook her head wordlessly, then slowly began pulling his mouth down to meet hers.

He looked at her vacantly for a moment, then comprehension began to sink in as he swore under his breath softly. "What is this . . . Cass . . . ?" Their mouths touched briefly and he felt his whole body go limp with desire.

"Rainy nights make me sort of . . . crazy," she excused lamely. It was a flimsy excuse, but she couldn't think of anything else to explain her sudden irrationality.

At first he thought he was dreaming, but when her hand began to pull him back to her once more, he went willingly, but by now his mind was whirling with indecision. What was he suppose to do now? If he ever once touched her, he was gone, and he knew it. So don't touch, Travers. Walk away before this gets out of hand. . . .

"Uh . . . yeah . . . they sort of have the same effect on me," he admitted, and kissed her again.

But his silent warnings went unheeded, and it seemed only too natural for the fleeting kisses they were temporarily exchanging to grow longer, deeper, more intense.

Sliding into the chair with her, he took her more fully into his arms and their mouths met hungrily. A few moments later he knew there would be no turning back. He would make love to her and he would enjoy every moment of it, no matter what tomorrow brought.

"Uh . . . Cass . . . do you want to . . . ?" He was still afraid to put words to what was taking place for fear it would all shatter in his face.

She nodded and nipped his lower lip seductively.

"Why?" His voice cracked nervously.

"Does there have to be a reason?" she prompted softly.

"I'm having a hard time understanding you," he confessed with an agonized groan. "At times you act as if I'm a leper and at others . . . well . . . what do you want from me? I'm only human, and if this is some little game you've decided to torture me with, I want to warn you you're playing with fire. I'm not the young boy you used to know who wouldn't dream of actually touching you because he held you in awe. I'm a man now, and I just might take what you're offering," he warned gruffly.

She laid her cheek against the rough palm of his

hand and gazed at him tenderly. "You never held me in awe," she chided.

"Yes, I did, and you knew it."

"I did not," she objected. "You always acted as if you couldn't stand me."

"I seem to recall it was the exact opposite. You were the one who couldn't stand me."

As long as he had brought up the subject, it seemed like a good time to confront him with a question that had nagged her for a long time now. "If that's the case, how come you took Sybil Wilson to that dance!"

He shrugged and replied cockily, "To get even with you for being such an uppity little snit." A slow grin tugged at the corners of his mouth. "Did that really bother you?"

"No . . . Well, yes, it did, come to think of it. It was terribly embarrassing to have you treat me that way in front of all our friends. I was miserable for days."

He chuckled and pressed his forehead tightly against hers. "I can't tell you how happy it makes me to hear you say that. I couldn't begin to tell you how many of my days you made miserable."

"You're terrible, but I must admit you're nothing like the Luke Travers I knew twelve years ago," she confessed, smoothly tracing the outline of his face with her fingertip.

"Is that a fact?" He captured her hand and brought it back to brush his mouth across the fingertips as the blue of his eyes deepened to an even darker hue. "Well, you're not exactly as I remembered you, either."

By his low, intimate tone, she knew it was the most sincere of compliments.

321

"Then why must you ask . . . why? We're two consenting adults now, accountable for our own actions."

"Because I don't think there could ever be any sort of commitment between us, Cass," he said raggedly. He knew that as well as she did.

"I'm not talking commitment," she teased as her fingers gently traced the outline of his nose, then his mouth, and paused as his lips closed over her fingertips once more.

"What if I were to say I'm not sure I could accept such an offer from you without a commitment?" he parried.

She lifted her eyes in disbelief. "Are you asking that of me?" She found it impossible to believe that he could be serious.

"No, of course not," he murmured, and Cass had the impression that question had slipped out unintentionally.

Her arms slid back around his neck invitingly. "Then you're just hedging. Do you want to make love to me or—"

His mouth closing over hers prevented her from finishing the sentence. Moments later, when their lips finally parted, he whispered against them suggestively, "I'll give you five minutes to reconsider your offer, then you're on your own."

"I don't need five minutes."

"Are you sure?"

"Let's just say I've always been fascinated by your unsavory reputation and I want to see if any of the gossip is true," she bargained, then grinned at him impishly. "But I hope you're aware a lot of people in

322

this town have stripped you of your horns and tail and put a nice, neat little halo around your golden head."

"Don't worry. I've changed my morals," he comforted. "But not my technique."

"And apparently you're going to make me beg to see this miraculous transition," she breathed against the hollow of his throat.

"You're sure you want to see it?" he pressed.

Her arms tightened around his neck and their mouths came down to meet each other's eagerly. With a low groan, he slipped his arms beneath her and gently gathered her up against his chest. His mouth met hers once more, hard and demanding.

"Okay, lady. But remember, this was your idea," he cautioned a few moments later.

He carried her through the darkened living room and up the carpeted stairway, their mouths never leaving one another's for more than a moment.

She could not seem to get enough of the taste of him, or the smell, or the feel of him.

"I know this is shameless of me," she murmured, pressing warm kisses on his neck as they entered his bedroom. Like the rest of the house, it was decorated in tones of blues and browns. The large king-size bed dominated the room along with a highly polished oak armoire and dresser.

"You don't hear me complaining, do you?" he whispered against the sweetness of her mouth. "I just want you to be sure. . . ."

She pulled his mouth back down to meet hers in a kiss that put all his fears to rest as he lay her carefully on the bed, then lay down beside her.

"Luke, there really isn't any other woman in your

life right now, is there?" It seemed a little late to be inquiring about such matters, but it would shed a different light on what was about to happen.

"No. Is there someone special waiting for you back in New York?" He began to undress, watching her as they talked.

"No, I'm not involved with anyone . . . but about Marilyn?" She was afraid he wasn't being truthful with her.

He removed the last of his clothing and her breath caught. He was truly magnificent. "What about her?" he countered.

"Is it serious between the two of you?"

"If it was, I can assure you I wouldn't be standing here stark naked discussing her with you," he returned dryly.

"Then it isn't serious?" They were about to share an intimate moment, one that no doubt would be highly pleasurable, but it would change nothing in their relationship and she wouldn't think of letting him make love to her if he was involved with another woman.

He lay down beside her and began to kiss her, long and passionately, until all thoughts of anything or anyone else were completely obliterated from her mind.

Her hands buried in the golden dark blond hair that covered his chest as his hands slowly began to explore her.

Piece by piece, he removed her clothing, masterfully, skillfully, and with the breathtaking expertise she had expected.

"You are so beautiful," he whispered reverently. "So very beautiful." His mouth began an exploration of her body, his tongue touching and tasting, then lovingly kissing what until now had been the most forbidden of places.

"Methinks you haven't changed at all," she accused as her mind became increasingly muddled with the growing, sensual haze he was weaving.

He raised his head to look at her as the last obstacle of cloth was disposed of neatly and without ceremony. "You're too well practiced to be the saint you're reported to be," she scolded breathlessly.

"Naw, I'm just a real natural when it comes to this," he teased.

"Then you're exceedingly talented," she pointed out, trying to control an unexpected surge of jealousy. This was not the time to think about how he received his training, she reminded herself. A thirty-year-old man with Luke Travers's looks was not going to be completely celibate, even though that would have been extremely nice. . . .

"You're not bad yourself." He returned the compliment easily as he urged her hand to become more aggressively involved. He drew a sharp intake of breath as she willingly complied.

"It always amazes me how men take this sort of thing so . . . so casually," she pondered.

He groaned and rolled over and positioned her on top of his broad chest, his hands cupping her face gently. The feel of his masculinity against her bare stomach was a new and disturbing feeling for her. "Have you changed your mind about this?"

"Oh, no." After all, she shouldn't be blaming him for taking full advantage of something that she had instigated, yet it bothered her he had been almost . . . easy.

"Then can we discuss this at another time?" He ran the calloused tip of his thumb across her moist bottom lip, then lowered her lips back down to meet his with a hungry urgency.

"Luke, I think there's something you should know," she murmured against the pressure of his questing tongue.

"Later," he commanded in a voice that had grown weak with passion.

From that point on all conversation willingly ceased as he took full control of her reeling senses and began tutoring her in the joys of being Luke Travers's woman. He evoked new and provocative feelings within her, feelings that all too soon had them both crying for release from the exquisite torment that was threatening to consume them.

Later, as he became a part of her, he suddenly pulled away, a stunned look overtaking his passion-laden features. "Don't tell me . . ."

She shook her head mutely. "I tried to, but you wouldn't let me."

He was clearly aghast at the situation he now found himself in. "You mean you've never . . ."

"Well, it wasn't because I haven't had the opportunity," she quickly clarified. "It's just that I've never met a man I thought I wanted to do . . . this with . . ." her voice trailed off lamely.

Having been raised on a farm and watching the way the animals mated, she had convinced herself that a man would have to be something extremely special to warrant that sort of total involvement from her.

"You're thirty years old and never . . . well . . . you should have stopped me. . . ." He immediately

326

began to move away, but she determinedly pulled his lips back down to meet hers. "If you stop, I'll never speak to you again, Luke Travers."

By that time the issue was a useless one, anyway. It was far too late to discuss the advisability of what was taking place. His unexpected discovery only served to add prudence to a smoldering inferno that quickly recaptured precedence over all.

Later, as they lay in each other's arms, satiated and incredibly relaxed, Cassie thought she could finally understand why her sisters were so darn happy and optimistic all the time.

If the men of Rueter Flats were anything like Luke, she had been bad-mouthing them unjustly.

"Are you asleep?" she murmured drowsily. She was lying on her side, pressed tightly against the warmth of his back. The rain was falling harder again outside, the low rumble of thunder periodically breaking the silence. She should be getting up and going home, but somehow she wanted to lengthen the time she had with him.

"No, just thinking."

"About what?"

"About you." He rolled over and reached for his shirt beside the bed and withdrew a cigar. Propping himself up on a pillow, he lit the thin cylinder and then drew her into the crook of his arm. "That was a dirty thing to do to a man."

"I tried to tell you. You said, 'Later.' "

"I wouldn't have said 'later' if I'd known that was what you were trying to tell me," he protested.

"You could have stopped," she pointed out.

He raised a brow in patient tolerance as he drew on

327

the cigar and let the smoke curl around their heads in a blue cloud. "Right."

She smiled and impishly traced her finger around his bare navel. "Are you saying you're sorry for what happened?"

"No . . . but I should be," he admitted.

"No you shouldn't. I was the one who started it."

"That doesn't make any difference." He inhaled again and looked over at her, then a wicked, devilish grin she had seen a million times before broke out on his face. "I was really the first, huh?"

She smiled back at him. "Yeah . . . why I picked you, I don't know," she teased. They both would have readily admitted that Luke Travers would seem like a highly unlikely candidate for Cass McCason's favors.

"It was a hell of a shock," he confided.

"Why?"

"Well, I thought with you moving away and all there had probably been numerous men in your life."

"No, not intimately anyway. I know it's highly unusual for a woman my age to be inexperienced in these matters, and I have dated a lot of men. I'll even confess there was one time that I came close to letting a man make love to me, but I backed out," she confessed sheepishly.

"At the last moment?" Luke shook his head in sympathy for the poor man. "I bet that made his day."

"No, he wasn't very happy about it, but it wasn't right for me and I realized it in time. I have always promised myself that that's how it would have to be before I could let that happen."

Luke gazed at her thoughtfully. "And tonight was right for you?"

She smiled. "Tonight was very right for me," she affirmed softly, then sighed and pressed a kiss on his bare stomach. "And maybe I'm a little bit old-fashioned too. Throw it all in together and you have a thirty-year-old virgin, like it or not."

Luke instinctively pulled her closer and tilted her face up so he could give her another long kiss. When their lips parted several moments later he smiled at her tenderly, his voice strangely emotional now. "There's nothing wrong with a woman being old-fashioned. Thank you, Cass. That's the nicest gift I've ever had."

Cassie felt her heart overflowing with something suspiciously close to love as she smiled back at him. "My pleasure, Dr. Travers." By referring to him as a doctor, it was as close as she had ever come to letting him know she was terribly proud of him.

He bowed his head to her respectfully. "No, it was all mine, Ms. McCason."

Ms. McCason? She grinned.

She thought they finally understood each other.

CHAPTER NINE

Had she been wiser, she would have realized that the blissful hours she was spending in Luke's company could only complicate a situation that was already out of hand.

She had no intention of becoming seriously involved with a man from Rueter Flats, even though a certain veterinarian's electrifying kisses and captivating smiles were capable of making her a blithering idiot at times. Already he was occupying her thoughts far more than he should be, and events were moving along entirely too fast to suit her.

It seemed like every spare minute they could find in the following days they would immediately seek out each other's presence, whether it was to take Wylie to a movie or on a fishing expedition, or the times that she secretly enjoyed the most, when she and Luke would sneak away for a few stolen moments of their own.

Their relationship was reckless and exciting and a totally unthinkable one, and yet they never spoke about their new feelings for fear they would have to do something about them.

The three had gone to a rodeo one night and spent

the entire time eating hot dogs and cotton candy and laughing. It seemed like she could laugh so much easier with Luke than she could anyone else.

And another time she had coerced him into accompanying her on a shopping expedition to find Uriah a new recliner. Her father's favorite chair was old and worn out, and Cassie wanted to buy something new and more comfortable for him when he returned home, although Luke warned that Uriah would not give up the old chair without a fight.

The church had its shiny new piano now. Luke and Cassie had selected the instrument with care. Luke insisted on donating it to the church in honor of Uriah and Neoma McCason, and Cassie's heart was touched.

Morgan Pixley sat in his pew Sunday mornings and beamed with pleasure as the Widow Neely played the old hymns in clear, resounding tones. In a way it seemed like he was much happier that Louella's piano wasn't there to remind him of happier days.

Luke, Cassie, and Wylie attended services together and then on Sunday afternoons, much to her surprise, he took her up in his small plane. They flew around Rueter Flats and Macon while he pointed out every landmark in the area to her.

On those afternoons her attention was diverted from sight-seeing because she enjoyed watching the pilot more than the sights! She had never acted this way around a man before and she was at a loss as to why she had suddenly picked Luke Travers to become so infatuated with.

If she was going to go off the deep end, why couldn't it be with one of the men she knew in New York? Tony

Jackson or Ed Flannery or Larry Ellison—or anyone but Luke.

It was really quite senseless to be so giddy about him. She reminded herself of that a hundred times a day, but it didn't seem to do any good because her pulse still raced like a sixteen-year-old's and her knees still turned to jelly every time he walked into the room.

She was in the process of giving herself another stern mental shakedown concerning Luke as she mucked out the stalls in the barn Wednesday morning. She had been home a little over five weeks, and every day she could feel herself growing a little closer to him.

This is exactly how the women of Rueter Flats get in their predicaments, she warned. They meet a good-looking man and before they know what hit them, Wham! they're on their way to the altar, then on to the local maternity ward.

Well, not her.

She would be leaving any day now. She would look back on this time for what it was—a pleasant interlude with a man she would no doubt always remember. When she returned home periodically she would speak to him when they bumped into each other at local gatherings, but that's as far as it would go.

By then he would be married. Her thoughts skidded to a screeching halt at the unpalatable prediction. Well, maybe not. It wasn't unheard of for a man to remain a bachelor.

Luke and Wylie entered the barn as she was still trying to convince herself of that feeble possibility. His gaze was unwillingly drawn to the way her tight jeans hugged her bottom. She was wearing another one of those clinging T-shirts that dipped low at her neckline and fit snugly to her breasts. She had acquired a smooth, even tan from working outdoors the past few weeks and a fine sheen of perspiration lay on her skin. Her face was flushed from the mounting heat and her hair was mussed and full of bits of hay, but she was still able to send his blood boiling to a fever pitch.

He had lain awake every night for hours the past few nights torturing himself with the remembrance of her in his arms, unbelievably soft and giving, unbelievably his. . . .

He would only be kidding himself if he thought anything serious could ever come out of their brief affair. But the searing memory of that rainy night still wielded the power to make him toss and turn between tumbled sheets until the wee hours of morning.

Why couldn't Marilyn make him feel this way? He would agonize as his new feelings continued to bewilder him. It seemed with increasing regularity that he was watching yet another dawn break peacefully outside his bedroom window. Marilyn was beautiful and talented and had no thoughts of leaving Macon in search of greener pastures. They could have a good life together. Even though they had never discussed the subject of marriage, Luke knew she would welcome his proposal, and yet for some reason he had always held back.

And he had no idea why he continued to delay. He was thirty years old, his practice was growing every day, and he wanted to get married and settle down. He could think of nothing that he would want more than a wife to come home to every night—a woman he could hold in his arms and share all the pent-up love he had kept so carefully hidden from the world with—a woman who could set his senses on fire and turn his insides to mush, one who he could argue with, make up with, share his dreams with, grow old with. . . .

His eyes followed the woman raking hay with reckless abandon and he felt an overwhelming sense of frustration wash over him. A woman like Cassie, dammit! Even if she was stubborn as a jackass at times!

This morning had been set aside for fishing, and Luke was sorely tempted to send Wylie on to the river by himself and spend a few moments alone with her, but he quickly checked his thoughts. After yet another interrupted night's sleep last night he had promised himself that he was going to have to begin cooling it where Cass was concerned. It was hopeless between them, and he'd better get used to the idea.

The redolent smells of hay and manure filled the air as her pitchfork paused in midair when she spotted him. She broke out into a radiant smile. "Hi!"

Against his will, his face had that same illumination as he grinned slowly back at her. "Hi."

"I suppose you guys are ready to go fishing, but I'm afraid I won't be able to go with you. I'm only half through with my work," she confessed. If she hadn't spent so much time daydreaming about him, she would have finished long ago.

"Okay," Wylie accepted easily. "Me and Luke will go ahead and you can bring us some sandwiches later on."

Cass frowned. "Thanks a lot."

Luke chuckled and reached for the extra pitchfork leaning against one of the stalls. "Why don't you go on down to the river and I'll help your sister finish up in here?"

It was Wylie who frowned this time. "Aw, Luke. Can't she finish it herself?"

Luke swatted him playfully on his behind and gave him a gentle nudge out the doorway. "We'll be down in about an hour. I want to see at least two big old flatheads on your stringer when I get there."

"Oh, all right. But be sure and bring plenty of sandwiches and cookies when you come." Wylie was back to his old self after the time he had spent with Uriah, but he was still grumbling something under his breath about "girls" as he headed for the river.

With two of them working, the stalls were soon tidied up and the tack room was put back in order. Luke was transporting sacks of grain to the storage room when Cassie began to feel playful. She had watched the way his powerful muscles bunched enticingly across his broad back as he lifted the heavy sacks and transported them into another room. He had stripped off his shirt in the intense heat and sweat now rolled in wet rivulets off his bronzed body and dampened the thick blond hair on his chest.

It took very little for her mind to conjure up what it felt like to be held tightly against that soft mass and the feel of it tangled beneath her fingers. . . . Her mind continued to torture her with the remembrance of the feel of those muscles, firm and bare beneath her fingertips. She bit her lower lip thoughtfully, then leaned over and waited for him to walk past the loft again.

When he did she pitched a huge forkful of hay down on his head.

Shifting the bundle more evenly on his shoulder, he glanced up and shot her a warning look. "I would watch that if I were you."

She smiled at him prettily. "Ooops, sorry. My fork just slipped."

But when he carried another sack by a few minutes later, another forkful of hay bombarded him.

Glancing up once more, he paused and carefully sat the sack down at his feet. Hooking his thumbs in the loops of his jeans, he leveled his blue gaze on her sternly. "Are you lookin' for trouble, lady?"

"Heavens no! I don't know why I'm so clumsy today," she apologized, a tiny grin threatening to give her away. She lay in the loft hanging over the side, looking at him invitingly. "You have hay all down your back," she divulged sympathetically.

He shifted his weight to one leg impatiently. "Yes, I'd noticed that."

"Bet it's miserable, huh?"

"You got it." He reached down and hefted the sack of grain back to his shoulder and carried it on into the storage room.

She shrugged, deciding he wasn't going to take the bait, and resignedly turned back to her work. She could hear water running outside a few moments later and she peaked out the loft door, but she couldn't see him anywhere.

The next thing she knew a whirlwind of hay came swirling through the air and literally engulfed her. She yelped and lost her footing as a heavy object came hurtling toward her.

"Luke Travers! I'm going to murder you!" She tried to sound authoritative but she was laughing too hard.

336

"Ooops, pardon me," he mocked. "I don't know why I'm so clumsy today." He cupped the back of her neck and started to kiss her as their legs became entangled and they fell in a heap on the hay. She started to giggle as he momentarily forgot the kiss and began energetically stuffing hay down her pants.

"You stop that this minute!" she sputtered as she tried to slap his hands away from the snap on her jeans. In addition to stuffing hay, they were becoming awfully familiar!

"Make me," he taunted as another handful of hay plummeted down the front of her T-shirt.

They tumbled over and over in the sweet-smelling hay as she tried to free herself of his mighty hold, but it soon became apparent she was no match for his strength.

Not even if she had wanted to be . . . which she didn't.

She couldn't deny that it felt wonderful to be pressed up tightly against him again, to touch him, to smell him, to feel his bare chest molded next to hers. Scooping up a handful of hay, she rammed it down the front of his pants and heard him suck in his breath as she encountered more than they both had bargained for.

He hurriedly rolled over and pinned her flat, all the while keeping her hand firmly trapped in place. He gazed down at her, his eyes deepening to the dark, passionate hue she had seen one time before, and she smiled up at him lamely. "Take that, you big bully."

He grinned wickedly. "Gladly."

She blushed and pushed at him ineffectually for a few moments, then finally shrugged and with her one free hand pulled his mouth slowly down to meet hers. "Well, if you're going to enjoy yourself so darn much, I might as well join you."

Their mouths touched briefly as he murmured unevenly against her lips. "Are you wanting something?" he teased as he ran the tip of his tongue lightly over her bottom lip.

"What you got to offer, sugggaarrr?" she teased back in a long Texas drawl.

"For you?" He growled suggestively, then playfully nipped her lower lip with gentle roughness. "Anything you want."

And once again their earlier avowals of prudence and temperance and all those other promises they had adamantly made to themselves went up in a puff of smoke.

Cassie wasn't sure how it happened, but it seemed their clothes were shed with alarming swiftness. She vaguely remembered murmuring a soft protest that someone might see them, but her protests were met with another mind-boggling kiss.

"Close the loft door," he murmured between kisses.

"But, Luke . . . it's broad daylight," she protested once more, but it was hard to sound very convincing . . . not when she reached out and slammed the door to the loft herself.

And then he made love to her again.

Not in the tender, almost reverent way he had the first time, but with a seemingly pent-up passion that was turbulent, restless, hungry, and yet so incredibly gentle.

Only this time he took the time to introduce her to the pleasures of pleasing a man, and when his lessons were readily learned she became almost giddy to find out she could weaken such a strong man to the point where he lay slack and drained of strength in her arms. She placed sultry kisses over his smooth, taut skin, and discovered anew the treasure of his lean, brown body, toughened by hard work and nature's elements.

And then when he could stand no more of her exquisite torture, he turned her over on her back and began his own virile assault, one of teasing and arousing to the point of madness, then dropping back to arouse and tease once more until she begged for fulfillment.

"Oh, Cass." He hated this feeling of such helplessness when he was in her arms. She was like no other woman he had ever known . . . searing his senses, invading his mind, penetrating his heart until he wanted to cry out for her to stop, to have mercy.

But instead he only muffled her cries with his own as their senses exploded in a brilliant shower of wild delirium while the sensations went on and on and on. . . .

When the fiery storm finally abated, he held her in his arms and buried his face in her hair, drained of strength, yet feeling strangely alive and vibrant.

"I don't know how that happened . . . but it was wonderful," she murmured as she sighed and snuggled closer to him.

The heat was so intense inside the loft they could barely breathe, and yet neither one made an effort to move.

Bits of hay were stuck in their hair and their bodies glistened with a fine sheen and still they stayed locked in one another's arms.

"I don't either." Luke kissed her again softly. "I didn't want this to happen again, Cass."

She felt a sharp twinge at his admission. She hadn't planned on it either, and yet now that it had happened, she didn't regret it. "You mean . . . you regret it?"

"No . . . not regret." He would never regret what they had shared. "I . . . I guess I really don't know what I mean," he sighed.

It wasn't hard to understand his confusion. She had plenty of her own.

"I know. Sometimes I wonder how this all started, don't you?" They lay together in the loft, gazing up at a patch of blue sky that was showing through the tin roof.

"Yeah, it is strange, isn't it? Luke Travers and Cassie McCason." They rolled their heads to one side and grinned at each other knowingly.

"Unlikely combination, huh?"

"Oh, I don't know." He reached over and caressed her cheek thoughtfully. "I'd say we weren't all that bad together."

"No, not bad at all," she agreed.

But he knew that no matter how wonderful this afternoon had been, he wouldn't be doing it again. The whole relationship was just becoming too painful for him. While he couldn't deny she shared the depth of his passion, he didn't dare let himself hope that she was falling in love with him.

And for some reason, that tore at his heart, because he was in love with her.

As crazy as that was, he could no longer shove the fact aside and pretend it didn't exist. It did exist. But as strong as his love was, he wasn't about to confess it to her for fear she would laugh at him the way she had when they were young and remind him this was only a summer fling. Surely he would be the last man she would actually fall in love with.

He couldn't stand that.

He raised his eyes to meet hers and they stared into each other's depths for long moments before he sighed again and admitted, "You're a hell of a woman, Cass."

She ran one finger lightly across his full lower lip. "Thank you, sir."

She waited, breathlessly hoping he would mention the word *love,* yet praying he wouldn't. Because if he did, she honestly didn't know what she would say to him.

It was becoming increasingly hard to think about a life without Luke Travers in it, and yet what could she do? Move back to Rueter Flats? At one time the thought would have been laughable, but that was before the last two weeks had occurred. Could she actually entertain the thought of giving up a successful career with an impending promotion just for the chance to be near him?

The thought was ludicrous, and yet she found herself frantically sorting through what few alternatives there would be if she did decide to do anything that frivolous. She supposed she could always find a job in Macon, but it wouldn't be doing what she loved. And what made her think that just because she was having these crazy feelings toward him that he returned them? He had never indicated that he was in love with her. Far from it. He seemed to avoid any talk of personal involvement. Not even at the pinnacle of his passion had he ever murmured the words *I love you, Cass,*

341

yet they had been on the tip of her tongue more than once.

Yet the way he was looking at her now, with such longing . . . such . . . well, if it wasn't love she was seeing, then she was at a loss to describe what it could be. Maybe, just maybe if he would bring up the subject of their growing relationship, then she could admit she was beginning to care for him. . . .

But he didn't mention the word.

Not then as they were getting dressed or later as he helped her make sandwiches for the delayed fishing trip.

She could only assume the word had never occurred to him, and it was a stunning revelation to her.

It was late afternoon when they cleaned the fish they had caught and Cassie put them in the freezer for Uriah to enjoy when he returned home.

She walked out to the truck with Luke to say goodbye, trying to appear casual in front of Wylie. "It's still early. You could stay for supper," she invited. "I'd even fix macaroni and cheese." It was another one of his favorites and she hoped to entice him into staying.

"I'd love to." He smiled at her and that strange light came into his eyes once more. "But I can't."

"Big date tonight," she teased lightly, praying that he would say that was not the case.

"Just with a sick horse."

"Oh." She knew she sounded unduly relieved, but at this point she didn't really care. "You going to the party the Murphys are throwing tomorrow night?"

"I was planning on it. How about you?"

"I thought I would. Dad should be coming home day after tomorrow and I'll be leaving. The party will give me a chance to say good-bye to everyone," she finished hurriedly.

At the mention of her departure, Luke turned and opened the truck door, then asked in a short voice, "You want to ride to the party with me?"

"Yes, I'd like that."

"Fine. I'll pick you up around seven." He got in the truck and slammed the door sharply.

"I'll be waiting."

It seemed like it took unusually long for seven o'clock to come around the following evening, but Cassie was dressed and sitting on the porch waiting for him when he finally arrived.

Her first impulse was to run over and shower him with kisses as he got out of his truck, but she quickly quelled the urge.

She would wait and see how he greeted her.

"Hi."

"Hi." He walked up and paused, his eyes inspecting her lazily. She was wearing a white cotton sundress with some pretty pink embroidered flowers around the neckline. Her shoulders were bare again, displaying the dark tan she had acquired, and he marveled anew at how beautiful she was.

"You look nice," he complimented.

"Thank you. You do too." He had to mean it, because he was looking at her as if she had just been declared the winner in a wet T-shirt contest.

The evening was to be another informal gathering, so he had dressed accordingly. Denims and a blue checked Western shirt, yet he was as devastatingly handsome as if he had been wearing a black tie and tuxedo.

"Ready?" He offered his arm and she stood up and placed her hand in it.

"Ready."

They strolled out to his truck and she paused and grinned at him knowingly. "Want to take the Jag?"

He pretended to have to think the suggestion over, but she knew what his answer was going to be. He was dying to drive that car. "Sure, why not," he finally agreed with an indifferent shrug.

He was in the car in a flash, busy inspecting all the gauges and accessories the car came equipped with before she could get in the passenger side.

"You big faker. You've been dying to get your hands on this, haven't you?" she accused as she snapped on her seat belt. He turned the key in the ignition and shifted down into low, then gave her a sexy wink.

He wasn't fooling her one bit with this so-what-if-it's-a-Jaguar act.

She could see boyish anticipation written all over his face.

But her words were drowned out as her head snapped back and the high squeal of rubber meeting pavement rent the air.

They blasted out onto the highway like a rocket and he began to wind the motor out until they were careening down the highway like a silver bullet.

She could honestly say it was the fastest trip she had ever made to the Murphys—or anywhere else—in her life.

When they finally zoomed up the drive she let out a huge sigh of relief and snatched the keys out of the ignition the minute they rolled to a stop. "You just see if I ever let you drive again!"

He looked at her solemnly. "You realize it's a little doggy."

"Doggy!"

He grinned and leaned over to kiss her. "Okay. I'll admit it. You've got a nice car, and I'm envious as hell."

"Good. It's been a long time comin'." She returned his kiss with full measure, which consequently delayed their arrival by another ten minutes.

They were greeted enthusiastically when they entered. Most of Cassie's brothers and sisters were there with their husbands and wives, all except Rowena and her family, who had decided to take Wylie and go to the county fair instead.

The party turned out to be a boisterous one. Sawyer Middleton spotted her immediately and claimed the first few dances as his.

Luke smiled and handed her over willingly, but Cassie thought he seemed disappointed that they wouldn't have the first dance.

By the time the small band swung into the third number, Cassie was pleading mercy and Sawyer promptly escorted her over to old washtubs iced down with beer and soft drinks. "What's your pleasure?"

She chose a soft drink and he peeled off the tab and handed her a bright red can. Seth Holoson stopped by to ask for a dance later, and she motioned with her free hand that she would be available as she took a long, refreshing drink.

"Good boy, that Holoson," Sawyer commented as

he ripped the tab off a beer and took a long swallow. "Make someone a fine husband."

She smiled and took another sip of her drink. Sawyer was a born matchmaker, but you would think with his less than perfect record with women, he would look for another hobby.

"When I was over in Macon the other day I stopped by the hospital and visited with your daddy. Said he might be comin' home soon."

"Yes, tomorrow."

"That soon? Well, that's just great!"

"It is wonderful, isn't it? The doctor says he should be as good as new if he'll take care of himself."

"Well, we'll all just have to make sure he does." Sawyer leveled his gaze on her sternly. "You give any more thought to what we talked about the other day?"

He could tell she hadn't by the way she grinned back at him sheepishly.

"I thought so. Well, little lady, you're makin' a big mistake by not givin' it some serious consideration," he warned.

"Sawyer, I can't visualize me opening my own agency," Cassie protested. "That takes a lot of money and I'm afraid I spend mine as fast as I make it."

"Missy." Sawyer had obviously never heard of the ERA. He "missyed, "little womaned," and "honeyed" every woman he met. "Any bank around here would be itchin' to loan you the money if you went to them with two or three big accounts already in your pocket," he insisted.

"But I don't have two or three accounts already in my pocket," she argued.

"Well, you could have if you'd get busy! I saw Wally

Henson and Oscar Miller over at the Elks Club last night and we got to talking about how hard it was to get good advertisin'—you remember Wally and Oscar, don't you, honey? Wally owns the poultry plant over in Macon and Oscar owns that big fleet of semis."

She nodded patiently.

"Well, they said to tell you they were sick of dealing with these eggheads around here and they'd sure be glad to throw their business your way if you decide to open up your own agency. There's your three accounts right there."

Her gaze unwillingly found itself centered on Luke again as Sawyer droned on. He was dancing with one of the younger girls in the crowd and she had to smother a smile to see how mesmerized she was. He was charming and handsome and totally capable of capturing any woman's heart, no matter what their age.

"Throw in the fact that Uriah and Neoma would plumb be beside themselves if you'd come on back home, I can't see what you're waitin' for, sugar," Sawyer challenged.

Pulling her gaze away from Luke, she smiled and started to explain to Sawyer about her upcoming promotion with Creble and Associates when Seth came back to claim her for his dance.

Cassie gave Sawyer an apologetic smile as he led her back to the dance floor, yet she was relieved to have the discussion interrupted.

The idea of opening her own agency was ridiculous, yet for some reason she did find herself tucking it in the back of her mind to give more serious thought to later on.

For the next hour she danced and laughed and forgot all about illnesses and advertising agencies and the endless decisions that suddenly seemed to be raining down upon her.

The only incident to mar the evening was when she came back into the room after catching a breath of fresh air with Bray Williams and found Luke dancing with Marilyn. It was a slow, romantic waltz and it made Cassie feel as if she were coming unglued.

To see Marilyn in his arms had a devastating effect on her and she couldn't keep her eyes off the attractive couple as Bray whirled her around the floor.

They smiled at each other as they brushed shoulders on the dance floor and Cassie fought to keep her expression pleasant.

"Hi. Having a nice time?"

Luke grinned at her, one of those sexy suggestive grins he was so good at leveling at her when he wanted to irritate. "Great. How about you?"

"Great."

Later, as he pulled her into his arms without even asking, she wanted to pull away and make him miserable for a while! But as their bodies blended in heavenly reunion, she found herself nestling much closer than was required.

"Are you still enjoying yourself?" she inquired nicely.

"It just got better." He winked. "How about you?"

"Yes, I'm having fun," she replied coolly. "How is Marilyn?"

"At what?" he asked innocently.

She eyed him sternly. "Dancing."

"Oh. She's just fine. How is Seth?

"He's just fine."

"And Bray?"

"Fine . . ."

"And Ron?"

He had made his point.

"Fine! She looks lovely tonight."

"Who?"

"Marilyn!"

He angled himself around until he could see the petite blonde, who was dancing in Brad Younger's arms now. "Yeah, she does, doesn't she." He glanced down at her warily as she inched even closer.

Her eyes narrowed and she slid her arms around his neck possessively. "I don't think she looks all that good."

"Well, you just said she did. . . . Uh . . . you mind to tell me what you're doing?" he groaned miserably as her suggestive actions began to affect him.

She had an uncanny way of arousing him to such a fevered pitch and getting him there in record time that he was afraid it could get mighty embarrassing for him at any moment if she kept this up.

"I'm just dancing close to you like Marilyn was," she murmured, but she wanted to make it perfectly clear to whoever happened to be watching that she was staking her claim.

"She wasn't dancing this close to me," he denied swiftly.

"It certainly looked that way to me!"

"Cass, look"—He carefully maneuvered her away from him to a more comfortable distance—"I think if you're going to make a pass at me, which I have no objections to," he assured hurriedly, "don't you think we'd enjoy it more if we found a little more privacy than a crowded dance floor?"

"Am I embarrassing you?" She was pressing so tightly now he was beginning to perspire heavily.

He groaned and pushed her back again to a safer distance. "No, I'd say torturing would be a better word."

She smiled smugly as she felt the ever-growing evidence of his words pressed against her middle. "You don't care if Marilyn gets the wrong idea about us?"

"Marilyn? Is that what all this is about?" He paused and looked at her with annoyance.

"Well, for someone who isn't serious about someone, you sure looked like you were having a good time a minute ago."

"Me! What did I do?"

"Pasted yourself to her, that's what!"

"Well, if I remember correctly, you and Seth weren't exactly dancing like brother and sister," he returned curtly.

"Me—Seth," she sputtered. "We were merely dancing. You and Marilyn were . . . were . . ."

"Dancing!" he supplied stubbornly, then set their feet back in motion. "You're making a scene," he grumbled. "I was only dancing with Marilyn because you weren't available."

"When did you ask?"

"I never got the chance. You were always occupied!" He glanced around uneasily and found that people were beginning to stare. "Let's just drop the subject, okay?"

"I'm not making a scene. I only pointed out that you look like you were enjoying yourself."

"Well, I'm sorry. Okay? Next time I'll try to snarl and frown and look perfectly miserable the whole time I'm dancing with her."

"The next time you dance with her I won't be here to see it," she snapped, and her words sliced deeply within both of them.

"I'm fully aware of that," he said calmly. "You don't have to keep reminding me."

They danced in strained silence for a moment, then she said in a more appeasing tone, "I know I've been taking up a lot of your time lately with the farm and all, and I know it's been because of Dad that you've helped me the way you have, but I want to thank you for all your help. I know I've interfered with your personal life, and now that I'm leaving, you can get back to normal." She paused and warned herself not to say it, but she went ahead anyway. "I suppose you'll probably have more time to spend with your friends when I leave."

"I haven't been neglecting any of my friends," he denied.

"You mean you've been seeing . . . her . . . while I've been here?" That thought nearly killed her. He had made love to her, then still dated Marilyn!

He heaved a long, put-upon sigh. "Now who in the hell may I ask is 'her'?"

"Marilyn!"

"Oh for heaven's sake! No. I haven't been seeing her." You would think by the way she was acting she would actually be offended if he dated another woman.

"Oh." She realized she was being a little pushy. After all, he could see who he wanted. She had no strings attached to him. But she was curious as to what he

351

would be doing after she left. He had obviously spent every spare moment he had with her since Uriah had taken ill. "Well, not that it matters, but I was only trying to find out what you were going to do with all your time after I leave."

For a long time he didn't answer her and she thought perhaps he was only being stubborn again, but then he buried his face in the cradle of her neck and confessed in a very small voice, "I don't know what I'll do when you leave, Cass." Then as quickly as he had lost it, he regained his composure and added more firmly, "I make it a point to live one day at a time," he stated curtly.

It wasn't what he said but rather the way he said it that made her suddenly want to cry. No matter how she had felt about him in the past, she didn't feel that way about him now. The Luke she had come to know seemed so vulnerable that she wanted to fold him in her arms and keep him forever.

For a brief moment he had actually sounded as if he would miss her. But that was crazy. All he would have to do is tell her what he was feeling and then she would gladly confess her love.

"I . . . I can't thank you enough for being with me these past few weeks, Luke." Her own voice was a little unsteady now as she continued in a gentle tone, "I don't know what I would have done without you." Her hands tightened in his hair and she closed her eyes painfully as he moved her closer to him. She was giving him every chance to open up to her.

But the moments passed and, other than a perceptible tightening of his arms around her, he said nothing.

She choked back the tears and decided the only

good and noble thing to do at this point was to wish him the very best of luck, but it was like trying to squeeze blood out of a turnip to get the words past her dry lips. "And I just want to say that I . . . hope you and whoever you choose to marry will be very happy. . . ."

He finally paused and looked down at her for a very long time, then suddenly began to maneuver her off the dance floor.

Amid her confused protests, he pulled her out onto the terrace, where he pushed solidly up against a vine-covered wall that was in the darkest corner of the building and trapped her between his two arms. "You know what your problem is?"

She looked at him worriedly. "No, what?"

"You talk too much." He then proceeded to kiss her until she went limp as a rag in his arms.

"My goodness, what brought this on?" she managed when she was finally able to catch her breath.

He sighed and stole another smoldering kiss before he answered. When he spoke he dropped a bomb she wasn't expecting. "I wanted to be alone with you when we said good-bye."

"Good-bye? What do you mean, good-bye? I don't leave until Saturday."

"I know, but I figure there'll be a lot of confusion around your place when Uriah comes home, and besides that, I have to fly over to Seeny County sometime tomorrow to tend to business." The tips of his thumbs gently caressed her mouth, which was slightly swollen from his ardent kisses. "I want to say good-bye to you now, Cass."

For a long time they stared at each other in the

moonlight, both at a complete loss for words. There were so many things they wanted to say to one another, and yet they were afraid.

Afraid the other one would laugh if they would dare confess that Luke Travers loved Cassie McCason or Cassie McCason loved Luke Travers.

"John said he would drop me by your place later so I can pick up my truck. And he has a heifer he wants me to take a look at before I leave tonight."

"But, Luke . . ." She wasn't even going to have these last few precious hours with him because John Murphy had a sick cow!

"I . . . let's just make this as easy as possible, Cass." His eyes pleaded with her for understanding, yet she didn't know what she was supposed to understand. "Can't you stop in later? Wylie is staying all night with Rowena. You could stay with me tonight," she offered, casting all pride aside now.

"Thanks, but it will probably be too late." It was going to be hard enough to walk off and leave her. One more precious night would only add salt to an already gaping wound. He gazed at her lovingly as he smoothed back a stray lock of hair from her face, trying to memorize everything about her so that after tonight he could hold her in his heart if not in his arms.

God, how he loved her. Oh, she made him mad as hell at times, and yet she could make him feel emotions that no other woman had ever been able to. He supposed deep down he'd always loved her, even when they were children. But she was no more obtainable to him now than she had been then. What was it she had

354

said the first time he had made love to her—she wasn't looking for a commitment?

His mind churned with confusion. It would be so easy to tell her that he loved her, to confess that if she would marry him it would make him the happiest man on earth, that he would go out of his way to make sure she would have that same happiness, even though she would be living back in Rueter Flats. But he knew without asking she would never settle for that kind of life.

And he could never uproot his life and move to New York.

So it was best to end it now, swiftly and cleanly, while he still had a small remnant of sanity left in him.

He kissed her once more, long and passionately, then raised his head and touched his nose to hers affectionately, then whispered softly, "See you around, kid."

"Luke . . ." She was so confused and miserable, she thought her heart would break. That was it? After all they had shared together he was going to walk out of her life with a simple "See you around, kid"?

But her silent plea went unanswered as he quickly turned and left her standing in the shadows, alone and lonely, feeling as if part of her had just died.

CHAPTER TEN

Many thoughts raced through Cassie's mind as she drove to New York.

As predicted, Uriah's homecoming was boisterous and happy and sad all at the same time.

Happy because he was home and recovering from the stroke nicely, but sad for his children to realize that no longer could they think of their parents as being invincible. It would seem nature had a way of pointing that out when it was least expected.

For Cassie it was a more emotional time than it was for the others. She hated to leave the safety and love of her parents' home, and yet she knew she had another life waiting for her when she returned to New York.

And Luke. How in the world had she allowed herself to fall in love with him?

She still bristled when she thought about the way he had chosen to say good-bye to her. She had felt confident that he would change his mind and come to see her before she actually left. There were too many unsaid things between them for him to end it this way.

But he hadn't come by to see her and she had been too stubborn to call him, so consequently she was still angrily jerking tissues out of a box and wiping at the relentless stream of tears when she entered the city limits of New York on Monday evening.

The apartment smelled musty as she let herself in and switched on the air conditioner. There was a pile of papers and a stack of mail on her kitchen counter, left for her by her cleaning woman. She looked around her and everything was the same.

Except nothing was the same at all.

She was exhausted from crying halfway across the United States so she went directly to the shower, then fell into bed. She was sure she would quickly shed this miserable feeling of despondency the moment she returned to her office tomorrow morning.

It was going to leave anytime now, she continued to remind herself as her life gradually settled back into a routine pattern. She couldn't go on forever mooning over a man who apparently didn't care one whit for her. She had known Luke Travers was trouble from the day he had tied her braids in a knot when they were in the first grade.

She stood in her office staring down at the traffic late one Thursday afternoon when she had been back at work almost three weeks. It was the height of rush hour and she was glad to have a desk piled high with work. She planned on working late tonight, as she had done almost every night since she returned. It wasn't that she couldn't get caught up, it just gave her a reasonable excuse to be away from the apartment. The nights were far too lonely now, and she had found herself calling home at least three times a week to check on her father. She had asked about Luke each time, and Neoma had told her they hadn't seen as much of him as they usually did.

Then she had lain awake all night wondering just what he was doing that took up so much of his time!

Her gaze was drawn to the west, where the sun was a blazing red ball of fire. It was just beginning to sink behind the tall skyscrapers and she was reminded of the way the sun sat in Rueter Flats.

There were no tall buildings to conceal its resplendent beauty, only miles and miles of rolling farmland to bathe in its soft rosy radiance. With great pain, she recalled the last sunset she had watched with Luke.

They had stepped out of the barn just as the daily spectacle was taking place. They had paused to watch the fiery round ball slide gently behind a hilltop and disappear. The sky was still ablaze with reds and oranges and they had both looked at each other and smiled. They had shared a beautiful moment together. . . .

A soft knock sounded on her door and she turned away from the window, hurriedly dabbing at her eyes. "Yes?"

Ed Flannery stuck his head in the door and smiled. "I'll spring for the pizza if you'll buy the suds."

She shook her head and smiled back. "Thanks, Ed, but I'm going to be here at least another two or three hours."

"Again?" Ed was an attractive man whom she had dated several times in the past and he was always fun to be with. In a way she was tempted to accept his offer. It would be good to laugh again. But she would make miserable company and she knew it.

"Yes, I'm afraid so. I can't seem to get caught up."

"Well, I'm pretty good at lending a helping hand," he offered lightly.

"That's really nice of you, Ed, but most of it is a one-man job. Thanks anyway for the offer."

"Sure thing. Don't work too late," he cautioned.

"No, I won't."

But it was past eleven when she finally let herself into her apartment and switched on the light. She glanced at her watch again. It was late, but Texas was in a different time zone. . . .

Her mind toyed with calling Luke just to say hello and see if he thought Uriah was doing as well as had been reported. It was a viable excuse, even if it was sort of a lame one. Before she lost her nerve she jerked up the receiver and hurriedly punched out his number by memory.

The phone rang for a very long time before he finally answered. "Dr. Travers here."

Her knees turned weak at the sound of his voice and she was afraid she was going to lose her nerve and hang up.

"Dr. Travers!" he barked again.

Would he think she was out of line by calling him this way? Probably. And what if he was with Marilyn or entertaining some other woman from Rueter Flats? She suddenly felt sick to her stomach as she hurriedly placed the phone back in its cradle.

For the next few minutes she paced the floor in front of the phone, reviewing all the reasons why he should be the one to call her. But when all the evidence had been presented she decided he really didn't have more of a reason to call her than she did him.

The fact was, she had more. She wanted to know about Uriah.

Quickly snatching up the phone once more, she

punched out the numbers and waited while it rang only twice this time.

"Dr. Travers."

And once again she was struck speechless and hung up.

But the third time his phone rang the receiver was snatched up on the first summons and an impatient voice boomed out, "Damnit, Cassie! If you're going to keep getting me out of the shower the least you can do is say something!"

For a moment she was so astounded that he would know who was calling, she couldn't talk.

"Cass," he admonished sharply.

"What?" Her thoughts were now honed in on the fact that she had gotten him out of the shower. He must be standing there dripping wet . . . nude . . . nude . . . nude. . . .

He let out a rush of relieved breath. "Then it is you," he confirmed softly.

"Yes. How in the world did you know?"

Maybe it was because he had spent the last three weeks thinking about her every hour of the day. Maybe because every time the phone rang he had been praying it would be her. Maybe he had suddenly turned psychic. He couldn't explain it. Somehow, he just knew.

"I don't know . . . I just did." He propped a wet hip on the side of the cabinet and closed his eyes for a moment, visualizing the curve of her mouth, the way it was moist and sweet when he kissed her. "What's up, babe?" What's up, babe! Couldn't he think of anything more eloquent to say to her than "What's up, babe?" he agonized. Couldn't he tell her how much he had missed her, how he was dying inside day by day, how he longed to touch her, to taste her. . . .

"Nothing." She closed her eyes and tried to remember his touch . . . his smell. The musky aroma that sent her blood pounding through her chest and her senses reeling. . . . "I was just wondering how everything was going back there."

"About the same."

"Have you seen Dad lately?"

"Yeah, Wylie and I took in a movie last night. I visited with Uriah awhile when we got back."

"Is he doing as well as Mom says he is?"

"Seems to be. His color's back to normal and his appetite's picking up."

"Oh, good. Good." *Say you miss me, you big oaf! Tell me since I've gone your life's been as miserable and bleak as mine has!*

"How's the Big Apple?"

"Hot."

Ha. She didn't know the meaning of the word. He bet it couldn't hold a candle to the way he had been since she had left. "Yeah. It's been warm here too."

She bit her lower lip thoughtfully. "You ever been to New York?"

"No, never have."

"No? Oh, that's terrible. Everyone should see New York at least once in their lifetime."

"Yeah, that's what they say." *Just say the word, babe, and I'll be up there so quick it'll make your head swim,* he pleaded silently.

All right, you stubborn jackass! I'm going to make a complete fool out of myself and ask, but I'm warning you—you better not laugh in my face!

"Why don't you fly up here sometime? I'd be glad to show you the sights," she offered nonchalantly, then held her breath as she waited for his answer.

"Fly up there?" He managed to sound as if the idea had never occurred to him. He reached over on the counter and fumbled for a smoke with trembling hands. "Uh . . . when would be a good time for you?"

Good time? Good time? She willed herself to think straight. It was already late Thursday night. Should she dare invite him for this weekend?

His alleged state of undress on the other end thundered through her mind like a herd of wild buffalo. The width of his chest, the touch of his hand, the way the tight muscles in his forearms gathered tautly when he held her in his arms. . . . "Would this weekend be convenient?" she inquired meekly.

"This weekend?" His insides jumped with anticipation. "Sure, that sounds all right to me." He reached over and draped a towel around his middle as the tension in his loins steadily increased.

"You can? Great!" She clapped her hand over her mouth and was mortified that she had been so appallingly transparent.

Grinning to himself, he fought to remind himself this was not to be taken as a sign that she actually cared and had missed him. She was probably experiencing just a touch of homesickness. "Why not? I think I can get Milt Turner to take my calls for the weekend."

Clearing her throat nervously, she managed to regain a thread of her composure. "Oh, well that will be wonderful. I'll pick you up at the airport."

Since he would be flying his private plane, they discussed his possible arrival time the following evening and she assured him she would be there waiting for him.

"Great! I'll see you tomorrow afternoon."

"Well . . . good night. . . . Oh, I hope I didn't call too late."

"No. I hadn't gone to bed yet."

Was he alone? God, let him be alone. "Uh, you don't have company, do you?"

"No. Why?"

"Oh, I just thought I heard voices in the background."

"The television is on, that's probably what you hear."

Once more a tremendous sense of relief washed over her. "Yes . . . well . . . good night again." "My darling" she added silently.

"Yeah . . . good night." "My love" he added silently.

Then they both hung up to spend another restless night alone.

When the blue and white, twin-engine Cessna came rolling into the hangar late Friday afternoon, Cassie was there, jumping up and down, waving exuberantly at the pilot.

There was something to be said for discretion, but she couldn't think of it at the moment.

Luke climbed out of the cockpit as she ran across the tarmac to meet him.

Did she throw herself in his arms and kiss him

senseless, like she longed to do, or did she wait to see how he would greet her?

Deciding that it would be prudent to rely on the latter, her steps slowed and she waited until he gathered his belongings and began to walk toward her.

Her eyes eagerly drank in the familiar sight and her smile was nothing less than radiant as he approached carrying a blue garment bag draped casually over his shoulder and held by the tips of two fingers.

He paused when he reached her and they looked at each other hungrily.

You're even more beautiful than I remembered, his eyes told her wordlessly.

How could I ever have thought I could live without you, her gaze confessed lovingly.

"How was the flight?"

"Not bad. A little bumpy at times." He glanced around him. "Big place."

She laughed. "Yes, pretty good size."

They fell into step with one another and started in the direction of her car. They talked about the weather and Uriah. He told her Wylie's baseball team had won the championship last week and Rosalee was wearing maternity clothes again.

When they reached the car he paused and looked at the plain two-door sedan parked at the curb. "Where's the Jag?"

"In the body shop. This is a loaner."

"Did you wreck your car?"

"No, just having the hurricane 'Rueter Flats' corrected." She grinned.

On the way home she made several detours to point out various sights she thought he should see and he was clearly impressed by the city. They decided it was still too early for dinner, at least by New York standards, so she drove directly to her apartment to rest for a while before they began the tour of the city she had so lavishly planned.

When they arrived she took him on a brief excursion of the two-bedroom flat and almost popped a button when he told her it was nice. Really nice. And she wanted to hug his neck when she realized he was sincere.

Gliding over to the window, she pushed a button and the drapes gracefully folded away, revealing a spectacular view below them. The lights of the city were just beginning to twinkle on—a beautiful, breathtaking sight—and Luke chuckled and said he felt like he was in a spaceship looking out.

They stood gazing over the vista, saying nothing for a moment. It just felt good to stand there next to each other and know they were together again.

Her hand hesitantly slid over and reached for his.

His hand closed over hers warmly.

They turned and their eyes met in the gathering twilight.

"Hello," she said softly.

"Hello," he said in the same tone.

She wasn't sure how she suddenly found herself in his arms, or how they were suddenly kissing with a wild, insatiable urgency, or how he was murmuring her name over and over in a husky, pleading voice as he lifted her into his arms and carried her into the bedroom—but it all happened. The only thing she was totally sure of was the love they shared in that next glorious two hours.

Somehow the unbelievable ecstasy they found in each other's arms seemed to make up for all the loneliness and agony of the past few weeks.

Darkness had long ago spread its velvet mantle across the city when their frenzied lovemaking slowed then finally abated.

They were still lying in the ebony shadows, leisurely exchanging long, drugging kisses when the mantel clock struck ten. The searing urgency was over now. They could simply lie in each other's arms, contented, happy . . . at peace with themselves and the world for the first time in a long time.

"Are you getting hungry?" she asked sleepily.

"I think I could eat a ten-pound steak," he acknowledged in the same drowsy voice. He was sprawled flat on his stomach, dozing now.

She slid on top of his back and hugged him tightly. "I know where they have delicious steaks and huge baked potatoes dripping with butter and sour cream and chives. . . ."

He grunted as her weight smashed his nose farther down in his pillow. "If you'll quit trying to smother me, I'll let you take me there," he promised in a muffled voice.

"I will grant you your life on only one condition," she threatened.

"What's the condition?" His voice was even more drowned out as she suddenly sat up and smacked his bare bottom affectionately.

"I want you to say it."

"Say what?"

This was his hour of reckoning. She had come to grips with hers long ago.

Not once had he told her he loved her, but she knew he did. She just knew it. And he wasn't going to leave this bed until she heard him admit it!

For agonizingly long moments he didn't say anything and she felt like she suddenly had a hedge apple wedged in her throat. What was he waiting for? Would he actually pretend indifference and say "You didn't really take all of this seriously, did you?"

But he didn't. Instead, he slowly removed the pillow off his head and rolled over. It was dark in the room, so she couldn't see his face, but she knew by the timbre of his voice, he was stunned by her request. "You want me to say I'm in love with you?"

Her eyes dropped shyly, then she laid her head on his chest so she wouldn't have to look at him. "Yes . . . Oh, Luke, I think I'm going to die if I don't hear you say those words."

He suddenly felt as if all the air had gone out of him. "You wouldn't . . . laugh at me if I did?"

Her head snapped up. "Laugh at you!"

"Yes! Laugh at me." He reached out and cupped her face between his two large hands and his gaze bore into hers solemnly. "You think I haven't wanted to tell you that I love you—you think I haven't died a thousand deaths knowing that I've fallen in love with a woman who couldn't stand the sight of me. . . ."

"Oh, that was years ago," she scoffed. "I was young and foolish—"

"And a mean, feisty little heifer," he added tartly, "that wouldn't have thought twice about slicing my heart out and feeding it to her dad's hogs."

She blushed at his callous—yet surprisingly astute—

assessment of her earlier feelings. "Now, really, Luke, I wasn't that bad, was I?"

"Every bit and more."

"Well, you weren't exactly Mr. Nice Guy yourself. I remember all the bad times you gave me," she defended.

He waved off her objections curtly. "I was only fighting fire with fire."

"Well, I'm tired of fighting," she announced.

"Oh?" His left brow came up challengingly. "Well, what do you want me to do about it?"

She grinned and he blushed. "Say that no matter how cantankerous I was, you managed to fall in love with me anyway."

With a gentle touch of his hand to her cheek, he complied willingly. "That's too easy. I do love you, you feisty little heifer."

"Say it nicely!"

He flashed her a contrite grin. "I love you, darling. I think I always have."

And then they were back in each other's arms once more, pouring out their love, their words tumbling over each other's in their eagerness to confess what they had felt all along. The hours slipped away and dinner was completely forgotten.

The following day proved to be hectic. Cassie had planned enough activities for an entire week, so they were kept busy from early morning until late evening. When they had seen all they could see by daylight, Luke took her up in the plane and they flew over New York at night.

But even though they had finally confessed their

love, they still couldn't bring themselves to discuss the future.

For Luke the future still loomed bleakly ahead, since he knew her feelings concerning Rueter Flats and he had no idea what he could do to change them.

For Cassie the decision had not been easy, although a relatively simple one. She knew what she was going to do about it.

So when Sunday afternoon was upon them and it was time for Luke to leave and he still hadn't said anything about their future, she resigned herself to the fact that she would have to make the first move again.

But that didn't bother her. She loved him enough, and even more, to do that. Still, she wanted to see if he would actually depart without proposing to her.

They had arrived at the airport a little before two, and she had walked to the plane with him. He had been pensive all day, a little jumpy, a little irritable, yet so darn lovable they had made love twice before they left the apartment.

"Be careful," she warned as he slid his gear into the plane. "I'm not sure I like these small planes." Actually she wasn't sure she liked any plane. They all made her want to throw up.

"I'm always careful." He draped the garment bag over the passenger seat and turned around to kiss her again.

They stood locked in a passionate embrace, kissing and patting and hugging until she was sure the men in the control tower wished they'd get on with it.

"I can't tell you how nice it's been to have you," she teased in a pleasant voice. "You have to promise to look me up if you ever get up this way again."

He eyed her sourly. "I'll do that. And you be sure and do the same when you're in Rueter Flats."

She nodded solemnly. "Oh, I will."

"Well." He cast a hesitant glance around him. How in the hell was he going to leave her here? What would she say if he got down on his knees and begged her to go home with him? No—she wouldn't go. She still had her fancy job and hated small-town living. "Guess I should be shovin' off."

That's right, you stubborn, adorable oaf! Just stand there and ignore the fact we just spent a weekend that will change our lives forever. "Yeah, I guess it's a pretty long flight."

"Yeah . . . pretty long."

He gazed at her longingly. "Cass . . ."

"Yes?" She smiled at him, trying to give him the courage he was so desperately seeking.

But once again his shoulders sagged dejectedly and he let out a long sigh. "Nothing. I'll give you a call sometime next week."

"Okay."

He kissed her once more and then turned to climb aboard the plane.

"Luke."

He turned. "Yes?"

"Aren't you even going to help a lady with her luggage?"

"Her luggage?" he asked blankly.

"Yes. There're four bags in the trunk of the car, and then we have to take the car to the parking area because the body shop is coming over to pick it up tomorrow morning, then I'll have to fly back soon to pick up the Jag and take care of the lease—"

370

"Hold it!" Luke slid off the plane slowly. "What are you yammering about?"

"Yammering? Really, Luke. Yammering? I'm standing here about to ask you to marry me and you accuse me of yammering?" She shook her head chidingly.

His face was totally confused by now. He shifted his weight to one foot and put his hand on his hip. "You're asking *me* to marry you?"

"Yes! You will—won't you?" Suddenly all her earlier bravado started to falter. What if he wouldn't? She couldn't stand it, that's what!

Keeping his face without expression, he reached into his pocket and withdrew a cigar. Inside he felt like jumping for joy, but he couldn't believe this was for real just yet. "What about your job?"

"Oh, haven't you heard? I've decided to open up my own advertising agency in Macon." She was still holding her breath, hoping. . . .

"And that fancy promotion?"

"Being my own boss is better."

He struck a match and lit the smoke. Then, holding the cigar in his even white teeth, his eyes narrowed in challenge as he said, "Oh, yeah? Well what about living in Rueter Flats again?"

She shrugged sheepishly. "Mom and Dad are getting older. I need to be around more often . . . and my nieces and nephews need to get to know their Aunt Cassie a little better."

"Well," he took a long, thoughtful drag off the cigar, pretending to think about her proposal. When he saw the absolutely miserable look keep deepening on her face, he quickly discarded his insincere theatrics.

"Well, hell. Why not?" He grinned and winked at her conspiratorially. "The town could use a little class."

She returned his grin, ear to ear, replying in her worst Rueter Flats drawl, "Ain't that the ever-lovin' truth, sugggaarrr!"

Then their faces grew serious, and they held each other for a long, loving moment.

They quickly disposed of the car and gathered up her luggage, pausing to clasp each other in lingering smoldering kisses every now and then.

Within thirty minutes they were walking back across the tarmac and Cassie was yammering away happily.

"Now, I want to make one thing perfectly clear. Just because I gave in first doesn't mean I'm going to be a real pushover after we're married," she was saying as he proceeded to help her into the plane. "I still plan on having my career and my life—"

"I sort of had that one figured out all by myself," Luke said dryly.

"And there are still things I will never change my opinion on. Number one! You are not going to keep me barefoot and pregnant all the time. . . ."

He pinched her on her behind affectionately. "I have every intention of keeping you in shoes!"

She turned around and shot him a dour look. "Having shoes is not what I was worried about." She proceeded to climb into the plane. "Now, maybe someday we'll have one—possibly two children, but I certainly don't plan on being like the other women of Rueter Flats who have a baby every nine months like clockwork—and I seriously doubt if you will ever catch me in Nellie Sooter's beauty shop having one of her revolting permanents. In fact, you may even have to fly me back up here occasionally so I can go shopping and let Stephan do my hair—and do you realize, Luke Travers, I don't even know your middle name—"

"Luke Raymond," he supplied easily.

She whirled around and her mouth dropped open weakly. "Your middle name is . . . Raymond?"

He nodded. "Yeah, why?"

"Oh, no reason." She sank down on her seat lamely, realizing what they would probably name their first son.

But there would be only one Ray among her children—no more!

"What's yours?"

"Cassandra Beth."

Leaning over to fasten her seat belt, his mouth found hers again in the process. "Hello, Cassandra Beth."

She sighed hopelessly. "Hello, my darling, Luke Raymond."

SPEND YOUR LEISURE MOMENTS WITH US.

Hundreds of exciting titles to choose from—something for everyone's taste in fine books: breathtaking historical romance, chilling horror, spine-tingling suspense, taut medical thrillers, involving mysteries, action-packed men's adventure and wild Westerns.

SEND FOR A FREE CATALOGUE TODAY!

Leisure Books
Attn: Customer Service Department
276 5th Avenue, New York, NY 10001